'Barry

A Novel by
John A Ward

All the characters and events in this novel are fictitious. Any resemblance to persons, living or dead, is purely coincidental, locations used are mainly actual.

The picture on the inner title page shows the Seal of Dunwich.

Dunwich was probably the most flourishing of the medieval Ports of Suffolk. It was a self-governing borough and the official seal depicted the main source of prosperity: ships.
This seal of 1199 shows a clinker built sailing ship with two fighting platforms - fore and aft - and another atop the mast. Note the large sized rudder for steering.

'Barty'

Principal Characters appearing in this novel

Kaleb Bartholomew (Barty)	
Walter James Bartholomew	Kaleb's father - aka Bill Marriott
Doris Bartholomew (nee Gill)	Kaleb's mother
Frederick Green	Farmer at Sunrise Farm
Charles & Mary Carpenter	Workhouse Master & wife
Ben Chapman	Head grounds man at Mill Hill
Jed Slater	Mudlark
Ben Osbourne	Lodging House owner
Sir James Middleton	Owner of Mill House & Farm
Jim Crawford	Mill Hall House & Farm Charge hand
Reuben Young	Mill Hall Farm - stable hand
Thomas Black	Army pal & co-worker
Donald McLean (Skipper)	Owner of 'Ellie May'
Arthur Spalding	Owner of the Tide Mill Complex
Sarah Spalding	Arthur Spalding's daughter
Ted Moore	Farmer of Easton Farm
Joseph Smalley	Barty's solicitor
Noel Baxter	Company solicitor for Tide Mill Associates
David Lloyd	Bank manager TMCC & TMA
Bill Marriott	Barty's father adopted name
Marie & Matthew Arnold	Skipper's daughter & her husband
John & Rebecca	Son & daughter of above

'Barty'

Glossary

Mudlark: Scavenger of a tidal river
Freeride: Trade in untaxed goods
Crop: Illegal cargo
Flink: Warning light
Brig: Two masted, square rigged vessel
Cutter: Small, single mast vessel
Ketch: Small two-mast, fore & aft rigged vessel

In the poem 'The Smuggler's Song' (Page 163)
Gentlemen: The Smugglers
Woodlump: Woodpile
King George's Men: Soldiers hunting smugglers
Valenciennes: Lace made in Northern France

To my Grandson
Kaleb Michael John Haynes

also

my grateful thanks to a
dear friend **Lynne Gadd** for her
computer expertise for correcting my
typographical errors of which they were too many!

Barty

A sliver of sunlight managed to force its way through the filthy grime encrusted window pane of the basement room forming a little puddle of light on the earth floor of the tall building fronting the Dock Road just opposite the Millwall Embankment. It was late spring and the sun was rising at about 5.15am giving scant warmth to the many pairs of feet making their way to the warehouses and docks along the River Thames. The small pool of light slowing grew but gave no comfort to the curled-up figure on the small wooden bench on the opposite side of the room. The figure lay motionless as his eyes became accustomed to the semi-darkness until he could clearly see all the inside of the room revealing two bench beds, two chairs and a small makeshift hearth that served as a cooker and the only means of warmth. The single door led to a short flight of steps up to street level. There was a pile of dirty clothes on one chair, these were street clothes that were absolutely caked in mud and filth from the river, a river that appeared to hold all the effluent and rotten waste of the City.

    The figure on the bed moved to find a more restful position but his bones were aching painfully from the hard work of trying to make a few pennies to pay for food and the pathetic roof over his head.

The noise from the passing traffic filtered in through the door and broken window to where he lay keeping him from any further rest that morning. He had lain awake most of the night, deprived of sleep and he could now see the shadowy outline of people passing in the street, their footsteps echoing on the cobbles as some pushed their handcarts towards the early morning markets.

Early morning! Today, he thought, would not be a good day to go out as the tide would be high and he would be unable to search for his 'treasures' until it receded, the pieces of coal, wood, rags and metal, almost anything that could be found only at low tide and then could be collected and sold to various merchants for a few pennies. Kaleb was, like many other children and some adults, a mudlark; mainly surviving on the few coins they collected for their living – a miserable dirty way to exist.

The circumstances of his very existence had forced him to seek some way of earning money to stave off begging and starvation. He had only been wading in the dirty polluted waters of the Thames for the past three months or so. His mother Doris, a relatively young woman had left the tenement building to seek employment at a gentleman's residence somewhere in the countryside. Kaleb hadn't seen her since; living alone in that tiny cellar room called home! He had no idea where she had gone and presumed that she didn't find work and went elsewhere without leaving any message for Kaleb, which was nearly three months ago,

The sun struggled in between the warehouse buildings allowing more light to enter the room revealing the shocking state of his clothes and bringing harsh reality of what the days had in store for him. He suddenly remembered that after midday the future was totally unknown to him. The reality was that at midday he had to leave this hovel he called home what to do next now occupied his mind. He realised that his sleepless night was due to partly to not knowing where his mother had gone coupled with a letter received from the landlord. Today was 21st September 1910, it was Kaleb's 12th birthday but he had not recognised it at all, he had more pressing thoughts on his mind.

Mr Sykes was the landlord of the tenement block and another large warehouse complex over the other side of the river. Mr Bernard Coles, agent for the property, had delivered the letter almost three months ago, when Doris was given just one month to settle the arrears for rent, that was three months ago, and Mr Coles had been sympathetic in trying to console her but all to no avail. Realising that the future looked very grim she had left after frantically searching for employment. Mr Coles had not seen or heard from Doris since that time. Did he gain employment? Where else could she have gone? What had happened to her? All these questions were in Kaleb's mind as he struggled to come to terms with his present predicament. Mr Coles had told Kaleb that if the arrears were unpaid at midday today, the bailiffs would affect entry to the room, not that there was anything of value for them to seize but they would change the lock on the door.

The time was now roughly 7am and low tide would be about 10am this morning so there was no immediate rush for him to vacate the room Suddenly he became aware of the thought that had earlier evaded him. Today was his birthday. He had quite forgotten, he was 12 years old on this very day when his future held no promises: no one to even wish him a Happy Birthday, no wonder he wasn't looking forward to anything, no work, no friends or relatives and he was being made homeless at 12 o – clock.

He slowly rose from the bed, put on his cardboard stiff clothing and stepped outside to answer a call of nature. The lavatory was at the end of the communal yard, five cubicles had to serve the sixteen families that live in the block so he had to wait awhile for he could take his turn in the lavatory. On leaving the yard he climbed a few steps and went to the front of the building. People were still scurrying along the dismal thoroughfare to their places of business. Kaleb returned to his small abode and sat on the edge of the bed, still thinking. He casually glanced about the room just to ensure that there was nothing to take with him when he left. His mind was still wandering, it hadn't always been like this, there were times when he recalled happier occasions before he and his mother came to London. His memories of his formative years weren't great but some of the better ones lingered in his mind. He must have been 5 or 6 years old when the pattern of his life became clearer.

Kaleb was born in the little town of Leiston in Suffolk on 21st September 1898 to Walter James and Doris Bartholomew (nee Gill). He was a very healthy baby that grew strong during those early years. They moved from their small terraced house to a tied farm cottage on the outskirts of Friston where his father had secured a job as farm hand at Sunrise Farm owned by Frederick Green. It wasn't a large farm but to young Kaleb it seemed enormous and he enjoyed the freedom of being able to roam about the farm when on occasions he went there with his father. Walter was a well-built man of 28 years of age, a very capable and likeable man, his mother Doris was 3 years his junior and had part-time domestic work at one of the larger houses on the outskirts of Aldeburgh, the master of the house being the owner of a mill at Snape.

Kaleb had the benefit of a basic education at a small school in Friston. He was a popular boy at school and was accepted by both the pupils and the teachers alike. The rules and regulations in the small Victorian school were quite rigid and Mr Boswell enforced them without exception. During his time at the school Kaleb fell foul of the rules a couple of times and found guilty of misdemeanours that really didn't warrant punishment but boys will be boys and Mr Boswell carried out his duties. On the whole Mr Boswell was pleased with Barty's conduct and progression and didn't hesitate to tell his parents of the pleasure he felt in teaching him. As for Kaleb, he enjoyed his schooling within reason but looked forward to the day when he finished school. His father obtained permission from Mr Green for him to take Kaleb to Sunrise Farm where he would be employed with some of the lighter work. He was a hard worker, happily carrying out most every job he was capable of and on occasions he would earn a penny or two from Mr Green. Of all the odd jobs, he did at the farm he enjoyed the animals, especially the horses. This arrangement carried on for three years or so when things started to go wrong. He was growing into a very dependable farmhand for a lad who was only eight or nine years old, growing stronger every day. He was about five feet 4 inches tall with a mop of dark brown hair, brown eyes and a wide happy smiling face, a very attractive lad. He continued to attend school and on the fine evenings he would visit the farm after school. He was eager to learn more about the horses and he learnt a lot from Mr Green who specialised in breeding and showing the famous Suffolk Punch heavy horses. Kaleb quickly learnt so much about magnificent animals, which appeared so very big to him, the horses reaching some 16 to 17 hands (65" – 70") in height, powerful agricultural workhorses and always chestnut in colour.

Mr Green had three horses he kept mainly for showing and Kaleb's knowledge and care became quite comprehensive He was forever asking questions and seeking more knowledge. This happy and satisfactory way of life lasted for roughly three years then things began to happen that brought much sadness and a complete change of life for him.

Still sat on the edge of his bed in that tiny squalid cellar room Kaleb revelled in these carefree memories but now, unfortunately those lovely bright sunlit days had come to an end as his thoughts returned to his present predicament. He inwardly cursed himself for allowing his thoughts of the past to take precedence over today's plight but it was hard to dismiss those happy days.

The year of 1907 was a year of disaster for the farming community. Disease and crop failures caused many farmers to lay off their workers, it was no different for Mr Green who had to give one month's notice to

Barty's father to quit. That was when Walter Bartholomew committed his greatest crime. There was no possibility of employment at surrounding farms; they were all in the same boat. The fields were flooded from the early spring rains; the crops failed leaving an acute shortage of food for everyone and the animals. The grain harvest would be completely ruined for the year and there would be no work at the mills. A limited amount of grain was obtainable from the neighbouring counties and that was at an inflated price. Many families were on the breadline and there was a spate of thieving from barns and storage depots. The Bartholomew family was no exception. Walter had tried to get work at many places, any job that would pay a wage but all without success. Doris still had her domestic duties at the house at Snape but her hours were also cut leaving even less of her meagre pay for the family to live on. Times were getting hard.

About two weeks after Walter had been laid off from Sunrise Farm the situation was becoming critical, there was hardly any food obtainable and little money to buy anything that was available. Walter recalled that he had seen in the back larder at the farm several carcases being ready for sale at the local meat market. He remembered the recent slaughter of a few animals, sheep, cows and a few chickens all ready for the market and a few more put by for use at the farm.

Saturday was the local market day when the clear majority of this stock would be taken for sale. And Mr Green also took some livestock to be sold at the auction. He had foreseen that feeding his livestock could present a huge problem as the months shortened and the onset of a meagre winter threatened his own family's living.

In sheer desperation to feed his own family, Walter left his cottage and made his way to Sunrise Farm knowing full well that Mr Green would be at the market. Mrs Green always accompanied her husband to the market as it gave her the opportunity to visit the town to buy any other items they needed. Walter didn't take his usual route to the farm but skirted the house through the neighbouring field and the woods in an effort not to be seen by anyone else. The day had dawned brightly; it was dry and sunny when Walter set off. The only person he saw on his half-mile journey was the old charcoal burner man who lived just on the edge of Hillside Wood. Walter didn't know his name, the man always kept himself to himself but seemed to have lived and worked there for as long as anyone could remember. Although the day was dry the ground underfoot was still very wet and muddy from the excessive rain and flooding. He reached the farm and crossed the yard where the farm dog ran to greet him, running and jumping about him. The dog had given no warning bark as he knew Walter so well. He knocked on the farmhouse door and receiving no response he tried the handle. Locked! Believing there was no-one around he went to the back of the house and with hardly any effort he forced a small window, climbed through and accessed the kitchen store quite easily. It took him but seconds to slip two legs of lamb and a few vegetables into the small sack he had brought with him. Departing the house, he made his way back by the same route as he had arrived believing that no-one had seen him, he saw nobody either.

He was very conscious of what he had just done, petty pilfering as rife almost everywhere and Walter, had in the past taken his opportunities as they presented themselves but this was the first time he had committed an offence that was pre-planned. Housebreaking and Theft, he was so desperate to provide food for his wife and family that caution had been cast to the wind. He was also aware that if he was caught he would lose the tenancy of the farm cottage that Mr Green had generously agreed to allow him to remain until he could find new employment

As Kaleb sat on the edge of the bed in the cellar room he imagined how his father must have felt, he was now experiencing lean times himself. He hadn't understood the details about his father's crime until more of the evidence came to light after the arrest. At only eight years of age it all appeared quite hazy to him. Now, four years later and alone in London his previous life in Suffolk seemed to be falling into a pattern that had brought him to his present situation.

The Officers who entered the house, after a brief questioning and search found a leg of lamb together with another partly consumed joint. Walter was arrested and taken to the Police Station for further questioning. Doris was quite distraught and Kaleb did his best to comfort her. This was the first occasion that the family had had any contact with the law, now the future was unclear. Basically, Walter was an honest man and a valued employee of Mr Green. Why Walter had, in his desperation, succumbed to dis-honesty was understood.

The following day he appeared before the town's magistrates and was referred to the Court of Quarter Sessions in Ipswich in a few weeks' time meanwhile he was to be kept at His Majesty's pleasure at H.M.P. Hollesley Bay known locally as Hollesley Colony, about 8 miles from Woodbridge. Doris was unable to make regular visits to see her husband as travel to the prison was awkward, no direct connections, and rather costly to travel by other modes. Kaleb never visited his father at all. Mr Green let them stay in the cottage at a peppercorn rent that was quite a drain on her meagre wage as a domestic. It was obvious that they would have to abandon the cottage and for Doris to find a more lucrative employment. Mr Green, although he had been wronged was very understanding and for a short while permitted Kaleb to visit his beloved 'Suffolks' and receive a few pennies payment for the work he performed but the financial rewards were of little use as Mr Green was experiencing hard times on the farm just like everyone else.

It was six weeks later when Walter Bartholomew appeared before Judge and Jury at the Ipswich Quarter Sessions. The case was soon heard as Walter, in a bid for mitigation, pleaded 'Guilty' to the two charges of Housebreaking and Larceny and subsequently sentenced to ten years' imprisonment. Since Walter had been in prison awaiting trial the only money coming into the house had been his mother's pittance. Slowly the rent arrears, low as they were started to mount up and Doris realised that she would have to leave the tied cottage earlier than anticipated, where could they go, they had no relatives they could stay with and with employment being so scarce the future looked grim. She frantically searched through newspapers, made enquiries but all to no avail. As a last resort, she applied to the Parish Council for poor relief. She had no experience of claiming such benefit through the local council and her efforts fell upon stony grounds Doris was at her wits end, no wages, her husband in prison and her son too young to possess any form of skill that would bring in a wage was unable to assist in supporting himself and his mother.

Charles Carpenter stood at the large window of his office on the first floor of a rather grim looking building that was surrounded by open land that was being tended by several people in the process of growing vegetables when there was a light tap on his door.

"Come in", a small boy entered clutching some papers that he placed on the desk facing the office window. The boy hesitated for a moment until he was dismissed by a wave of the hand from Mr Carpenter who watched the boy quietly leave the office. His attention then turned to the papers that had just been delivered. Mr Charles Carpenter was a somewhat sour faced moustachioed man of about 55 years of age, he was the Master of the Union Workhouse at Shipmeadow, Woodbridge, locally known as 'The Spike' It had the reputation of being one of the strictest establishments in the County and it was run by a very strict Master in Mr Carpenter giving no quarter to misdemeanours, rules were rules and made to be obeyed. Any infringement of those rules was not tolerated in any form and certain punishments were sure to be exacted.

Entry into the Workhouse, in the main, was voluntary but anyone in dire need and not in entitled to Parish relief payments could be referred by the Parish Relieving Officer for entry into the Workhouse, as it was in the case of Doris and Kaleb Bartholomew.

Thinking back, Kaleb was still not aware of all the efforts his mother had undergone trying to find an answer to their problems or of the degrading facts she had had to disclose to the Parish Council about his father, after all he was still only eight years old and didn't understand a lot of what had happened during the various processes. He did well remember that day when his mother took him to 'The Spike' and the reception that they received on that first morning, that would live in his memory forever. They were taken up a flight of stairs to the Master's office and introduced to Mr Carpenter and his wife Mary. The Master asked a few questions as he laid out the rules of the 'house' and asked them if they accepted the rules. They both agreed. At least they could expect food, shelter and some prospects for the future, the lack of the very things that had brought them through the doors of that establishment. When all the formalities were completed they were taken to the Reception Area to be classified, medically examined and bathed to ensure that that no infections would be spread to other inmates. Kaleb had his head shaved for similar reasons. a process he remembered vividly. Their day clothes were taken from them and they were issued with workhouse clothing that had been obtained from rag shops or from previous inmates that had passed away. The treatment was harsh and unforgettable. The came to final blow, they were given one of seven categories. Doris and Kaleb were separated. Doris was classified as "female, able-bodied, over 16 years of age". Kaleb was "male youth and boys above 7 and below 13 years of age" They were then sent to their separate classification group dormitories.

Woodbridge was a large workhouse with some 350 inmates and changes over the years had been slow in the implementation of various Acts of Parliament. In the earlier days, the Parish Poor Law Unions were required to provide at least three hours a day for schooling, reading, writing, arithmetic and the basic of a Christian religion. Over the years, Acts were past to improve the educational standards. Kaleb had reached an acceptable standard at his junior school and could read and write well. He attended further schooling at the workhouse under the guidance of a Mr George Brown, an amiable reasonable young man who possessed quite revolutionary ideas about improving the conditions in the workhouse school but was never allowed to put them into practice. With his help and encouragement Kaleb had the opportunity to join the workers in the gardens as part of his skills training. He always enjoyed being in the fresh air, rain or shine, as it was reminiscent of his carefree days at Sunrise Farm

Occasionally Doris and Kaleb would meet in the library room in the evenings after supper. During the day, Doris worked quietly assisting in the day to day running of the workhouse' finding the time each evening to go to the library room where there was a small stock of reading material mainly donated by well-meaning parishioners together with a daily supply of newspapers that were delivered from the town. Doris devoured the adverts in the papers searching for a suitable post but there was always some reason for eliminating them. It was hard to find work when you are the mother of an eight-year old son and jobs were still scare everywhere.

Life in the workhouse was quite mundane, repetitive and boring although a certain amount of relief could be gained by attending the occasional handicraft sessions brought in by visiting trades people and local craft workers after the days' work had been completed, #readings, lectures and a minimum of entertainments staged usually by talented inmates or visiting players but they had little effect on Doris who had her heart set on leaving the workhouse as soon as she was able to find work. The workhouses were not prisons and inmates could discharge themselves having given at least three hours' notice to the Master. This time allowed for the completion of the administration and the retrieval of their own clothes and property from the store. If inmates left the workhouse wearing issued clothing they could be arrested and charged with theft. Some workhouses granted 'liberty days' that allowed inmates to leave the workhouse to pursue job applications and sometimes even to visit relatives.

Some workhouses granted 'liberty days' that allowed inmates to leave the workhouse to pursue job applications and sometimes even to visit relatives. Doris had left the workhouse on previous occasions to attend interviews nearby but she was tired of all the petty rules and regulations, the pettiness of the rules and the lack of freedom weighed upon her so much that she vowed to take any job, no matter how menial that would support herself and Kaleb., but every avenue to leave was blocked by the shortage of opportunities. After about three and a half years in 'The Spike' Doris found an advert in one newspaper for a domestic 'live in' housekeeper at a large house

After about three and a half years in 'The Spike' Doris found an advert in one newspaper for a domestic 'live in' housekeeper at large house just outside London. She applied for a liberty day, which was granted, and she went to Woodbridge to answer the advert,

She visited the Poor Relief Office at 10 Water Street, to seek advice and the best way to approach her pending application. A well-dressed middle-aged lady invited her to be seated while she asked a few questions and said that she would contact a Mr & Mrs Middleton who had placed the advert in the newspaper. Doris had been very truthful in answering all the questions, telling of her present position and that she had previously worked as a domestic and lived on a farm prior to her husband's imprisonment but she never mentioned Kaleb.

As she left the office she sensed a certain feeling of satisfaction, having been so honest about her previous employment and her work experience. She had liked the lady who interviewed her and felt confident that she would be given a good reference to support her application.

Mr Carpenter called Doris to his office about two weeks after the visit to the Poor Relief Office. He was pleased to tell her that he had received a positive reply from the Middleton's via the Relief Office and to be prepared to start her new employment at the beginning of next month. He told her that the job would entail a lot of domestic work; she would also be expected to work on the land around the house, which appeared to be quite extensive, and under the control of Mr Ben Chapman, the Head Groundsman. All this sounded like a big job, housekeeper, domestic work and help in the gardens and being 'live in' she would be expected to be available at all hours. Being desperate to leave to workhouse she agreed to accept the job and take the chance. She would be given living quarters in the west wing of the house and her meals would be provided from the kitchens. The pay wasn't that good but she would have food, shelter and that was most important to her. She recognised that she hadn't mentioned Kaleb in her plans but had decided to just go and give it a try and if successful she would send for him. Nothing of the plans were revealed to Kaleb when they next met in the library room, she just said she would be going away for a couple of weeks while she was job hunting in London. This Kaleb accepted without question. He would be allowed to stay at the workhouse until his mother was settled then he would have to leave as the rules stated that if the parents of children under the age of 13 years left the workhouse then they too would be required to leave.

Life at the workhouse continued with the same monotonous routines. Kaleb still went to school and at his age, nearly 12 years old, he had learnt to read and write perfectly well, whenever he managed to have time to read the newspapers he made the most of it asking Mr Brown many questions about the things he didn't understand. For his part, Mr Brown was delighted to have such an interested pupil with such an appetite to learn.

Kaleb also valued the time he spent in the gardens and appreciated the changing seasons and the variety of fruits and vegetables that were produced to be used in the workhouse kitchens. Although contented with this side of his limited existence he longed for the day when he could be totally free to make his own way and make his own choices but, now he had no idea of what he wanted in the way of employment outside the walls of the workhouse.

Doris was due to report to Mill Hill House at 8am on 1st June to take up her duties. She stayed at a close by B & B overnight so that she would be in good time to report. On reporting to the house she was met by Mr Ben Chapman, who would brief her as to her responsibilities and show her around the large house. It was during the tour of the house that she learnt that the owner was Sir James Middleton and not Mr Chapman as she had been lead to believe. The room she was to occupy was in the attic, a small room containing a single bed and just enough furniture to make it comfortable. Doris asked where he son would be accommodated only to receive the reply that Mr Chapman wasn't aware that she had a son and therefore he had not been allocated a room. This news came something as a shock to Doris especially when she heard that no other rooms were available as other members of the staff lived in them. Had the correspondence relating to her appointment not mentioned the fact that she would require accommodation for her son or had it perhaps just been overlooked?

Doris immediately apologised for the oversight saying that she could not possibly accept the post as her son was still in the workhouse waiting for her to send for him. Mr Chapman said he would contact the workhouse and the Poor Relief Office to explain the situation and, in the meantime she could perhaps find suitable employment whilst she was in London. The Poor Relief Office had given her enough money to tide her over for two or three days so she would have to go into a lodging house while she again searched for work.

The very next day Kaleb received the news that his mother's employment had not been accepted. The Workhouse Master broke the news to him and told him that he would now be required to leave the workhouse and join his mother in London but he had no address for her and Mr Chapman at Mill Hill House had no idea where she had gone. The following morning Kaleb went to the Reception room to claim his clothing only to find that the clothes he wore on entry, three and a half years ago, were much too small for him so other suitable clothing was found for him. With no other baggage, he left the workhouse and made his way to the Poor Relief Office as he had been advised. On completion of the necessary forms he was given a travel warrant to London and enough money for roughly a week's stay in a lodging house. His prime object now was to try and find his mother in the big City. He knew that she had applied for the job at Mill Hill House but he didn't know where it was located. He travelled to Ipswich and had to wait a long time for a train to take him to London. At 12 years, old he had little idea of where to go and what to do.

He arrived in London late afternoon and made his way to the dock area where he understood there could be the chance of work on the docks and where the cheapest lodging houses were to be found. He wandered about for some considerable time and as the light began to fade he found himself on the West Ferry Road on the Isle of Dogs, had had walked quite a distance from the railway station. It didn't take long for him to find a small dingy room to rent and paid a week's rent in advance. Again, it was a cellar room fronting onto the street and sparsely furnished. He just couldn't afford anything better. He slept fitfully that night worrying about tomorrow. He had 6d in his pocket, no food and no prospects of earning a few pennies and a roof over his head for the coming week only.

Kaleb cut a pathetic figure as he walked down the West Ferry Road past the Harbourmasters compound where he and another man were preparing the launch for one of the regular river patrols along the docks and waterways of this busy stretch of the River Thames. He had been living in the hovel for two days but already he could recognise the launch and the other launches belonging to the river police who would often stop and approach poor people along the river to find out what they were doing and what they had in their possession always suspecting that they could be in possession of stolen property. He hurried past the compound without looking at the launch and headed for the West India Dock Pier where he was surprised to see a few people, all busy and up to their knees in the muddy water They were all very intent upon their efforts to find some 'treasures' that they would be able to sell for a few pence to provide them with food for the day. He counted twelve people ages ranging from about five years to quite elderly men and women all dressed in stiff muddy clothing and engrossed in finding anything that might be of little value no matter how small; no one spoke to him. These people were the mudlarks who he had seen a few short days ago. It was a bright morning and the weak sun shone down on the pathetic figures each carrying a basket, large empty tin or a bag in which they would put their 'finds' Kaleb started his search close to the river wall where only a couple of the boys were working, his old worn shoes tied around his neck as he probed the muddy river bed with his feet and his hands as he bent nearly double to identify the various odds and ends he came upon; small pieces of coal, wood, rags, bits of metal in fact anything that could be sold for a few halfpennies. The items he found would be sorted and taken to dealers who would resell them to interested parties - small bags of wood and coal for the fires of people living in the network of alleyways and courts in the neighbourhood, where many of the mudlarks also lived. Metal that could be weighed in, the rags would be dried and sold to the ragman, even small lengths of rope, anything! Rag shops would pay about one penny for 5lbs of iron, bones one penny for 3lbs. of wet and dry ropes – one halfpenny wet and 3 farthings dry. The best 'finds' was copper and copper nails, which were sometimes to be found in the dry docks after ship and boat repairs had been completed and the vessels moved out.

Going into the dry docks to retrieve the copper was a hazardous affair as it was private property and people found there may be arrested and charged with stealing, copper was selling for 4 pence for 4lbs.

The average earning for a mudlark would vary from two and a half pence to 4 pence a day although on rare occasions, if they found lost tools they could earn as much as 8 pence but that was rare indeed.

Kaleb soon learnt the going rate and where to take his hard earned 'finds' for the best price by following the more experience mudlarks to their dealers. He found it more lucrative to collect coal as this was the main cargo carried by most barges and lighters so he preferred to work nearest to the jetty wall, as spillage was greater there. While searching, he was mindful that he would again be homeless when his small amount of cash ran out and he wasn't earning much so he made up his mind that he would go to one of the cheap lodging houses in the dock area before he was penniless.

He worked until the tide began to turn when he was startled by a cry for help nearby. Glancing about him he saw a boy just a few yards downriver, he was up to his neck in the water as the tide was swiftly rising and at a fair rate. The boy was evidently in trouble and Kaleb, who was close to the jetty wall, hanging on to a mooring chain kicked out from the wall towards him; he was in danger of being swept towards the middle of the river. His actions were very quick as he stretched out and caught the boy by his shirt collar whilst still clutching the mooring chain and dragged the boy into the side of the wall close to the jetty steps. They scrambled towards the steps but the boy was obviously in pain and had difficulty in climbing them. He had large cut to his lower right leg which Kaleb presumed had been caused by some underwater object, glass, a piece of metal or something similar. Although he was hurt and bleeding freely it looked worse than it was as the blood mixed with the water but luck was smiling on them. As they reached the top of the jetty steps a motor launch came alongside, it was the Harbourmasters boat. Seeing the boys were struggling and obviously in need of help the Harbourmaster approached them. They were on the private property of the Harbourmaster's Compound although they didn't realise it.

"What's going on here then?" the Harbourmaster asked then he spotted the boys injury that looked quite nasty. Up until this point the boy hadn't said a word but suddenly spoke "I can't swim you know"
The Harbourmaster said, "Just stay here a minute, I've got a First Aid Kit in the boat" and off he went. On his return, he started to dress the boy's leg whilst asking how it had happened. Neither could say only that it was cut by something in the river. Both boys had a shoulder type satchel bag that the Harbourmaster had spotted; he looked into the bags that just contained a few bits of wood and coal. He was used to seeing mudlarks on this stretch of the river and just grunted. He chastised the boys for their misdemeanour but mainly because they had trespassed on Crown property. He finished dressing the boy's leg, the wound wasn't deep and the Harbourmaster was happy that the treatment rendered was sufficient. He was however, obliged to report the incident and when asked their place of abode, both replied, "We don't live anywhere" but willingly gave their names. They thanked him for the trouble he had taken and apologised for their presence on Crown land.
The Harbourmaster let them out of the Compound and into the street before resuming his normal duties.

Kaleb had saved the boy's life, being unable to swim the boy had trod on a sharp object and lost his balance. He was foundering when Kaleb caught him by the collar and pulled him to the jetty wall. The unfortunate thing was that the Harbourmaster had confiscated their bags so there was a mixed feeling of luck.

The boy was Jed Slater, aged 11 years, an orphan who had been mudlarking for almost three years. This was the first moment that the two boys had had the chance to talk to each other. Kaleb told Jed of his present predicament and the fact that he truly had nowhere to live. Jed on the other hand had lodgings in a cheap lodging house just off the West

Ferry Road; he didn't want to tell the Harbourmaster that he lived in a cheap lodging house although he suspected that he knew anyway. On learning that Kaleb had a worldly wealth of just sixpence he invited him to go back to the lodging house with him. This was extremely helpful, as Kaleb had planned to search for such a place. They slowly made their way along the West India Dock jetty, Kaleb giving support to Jed until they came to Brighton Place, a small courtyard of six houses, most of which would benefit from maintenance and a coat of paint, especially the three facing the gateway to the courtyard. The time was about 5pm as Jed entered the building beckoning Kaleb to follow him. The room as very long and scattered with an odd assortment of chairs and tables, most of which had seen better days. There was no-one in the room as they made their way towards a curtained door at the far end. Jed knocked quietly on the door and on receiving a gruff reply of "Come in" they entered and approached the man sat behind a desk. The man glanced up from some paperwork that was holding his attention and said, "Come back at 6 o-clock, that's when we open" He caught a sight of Jed's bandaged leg and continued, "What 'ave you been up to?" He had recognised Jed as one of his lodgers, "and who's this?" he enquired looking directly at Kaleb. Jed explained what had happened and how Kaleb had prevented him from being swept into the river by the tide. The man, Mr Ben Osbourne said to Jed, "I 'hope you didn't tell then where you lived, I don't want no trouble here" Jed assured him that he hadn't said a word and asked if there was a vacancy for Kaleb. Ben Osbourne, despite his looks and gruff nature was a sympathetic man. He was aged about 50 years and stood roughly 6'.2" tall with a massive frame and arms to match, the type that no sane person would pick a fight with. In his younger days, he had been a bare-knuckle fighter and billed as "Battling Ben Osbourne" he had been quite successful in his chosen profession and had won some lucrative purses.

However, he had the sense to know that his heydays would not last forever, he retired and put away his hard-earned money for a rainy day That day arrived when he bought three of the houses in the courtyard and eventually opened as a cheap lodging house, mainly for dock workers and other unfortunates that had fallen upon hard times.

He made a few notes in a large ledger, recording Kaleb's full name, place and date of birth. The information was required by law as an attempt to keep a trace on the many offenders that also frequented this type of dwelling Having completed the entry Mr Osbourne said,

"That will be 2 pence for tonight and 2 pence for every night you stay here. Now go upstairs and find a bed" and pointing to Jed, He'll show you, then wait in the room outside this office".

Kalen paid him the 2 pence and thanked him. There were 12 beds in the room upstairs, each with a small cupboard beside it and a 4-foot partition dividing the bed spaces. Luckily the bed space next to Jed was unoccupied so Kaleb left his dirty muddy coat at the foot of the bed to show it was taken. They both went back downstairs to wait where they had been told, looking around the room it was evident that it was a shared Common Room with a row of cookers along one wall that was sooty black and grease stained. There was a stack of well-used cooking pans at the far end. This was the Common Room, as well as the kitchen, dining room and a washing room used by all the lodgers

The boys sat quietly not saying very much but taking in their surroundings. Kalen asked one or two questions of Jed to which he had the answers, he had been staying there a few nights now.

At 6pm, Mr Osbourne went to the front door and opened it wide. It hadn't been locked but nobody had dared to enter before 6pm. Rules were rules! Slowly people started to come through the door and occupy the main room. Men and women, some quite decrepit, sat around at the tables talking and sorting through the assorted articles that had procured during the day while the younger one, some as young as 8 years chased about between the tables. Jed had seen all this before but Kaleb was surprised at the age differences and the appearance of them. It was obvious that most of the children worked as mudlarks, bone collectors and beggars. There were others who pursued their chosen professions as pickpockets, thieves. shop-lifters, handkerchief stealers, dock labourers, market porters and costermongers, who left their handcarts in the large open space in front of the house. Some lodgers went straight to their bed spaces but all of them were in need of a wash but the only source of cleaning themselves was a cold-water supply to two or three hand basins in the back yard. Jed pointed out several of the men telling Kaleb how they obtained their money, he particularly told him which men would buy goods – usually stolen, from others and sell them on again at a profit or, in the case of jewellery to a 'fence' who would trade with one of the Jewish shops in the area. One exception to this were the men who were housebreakers; they wouldn't frequent the lodging houses but lived with prostitutes who between them generated a better standard of living.

    This then was Kaleb's immediate future; he could see no reprieve from his present existence so he listened intently to what Jed was telling him. True, Jed was a little younger than Kaleb but he had been staying in lodging houses for quite some time now.

The smell of cooking pervaded the room as some of the lodgers prepared their food. Jed and Kaleb had a few vegetables that they had stolen from a market stall, from which they concocted a soup. From the original 6 pence Kaleb had when he left the cellar room he had spent 2 pence on his bed space for the night before realising that tomorrow would be Sunday and the mudlarks, like the dockers, did not work on the Sabbath. The day would be spent roaming around the wharfs noting where the ships and coal barges were berthed, loaded or not, as that could be a great place for 'finds' the next day. The boys continued talking and planning until late when the gas lighting was switched off at 11pm and no further admittances to the house were made. The kitchen would not open again until the next morning at 5am so the lads groped their way upstairs to find their beds.

They were awakened before 5am by the noise made by two or three dockworkers, as they got ready to start their day that began on the docks at 6am. Normally there were no activities on the docks on Sundays but these probably had special duties to perform. The boys dressed and went down to the kitchen mainly to escape the overwhelming stagnant odours of the dormitory, it was only then that Kaleb realised how many people had spent the night at the house as there were other rooms he had not seen the night before. Jed made a drink of tea but they had no breakfast as they had no food at all.

It was a fine brisk September morning when they left the house after booking in for the next night. The autumn air was still quite warm as they walked down an almost deserted West Ferry Road pausing now and again to watch the river traffic leaving London for the open sea. As they approached the docks about 7 to 8 o-clock some of the shops nearby began to open as groups of men were appearing in the streets and returning to their ships after a 'night out on the town' some were still the worse off for drink so they carefully avoided them as best they could, they came to a couple of shops that had their goods displayed on tables outside the doorways, seeing the shop keepers was busy inside the shop they managed to steal two apples and a small loaf of bread, their breakfast! This was a common practice of the penniless and homeless but woe betide anyone caught stealing; the law was very heavy on them. They took their spoils to the riverside and sat on a bollard to eat them idly watching the passing parade of small boats and ships. As they sat watched Kaleb's mind went back to his early days in Suffolk and his life with his parents. His memories were fairly limited, quite vague in certain areas but he could recall going to a harbour somewhere with his father, it could have been Ipswich, where his father had to sometimes deliver goods for his employer Frederick Green. Kaleb could remember the word Ipswich on the stern of some of the barges. He was also interested to see the names of faraway places on the sterns of foreign ships and his mind was entranced by some of the exotic names although he hadn't a clue where they were from, he saw the crews working, heard them speaking and fantasised of a life he knew nothing about. He was now 12 years old and hadn't had access to any books that could satisfy his puzzled mind. He could read perfectly well and had read of great changes that were taking place in the world. He found old newspapers in rubbish bins and at the lodging house and eagerly read of many happenings. He remembered that Queen Victoria had died in 1901 and that King Edward the Seventh had been crowned the following year and that this year 1910 another new king had come to the throne, King George the Fifth. At his young age, much of this meant little to Kaleb as he struggled to earn a pittance for his work. One thing that did stick in his mind was that about time was that the trams of London were starting to be withdrawn. His mind went back to the Suffolk Punch horses on Mr Green's farm that had given him the idea that when he was old enough he would try for work at the transport depot but now that dream was gone although it would have been a few years before the withdrawal was complete.

 Suddenly he was jolted back to reality as Jed suggested that they take a walk around the business area near the docks and look at the rag shops and second hand shops just out of curiosity. Even though it was Sunday the whole population of the Isle of Dogs seemed to have come onto the streets, many dressed in their best clothes on their way to a church service. Sailors of mixed nations began to throng the alleyways and back streets looking for entertainment and drinking houses. Kaleb was impressed by some of the horse drawn carriages that drove through the better parts of the area

The day passed quickly and the boys returned to the lodging house having first purchased some food for supper, cheese to go with the small loaf they had stolen earlier together with a few potatoes. Jed had told Kaleb to leave nothing of value in his bedside locker, not that he possessed anything of value and currently had only 2 pence of the original sixpence left, Jed had paid for the cheese and potatoes. They went to bed reasonable early to try and get some sleep before the dockers awoke early again next morning.

Monday morning dawned overcast and miserable but the boys realised their urgent need for money, after paying the next night's stay they were stony broke. They went down to the Customs jetty and started to work. They worked separately where they had noted the empty coal barges the day before. They both did reasonably well and took the 'finds' to a rag shop to be weighed in – Kaleb received 4 pence and Jed 6 pence this made then feel fairly cash secure for the next two days Before leaving the river they had gone to the hot water outflow of one of the factories and washed themselves and their jackets. Which they dried in the kitchen of the lodging house, the days were now getting colder so they needed to wear the coats while they were working. Similar days followed and their earning very slowly increased especially when they found a box of new copper nails that weighed in for 5 pence per 1lb, netting them a whole 10 pence. They pooled the money they had earned but were very cautious with their expenses. Returning to the lodgings one night they learnt that an overnight stay had gone up by a penny to 3 pence per night, but they were quite able to pay two days in advance. They also cut the risk of being caught stealing food by buying it from other lodgers at the house. Most foods were obtainable, no questions asked!

After long days of work the boys would have accumulated a fair amount of rags, bones, small pieces of ironware, coal, wood and rope ends which they kept hidden beneath the jetty steps until they could find time to sort it all out and take it to the dealers. They were still very fugal with their outgoings but realised they needed some new clothing, their filthy old working clothes soon wore out with the constant everyday washing that it needed. Whist in one of the rag dealers' shops they could each buy a second-hand jacket for 5 pence, a thick shirt for one penny and a pair of trousers for 4 pence. They had some money left but could not afford to buy any shoes, pay their lodging house fees and eat. The clothes would not last them for long doing the job that they were doing!

Winter was really starting to set in and the cold began to bite. As the days grew colder less people came to the river in search of things to sell. The boys persisted and were rewarded for their efforts in the absence of the less hardy mudlarks that normally scavenged the mud banks. They regularly visited the hot water outlet at the factory to wash some of their clothes and to warm themselves. It seemed that more poor people were coming to the area every day seeking shelter from the coming weather.

The Asylum for the Homeless only opened in the winter months when the thermometer reached freezing point and offered nothing but dry bread and shelter for the night. The penniless and homeless flooded to find somewhere to sleep, out of work seamen from many nations, beggars and wanderers all looked for relief and Kaleb and Jed were thankful for the little cash they had to secure their accommodation at the lodging house by paying in advance. The Asylum houses were degrading places, there were no beds in the large dormitories and only old boxes dividing each berth space that contained a straw stuffed tarpaulin to sleep on even they were riddled with insects after a few nights. A pot-bellied stove occupied the centre of the room around which most of the 'down and outs' crowded looking for the comfort of a little warmth. Some of the luckier ones may have been awarded a few pence from the Parish Relief Fund and they sought better accommodation at the lodging house where the boys were staying. But places were few and far between. The lodging house became almost over-crowded during the winter month then many returned to their previous pursuits. The boys immersed themselves in their boring life but always looking for better prospects. As time passed they became older and wiser in the ways of making extra money and in their dealings with the various shop owners to whom they sold their 'findings' by gaining extra pay for their loyalty of using the favoured agents

One day Kaleb was in the town when he saw a horse and wagon stop outside a bank, he noticed the name on the wagon, 'MILL HALL FARM ESTATE'. The name seemed familiar to Kaleb who soon connected it to the Hall that his mother had visited for interview for domestic employment. Wanting to speak to the driver who appeared to be in a hurry Kaleb said. "Hold your horse Sir?"

He eyed Kaleb, noting the state of his dirty clothing and his general appearance but decided to take advantage of the offer

"Here", he said, "I'm in a hurry" and handing him the reins he added, "and stay off the cart" He was obviously aware of the thieves that frequented this part of town and in a few short minutes he was out from the bank and hurriedly climbing back onto the wagon whilst taking the reins from Kaleb as he did so.

"Here you are lad" said the driver handing a sixpence to Kaleb.

"Thank you very much Sir, can I ask you something?"

"Aye lad, what is it, be quick though I'm running late today."

Kaleb quickly told him the story of his mother's acceptance of work at Mill Hall, how she had left him weeks ago, and that he had never seen or heard from her since. The driver looked long and hard at Kaleb his air of hurriedness seemed to be forgotten. His deliberation in replying gave Kaleb a feeling of great expectation, would he now get news of his mother's whereabouts?

The driver had listened to Kaleb carefully; he climbed down from the cart "I am the Head Groundsman at Mill Hall" he said, and continued, "I do remember a woman coming to the Hall a while ago, what is her name"?

"Doris Bartholomew, Kaleb replied.

"Oh yes, I remember, she came to the Hall and was going to live in but she never told us that she had a son who she expected to live in as well, there was no room for him so she chose not to stay".

Disappointment welled up inside Kaleb; he had felt sure that he was on the verge of tracing his mother.

"Are you her son?" asked the driver

" Yes, do you know where she went?"

"No, I'm sorry she just left without leaving a contact".

The driver, Mr Ben Chapman sympathised with him and said he would ask the Master of Mill Hall if he had any idea where his mother could have gone. Ben Chapman felt a little helpless on hearing this poor lad's story

"I call here every week about this time so if you are here next week I will tell you if I have any news for you".

Kaleb nodded, thanked him for his kindness and said he would definitely be there next week.

To earn sixpence for a few minutes' wait was like Christmas to Kaleb and he couldn't wait to tell Jed. That evening they sat in the kitchen and discussed the day's happenings. Normally they would go to bed at 9pm after a hard day's work but tonight they talked until lights out at 11pm. The ideas that they had the night before were put into action next day when they again visited one of the better rag shops and bought some decent cloths and a pair of shoes each. They also bought a padlock each to fix to their bedside lockers as they had nowhere else to store their clothes, which they carefully folded and stored away. Their new purchases had cost them more than they had anticipated and the following week they continued mudlarking and taking their 'finds' to the dealers. The prices being pad were lower than usual which made their efforts even harder but they were wise enough to keep enough money for food and lodgings.

Kaleb went to meet Ben Chapman as arranged but was again disappointed to hear that there was no news about his mother. Kaleb held the horse while Ben attended his business at the Bank for which he again was given a sixpence. During a short conversation, Ben told Kaleb where Mill Hall Farm was and invited him to call should he perhaps be looking for a farm work? This was wonderful news but on thinking about it Kaleb was reluctant to leave his good friend Jed and the plans they had made together. They sat quietly talking of their future. They spoke about the change in their lives that would hopefully earn them a little more money. It was difficult to concentrate, as there were always petty squabbles in the kitchen and frequent interruptions from other inmates trying to buy or sell something the arguments sometimes developed into fights and Ben Osbourne, the lodging house keeper was always having to settle these petty fights that often culminated in the culprits being thrown out and barred from the house. The ex-bare knuckle boxer, "Battling "Ben Osbourne was a very large fearsome looking man and was more than capable of dealing with any trouble makers, he was also a very fair man, give him respect and no-one would have cause to fear him.

Jed had left the kitchen for a short period to clean himself up and returned to find Kaleb in a heated argument with a dour looking man who was a known thief. The man alleged that Kaleb had stolen a pair of fresh herrings from him and was in the process of cooking them. This was totally untrue as Kaleb had stolen the fish from the market when the seller was loading his barrow ready to leave his stall. Such was the noise and fuss made by the little weasel-faced man that it attracted the attention of many of the other inmates and that of Big Ben Osbourne as well. A couple of other men were backing Kaleb's accuser and the situation appeared to be getting out of hand. Big Ben appeared from his office and to confront the group gathered around the cooking stove. Ben didn't have to ask many questions and turning to Jed he asked if Kaleb was telling the truth.as he doubted what the little weasel faced man had said to him, he was a well-known liar as well as a thief. Several of his backers had shied away as Ben entered the room but the little accuser persisted in his allegations and foolishly offered to take both Kaleb and Jed outside to prove his point. Kaleb had admitted stealing the fish in the first place and Ben was starting to lose his temper he turned to the little man very red faced and said "I'll come outside with you, not these two young boys" but the man, not very politely declined Ben's offer

"You will go outside and what's more you'll stay out" said Ben", this isn't the first time you have caused trouble, now get out, and stay out." There was no further trouble and the man quickly and quietly gathered his few sparse belongings and went towards the door that was kindly held open for him by Ben! As he left he gave a sidelong glance at Kaleb and said, "I'll be seeing you again mi lad"

The menace in his voice and the threat made to Kaleb caused Kaleb to believe that he was telling the truth this time.

The incident worried Kaleb for a few days and made him more determined to get away from the lodging house for good even though he had not experienced that kind of trouble before. Being so young most of the inmates just left the two boys alone to get on with their own business The boys sat awhile talking about the incident and gradually their talk harped back to their original plans for the future. Now that they each owned a presentable set of clothes they planned to split every day between them. For half the day Kaleb, would dress reasonably well and spend the morning in the streets of town offering to hold the gentlemen's horses whilst Jed would spend half the day mudlarking as usual. The following day they would change roles. The only problem was that the duty 'horse-holder' would have to leave the lodging house in his river clothes and take his good clothing with him ready to change over their roles. They couldn't leave a set of clothing at the house, as it would be closed until later in the evening. They had nowhere to leave the clothes and the timing of the changeover would depend on the tide times but Jed hit upon a solution. He remembered the kindly Harbourmaster's assistant who had tended his Jed's wound after Kaleb had fished him out of the Thames, He may be able to help.

They saw the man who was pleased to see them both well and listened to their plan they had made and their small problem. He agreed for them to use a little shelf inside the small hut situated just inside the jetty gates where he had looked after Jed. The arrangement was fine as the gate and hut were never locked during the day and contained nothing of any value. They came to know the man as "Old Jim" who would prove to be a good friend to the boys over the next few months. The tide governed their working arrangements and while Jed was in town at high tide Kaleb would sit near the river engrossed in the constant parade of boats and ships using the river as they made their way to and from the Pool of London and the nearby docks and dry docks serving the area. His mind wandered with each new flag he saw although he was unable to recognise their countries of origin. He thought about the wonderful and mysterious places thinking that one day he may be able to sign up with one of the shipping lines and explore these faraway places himself. He noted the local traffic too, the small coasters laden with coal, cereals, timber and the varied cargoes they carried as he tried to read the names and ports of registry displayed on their sterns. All this brought back more memories of the times when his father had taken him on the occasional trip to Ipswich. The sights and sounds of those outings were now very much in the misty past but still lingered in his memory.

    The arrangement with Jed started to show profits especially the horse holding which always paid a good tip for a short time. They shared all their earnings; no more stealing from the market stalls and open fronted shops always looking out for the shopkeepers and the police. Kaleb insisted that he continued to meet with Ben Chapman each Thursday lunchtime when he came to the Bank in town he felt that there was a connection there with his mother although that wasn't the case but Ben had become a good friend advising Kaleb whenever he had a need for his advice and always gave him a sixpence tip for holding his horse. Kaleb felt that he was one man he could really trust.

    Life at Prospect House, the lodging house, never varied and had become quite mundane. The boys spend as little time as possible there much preferring to remain in town or around the docks where they could meet with sailors and workers and taking the opportunity to look for better-paid work and lodgings. They could also obtain wholesome meals quite cheaply at the Seamen's Missions on the docks. Prospect House was just a cheap shelter for them and they tried hard to avoid contact with the other lodgers who were nearly all petty criminals., not many prospects for two healthy, strong and willing workers. They had been living at the lodging house for about two years now and had managed to scrape by without any major problems but they felt that the future held nothing in store for them.

    One Thursday morning when Kaleb had gone to meet Ben Chapman, Jed was down at the riverside when he happened to meet one of the dockers that he knew. They talked for a while and Jed learned that he employed on the dock railway. He suggested that Jed apply for work as a porter with the railway. When they parted, Jed cleaned himself up as best he could and made his way to the Docklands Light Railway Office about half a mile away where he told the attendant of his mission. As it happened the railway company were looking for strong young men for work that could be too hard for some other men. The attendant noted his name and told him to return to the office the following week, on the Thursday at a certain time as 'the boss' was away for the rest of the week and he would be interviewing applicants on his return.

When Jed saw Kaleb that evening he had decided for some unknown reason to say nothing about his visit to the railway office. The weekend passed, Monday and Tuesday brought more monotonous days but on returning to the lodging house on Tuesday evening to find it was on fire. The tenants were all assembled in the courtyard as the Fire Department fought the blaze. The fire was confined to the communal kitchen. This came as no surprise as the open domestic fire was kept alight all the time as a source of heating in the room. The kitchen had been a sooty mess urgently requiring decorating. It certainly did now!

Following the departure of the Fire Brigade the tenants were allowed back inside but unable to use the kitchen and communal area at all.

Luckily the fire had not affected the upstairs rooms so all the lodgers were confined to the dormitories. With the fire not affecting the dormitories their personal belongings were safe in the bedside lockers. The boys needed their few belongings mainly clothes to carry on with their daily work. Living in the dormitories became increasingly difficult being crowded into these confined spaces was very unsettling and the boys had no private space and the fear of being attacked and robbed. Kaleb remembered the threat made by 'weasel-face' and hoped that he would not be allowed back into the house at any time.

Came the appointed day for Jed to attend his interview and he still hadn't said a word to Kaleb. It was a Thursday and the boys left Prospect House as usual, Kaleb to meet Ben Chapman and Jed went to attend his interview but first went to the hut on the jetty to change his clothes.
At 10am he presented himself at the railway office and was led to a large room where several other men were already seated. Glancing around the room he observed that most of the applicants were not so young and the majority were poorly dressed. Jed was probably the youngest applicant at 14 years of age but he looked older than his age. He had changed into his horse holding clothes so he appeared clean and alert. Time slowly ticked by and he eventually followed the succession of men who had been called into the inner office and took the indicated seat in front of the large desk behind which sat three bespectacled, well-dressed gentlemen all seemed very old to Jed.
He was asked several questions, where he lived, his present circumstances, his parentage, where he was born and his educational achievements. Jed answered all the questions honestly and without hesitation. The men seemed relatively pleased his answers and dismissed him saying they would contact him at Prospect House if he was successful. He had been pleased with his performance thinking that he

may have secured a chance of regular work on the railway. Several vacant positions had been explained to him together with the prospects, pay and future with the company dependent on which vacancy he may be offered if any. He decided to say nothing to Kaleb until he learnt the outcome of the interview. Oddly, it was only that day that Kaleb thought he would speak with Jed about finding alternative accommodation, since the fire things were gradually getting unbearable at Prospect House, it was now overcrowded, the larger room the communal kitchen and common room was unusable with all activities being restricted to the dormitories making the overpowering smell of cooking and stale body odours quite sickening. Kaleb had been reluctant to speak of it to Jed as they had formed a working liaison that may be threatened if they should be parted. With so many people crowded into the limited space, 'weasel-face could easily gain entrance to carry out his threat. They spent the time that evening by going out for a walk and talking of their day which to all intents and purposes was just another routine one. returning to the house just as Ben was closing the doors.

They got up next morning nice and early, to avoid the crush and to catch the tide so that one of them could change his clothes and go into the business area to hold the horses of the visiting businessmen. Horse holding ws becoming less popular as motorised traffic increased but both boys were now well known and trusted to satisfactorily carry out any chore they were given but this morning there was very little for him to do so Jed met Kaleb and they both went to try and sell their meagre findings. On their return to the Harbourmaster's shed to pick up their better clothing they received a shock. The Assistant told them that a man who said that Kaleb had asked him to collect them on his behalf had taken the clothes. Kaleb asked the Assistant Harbourmaster to describe the man who had taken them and after only the briefest of a description he knew who it was – weasel-face! Described, as of similar build to Kaleb but much older there was little doubt that his guess was correct. But how did he know where the boys kept their nets, boxes and clothes? The items held hardly any value, just a few pence at the rag shop but they enable them to earn a few pennies each day. It was a low, mean way of getting his revenge on the boys for something that they hadn't done and the consequences were that their small takings for the day would be even more depleted as they would have to buy some more clothing. They went back to the house at 6pm having spent a little money on food for their supper and to discuss their situation, neither of them had had a good day but Jed decided that the moment was right to tell Kaleb of his interview even though he hadn't yet received a reply. For the second time that day Kaleb felt the bitter blow of disappointment. They stayed in that evening huddled in a corner to talk about the future. They had some money but were reluctant to spend any of it as the coming week was so uncertain. They would certainly have to visit the rag shop for some more clothing and decided to spend no more than was necessary for the coming week until Jed knew if he had been successful in his application.

Kaleb had a disturbed night but lay awake thinking of what he would do if Jed did leave for regular employment. He had known Jed for over two years but he really didn't know very much about him. He had been brought up in an orphanage but never knew his parents. The orphanage was in Birmingham and Jed had run away prior to his 11th birthday and after the routine search as a missing person there was no trace of his whereabouts. He slept rough for a while begging for money to buy food and gradually made his way south to London. He became a mudlark and took accommodation at Prospect House, met Kaleb, both stayed in the lodging house since that day. Kaleb knew that he could possible lose his friend, his only friend as the time was now near when they both must look towards the future

Thursday morning dawned bright and clear, both the boys had endured a rather sleepless night being apprehensive of what the future could hold. The day before they had visited the rag shop and bought some presentable clothes at a price greater than they intended. High tide was at midday so they dressed in their new clothes as Kaleb went to meet Ben Chapman as usual and Jed had an appointment to attend the railway office. Weasel-face had cost them cash in his misguided revenge as they needed to replace their tackle as well but somehow, they didn't feel the threat of meeting him face to face anymore.

They left Prospect House at 7am and walked down the West Ferry Road Jed clutching the letter he had received from the railway company telling him to be at the office by 9am. It was the first letter that Jed had ever received in his life – Mr J Slater. c/o Prospect House, Bullion Yard, off West Ferry Road, London. It read "Dear Sir" followed by the instruction to attend the office. "Sir". He had never been addressed as Sir and he felt that he was now being considered as a man at only 14 years of age.

The two boys parted company, Jed heading further along The Reaches whilst Kaleb turned towards town after wishing Jed 'Good Luck'

Jed reached the office at 8.30am and was invited to wait the arrival of the Personnel Manager who wasn't due until 9am. During his wait two other young men entered the room and were bade to wait with Jed, no conversation ensued but Jed formed the opinion that they were both waiting for the same man as they both held a letter like that which Jed still clutched.

Mr Samuel Johnson didn't arrive in the office until 9.15am.amd left the door of the inner office open so that Jed could see a small, pompous little fat man shuffling through numerous papers presumably looking for the wanted documents with the applicants' details recorded. After about 10 minutes and the use of the desk telephone that swiftly brought another man to his office, he called the first young man in and shut the door. He re-emerged about 10 minutes later and the next youth was called into the office. Jed was now becoming anxious, as the first lad had left his face showing no emotion whatsoever. Eventually it was Jed's turn to sit in front of the large desk and to answer several questions some of which he had been asked during his first interview. He was honest and truthful about his answers and began to warm to the two men who appeared to be quite interested in his current way of living. His interview seemed to last longer than that of his predecessors and on completion he was asked to go back and wait in the outer office – a good sign thought Jed, at least he hadn't had to leave the office as the others had done. A fair time elapsed before Jed was called back before the two men. Mr Johnson did most of the speaking and had rather a lot to say, the time culminating in Jed being offered a position with the Docklands Light Railway Company. From what Mr Johnson, had said it appears that Jed was accepted for employment by the mere fact that he was a strong looking healthy lad who could read and write. The plans for his future with the Company were outlined to him and with his agreement he was told to report for duty the following Monday morning at 8am.

    It was a warm pleasant evening as the boys sat in the courtyard of Prospect House for their supper. The dormitories, now a little tidier were overcrowded as usual and smelt grim so the relatively fresh air outside was much appreciated. Jed told Kaleb everything about the interview and the offer that had been made to him also that he was expected to start next Monday at 8am. Initially he would be on a six-month trial period when he would be required to undertake all kinds of work and gain a general knowledge of the workings of the Engineer's Department. He would be

given a uniform and start with porterage duties for the first month, he would be paid weekly and accommodated in the Apprentices Hall a few miles away and expected to attend the Engineering School once a week. The wages weren't great by they would be regular and he would have somewhere safe and secure to live. He would certainly receive enough money to feed himself and his work clothes would be supplied.
Jed thought that Christmas had arrived early!

Kaleb listened attentively to everything that Jed told him, with all the good news he felt quite envious but wished Jed the very best of luck and suddenly realising that in just a couple of days they were destined to part company, he would be saying goodbye to his best and only pal.
Kaleb would be alone again.
He had no intention of staying at Prospect House and had already been searching for alternative accommodation for the two of them nearer to the town. Kaleb was fed up with mudlarking, the rewards were very low these days and security at his present lodgings was practically non-existent now that everybody was crowded into the dormitory rooms. The more he thought about the future the more a knew he didn't have one.
The boys would work tomorrow and Saturday, spend Sunday together before they went their separate ways. The parting was never off Kaleb's mind and he wondered if he would ever see Jed again. They had made a promise to keep in touch but once their new lives had swallowed up their present commitments, would they ever meet again?

Friday and Saturday passed without incident and on Sunday they sat on the bank of the River Thames just talking and watching the river traffic going uninterrupted about their business. They had picked up a couple of discarded newspapers from the rubbish bins and read of the happenings in the world. Everything seemed very unsettled and the threat of war with Germany was imminent. All that they read seemed so very far away and certainly didn't affect them in any way. Jed was very assured about his future but Kaleb was quite perturbed especially about tomorrow.

Monday morning at 6.30am, Jed packed his few belongings into a bag and told Ben Osbourne that he was leaving and would not be returning that evening but Kaleb would be back as usual. It was very strange after over two years of living there it would be the last time Jed would see the place.

At 6.45am they set off, each wearing their better clothes, Jed to report to the railway office at 8am and Kaleb intending to go into the town and hopefully run a few messages where ever he could. It was no good going down to the river as the gleanings were sparse and the prices low. He had lain awake the past night wondering how he could earn extra money now that he would be alone. He had a little money saved as he and Jed had always pooled their earnings but his share would only last for a few days. He would meet Ben Chapman on Thursday when he came to town on business and would ask if the work he had been offered on the farm some months ago, was still available the next few days passed slowly, not much work and Kaleb felt quite lost on his own each evening.

On Thursday morning, he was up early and waited outside the Bank. Ben was on time' Kaleb holding the horses while he completed his business. Kaleb told him of the happenings over the past few days, Ben carefully noting his feelings that he had lost his only friend. Kaleb was reluctant to mention the farm work he had been once offered but it had been many months ago, since they had first met and his overpowering need to find work now outstripped all other feelings. He need not have worried though as Ben explained to him that the farm had employed many workers with seasonal jobs and he was sure that work would be available for Kaleb. He would be initially employed on different jobs about the farm and in the grounds of Mill Hall House. This was music to Kaleb's ears and immediately again brought back memories when he went with his father to Sunrise Farm in Suffolk as a young boy, the beautiful Suffolk Punch horses that the farmer Frederick Green bred and the magnificent sight when they were dressed for the agricultural shows. Great memories. During his day dreams Kaleb forgot to thank Ben for the kind offer and when he could start and where Mill Hall Farm was located. Ben could see the happiness in Kaleb's face and told him to be at the Bank the following Thursday with any baggage he may have, ready to travel back with him in the carriage to the farm. Only one week to wait but it would seem like a lifetime. Ben paid him the customary rate for holding the horses even though he had spent most of the time sitting in the carriage talking to Ben. Kaleb spent the rest of the day running a few messages with a spring in his step. Things were looking up. He thought of many things he'd wished he had asked about, where would he live, how much would he be paid, were there many others employed at the farm and gardens? He wasn't really perturbed by these unanswered questions; he trusted Ben implicitly and knew there would be satisfactory answers to his questions. If there had been any problems Ben would have mentioned them but he knew of Kaleb's present conditions and he had told Ben about his parents many months ago.

    The week was longer than any other he could have imagined; the pickings were poor and the rewards extremely low. That didn't bother Kaleb unduly; he had something exciting to look forward too. Thursday dawned, a dull overcast morning that didn't dampen Kaleb's spirits at all, he still had a little money in his pocket, no debts and a new life ahead of him. He threw away his old muddy clothes, said goodbye to mudlarking and after packing his few belonging into an old fabric bag, dressed in his better clothing and went to say goodbye to 'Battling' Ben

Osbourne. Old Ben wished him all the luck in the world and said he was sad to see him leave as he had been a good tenant and never caused any trouble or problems.

Kaleb took a slow stroll into town and was waiting outside the Bank long before 10 o-clock. The roads were busier than he had seen them before, motorbuses, lorries and cars wending their noisy way to their varied destinations. A funeral passed by, the hearse being drawn by four black-plumed horses that slowed the traffic along the main street. A nearby clock struck 10am and Ben Chapman appeared around the corner as if by magic.

"Jump up on top lad" said Ben motioning towards the driver's seat of the carriage. As Ben emerged from the Bank Kaleb had been holding the horses and caressing them on their noses. He jumped up beside Ben as he gently guided the pair out into the busy traffic. Kaleb felt very important sitting up there, he had never ridden on the road before and again the memory of riding with his father on the farm cart through the fields came back to him.

    They travelled in silence, down the West Ferry Road towards the Port of London Wharf at the Greenwich Road then turning left into the East Ferry Road/ Kaleb was on new ground now, he had never been this far from the Limehouse area before. He had noticed that they had passed the back of the Millwall Dock on his left and continued along the road until they reached the Millwall Dock Station.

The sign on the gate on the right read PRIVATE PROPERTY – MILL HALL FARM. It hadn't been a long ride, about 20 to 30 minutes but this area was new to Kaleb. As they drove up the tree-lined approach he saw the big Hall for the first time. The towering building stood at the top of the long drive, the first sight of it reminded Kaleb of a book he had read and a picture in that book of a large mysterious house with a haunted aura about it, he shuddered when he thought of it but quickly turned his attention back to the building before him and dismissed the vision of the haunted house from his mind. Ben drove the carriage through the gabled entrance and into the stable yard bringing it to a halt outside a large open barn door from which appeared a man of about sixty years of age.

"Good morning Sir" said Reuben Young taking the reins of the horses and tying them to a post near the barn.

"Shall you be wanting the rig anymore today?" On receiving a negative reply Reuben started to remove the horses from the carriage and taking off the harnesses.

Ben turned to Kaleb and said, "Get your bag off the carriage and give Reuben a hand, I'll see you shortly" and with that he left the stable yard.

"Right lad, do you know what to do?" asked Reuben.

Kaleb told him that he had dealt with horses many years ago, when he was a young lad with his Dad on Sunrise Farm. Reuben showed him how to take off the harnesses and helped him push the carriage into the barn. They carried the harnesses through the barn to the Tack Room and started to clean and oil them

They worked in silence for a time before Reuben said, "So you are the new stable hand, are you?" to which Kaleb replied that he didn't know what job he was going to do yet as he hadn't been told.

Reuben had been the, family's Stable Master for several years, the Middleton Family having owned Mill Hall House and farm for longer than old Reuben could remember. He was just about to tell him more about the Middleton's when Ben returned to the barn.

"Right then, let's show you round and get you settled in, shall we?" and he led the way firstly around the outside of the grand house and then through the gardens. The sheer beauty of the formal gardens took Kaleb's breath away; he had never seen such a wonderful and colourful display of plants trees and flowers in his life. The riot of colours and the smells intoxicated him and he stood in awe of the splendours all around him. It was midsummer and the gardens were looking their best he was only a short distance from the back of Millwall Dock and never thought that such a beautiful place could exist in the conurbation of the dirty noisy docks and shipyards.

Ben's voice interrupted his reverie, "Come along lad, we haven't got all day" They moved to the rear of the gardens and across a field where Kaleb could see a collection of buildings in the next field. This was Mill Hall Farm. It was much bigger that he had imagined, most the buildings were grouped around the crew yard. One barn-like structure was facing away from the crew yard. They entered that building Ben calling "Mrs Hudson" as they did so. A homely looking lady who looked at Ben and just said "Sir" answered the call. Ben introduced Kaleb to her and turning to Kaleb he continued, "This will be your new home and Mrs Hudson will look after you. I'll leave you in her capable hands and you come to my office at 8 o-clock in the morning." And having said that he disappeared over the field back towards the big house.

"What's your name?" enquired Mrs Hudson who had probably missed it during the introduction" Kaleb, Kaleb Bartholomew" he replied.

"Well now Kaleb Bartholomew, let me show you where you will sleep, follow me" Mrs Hudson took him through the large kitchen dining area through a short corridor to the rear of the building where a notice bearing two arrows announced, 'Men to the left, ladies turn right"

She turned left to reveal about twelve doors leading off the corridor. "You are in number seven, she told him "Come back to the kitchen when you have settled in"

Kaleb opened the door to number seven to reveal a room, about 12 feet by 12 feet with a window at one end. It was furnished with a bed, a table and chair and a chest of drawers. There was a small fireplace on the left-hand side. Kaleb couldn't believe it, a room of his own and much better than anything he had ever rented. With so few belonging it didn't take him long to unpack and stow his gear in drawers before returning to Mrs Hudson in the kitchen.

Mrs Hudson was busy preparing the evening meal, "It will soon be supper time and the boys will be here shortly" she said. "Now Kaleb Bartholomew, I expect you have a lot of questions you would like to ask, Kaleb Bartholomew, that's quite a mouthful, can I call you Barty?" she asked. Kaleb readily agreed Mrs Hudson was a lovely lady, she spoke kindly and seemed more like a 'mum' already.

Mrs Hudson told him to be respectful to all members of the household and on meeting the owner Sir James Middleton to always address him as Sir. Mr Chapman was also to be addressed as Sir as he was the Head Groundsman and farmer and in full charge of all the ground staff. Kaleb had always called Mr Chapman, Ben, as that was how he had introduced himself when they first met. He must remember.

Slowly other people drifted into the kitchen until there were five young men and three girls. They all lived in the converted stable block and that meant that six male rooms were unoccupied. The three girls were also employed on the farm as milk and dairymaids. Mrs Hudson introduced everyone as the entered the room but Kaleb soon began to forget names and couldn't get used to now being called Barty. Next morning Barty reported to Mr Chapman as instructed.

His first day was spent working in the gardens of the house where he saw many visitors coming and leaving, he noted that there were also a lot of domestic staff and was told that they were accommodated upstairs in the rear of the big house. It was like two separate communities and the only time the farm workers were allowed at the Hall was to deliver produce from the farm to the kitchen. Barty worked closely with one of the other gardeners who had been at the Hall for a long time and could instruct him in the jobs he was given to perform that day. When they all gathered in the Bunkhouse that evening Barty felt that he had had a good day and enjoyed the work. The other workers were telling him of life at Mill Hall both on the farm and in the gardens. He found difficulty in responding to his new name after all he had been known as Kaleb for the past fourteen years, but it now appeared that Barty would be his name henceforth or at least for the time he would be at Mill Hall.

Mrs Hudson's meal that evening was as good as he could ever remember for a long time. His mind went back to Jed, how excited he had been to get a job that provided a fair wage and shelter and he thought that his job now was like Jed's except that his provided him with food as well, good food fresh from the farm and plenty of it. He still had no idea of the wage he would receive but he believed it would be fair taking into consideration his food and shelter and it would be regular, not like the pittance he earned as a mudlark.

    He was awake early next morning when he heard the other workers preparing for the days' work after breakfast. He had been told to report to the Hall office again as yesterday only to learn that he was again to be employed in the gardens. As he crossed the field at the back of the Hall the birds were singing as a gentle breeze disturbed the trees, everything was so peaceful and unhurried suddenly life seemed so good and his life seemed to be slipping into place. What a world of difference from walking along the Limehouse Reach to the steps of the jetty where he had spent so many hours wading in the dirty muddy waters of the River Thames. He enjoyed the short walk to the office arriving there five minutes early to be given his work for the day. Mr Chapman had met him at the door.

"Good morning Kaleb, have you settled in alright"? he asked as he motioned him inside, to take a chair in front of his desk.

"Yes, thank you Sir" remembering to address him as Sir, not Ben.

Mr Chapman said he had certain details to ask him that he required and to tell him that Sir James would meet him in the office at 9.30am.and not in the gardens as previously arranged as Sir James had some other business to attend. This made him feel a little uneasy, as he always felt better out of doors than in an office.

Sir James didn't arrive at the office until 9.45am after being detained at the Hall for some reason. This gave Kaleb time to speak more freely to Mr Chapman and ask about his work at the Hall to which Mr Chapman replied that he would know more after his talk with Sir James. He also took the opportunity to tell him that the workers now knew him as Barty, the name given to him by Mrs Hudson.

Sir James entered the office looking slightly flustered but smiling as he greeted Mr Chapman and Barty. He was a stout man, about 5 feet 6 inches tall, grey thinning hair and a round smiley ruddy face. Barty estimated him to be in his fifties and immediately liked the look of him. He apologised for keeping them both waiting but Mr Chapman and Barty had filled in the time quite usefully as they had known each other for several months and confided on many occasions. Barty was introduced to Sir James as Kaleb Bartholomew, a name with which Sir James wasn't totally unfamiliar, as Ben Chapman had mentioned him often. Sir James asked very few questions of Barty saying that he had full trust in Ben Chapman when it came to hiring staff and hoped that Barty would he happy and work well while in the employ of Mill Hall Estates

The meeting ended and Ben told Barty to find Jim Crawford, the Charge hand at the stables where he was to be employed for the present. He crossed back over the field feeling as if his bread had been buttered on both side, especially after he had just learned that he would start on a wage of £1 each week. With his food and shelter supplied he would need only a few personal bits, he felt positively well off.

He quickly found Jim Crawford, who he had seen at the bunkhouse, a young man of 22 years who had worked at Mill Hall since he was 16 years old. He had worked his way from stable boy to become Charge hand only last year.

Barty's first job was 'mucking out' the stables of which there were ten and depositing the muck in the crew yard. On completion, he was shown how to feed and groom a couple of the horses. All the ten stables were full, four riding horses at one end and six working horses at the other. Barty took great pleasure working in the stables and put great effort into doing everything properly. Again, his memory went back to the fantastic Suffolk Punch horses at Sunrise Farm. The horses here were not Suffolk Punch but Clydesdales, heavy horses used for working the land. Barty had read how tractors were fast replacing these plough horses and hoped that they wouldn't be replaced at Mill Hall Farm. He did learn that at a certain time of the year, two or three of these wonderful horses were entered an agricultural fair and ploughing match but he didn't know where or when. Apparently, Sir James was keen on entering these shows in many categories, horses and pigs, dairy and horticultural produce he apparently spared no expense to secure a win wherever he could. Barty would learn more of this as time went by.

Meantime he was to work mainly in the stables with additional time spent cleaning the pigsties and chicken coops. He loved working with animals especially the horses and he soon developed a good working relationship with the horses. Jim Crawford who left him more and more on his own trusting him to keep the stables spick and span and to maintain all the equipment in the Tack Room.

Barty developed the habit of getting up about 5.30am each morning but he seldom saw Ben Chapman and never Sir James, he was left in the care of Jim Crawford who was happy to leave him to do his work unhindered. He loved his work and took great care of all the animals and spent a great deal of time grooming the horses. The riding horses were sleek beautiful animals ridden by members of the household and Barty got to ride them in the exercise yard but his main interest lay with the working horses and Jim took time to tell him that Sir James entered a pair of teams into the All England Ploughing Match held in Hampshire in October each year. The Clydesdales weren't quite as heavy as the Suffolks having an average weight of 1600 to 1800 pounds, some a little heavier and stood 16 to 18 hands high (a hand being 4 inches in height). They are a very friendly breed from Lanarkshire, Scotland and known as 'The Gentle Giants'. At the end of the working day he would often go to the stables to check that all was well and often stay there talking to the horses, he was besotted with their care and well-being that he forgot everything else while he was there. Sometimes, just to get away from the bustle of the bunkhouse he would take a book with him, he read a lot, but there were very few books at the bunkhouse that were of interest to him. but if he came across a book on exploration, the sea or a classic like 'Treasure Island' or 'Kidnapped', he loved stories of adventure. He would read continuously until he finished the book. Occasionally odd newspapers would appear, always a few days old but enabled him to keep up to date with world affairs. Whenever he got the chance he would seek Jim 's attention and if he wasn't busy, to ask him questions about the horses and the Shows that they attended.

It was 1912 and Barty had just celebrated his 14th birthday, well, not really celebrated as he told no-one, when Jim said they must start preparing the horses and plough tackle for the ploughing match in

October. The harvest had finished and the ground was to be ploughed ready for next year's crops, Barty had never been behind a plough team before and was very disappointed when four men arrived at the farm to undertake the ploughing for the coming season. He learnt that the four men also represented Mill Hall Farm at the All England Match. The men were very affable and told Barty of many tricks of the ploughing trade, the parts of the plough and how to harness up the team. Barty hoped that he would be included in the staff that would travel to Hampshire. Sir James hired a large horsebox and a lorry to take the team of four Clydesdales leaving the riding horses and two heavy horses for him to look after. The team of four ploughmen, Jim Crawford and Reuben, the Charge hand accompanied the horses in the transporter. Sir James and his Lady travelled by themselves in a chauffeur driven motorcar   There was extra work to be done on the farm, the plough team had vacated their rooms and Mrs Hudson was busy cleaning and cooking for those who were left.

Barty thought of an earlier time when four men came to the farm to help at harvest time. They were the threshing crew with their huge machines and a traction engine and they occupied the spare rooms during their stay and although Barty didn't take any part in the harvesting he did have the chance to see the team working and to understand the basic functions of the machines. Two men were employed in the 'chaff hole' just under the threshing machine, collecting up the chaff in sacks and carting it off to the barn. The threshing team came from Herefordshire and were hired annually to call at Mill Hall Farm as they travelled the southern counties during the season.

The two-day Agricultural Show in Herefordshire was coming to a close but there was no news of any winners, the staff at the bunkhouse would have to wait for the return of Jim and the others but the overall winners may not be known until the newspapers were published. With only the farm animals requiring attention this lull in the farming world gave Barty, a little more time to venture further than the confines of the farm. He was normally granted one full afternoon off each week, the day varied with the demands of his work so any time off was eagerly taken if only to relax. Farm work was very demanding but Barty was very happy with his lot. In the time he had been employed at Mill Hall Farm he had been able to make many enquiries of the long-term staff if anyone had met or even heard of his mother after she had attended for the job interview many months ago, but there was no-one there that could even recall seeing her. He took the chance to speak with the Housekeeper at the Hall she had a scant memory of Mrs Doris Bartholomew coming to the house as she had shown her into the office that morning. She remembered his mother declining the post as she would occupy a room at the top of the house and there was no provision for her young son, as she hadn't informed them of her family commitment. The Housekeeper, who had been present at the interview, had no idea where she went afterwards so he was no nearer tracing her.

One afternoon his walk took him up the Blackwall Reach and he sat for a while to watch the river craft. Ship buildings was all around him, he had passed four docks before reaching the Millwall Junction on the L.N.E.R. railway line and his mind went back to his old mudlark pal Jed and wondered if he would ever bump into him again. He decided to walk back along the line on his return journey to the farm but as he passed near the South Dock Station he was chased away by a railway policeman who probably thought that he was intent upon stealing railway property. It was getting near for the evening meal and Mrs Hudson didn't take kindly to keeping meals hot in the oven unless there was a plausible excuse like being detained on farm work so he hastened his step and arrived at the bunkhouse in good time. He had enjoyed a leisurely day and didn't realise just how far he had walked until his stomach started to complain of hunger. He ate a wholesome meal and then went down to the stables to spend time with the remaining Clydesdales He sat on a straw bale and thought what a fruitless afternoon he had spent; would he ever trace his mother or Jed for that matter? It seemed hopeless where his mother was concerned but there was a chance that he could find Jed if he called at the office of the Docklands Light Railway some time. The ships that passed him on the River Thames were still on his mind as he imagined their cargoes and their journeys from the foreign ports up to London. Seeing the names painted on the sterns conjured up exotic visions of a world he had only read about and he felt himself being drawn towards the sea. He had been intrigued by some of the stories told to him by the sailors that passed through Prospect House and the tales of the 'old salts' he had met in the town. He remembered that his father had told him that his Granddad had been at sea but he had no idea of anything more of his life at sea. With all these thoughts chasing around his brain he went back to the bunkhouse and turned in.

 It had become a habit to wake up early and today was no different and with fewer people moving about it was easier to wash at the back of the bunkhouse and reached Mrs Hudson's kitchen well before 6am. The atmosphere in the kitchen was light and happy – good news had been received from the Ploughing Match in Herefordshire – they hadn't won but took a 'Second' place in the ploughing and were 'Highly Commended' for the heavy horses. Barty had never received an Award of any kind, but it was so good to feel that he was part of a winning team Jim Crawford and old Reuben must have made a wonderful job of preparing, presenting and showing the four Clydesdales. He would learn much more when they returned.

The successful team arrived back at the farm the following day although the ploughman didn't come with them Sir James was so pleased with his men that he hosted a small garden party in a marquee in the grounds the following weekend. It was a cold day and the guests all gathered inside the marquee to keep warm. It was the first time that Barty had met most of the domestic staff that had been detailed to look after the farm staff. The silver cup and the rosettes they had won were on show and there were several people, obviously from well to do backgrounds in attendance. The food was plentiful as was the wine and beer; Sir James moved freely amongst his guests and staff seemingly savouring the success his men had achieved and saying, "Just wait until next year when we shall win more silver". He had even hired some entertainers to round off a very happy and celebratory evening it was early when the party broke up, as the cold was getting quite unbearable. Barty thought, next year he may be able to attend the Ploughing match and Show himself. He returned to the bunkhouse that evening with great satisfaction, feeling that he had left a mark on the occasion having taken part in the preparations and the general health of the heavy horses, a long way from the muddy dirt begrimed mudlark who had made his living in the back streets and waterways in the busy dock areas.

It was only a few days later when Barty had another big surprise. In the wake of Sir James's exhilaration, he had purchased a tractor, the first mechanical aid for the farm. Barty had mixed feelings about the purchase; did this mean that his beloved Clydesdales were under threat? Was his job under threat? Over his time at the farm he had undertaken most jobs that had been allocated to him and was quite capable of holding down all of them but with the acquisition of the tractor he thought he might be moved to other duties. No one had said anything to him but that didn't stop him worrying. It played on his mind so much that he decided to ask Jim Crawford about it. He need not have worried though, apparently, before the tractor had been ordered, Sir James, Jim and Reuben had discussed and agreed, the purchase. Jim and Reuben were to be responsible for the machine, both to be the drivers. His peace of mind restored Barty learned that the heavy horses would be retained for work on the land, competitions and showing, in fact Sir James said he intended to attend more Shows than just the one each year.

The tractor proved to be of much interest as they were rare in the early 1900s. It wasn't a new tractor having been built in 1903 it was a three-wheeled model known as an Ivel Agricultural Motor, an obvious progression from the steam driven machines but had only one gear and a reverse., it was, none the less a fascinating wonder especially to Jim and the other farm hands. Reuben took great interest in it, he had seen one before but knew very little about it. Such was his interest that Jim decided to make him responsible for its maintenance, cleanliness and learn how to drive it and even hired an engineer to instruct him how to use the tractor and the attachments that had been purchased with it.

Time at Mill Hall Farm passed uneventfully except for one instance. One of the hands went to the east field to tend the sheep and check the fences and was alarmed to see that some of the sheep appeared to be missing. A length of fencing on the land nearest the river had been damaged and about 12 feet of it was lying nearby on the ground. After a quick look around the farm he went swiftly back to find Jim Crawford, the two returning to the field to examine the scene much closer. They discovered distinct tyre marks into the field from the riverside.
"Thought so" said Jim, "Sheep rustlers, how many missing?".
The shepherd made a quick head count and thought that approximately thirty sheep were missing. The police were informed and after an initial examination of the scene said they would commence enquiries. The

examination of the land had revealed that one motor lorry had been used to remove the sheep and take them to a nearby river wharf on the Blackwall Reach, and from there, who knows? Barty and Jim spent the next two days repairing and re-enforcing the damage fence, which gave them time to look about the immediate area but they found no further evidence that would help the police with their enquiries.

The newspapers were reporting unrest in the world especially the political unrest in Europe. This didn't affect life on the farm but Barty noted how much busier the roads had become of late, more motor cars and lorries were on the roads around the Docklands, the railway and river traffic had also increased. Traffic passing the east field had also increased as he noticed when he went to check the boundary fences. Sir James had left strict orders that all the perimeter fences should be checked regularly since the disappearance of the sheep, a job that was taken in turn by all the hands. Barty welcomed his turn, whatever the weather, he loved to walk the boundaries especially those that skirted the river as it gave him a chance to watch any late-night shipping and gave him another chance to daydream although he was fully alert to his work.

He reflected on his life and that he had no friends of his own age at the farm but preferred the company of Jim and Old Reuben whose experiences in their own working lives he loved to listen too, more so Old Reuben who. Barty estimated was about 70 years old and was a mine of information and good advice.

The winter proved to be harsh, the snow meant that the animals had to be confined to the barns and stables. It was an early start most mornings to fetch the feed from storage and distribute it to the horses, cattle, sheep then a trudge through the snow to collect the eggs from the chicken coops and feed the hens. Back in the comparative warmth of the stables the horses were groomed and the tack needed attention even though it wasn't being used, the cold and damp could affect the leather. Reuben had occupied himself with the Ivel tractor and the attachments; he had managed to complete most of the winter ploughing before the snow came. With no heating in any of the outbuildings, a great deal of time was taken by just cleaning and drying much of the farm equipment.

Christmas 1913 was a swell affair, Sir James sent word that he wanted the occupants of the bunkhouse to have a good time. The weather was such that it was almost impossible to go far so Sir James sent for Mrs Hudson and told her lay on a special dinner and tea and not to spare the expense. She was to order whatever she required to have it delivered by motor van to the farm and direct the cost to him. A van would be able to cope with the road conditions where a horse and cart would struggle. It was most obvious that Sir James had been pleased with his staff's work over the past year, not just the relative success at the Herefordshire Show but with other small ventures that he had been involved with in the commercial world. He wanted Ben Chapman to take part in the celebrations on Christmas Day at the bunkhouse but none of these plans were mentioned to anyone else other than Mrs Hudson. None of the staff had any family living nearby so no one would be travelling from the farm.

Christmas Day dawned bright and clear but very cold as the hands went about their early morning chores as usual, returning to the bunkhouse just before midday to be greeted in the kitchen with a much warmer than normal atmosphere as Mrs Hudson had been cooking and using ovens, there was a large log fire burning in the grate. The room had been totally decorated and a Christmas tree stood splendidly in one corner, the table had been set with thirteen places and a Christmas cracker at the side of each place setting. Mrs Hudson had been busy all morning, how she had found the time to do all the work remained a mystery. As each shivering worker entered the kitchen Ben and Mrs Hudson offered a glass of mulled wine, a smile and a seasonal wish to greet them. Barty felt a bit overwhelmed by it all, he had never been at such a gathering before. He looked around the room everyone was present. They gathered around the beautiful six-foot Christmas tree and sang a few carols before dinner was served. What a dinner it was! Mrs Hudson and Ben served everyone as they were seated – a full turkey roast followed by a large plum pudding in which three silver sixpences were found.

When all had had their fill of the wonderful spread Jim Crawford stood up and proposed a vote of thanks to Ben and especially to Mrs Hudson who didn't seem to have sat down for more than two minutes all day. It was hard for Barty to understand that such a feeling of friendship and understanding existed as his past experiences had been in the workhouse and at Prospect House where he had known only passing acquaintances. Once again Barty was counting his blessings.

    A lazy afternoon passed with everyone getting to know each other better and just prior to teatime they received a visit in the bunkhouse by Sir James and Lady Jane. They wanted to offer their own Christmas wishes and to say thank you to all the ground staff for all their work in the year past and a prosperous 1914.

It was late afternoon when the party finally broke up as certain members of the staff had to go and tend to the animals. Barty went to the stables, fed the horses and then secured the chickens before returning to the bunkhouse. Mrs Hudson was just in the throes of cleaning up the kitchen while Barty made a hot drink for the remaining workers before they retired to their rooms. It had been a long busy day especially for Mrs Hudson, who had been working since 5am, but it had been a happy day for all.

Boxing Day was a normal working day except there was still a glut of festive leftovers to be eaten. At breakfast the farm hands were now more likely to talk to each other as the gathering from the day before seemed to have broken the ice between them and cemented some new friendships They normally didn't talk much to each other as they worked at different times and seldom together except perhaps the dairy maids. The social get-together on Christmas Day had improved the comradeship that was lacking prior to the event. Barty was still pleased to go out each evening to work the perimeter fencing, he took his time carefully noting anything that may appear unusual and reporting to Jim Crawford on completion; He attended to the horses whilst on his patrol but everything was quiet and peaceful as the old year drew to a close.

1914 began cold and cloudy and was to be a year that would be unforgettable for many reasons as news of world unrest grew stronger. Newspapers from the Hall were brought to the bunkhouse as they finished with them. The news had little effect on life at the Hall but the road traffic around the Docklands seemed to increase even more than usual. The area seemed to be developing into a gigantic warehouse and Mill Hall Farm was right in the centre of it.

On a shadowless evening Barty set off across the east field to check the fences after first calling at the stables to ensure that all was well for the night. He made slow progress, as it was quite difficult to find his way due to the lack of moonlight and he hadn't brought a lantern with him. He reached the boundary on the far side of the field and slowly picked his way to the fencing near the riverside. He paused momentarily as he thought he heard an odd sound. There were the normal background noises that he recognised, familiar noises that came from the river traffic taking advantage of the high tide. There it was again, this time he thought it sounded like muffled voices and fairly close by. He froze. He was very close to the gap, now mended, where the sheep had previously taken so he crouched at the bottom of the hedge and listened. He couldn't hear their whispered conversation but he soon became aware of two figures coming towards him. He was only about 12 feet away from the repaired gap when he could just make out two people climb over the fence. They obviously didn't want to use the gate as the hinges may creak and attract attention. The visibility was bad; he couldn't see their faces. They were so intent on being as quiet as possible and choosing their pathway that they failed to see Barty just a few feet away in the hedge bottom. He concentrated on the two figures but all he could see was two men of medium build and wearing flat caps. The moonless night afforded no other clear details. The men silently walked across the field to the derelict building opposite the gate. Barty left his hidden position in the hedge and skirted the building to take up a position where he could see the outline of the old barn He felt very tense, he couldn't tackle two men, anyway he didn't know what they were doing, but what should he do?

After a few minutes the men came out and started to re-trace their footsteps back towards the gate. Barty waited several minutes before he left his cover and slowly approached the building making sure that they did not come back. He waited for a short time until he was quite sure that they had left. He approached the building and went around the outside of it but could find no clues to what the men had been doing.

It was too dark to go into the old barn, he wouldn't see anything and he thought the building might be unstable; it hadn't been used for years. He felt he wanted to explore further but he was shaking with fear. What if there was somebody else hiding in the barn, He hadn't seen anyone else and he hadn't seen anything taken in or brought out. They had only spent a few minutes about the old place before they left. His excitement rose as he thought of the mystery that could surround his discovery.

He returned to the bunkhouse and quickly found Jim, tumbling over his words he tried to tell him his story but Jim had to calm him down before fetching Old Reuben to listen as well. They listened intently to Barty' tale and concluded that whatever they had been doing they had trespassed and so presumable they were up to no good. It was too dark to go there until morning. Jim praised Barty for not approaching the men as they could have been armed and a 16-year-old lad was no match for them. The three of them talked about the incident and decided that future patrols of the boundary fences should be undertaken by two people for the time being, certainly not one on his own.

Barty had trouble getting to sleep that night only to be awakened at 5.30am as usual. Time on a farm waits for no man! Jim delayed Barty, staying on the farm for the whole of the morning to meet with Ben and Sir James after he had fed the animals. The story was again told and an agreement reached that they should be coupled patrols in the evenings and extended to other areas. The dock areas were now so close to Sir James property and with the increased activities he was apprehensive about encroachment on his land, some of the dockworkers being of questionable backgrounds. The private land was fast becoming a small oasis in a world of brick, concrete and roadways.

The examination of the boundaries continued as planned and about two weeks after Barty's little adventure they again encountered something that aroused suspicion.

There was a quarter moon in the sky when Reuben and Barty set off on their patrol. They pursued their normal track after settling down the horses and proceeded across to the east field. On moving across to the riverside of the field they were surprised to see a barge tied up at the tiny jetty from where the sheep had previously been taken. This was most suspicious, more so because there didn't seem to be anyone about that could be connected with the barge. Everything was very quiet. The pair had a quick look over the barge but it was deserted so they decided to keep watch for a while. They found a suitable vantage point and secreted themselves where they could clearly see the barge and the old barn building just a short distance away, there was no one in their sight at all. They were just about to give up their observations when they became aware of two men approaching carrying a couple of ropes. It had been over an hour since they hid and Reuben was worried that Jim, back at the farm might think something had happened to them but they couldn't leave now. As the men approached the barge they were welcomed back by a third man who had been left on board all the time they were watching but they never saw him even when they had cast their glance over what they thought was a deserted barge. The vessel was quite small and of minimum displacement. They had seen the name on the stern *'SARAH JANE'* but there was no marked port of registration. The men exchanged a few unheard words before casting off and moving quietly downriver.

Given a safe period of time Reuben and Barty left their hiding place and went to the old barn. Making sure that there was no one else around they entered through the broken door and was immediately struck by the smell of fresh straw. Fortunately, they carried a lantern that Reuben lit and as their eyes became adjusted to the half-light from the lantern they saw a freshly broken bale of straw spread on the floor surrounded by several other complete bales around the walls. To the casual observer, it appeared to be just a conventional barn but Barty knew differently. It was many years ago, since this building had been in regular use. Reuben kept careful watch near the door for anyone that may be coming to the barn while Barty moved some of the straw from the floor with his foot to reveal it some sturdy planks of wood covered with a layer of soil, the earth was freshly spread. Realising that they had discovered something quite important they decided not to disturb things any further and carefully re-covered the find with the straw.

It was very late when the pair returned to the bunkhouse and reported to Jim what they had found. As late as it was Jim went to the Gatehouse of the Hall where Ben lived and related the story to him. Ben didn't appear to be unusually surprised by the news and said he would inform Sir James tomorrow morning as nothing could be done at such late hour of the night.

Reuben and Barty were summoned to the Hall at 10am next day to find Sir James and a Metropolitan Police Inspector in the study. The Inspector asked many questions of the two farm hands and requested that he be accompanied to the old building together with two plain clothed officers. They spent a very long time examining the scene and the surrounding area while Barty was given to job to keep his eyes open for anyone approaching the jetty. Apart from Barty standing near the east field gate it wasn't evident that anything untoward was happening. On completion of the search the police left the scene exactly as Reuben and Barty had reported finding it. The plain clothes officers were detailed to remain hidden near the building should the offenders return to collect the goods the police had uncovered, presumable the proceeds of crime. Other men would relieve the officers before darkness fell, the offenders would not return to collect their spoils during daylight hours as there ws too much traffic on the water and too many people walking about the immediate area.

Work on the farm was to continue as normal, the fences to be checked each evening but, of course the farm hands and the police officers keeping observations were aware of each other's presence.

Roughly a week later one of the police officers came to the bunkhouse to speak with Jim. Apparently, they had received a message from the Coastguard station at Sheerness that the *'Sarah Jane'* had been seen making her way inland up the Thames Estuary. The Barge appeared to be unloaded and manned by three persons. It was still early but the police suspected that the occupants might be returning to collect the goods hidden in the old building later that night. After a lengthy conversation, a plan was formed and the officer returned to the east field.

Jim called Reuben and Barty to the kitchen and told them of the visit and the plan that they should follow Sir James and Ben were also informed and were agreed that the police instructions should be followed. It was obvious that the men would not come to retrieve their goods until after dark; the forecast for that evening was for fine weather and a rising moon that would afford only minimum visibility for the time of year. The Police would have four other officers in the vicinity, well-hidden and fully aware of the timed farm workings.

Before dusk the horses were attended to and the chicken coops secured as Reuben and Barty followed their well-trodden path over the east field. Everything appeared to be as normal, they didn't see any of the police officers who were watching from their various vantage points and on completion of the rounds the two farm hands returned to the bunkhouse. Jim was waiting for them but there was no news for him.

Meanwhile, back near the riverside in the east field things were slowly starting to unfold. The barge had been seen coming up river and came alongside the jetty. Two men tied her up and after a whispered word they departed on a roundabout route for the building ensuring that no one had seen them or was following them and that the fence patrol had passed for that evening. They had done their homework by watching the farm movements and routines. On reaching the barn one man remained by the door to keep watch while the other entered and began to remove the soil and straw from the boards.

The police remained hidden. they wanted to wait until the goods had been removed from the barn and taken to the barge. The work continued silently and the goods were eventually loaded onto the barge. Still the officers remained hidden. Another pair of eyes was observing these happenings of which no one else was aware. The eyes were straining to see most of the movements in the overcast, conditions even with the aid of a pair of field glasses. Barty had sneaked back from the bunkhouse. He was enthralled by the incident taking place and was unable to resist the thrill of watching the story unfold. He felt sure that one of the men moving the goods to the barge he had seen before, a man of slight build and quick movement, was he one of the original visitors to the barn it was too dark to see his face clearly even with the field glasses?

Barty had no intention of intervening in any way as he had been told not to go near the east field after his patrol duty but curiosity got the better of him. He watched as what was presumably the last pack was brought out, the moment the police had been waiting for. The field suddenly erupted into a frenzy of activity as the six officers broke cover, four of them intercepted the two carriers while the other two ran down to the *Sarah Jane*. They swiftly boarded the vessel and arrested the third man who had been so busy stowing the goods that he didn't hear the officers until they set foot on the barge. The deck lights were switched on and the four officers joined their colleagues on the boat with the two other arrested men. Now that everyone had broken cover Barty moved closer to the boat without revealing himself and under the glare of the deck lights he could see the faces of the three prisoners. He was right in thinking one of them being familiar but it wasn't the man from the boat he had thought it to be, it was' Weasel face'!

Barty didn't reveal himself but walked back to the bunkhouse wondering how Weasel face had become involved with the smugglers, had he found out that Barty was at the farm or was it sheer coincidence that their paths had crossed again? He didn't speak to anyone about what he had witnessed, he couldn't really, having been told to stay clear, it was well past midnight when he got back and all the hands had turned in for the night. Barty had trouble sleeping that night his adrenalin was running high after seeing the thrill of the happenings of the night being played out in front of him. He didn't say a word to anyone at all and hoped that he hadn't been missed from the bunkhouse that evening. He arose early in the morning expecting to hear the' news' but found that everything was normal. No one even mentioned the incident so he assumed that no one had heard a word yet., not even Reuben although he had known of the raid but he didn't know that Barty had been present to witness it.

The workers all returned for the evening meal and that was when the news broke and became the sole topic of discussion for the rest of the evening. Barty didn't join in the discussions too much in the fear of giving away his secret observations of the night before. As the story was related it was magnified by additions to the facts thus making the whole affair seem much bigger that it had been. The strange thing was that there was no mention of it in the newspapers and neither Sir James nor Ben Chapman referred to it. Most of the planning in setting up the observations and the ultimate entrapment of the three smugglers was directed by Jim Crawford who thought that the fewer people involved the less were the chances of the plans going awry

Once again Barty's curiosity was aroused and in a quiet moment he brought the subject up with Jim. Jim told him that after the planning was complete and the arrests had been made could he reveal that the *Sarah Jane* had been suspected for a long time of smuggling activities. They knew she had rendezvoused with a French boat and good were transferred but the police and the Coastguard could not work out where the good were being landed. Enquiries were made without success but they were kept from the public in order not to raise suspicions among the smugglers that would make them change their Modus Operandi. The Police had suspected their operations for quite some time but were never able to find their landing place or storage place until Reuben and Barty had stumbled upon the old band. and when the Sheerness Watch had reported seeing *Sarah Jane* coming through the Thames Estuary that plans were put into operation and the smugglers apprehended. The ironic thing was that the smugglers only used the old barn once as they suspected that the Customs were watching them, it wasn't their usual landing place, it was only a small haul that consisted of boxes of tobacco and bales of French silk but it would offer a lucrative cash return sold duty free, of course. Nothing was ever published because the police still suspected that this was only a small part of a much larger operation, nothing more was heard of the whole affair and Barty's secret visit to the scene remained a secret.

The farming year went on with no interruptions except that the government were encouraging the farmers to grow more food due to the unrest in the world and the growing threat of a war with Germany. Life at Mill Hall Farm was still as active as ever with the concentration being mainly focused on the raising of livestock and the dairy industry but the building of warehouses around the farm perimeter was increasing giving a claustrophobic feeling. Sir James had other interests outside London and had hinted that he may sell Mill Hall Farm and move into a nearby county but, for the present things carried on as usual.

Jim obtained the details of an Agricultural Show that was to be held in Hampshire in August and Sir James gave permission for the farm to enter competition at the Show. Barty had been continuing his instruction with Reuben in ploughing techniques and dressing the Clydesdales and was delighted that he had been chosen to represent the farm together with Reuben and Jim, no expert ploughmen on this occasion. Barty had received instruction on ploughing using both the horses and the tractor so much attention was now to be paid in preparing the plough machinery and the horses tack that would be required. Everything had to be in top condition if they were to stand any hope of a prize the days became excessively busy with very little time to relax. Every evening after the animals had been fed and the fence patrol completed they had supper and an hour or so to discuss the next day's work and read the newspapers. There was a radio in the bunkhouse and now and again they listened to the newscasts that was causing such growing concern of the pending war. Things were fast coming to a head.

On 1st August 1914, Germany declared war on Russia and two days later they also declared war on France, the situation now almost touching the home shores. It was on 5th August 'The Guardian' newspaper headline read **"GREAT BRITAIN DECLARES WAR ON GERMANY"** confirming the news broadcast on the wireless the previous evening. None of this came as a surprise to the staff even though they hadn't heard that previous broadcast.

It wasn't very long before this devastating turn of events saw even more traffic thronging the roads around the farm and docks as munitions, food and men were being moved all around the country but mainly into the dock areas of London.

As the war developed the call to arms started to affect the manpower situation in certain industries, men were called up and women began to replace them in the workplace. At first, life at Mill Hall wasn't unduly affected and as the war developed the government again urged farmers to grow more food as supplies to Great Britain were greatly disrupted by Germany's submarine blockade of British ports.

It was in the very early days of the war on the 7th August, that Lord Kitchener called for 100,000 men to join the British Army. One month later it would be Barty's 16th birthday, too young for his entry into the army.

   It was expected that the Hampshire Agricultural Show would be cancelled but there was no such announcement as the time moved ever closer. Work on the farm became more intensified stretching into long days and long evenings everyone was suffering a creeping tiredness. One evening in mid-August, when all the routines had been finished a few of the staff gathered in the bunkhouse kitchen where Mrs Hudson had made a wholesome stew when another shock befell the little community. Reuben was missing. He hadn't returned after his chores.

This was most unusual as Reuben was always a stickler for time keeping. The rest of the staff, including the dairymaids were called and assembled in the kitchen to form a search party. They paired off and started the search in every direction. Reuben, by now was one and a half hours late and the growing concern for his safety was evident. Mrs Hudson remained in the kitchen in case he should return during the searchers absence that had made a time to return at 9pm, whatever the situation. Barty paired off with a young lad named Oliver, they were charged with searching the stables, outbuildings and adjacent outside areas. It was quite dark as they set off each pair carrying a lantern and a commitment to be very thorough in their search; it was quite unlike

Reuben to be late, he knew the farm layout probably better than anyone else having been employed therefore the past 25 years, something must have happened to him. It was an extremely thorough search that included the boundary fences, the old barn building near the river gate and all the outbuildings that housed the farming implements calling his name as they progressed.

Barty and Oliver were coming to the last outbuilding near the stables, the tractor house. The search so far had proved fruitless, everything was found to be in order, each building having been secured showing earlier. As they approached the tractor house Barty found that the lock was unlocked, he told Oliver to search the ground floor while he went up the ladder to the loft. He was halfway up the ladder when he heard a shout from Oliver, near the front of the tractor he had found Reuben lying face down. Barty descended the ladder to join Oliver who was talking to Reuben without response. Barty was shocked at seeing Reuben apparently uninjured but unresponsive. He immediately sent Oliver to the bunkhouse for help where he found Jim who had just returned from his own search Jim grabbed a couple of blankets and told another hand to accompany him the tractor house and Oliver to go quickly to the big house to tell Ben what had been found and ask him to call an ambulance. Meanwhile, Jim and the other hand went to the tractor shed, there was still no sign of life in Reuben, Barty had been talking to him and had him propped up by the tractor wheel. Jim found a long bin retainer board and between them they managed to roll Reuben onto the board and covered him with the blankets. With great difficulty, they managed to carry the improvised stretcher slowly across the rough ground and down to the bunkhouse where Ben and Oliver were waiting. Reuben was showing no signs of life when the ambulance took him and Barty to hospital. It was very late that night when Barty returned to the Gatehouse to see Ben bearing the sad news of Reuben's passing. The doctor had said that nothing could have been done to help Reuben and suspected that he was already dead when Oliver had found him. Ben went to the bunkhouse early in the morning to break the bad news to the staff that was half expecting the worse news. Mrs Hudson had just prepared breakfast and the staff ate a sombre and silent meal before leaving to attend their daily tasks. Ben told Barty to tend to the horses then take the rest of the day off, he'd had a late night and seemed to be deeply upset with the passing of Old Reuben.

Barty took a long time with the horses that morning preferring not to speak with anyone else for the time being. He went to the kitchen in the evening as Jim came back and said that he wanted to speak with him quietly after the evening meal.

Jim told him that he had spent a long time talking with Ben and Sir James that day and they had agreed that Barty should take over Reuben's role and duties on the farm, furthermore they had expected the Hampshire Show to be cancelled and assurance had been received that the event would still be staged. Jim, Barty and Oliver would now represent Mill Hall Farm with Barty showing the Clydesdales and doing the tractor ploughing., Jim would undertake the horse ploughing with the aid of Oliver as tack man. This news excited Barty who vowed to do his best in memory of Reuben who had taught him so much.

The day of the Show arrived and the three competitors had travelled down in two horse van and two trailers the evening before and trio took lodgings in a bed and breakfast in a large house near the showground. All the machinery, tack and the tractor was left on the showground overnight in the care of a night watchman., the horses had been exercised and fed before they repaired to the boarding house for the night. The rigs owned by Sir James had been driven by Jim and the second rig was hired and driven by Ben to everyone's surprise. Ben explained that Sir James was so interested in his team that he had spared no expense in providing all that was needed, he so wanted a success at the Show and the team were in high spirits when they left the boarding house for the showground next morning, which was fine and sunny. Barty groomed and dressed the Clydesdales ready for the competition that was to commence at 10.30am. Several teams of heavy horses assembled in the show area and the judging began on time, as some of the horses would be required for the ploughing match at 12 noon.

It was a very proud young man that led the two Clydesdale horses into the show ring, the sun shone and the polished leathers and the brasses twinkled like the stars. Barty did his utmost to remember all that Reuben had taught him and the tips he had been given. Jim stood to the rear of the horses as the judges carried out their detailed examination and making copious notes. They asked a few questions about care and feeding but gave no indication of their findings before moving on to the next competitor. Jim exchanged a few words with Barty and each felt that they had put on a good show and felt quite positive about it. The horses were de-harnessed and made ready for the ploughing match that was to follow in the open field at the back of the show ring.

Jim took the guide reins in hand and began to plough his allotted measure with Oliver in close attendance but not taking an active part in the match. Good straight furrows, neat turns and excellent control of the horses left Jim feeling quietly confident in his effort although he didn't say a word to anyone. Ben nodded his approval also without a word being uttered and that made Jim feel even more confident.

Immediately the horse ploughing had finished and the field vacated the tractor ploughing was announced. Ploughing with a tractor was a new event and there were only six competitors. Barty drove the machine onto the field where he was instructed to take the second position alongside a new Fordson. The Ivel tractor that Reuben had so lovingly tended looked resplendent gleaming in the sunshine and Ben had been giving it an extra polish for good luck. Only two competitions were held at a time so the whole affair was over very quickly. As he ploughed Barty kept glancing to the rear to ensure that his furrows were straight, the Fordson completed the stint before Barty but they both finished inside the allotted time. The overall results were not due to be announced until 4pm so the crew had time to clean the ploughs and get them loaded onto the trailers, ready for the journey home.

Ben, Jim and Barty would attend the prize-giving ceremony in the main arena while Oliver would stay with the horses and equipment. There was a little time to kill so the trio were able to admire the other competitor's livestock and talk to the owners. At the last show that Barty attended, the All England Show, he had looked after the transport, horses and equipment during the presentation ceremony so to be able to witness and take part in the whole proceedings made him feel great.

The loudspeakers around the ground crackled and burst into life, "Ladies and Gentlemen welcome to the Hampshire County Show. We have had a good day but before I announce the winners I would like to thank everyone for attending." There followed the customary acknowledgments to all concerned in the competitions, contributors and organisers in the many categories. Finally came the results and a hush descended through the ground,

"Heavy horses, individual heavy horse dressed category, First Place, Staines Farm, Middlesex, and in Second place, Mill Hall Farm, London" Barty didn't hear the third place result he was too busy congratulating Ben and Jim.

"Heavy horse ploughing, four furrows, The First place goes to Mill Hall Farm, London"

"In the tractor ploughing competition the First place goes to Mill Hall Farm, London."

Two First and a Second for Mill Hall Farm, what an achievement and a proud moment for the three of them as the winners went to the Judges platform to collect their respective rosettes and certificates, Barty for the horse dressing event, Jim for the horse ploughing and Barty again for the tractor ploughing event. What a result! They had bettered the All England result but then this competition was a smaller event and the competition was less but that did not detract from the feeling of all four of the team as they made their way back to Mill Hall Farm. These were four very happy men that Old Reuben would have been proud of also.

They arrived back rather late and after bedding the horses, a quick snack in the kitchen Barty went to his bed, again he found difficulty in sleeping, the adrenalin was still pumping and highlights of the Show kept returning to his mind.

    He arose early in the morning and following a substantial breakfast went to feed the animals and carry out is chores but was told to return to the bunkhouse by midday. He cleaned himself and went to the kitchen to find Sir James seated at the head of the table bearing a special lunch that Mrs Hudson had prepared. Sir James greeted each worker individually and seated Ben, Jim, Barty and Oliver on either side of him. He was in fine spirits and thanked everyone for their efforts and said that the whole year had been good especially the Show. He did stress that the only shadows, as far as he was concerned, was England being involved in a war with Germany and the passing of Reuben. Before he departed he said that the rest of the day should be taken as a holiday and wished them all Good Luck for the future. Several of the staff lingered to help Mrs

Hudson clear the table and wash the pots, she had been working hard since early morning, first the breakfast and then collecting the vegetables meat etc. and cooking a wholesome lunch for fourteen people, no mean feat, Mrs Hudson was a treasure.

   Reading in the newspapers of the war waging in France and Belgium Barty became aware of the massive loss of life and the injuries to both men and horses on both sides. He felt totally shocked but wasn't in a position where he could do anything about the situation; he was still too young to enlist in the army to feel that he was doing his bit. Christmas had passed and he wouldn't be of age to volunteer yet. He had read of the Christmas Truce on the Western Front when the fighting stopped and the opposing side played a game of football and exchanged gifts. Why couldn't the war and the entire killing stop, not only for one day but forever? The terrible battles at Ypres and the Somme only magnified the sheer futility of war. Every day as he tended the horses he thought more and more of the devastation and suffering that the war was bringing with no end in sight. Listening to the wireless and reading the papers he learned of the first zeppelin attack in London when a house on Askham Road in the Borough of Hackney had been damaged on 31st May 1915 luckily the family had escaped unhurt but 7 other people were killed in the raid and 35 more inured. This incident brought the war across the channel and into England.

Recently Barty had accompanied Ben on his weekly trip into town where he had noticed the number of people in uniform in the streets and in passing the Army Recruiting Centre he saw a long queue of men waiting to 'take the King's Shilling'. Posters glared out from the windows into the street seeking young men eligible to enlist into the army.

   'YOUR COUNTRY NEEDS YOU, SUPPORT THE SWORD OF
                              JUSTICE'

The queue of young hopefuls pressed eagerly forward to join Kitchener's Army, all enticed and fired with patriotism, the advertising obviously having had a great affect them. All this activity made Barty feel that he ought to be dong more than just feeding the horses and looking after the farm animals. They returned to Mill Hall Farm with him feeling quite despondent that he was not able to do his bit! Every evening the newspapers would come to the bunkhouse bearing more bad news, Barty never missed listening to the wireless mostly after work each evening and often stayed up late to discuss the war situations with Jim.

It was later in the year, just after the autumn harvest had been gathered and stored that the first finger of the conflict pointed in to the farm. It would be late September or early October, just after Barty's 17th birthday that two soldiers came to the farm in an army vehicle towing a horsebox. There followed a brief conversation with Jim and Barty was called to give a hand in loading two of the Clydesdales into the horsebox. One of the soldiers, a Sergeant handed Jim an official looking paper that informed him that the horses had been commandeered by the army for war service. Sir James had been contacted earlier in the month before the soldiers arrived informing him of the visit. The two younger horses had been chosen and put into the horsebox. It took a few minutes for Barty to understand what would happen to his beloved horses. The Sergeant explained the situation and the need for men and horses for the war effort, the need was now so great that the Government had approved a scheme that was affecting the whole Country where farmers and landowners with horses were required to hand over a certain amount of their stock. The Sergeant did his best to pacify Barty who was so broken hearted to see two of his beautiful horses leaving the farm; it was like losing two close friends. The rest of that day he could not be pacified no matter who spoke to him he just declined to answer, he didn't have any supper but just shut himself in his room until next morning. During the time he spent in his room he did a lot of deep thinking, was he soon lose the other two Clydesdales? He realised how much the horses meant to him and felt that half his purpose at the farm had now gone. He tried to foresee the future but all he could think about was the present. After much thought and deliberation, he decided what he would do next time he went into town.

    Thursday came and Barty went with Ben to accompany him to the Bank and they arrived a little later than normal as Ben had one or two other commitments to attend. Barty held the horses while Ben was in the Bank and on completion he asked if he could to in town for an hour or so and make his own way back to the farm. Ben agreed.

Later that afternoon Barty plucked up courage and entered the Army Recruiting Office, it was just about to close and there was no queue and he wanted to speak with the Recruiting Sergeant in private. Barty put his question to the Sergeant, if he was to volunteer for the Army would he be able to select which regiment he could join. He explained that he was employed in agriculture and was therefore exempt the 'call-up' The first thing the Sergeant asked was "How old are you son?" Barty fended the question by asking many others but the Sergeant was adamant and asked him where he worked, where he lived and about his parents and finished by saying "And how old are you? "Knowing he was compelled to answer he replied, "Eighteen Sir" Barty had answered all the questions quite truthfully except that final one when he added an extra year to his age. The Sergeant weighed and measured him taking note of his every detail while asking even more questions the final one being which regiment would he like to serve, to which he relied "The Army Veterinary Corps" The Sergeant seeing the potential in Barty, 5-foot-tall, 10 stone in weight, a well-built young man, extremely fit from his present employment. and quite knowledgeable about horses, a outstanding volunteer!

"I'll make some enquiries" said the Sergeant, "come back this time next week and bring a reference from your employer. He had been in the office for about 20 minutes but found Ben still in the carriage parked outside the Bank. Ben hailed him and asked if he was going back to the farm and did he want a lift which Barty readily accepted, his mind still on the Recruiting Sergeants words "Come back" he had said, he was obviously interested in recruiting him as he appeared to be a cut above the usual unemployed volunteers. Barty didn't say anything to Ben about where he had been and what he had been doing, in fact he didn't tell anyone back at the bunkhouse either. He felt a certain satisfaction although nothing had been achieved yet. He worried about his age and that bothered him, as he wasn't prone to telling lies. He had no birth certificate to show, as that had been lost years ago, when he was a boy living with his parents in Suffolk.

Friday morning, having completed his early morning duties after breakfast he asked Jim if he could go and see Ben over a personal matter. Jim agreed so Barty went to Ben's office at the rear of the big house. Ben welcomed him and very soon he knew all about Barty's intentions and when Ben approved Barty was overjoyed. He explained that he would need a letter of reference from Sir James and Ben said that he would speak to Sir James at the first opportunity. Ben also stressed how sorry he as that he may lose one of his best workers as good men were extremely hard to find when so many were signing up for the Army. Barty left Ben feeling very pleased but he still hadn't mentioned his age to Ben or to Jim.

Over the weekend, he went to the riverside and sat on a grassy bank of the Limehouse Reach, it was time for deep thought, was he doing the right thing and the more he thought of the suffering of the horses in the war, the more he wished he could help to relieve that suffering. The day was cold and overcast but he remained there for almost two hours deep in thought. Again, he was mesmerised by the boats and ships moving along the river and again he became lost in his thoughts of travel to distant lands and the romance of exotic places, but, all being well he would soon be in the Army so where would he go and what lay in store for him? He took a slow walk back to the farm enjoying the coming of the dusk and the moon casting its reflective glow beams on the now tranquil waters. He went straight to the stables to feed and bed down the horses. The stables seemed so empty now the two younger Clydesdales had gone. The riding horses were in a different stable, beautiful sleek animals probably worth a lot of money but Barty's heart lay with the heavy horses he now missed so much and knew he would never see again.

    The weekend passed without incident but on the Tuesday morning Jim came to Barty while he was cleaning the stables and told him that Sir James wanted to see him before lunchtime in his office. Barty tided himself up and went down to the Hall where, for the first time since he had worked on the farm, he was obliged to use the main front entrance as Sir James's office was at the front of the house. He was shown into the office immediately to find Sir James seated behind a large desk in the most luxurious room that Barty had ever seen. The walls were adorned with enormous paintings and pictures of horses and the wall cabinets displayed many cups and trophies that he presumed had been won at past agricultural shows.

Sir James greeted him and invited him to sit in a voluminous armchair near his desk and was soon discussing Barty's request for a letter reference. He said he was sorry to hear that Barty had his heart set on joining the Army but approved of his selection of how he wanted to serve. He praised him for his work on the farm and told him that he would do his best to assist him in gaining a place in the Veterinary Corps although he thought it most unusual that the Recruiting Sergeant asked for a letter of reference especially when men were so urgently needed as infantry men on the front line. He reached for a sheet of headed paper and addressed it to the Recruiting Sergeant by name. It appeared that he knew the Sergeant personally. He explained that Ben had written the letter to which Sir James had added his own comments and signed the letter, He handed the completed document to Barty and asked him to read it through, it was a glowing report on his work, his success at two Agricultural Shows he had attended and his deep interest in the upkeep and welfare of the horses ending the letter by emphasising his belief that Barty would be an asset to the A.V.C. (Army Veterinary Corps).

Sir James asked if anything had been missed from the letter and again thanked Barty for his time at Mill Hall Farm, he added that if his application was accepted and he joined the Army that should he wish to return to the farm after the war there would be a job waiting for him. He shook hands with him and accompanied him to the door wishing him good luck in his future.

Walking back to the bunkhouse he had mixed feelings, he enjoyed his work at the farm and the good friends he had made he felt reluctant to leave but he had still yet to be selected for an unforeseeable life in the future even though he was re-assured by Sir James comments that all would be fine. He decided that the time was right to tell Jim and all the others of his plans. Sir James and Ben both knew so it wouldn't remain a secret for much longer.

When the evening meal was over and everyone was still seated around the kitchen table, Barty made his announcement. The news was accepted with mixed reactions, mostly surprise. Jim said that he had half expected it since Barty was forever talking about the plight of the horses used at the front-line fighting. Mrs Hudson was quite upset at first and after the

initial shock went very quiet saying that it seemed like she would be losing one of her own sons, she had become very fond of Barty.
Barty finished his revelation by telling them that he hoped to have the answer regarding his acceptance on Thursday morning when he went into town. And tell them the news that same evening.

    Thursday morning found Ben at the stables busy harnessing a carriage read to go the town, Barty helped to finish the job and they departed a little earlier than normal. He was till apprehensive about meeting the Sergeant again in case he had found out about his true age but the possession of the Letter of Reference gave him added courage. How could he have found out, as far as he knew no-one else knew of his plans until a couple of days ago, and the Army had accepted boys who had lied about their dates of birth.

    At 9.30am, on the stroke he entered the Recruiting Office ahead of a small queue of volunteers waiting to see the Sergeant or one of his staff. Barty explained his presence and was taken through the main room into an office where an Officer asked him to be seated. After a short conversation, he handed his Letter of Reference to the Officer who took quite a long time to read it without saying a word. Placing the letter flat on the desk in front of him he looked over the rim of his glasses and looked directly at Barty before speaking.

"Well", he said, "Sir James certainly speaks very highly of you and your knowledge and interest in horses. There is quite a demand for qualified people in our field hospitals although technically you are not qualified, stable hands are still urgently needed as are assistants to the veterinary surgeons. Usually these are normally found from the civilian population but we do need soldiers to carry out some duties in the camps abroad. Now, providing you satisfy the physical needs for such a posting I am quite happy to support your request. I shall pass my findings and your letter through to the powers that be, recommending your appointment for specialist training."

Barty had listened intently to all that the Officer had told him and concluded the interview by saying that he should return to Mill Hall Farm and await a letter with the final decision in a few days' time. He left the Recruiting Office in high spirits. He was convinced that Sir James and the Officer were 'Old Pals' as the officer had placed great credence on what Sir James had written, the Officer would not have realised that the letter was the work of Ben but totally endorsed by Sir James. It had worked! Ben was again waiting for him to take him back to the farm and eager to ask how he had faired with the Recruiting Officer.

Barty was bubbling over with excitement and couldn't stop talking all the way home. As for Ben, he didn't say very much but he was so pleased to see Barty in such a confident mood. Back in the bunkhouse he was asked many questions, when would he be going and where would he be going, had he been accepted in the Veterinary Corps, scores of questions some that he was unable to answer until he received his letter of acceptance or otherwise? One good thing, nobody had questioned his age so he was quite relieved!

The stables next morning held even more attraction to him he paid extra attention to his chores thinking that if he was called up at short notice everything would be in tip top order. His mind was settled now, he would be leaving in a week or two, he didn't even consider the fact that he might be rejected, Sir James letter and his interview with the Recruiting Officer had made him feel very confident, but what if? - No, he wouldn't consider failure at this stage. He fully understood that to enter the Army with a recommendation of this type was unusual, it was almost unbelievable. So, satisfied with his situation he worked endlessly cleaning the stables and grooming the horses including the riding horses and was in the process of tidying up when he was interrupted by Jim. Barty had been so engrossed in his work that he had forgotten lunch and Jim came to check that he hadn't had an accident.

Having missed his lunch, he did justice to the meal that Mrs Hudson set before him at suppertime, he had certainly earned it. He went to bed early an enjoyed a long dreamless night's sleep.

The October mist was hanging heavy from the hedgerows and there was a definite chill in the air as Barty made his way across the field. He was still feeling quite elated from the previous days' developments and now resigned himself in patience awaiting the arrival of the letter. He worked hard that morning still trying to leave everything in order for when the time arrived. He saw nobody until he returned to the bunkhouse for lunch. Being alone all morning had given him time to reflect on what he would be missing at the farm and the job he loved, the horses and animals, the people that he had got to know so very well, they were more like family now, the secure life he had experienced over the last few years, all this would soon be in the past. It had been the newspapers and the street advertising that had persuaded him to look at a change in his life. The dreadful loss of life of men and horses in France had been the compelling factor in making his decision. The enlistment age for service was 18 but to serve overseas it was 19 years of age. He still had a background nag in his mind about lying about his age but he was physically fit and did look older than his actual age. He had read over the hundreds of underage young men that had joined the Army and only very few had been discharged, he also knew that some Recruiting Officers up and down the Country had not been averse to turning a blind eye and often received a small reimbursement for their considerations, after all the Country needed men desperately to enlist. He opened the bunkhouse door

to be greeted with the delicious smell of lunch, the kitchen was warm and welcoming and most of the staff were already seated and he realised that, once again he was late, but not too late this time. He took his place at the table to find a large brown envelope propped up in front of him addressed 'Mr Kaleb Bartholomew – Personal', and over stamped 'Ministry of Defence' Barty's heart missed a beat, he never received any mail and this one was the most official one he had ever set eyes upon. The letter had arrived days before he had expected it, as it was only two or three days ago when he had visited the Recruiting Office. Trembling slightly, he opened the envelope, all eyes around the table were watching him, they all knew what it contained but were eager to know the contents.
Slowly Barty read the letter to himself and on completion he felt obliged to tell every one of the contents of the letter. He told his work colleagues that he was to report to the Army Careers Office in Poplar at 3pm on Thursday 30th October to attend a medical examination with an Army Doctor. He paused a second then repeated, "30th October; that's only three days away", things were certainly moving quickly.

    The next three days passed in a flash and on the Thursday, he went with Ben to the Bank as usual then Ben drove him to Poplar, not so far away. Ben then returned to Mill Hall Farm and Barty took a slow stroll around Poplar killing time before 3pm and his appointment.
There were only five other volunteers waiting to see the doctor who took only a few minutes with each one. Only one of them spoke to Barty about basic training but he didn't know if they had been accepted or rejected after they had seen the doctor. His eyesight and reflexes were tested, he was weighed, measured and asked a few questions regarding his general health and past diseases the whole examination taking only about ten minutes. He was told to expect a letter soon.

He took nearly three hours to return to the farm deep in thought about what one of the five volunteers had told him about basic training. it sounded very disciplined. He understood that he would be required to attend 'boot camp' at first, as all volunteers had to attend but then transferred to another camp for those that had been earmarked for specialist training. He would be taught the rescue and care of animals at the veterinary hospitals including aftercare when they had received treatment from the veterinary surgeons. He had no idea where or when his training would take place.

He arrived back at the bunkhouse with plenty of time to spare before the evening meal but he was kept busy with a multitude of questions, where are you going for your training; when do you have to leave, did you pass the physical okay? He answered all he could and explained that he was to wait for another letter with his final results.

He didn't have to wait long as the letter arrived within a few days. It was now late November and the war wasn't going too well for Britain. Food was getting short due to the German submarines blockading the shipping lanes; there was a shortage of food throughout the country even though there were concerted efforts to produce more.

Once again Barty read his letter to his workmates. He was now ordered to report to Aldershot Barracks in Hampshire on the morning of the 12th November 1915.at 9am. Enclosed with the letter was a railway travel warrant together with a short list of personal items to take with him.

In the few days, he had left he enquired about train times ensuring that the time of arrival would be well in advance of his reporting time. He would have to leave late on the night before and Ben had promised to drive him to the station to catch the train. He would arrive in Aldershot in the very early hour of the morning, as there were no other suitable trains available.

Mrs Hudson had laid on a special meal that evening, a sort of farewell party and everyone attended. Sir James and Ben looked in for a short while but were unable to stay long due to a meeting being held at the big house that same evening. Sir James ensured that there was plenty of alcohol to toast Barty's departure but he declined a drink himself as he didn't drink much at the best of times and he wanted a clear head for his journey. He went, rather late to the stables to say goodbye to the horses he had grown to love returning to the bunkhouse to meet Ben after his meeting had finished, he ready to start his new life. Everyone was there to wish him well and Mrs Hudson handed him a large pack of sandwiches, just' to tide him over'. She gave him a big hug as the tears started to well up in her eyes, she had become very fond of Barty.

Barty didn't sleep on the train and arrived outside the Training Centre at 4am in the morning He entered the gates and reported to the Guardroom after being challenged by two soldiers in full uniform and carrying rifles. He showed his Joining Instructions and was directed to the New Entrants Block to spend at least two hours sitting waiting for the next move. The room slowly filled up as men came into the New Entrants Block each wondering what the day held in store for them, until there were approximately 40 new entrants seated uncomfortably on the hard-wooden chairs, their kit at their feet.

A bugle sounded, sharp and clear as 'Reveille' echoed around the mass of Nissan huts and wide-open spaces of the Aldershot Military Training Centre, waking hundreds of men reluctantly from their slumbers The Centre appeared to be deserted but within half an hour or so it became a teeming mass of men in khaki uniforms. The day for the men already in khaki it was breakfast in the Mess Room and another day of 'square-bashing', rifle drill and class instruction.

A small group of men in civilian clothing stood at the windows of the New Entry Block gazing at the scene outside. A Sergeant came into the room at 6.30am and told them to take their belongings outside and then, pointing across the expanse of the Parade Ground, to proceed to the Mess Room for breakfast instructing them that on completion of their meal they should report to 'D' Hut with their kit no later than 8.30am.

Barty was quite satisfied with his first meal in the Army, perhaps not as good as Mrs Hudson would have managed but perfectly satisfactory to the new recruits, most of whom had been travelling all night. They assembled outside 'D' Hut well before 8.30am. Two Sergeants introduced themselves as Instructors, unlocked the hut and told them to deposit their kit onto one of the beds and then go to the smaller room in the hut next door. For the next half an hour they were told what they could expect for the next six weeks. Six weeks? What, Barty thought, had happened to the specialist training for the Army Veterinary Corps? One of the Sergeants told them that all volunteers had to undergo the six weeks basic training to become a soldier, after all they were all to be trained soldiers and their specialist training would follow pending their successful passing out from 'boot camp'. Fighting men foremost before anyone qualified for special selections they had been promised. Specially selected volunteers and enlisted men were few and far between; most of the men under training were destined for the infantry divisions.

    The initial briefing over they were instructed to fall in outside in two columns of twenty men. One Sergeant took charge of each platoon and marched them around the block pointing out different buildings and stores then back to 'D' Hut that was to be their home for the next six weeks. Once inside, Sergeant Molloy again spoke to them of what he expected from his men. He was to be their Section Sergeant until the end of their basic training and wished them all every success in their Army careers.

Barty formed the impression that Sgt Molloy was a very fair man as long as all went well. He told them that they would take all their meals in the Mess Room and most of the lessons would be taken in the room next to D Hut. They would be responsible for the cleanliness of D Hut and the annexe. Any complaints were to be referred to him as soon as possible, He addressed them for a further half an hour and he finished his brief by saying, "Be fair with me, do your best and I'll be like a father to you. Wrong me and accept the consequences. I like a quiet life!"

He again told them to form up outside and he marched them to the large parade square in the centre of the camp together with the other twenty men of that day's intake, to be addressed by the Commanding Officer of the Centre and to take the oath of Allegiance to the King.

They were now sworn in members of His Majesty's Armed Forces and were marched to the Quartermasters Stores to be given a number, photographed and to draw uniform, bedding then marched back to Section D Hut. They were given the rest of the day to stow their kit in the lockers provided, make their beds and clean up the Hut from top to bottom ready for a formal inspection by an Officer after lunch the next day. Quite a tall order for some who didn't know one end of a mop and broom from another! Every man worked hard that evening both on his personal kit and the Section Hut that had been used by the departing intake the previous day.

Private Kaleb Bartholomew, 914531 Section D woke early the next morning to find several other members of his section already working on their kit. After breakfast, they changed into fatigues and cleaned the windows of Hut D and the annexe, swept and washed the floor and paintwork around the doors. The only form of heating was a pot-bellied stove in the centre of the hut, that had been used the previous night so it was cleaned, re-laid, but not lit. By midday the hut was ready for inspection. The new recruits cleaned themselves, put on their uniforms before marching to the Mess Room for lunch. On their return to the Hut they decided to wait outside for the arrival of the Inspecting Officer at 1.30pm. Uppermost in their minds was the consequences that Sgt Molloy said they would suffer if their quarters were not up to standard.

A Section Leader had been appointed, a man of about 35 years of age who appeared to have a good knowledge of army routines. At 1.30pm prompt the Officer appeared and the Leader called the parade to attention, With a rather ragged response, and reported to Sgt Molloy, "Section D Hut ready for inspection Sir" The Sergeant in turn reported to the Lieutenant who immediately started to inspect each man individually with Sgt Malloy following behind and noting any comments that were made by the Officer. They then went into Hut D where the rest of the men's kit was laid out on their individual beds in the approved manner. Again, the Officer made comments that were duly noted. The men were dismissed and told to fall in again outside the Hut. The whole inspection had taken nearly two hours before the Lieutenant finally addressed them. "At ease men, this is your first inspection after signing on for service with the British Army and I have seen many things which leave a lot to be desired. I found many beds that were untidy and dust on the upper casement window ledges. The floor although clean was unpolished and as for you, you are sloppy and un-drilled at present but all that will change and quickly, Sergeant, see to it that the points I have outlined are rectified and I shall hold another inspection in one week's time" He turned to face Sgt Molloy, who called the parade to attention, saluted the Lieutenant as he turned to leave.

Many comments were passed between the men concerning the inspection of both themselves and the accommodation The Sergeant said very little but handed his notes to the Section Leader saying "See to all this and report to me if you have any difficulties, By the way, it wasn't as bad as the Lieutenant made out, you've had no drill and very little time to adjust so don't take things too much to heart, just do better next week, dismiss the men"

The first week was a whirl of learning, parade ground drill, with and without rifles, bulling up boots and preparing the accommodation for the coming inspection. Barty had made a friend with the man in the bed space next to him. Thomas Black was a man of 22 years of age, an ex-dockworker from London. They would sit on their beds most evenings discussing the Army and the instructions they were being told during the day. They realised that all the 'bull' they were receiving was all for a purpose, the drills, the tactics and the fieldwork, early morning parades, attention to small details in dress and conduct and the comments they received from senior officer whenever contact was made. The attention to cleanliness of his equipment became most meaningful, no man could feel safe in conflict with a dirty ill maintained weapon. They were being taught to take orders without question.

At the end of the week the Section again underwent an Inspection by the same Lieutenant. The whole proceeding took place with very few comments and was deemed successful causing Sgt. Molloy to comment that his 'one week' soldiers had done very well.

The front line in France was desperate for more troops and brought the news that basic training would be cut to 4 weeks. This was received by most of the men as good news as they were eager to leave the camp early and do what they had signed up to do – fight!

Another week passed and Barty learnt from Tom that he had been employed on the docks as a driver; he had driven several different types of vehicles and was competent in maintaining their engines. He, like Barty had been selected for special training with the Transport Corps but neither would hear anything about their future postings until the completion of basic training here at Aldershot. Hundreds of men had in the past had completed training successfully to be released into the regular regiments of the Army. The camp turned out approximately 100 newly trained recruits each week

Barty listened to the newscasts every day and had access to newspapers, news of the happenings reported made him feel sick, like the terrible battles taking place in Europe and the dreadful loss of lives being suffered by armies on both sides of the conflict. The earlier sinking of the Lusitania in May 1915 had been one event that had shocked him as did the execution of Nurse Edith Cavell had just a few weeks ago.

It was late December when Section D completed their Initial Training Course and the men who were to join the various infantry regiments were sent off to their Units even though it was only a few days prior to Christmas. A piece of luck came to Barty, Tom and a few other men who were destined to go on Specialist Training Courses. As the Courses were being held at individual training schools that were staffed mainly by civilians, they closed for the Christmas period so the Army had decided to give them one weeks leave then join their respective Units on 27th December 1915.

Barty and Tom were given railway warrants back to London and Barty received a further warrant to take him to the Defence Animal Centre in Melton Mowbray, Leicestershire. Tom had also received his travel warrant and orders to report to a transport depot. After the beginning of the Christmas break they would not see each other again.

Barty's travel warrant was to London as he had given his home address as Mill Hall Farm, he had no real home and that was his last place of residence. Without really thinking he made his way to the railway station, it made sense that he should go back the farm, he didn't have anywhere else to go but he really didn't have any connection to the farm anymore even though it had been his workplace.

He sat in the railway carriage watching the now barren fields pass the window but his mind wasn't on the landscape but on his future with the Army Veterinary Corps. In no time at all the train was entering the terminal station in London. He picked up and shouldered his kitbag choosing to kill time by walking the rather long distance to the Farm. He arrived at approximately 9.30pm after taking a meal en route and it was a very proud young soldier in full uniform that knocked on the door of the bunkhouse, the door being opened by Mrs Hudson who was totally surprised to see him standing there. She gave a sharp intake of breath then flung her arms around his neck. "Oh Barty, it's lovely to see you, what a surprise, come on in, are you hungry? It was very clear how fond she had become of Barty and he had only been away for seven weeks.

"Where have you been, how long will you be here, where are you going next, do you want something to eat, are you tired? Mrs Hudson was bubbling over and Barty was unable to answer any of her questions before the next one was asked. She had Barty to herself as everyone was either busy elsewhere or in their rooms. Although Barty had tried to tell her he had eaten she interrupted getting the breakfast table ready for next morning to make him a sandwich and a cup of tea. It was close on midnight when they finally parted and Mrs Hudson took him to an empty room for the night. No one else had come to the kitchen so Barty's arrival remained a secret.

It was a dark, dull December morning when Barty awoke from a good night's sleep, dressed and went to the bunkhouse kitchen. Breakfast was being served and there was Mrs Hudson looking as if she had never left the kitchen last night. She hadn't said a word to anyone thinking that Barty's appearance would be a nice surprise for them as it had been for her. Suddenly the dull December morning suddenly brightened as everyone looked up as he entered the room and turned to greet him. They were all talking at once and Barty just stood there dumbstruck by their reception. He was wearing half uniform and a look of helplessness on his face. He didn't know what to say, only seven weeks away but it was at that moment that he realised this was his only family, these people with whom he had spent to last two or three years had accepted him as one of their own. It was Jim Crawford that was first to break the spell.

"Come and get some breakfast" he said as Mrs Hudson fussed about him. Again, Barty wondered if she had even been to bed, the kitchen as warm and the Christmas decorations added to the homely atmosphere. Yes, Barty felt that this was his home!

There was just one new face at the table, that of the new 16-year-old smooth faced stable boy who had taken Barty's job.

"What have you been doing then" Jim asked.

"I've just finished Boot Camp at Aldershot"

His reply unleashed a torrent of questions and he found himself telling of the training he had already taken and where he would be stationed next, he had his audience so engrossed in his story that they didn't notice Ben Chapman enter the door. "Come on you lot. Get to work, stop wasting time in here" and looking at Barty he continued, "I want words with you" Barty thought he was in trouble and when all the others had left to attend their duties Ben sat on a chair opposite Barty, after first shaking his hand and enquiring about his well-being, and about his training at Aldershot, and his future so Barty related his story for the second time that morning expecting at any time to be rebuked for staying at the farm last night with only Mrs Hudson's blessing. He explained that he would be joining his next camp at Melton Mowbray and that he had been granted leave until the 27th December. Ben listened intently and said that he was welcome to stay for the duration of his leave and he could earn his keep by doing a few jobs on the farm. This suited Barty admirably and Ben told him to get some overalls and work gear from Jim, he couldn't work in uniform!

He gave Mrs Hudson a hand in the kitchen until Jim returned at lunchtime, he was given some suitable clothing, and after lunch he made a beeline for the stables to be temporarily re-united with the two remaining Clydesdales and the riding horses. Nothing had changed and he had that same old feeling of 'belonging' again. The new stable boy was a most affable young man and they got on well together. Back at the bunkhouse he felt like he had never been away but the nagging in the back of his mind was the uneasiness that he would have to return to the Army in a few days' time. He hadn't got cold feet about his enlistment but this was his home.

What a wonderful Christmas it proved to be, everything he could have hoped for among friends, but the 26th of December came, Boxing Day, a bad day to have travel due to limited timetables but he had to be at his new posting by 9am next day, the 27^{th,} he would have to leave taking the only available train he made his farewells and left in full uniform.

The journey was uneventful and he enjoyed the sandwiches that Mrs Hudson had made for him. He took his time managing to find an early morning café for a cup of coffee before going to the Camp. He reported to the Guardroom and entered his presence in the Arrivals Book before being directed to 'A' Block, a large barrack complex comprising of offices, classrooms and accommodation for approximately 50 men. This was to be his new home for the next six weeks or more. The war was still raging and still not going well so the call for more men to serve was dominant on the many of the posters both in the town and on the barrack walls as were the posters urging to guard against 'Careless Talk' Eventually the same morning, he was inducted into camp life at the Centre and away from the Reception area, the 'advertising' posters was mainly given to instructions for discipline and care for animal notices. Training to become a veterinary nurse appeared to be quite complicated and prolonged but due to manpower shortage the present courses had to be of a shorter period with the expectancy that the trainees would self-educate themselves to a degree. Suffice to say that a very compressed training course followed looking at basic animal care, including horses, mules, dogs and pigeons and the handling of unbroken horses. Much of what Barty had learned at Mill Hall Farm was not new to him but the care of injured animals and the medical aftercare, he found particularly hard to tackle. More serious wounds were left the Veterinary Surgeons who also gave the lectures and introduced them to a little 'hands-on' practice. Barty never was one for book learning and found the course quite demanding however by the end of his six weeks training he was able to 'pass out of the Centre with satisfactory marks. The Centre staff had been very good in informing the trainees of the current developments on the war front, something they found very useful as they heard hardly any up to date news in their cloistered surrounds and the pressure of the training.

 The Training Course was completed and Barty was sent back to Aldershot to await his next posting. It was now mid-February 1916 and he was surprised to learn that at the beginning of the month National Service had been announced for single men, men of 18 years to 41, over 5 feet 3inches tall and a chest measurement of a minimum 34 inches were eligible for enlistment. If he hadn't lied about his age Barty would receive his 'call-up' papers even though he had grounds to be exempted as an agricultural worker. but here he was, not 18 until September and already a trained soldier with a specialist qualification. At Aldershot, he had met several other young men who admitted that they too had lied about their dates of birth but each eager to serve his Country with the British Army. It was only a matter of days before he received his posting for active service. He was to report to the Transport Office on the camp at 9am on Monday20th March 1916 for onward transportation to a Mobile Veterinary Unit somewhere in France. There was no indication as to where in France but he assumed it would be just rearward of enemy lines. Mobile Units had been established to receive sick and injured animals to receive first aid before being transferred to Veterinary Hospitals. The futility of war was sharply brought back to his mind, he had seen the horrific photographs at Melton Mowbray and heard the terrible stories of the men and horses who had been brought in from the front line. All this came vividly back to him; he was surprised how the thoughts affected him. Would he be able to stand to see the suffering, would he be able to cope with his work? Reality was slowly setting in, what if . . . ? No, he had to do his duty and resolved to dismiss these thoughts from his head. The two big Clydesdales from Mill Hall Farm, what had happened to them? It was hard to forget then especially after looking at the pictures he had seen at the Training Centre but he realised that they had been shown to the men in an effort to harden them against what they were going to experience in the field of conflict.

A blustery, rain-driven day greeted twenty young men on the Aldershot Parade ground as a large lorry pulled up beside them. They loaded their kit and other stores into the wagon then the twenty, now rain soaked soldiers climbed into the lorry grumbling about their discomfort,

"Don't you worry lads" shouted the driver "This is an April shower compared to where you are going"

'Job's Comforter', thought Barty as he tried to find the driest niche inside the canvas-covered truck. The journey to Dover was one of the most uncomfortable, bumpy, miserable trips he had ever experienced, many of the recruits never stopped moaning about the conditions, not that anyone could have done a thing to ease their plight.

On arrival at Dover, they de-bussed and marched to a large warehouse marked 'Troop Arrivals and Transportation, where they received a dinner before being marched away down the quayside to board a Royal Navy destroyer and taken below to an empty mess deck where the instant warmth was most welcome. Everyone had been briefed on what to do should the destroyer be attacked but the crossing to France was uneventful. Many other Units of the Army had joined the ship at Dover and all were discharged ashore, the twenty men of the A.V.C. with their kit, were taken to a church hall on the dockside to await further transport. Meanwhile, the rest of the Units were paraded on the dockside for a while then loaded onto a convoy of lorries that arrived about ten minutes after. The convoy moved off and a larger military vehicle pulled up outside the church hall and the men loaded it with the stores they embarked back in Dover then boarded a second truck. The first convoy had moved off destined for a camp in France while the twenty men of the A.V.C. 6th Mobile Unit learned that their destination was not to be in France, but at Hooge in Belgium, a long distance away, being about 4 or 5 kilometres from Ypres. The journey was rough and monotonous and they stopped twice for food and a hot drink from the stores they were carrying on the truck. For the first time Barty could see the countryside through which they were travelling, the roads were in a terrible state through bombing, ice and snow and almost impassable, no wonder the journey was so bumpy and rough. Suddenly he understood why the Army needed so many heavy horses to move equipment, as motorised vehicles were apt to bog down so easily, so far, due to their experienced driver they had managed well. They eventually arrived at the location that consisted of a sprawling conglomeration of heavy tents and more permanent structures to house the sick and injured animals. They were told to put their kit into one of the big tents and report immediately to the Control HQ in the next tent. They were detailed to their jobs and within 30 minutes of arriving at the camp they were working. They would be dismissed later when they could settle into the accommodation and sort themselves out. Permanent orders would be issued later that evening.

Barty was put to work immediately in the Receiving Bay and was shocked by the conditions in the Bay and appalled by the hideous wounds suffered by some of the animals. It was almost 10pm that evening when he returned to his tent to be told that a meal had been laid on in the Mess Tent. He hadn't even thought of food; he was so disturbed by what he had seen in the Receiving Bay. While they were having a meal, a senior officer welcomed them to the camp, he apologised for the conditions and the fact they had been 'thrown in at the deep end' so soon after their arrival. They were so short of men that an average day at the Unit was nearly always over twelve hours long.

He detailed each man to his duties, Barty being made a nurse in the Receiving Bay. He was issued with some special clothing and set to work with hardly any further instructions. The Veterinary Surgeons would brief him as they worked through each procedure they had to perform. This was how it would be for many days to come, the Unit moving forward slowly as the front line advanced. The heavy horses seemed to be the most frequent invalids as they hauled hundreds of tons of supplies, rations and ammunition through the mud, mire and the atrocious conditions to serve the fighting men on the front line. They would then return carrying the wounded men and animals on the piteous carts they dragged behind them. As time passed Barty grew to accept certain conditions. He saw the results of mustard gas attacks, being stuck in the mud, the damage done by the barbed wire and the seriously injured men and animals being left in 'no man's land', a strip of land between the two opposing forces. He did everything he could to comfort the injured but oft times it was never enough. Many people do not realise the acute sense of smell that horse possesses and how the horse is terrified by the smell of blood. He never could accept the reason behind all the waste and suffering of the stupid war.

After one battle, he heard that a General had outlined an incident that really brought home the futility of the war. The General said of his horse, "He had to endure everything most hateful to him – violent noise, the bursting of great shells and bright flashes at night when the white light of bursting shells must have caused violent pain to such sensitive eyes as a horse possesses. Above all, the smell of blood, terrifying to every horse"

Lieutenant R Dixon of the 14th Battery, Royal Garrison Artillery had written in his diary, "Heaving about in the filthy mud of the road was an unfortunate mule with both his forelegs shot away. The poor brute, suffering God knows what untold agonies and terror, was trying desperately to get to his feet, which weren't there. Jerry shells were arriving pretty fast – we made some desperate attempts to get to the mule so that I could put a bullet behind his ear into the brain but to no avail. The shelling got more intense – perhaps one would hit the poor thing and put it out of its misery"

All this was heard and in some cases witnessed by Barty whilst serving with the Mobile Unit.

There were thousands of animals brought in from the Battle of Morval and Transtoy during that year of 1916 and treated at the Unit. Other battles followed, Hill 70 and Cambria in 1917 and Flanders in 1918. These years of conflict caused Barty great distress in the things he witnessed and he became utterly sickened by man's inhumanity. The sights and sounds of the war would linger with him forever. It seemed an interminable time that he had been part of the conflict and it was with great joy that he and millions of other people around the world welcomed the Armistice on 11th November 1918 and it was with great resolve that Barty vowed he would never mention the atrocities and suffering he had witnessed.

Clearing the camp after the Armistice took a couple of weeks then the 6th Mobile Field Section moved to Germany as part of the occupying force stationed at Bruehl to remain there until February 1919 when he was transferred back to Aldershot for demobilisation.

It would take a long time for Barty to accept what had happened over the past three years, he certainly didn't want to talk about it so decided not to return to Mill Hall Farm for a long time to come although he craved the closeness of his friends, he knew there would be a lot of questions asked and that would put more pressure on the memories he wanted to forget.

The newspapers were still dominated by facts and figures gleaned throughout the conflict and it was startling to see some of the figures that were revealed. Nearly 900,000 British soldiers died in France between 1914 and 1918. Of the million horses sent overseas to aid the war, only 62,000 returned. The A.V.C. had done a magnificent job but what a price to pay! No. Barty didn't want to talk about the appalling revelations or his experiences so he decided to return to his place of birth where nobody would know him or even remember him, a fresh start. He was now 21 years old with no future again, a limited amount of cash and only the clothes he stood in. He knew about horses and very little else. There always appeared to be agricultural jobs in Suffolk, the more he thought about it the more determined he was to pursue that fresh start. He would find lodgings and look around for likely employment, his Army discharge monies would last him a couple of weeks, failing that he thought about travelling to Lowestoft looking for work with the fishing fleet, a hard job especially in the winter months,' He didn't really fancy that but he badly needed to find work.

The plan was set.

The roads in London were heavily congested as he made his way towards Liverpool Street railway station, it was midday and it felt like the world and its wife were going in the opposite direction to him. He was dressed in civilian clothing that the Army had provided prior to his final discharge and carried a small hand grip containing his toiletries, his discharge and identity papers. Fighting his way through the opposing crowd he managed to join the queue at the ticket office where he purchased a single ticket to Ipswich. He intended to make his way to Ipswich if he was unlucky in gaining agricultural work in the surrounds of the town.

The train cleared the smoky urban spread of the capital and slowly steamed into the open countryside. It was very re-assuring to him to catch the many glimpses of scattered farms near the trackside and to see the livestock grazing in the fields, very different to the bare, battered fire-torn landscapes he had seen lately in France and Belgium. He tore the memories away from his mind, maybe in the course of time they would fade away Seeing the tranquil scenes of the English rural countryside from the carriage window soothed his feelings and very soon the train halted at Ipswich railway station.

As he wandered slowly about the town he was unable to recall ever visiting before. His father, had on occasions taken him to various towns when he was a young lad but Ipswich appeared totally unknown to him. His first priority was to find somewhere to rent for a day or two. Ipswich had once been a very prosperous harbour town blessed with many flourishing industries. He made his way to the harbour and in no time at all had secured a room at a Bed & Breakfast for a moderate rent. It was getting late so after a good meal in a harbour side café he decided to retire for the night and read his copy of the 'Evening Star' that he bought from the newsagents. The 'Star' covered a wide area of the surrounding districts, Colchester, Bury, Woodbridge, Stowmarket and Lowestoft. He hoped that with such a wide scope he might find a vacancy in one of the varied industries. Unfortunately, feeling tired from the journey to Ipswich and the effects of the large meal he had consumed, he quickly fell asleep. He arose the next morning at 7.30am, washed and dressed and was taking his breakfast by 8.30am. Having no particular plan for the day and nothing 'ringed' in the newspaper, he asked the landlady if she would accommodate him for another night as he spent the day job hunting. She readily agreed and gave Barty the directions to the nearest Ministry of Labour Office. The landlady was a plump, pleasant lady that reminded him of Mrs Hudson back at Mill Hall Farm. She told him that the Labour Exchange was quite a long way off and advised him to take the tram and save himself some time.

He took the landlady's advice and boarded a tram for the other side of town, he found the Labour Exchange without any problem but was amazed to see many men queuing. He waited about twenty minutes before gaining access into the actual building and the chance to look through the vacancies listed on the notice boards. He chose two farming vacancies and took his enquiry to one of the clerks only to be told that both posts had been filled. The clerk told him that so many men had returned from the armed services that they were finding difficulties in satisfying the scramble for work, too many men, too few jobs. Barty had the presence of mind to ask where his best chance of finding work could be and received the answer 'Lowestoft', the very place that was in his original plan. He left the Labour Exchange rather disappointed!

He took the opportunity to look around Ipswich but soon became bored with the hustle and bustle. Seeing the directional board for the harbour he decided to return there. He had read how Ipswich had been a busy port in the past so what he saw was a disappointment as well. It was much smaller than he had imagined but there were several small vessels loading and unloading their cargoes. Now, as Barty had had such a fascination when he was at Mill Hall Farm, just sitting on the Reaches watching the ships going up and down the river and noting their names and ports of registration, it is of no surprise that he found himself a comfortable vantage point outside the Harbour Snack Bar. He noted there was quite a number of different types of vessels beside the quay and took great interest in reading the names on the stern of each craft, some of which he recognised from his days beside the Thames. There was at least one Thames barge but he couldn't see the stern as it was surrounded by several local wherries bearing such local names as *'Unity'* of Southwold, the *'Mary Jane'* of Aldeburgh and the *'Ellie May'* of Woodbridge. He watched the constant stream of boatmen and harbour workers that frequented the Harbour Snack Bar and longed to speak with some of the more affable looking men.

He sat there entranced for some considerable time until the pangs of hunger interrupted his thoughts. He entered the Snack Bar and ordered a sandwich and a mug of tea, he found himself a seat opposite an older man who looked as if he had spent many years as a boatman. Barty thought he looked the type of man who would be pleased to answer some of his questions. He was anxious to find out more about life on the boats and the inshore trade around the coast and rivers of Norfolk and Suffolk, even up to London. Barty broke the ice by asking the man if he minded him sitting at his table to which the man indicated his approval by the wave of his hand.

Don McLean seemed a friendly fellow; his weather-beaten face had a cheery smile about his mouth as Barty took a seat opposite him. He had the look of a real old salt about him and Barty broke the ice by asking which boat he was from and where he was bound. He replied immediately saying that he had just finished unloading his wherry and would be leaving for Southwold tomorrow morning. They exchanged small talk for a while and Barty learned that he had been born in Glasgow in 1850 and when he was a lad he shipped aboard a full rigged barque as a deckhand before taking to the deep-sea shipping trade He spent a lot of years in large sailing ships and only left as sail gave way to steam driven vessels. He hated steam ships saying they were dirty, noisy and like tin cans. There was something regal about sailing ships, beautiful to see under full sail and the joy of hearing the wind in the rigging had never left him. He just couldn't relate to the modern ships and at the age of 48 years he left the deep seas and settled for the coastal inshore trade.
His yarns intrigued Barty and Don's weather beaten craggy face reflected the satisfaction he had found in his life at sea. He quickly took to the inshore trade as a crewmember on a ketch working from Aldeburgh until he scraped and saved enough money to buy his own vessel, a Norfolk wherry, the *'Ellie May'* that Barty had seen in the harbour earlier that day. His questions to Don were endless but Don managed to ask a few of his own whenever Barty took a breath.

Barty told Don that he was on his way to Lowestoft to try and find work as he had just been demobbed from the Army. Don was sympathetic and they talked for a good hour before parting but as Barty reached the door Don called him back

" Tomorrow morning I'm leaving for Southwold" he said, "If you want a ride there be at the *Ellie May* by 8am, the passage won't cost you anything but I expect you to help with the boat"

The offer was something of a surprise and was gladly accepted so Barty returned to his bed and breakfast house with a happy heart and a mixed expectancy about life at sea. It would give him more time to enquire about the inter-river and inshore trade as such knowledge could assist him at Lowestoft He arose early and went to the quayside, he hadn't been too disappointed in not finding work in Ipswich but felt that is overall plan was still intact. He also had a strange feeling that the day held some sort of promise; perhaps Southwold would be a better place to seek employment. On his short walk to the quayside he saw two soldiers in uniform that made him think of his old pal Tom Black He wondered if he had survived the war and managed to find work. Briefly he remembered some of his old army colleagues, what they had endured together and that he would never know what became of them as they each pursued their individual lives as civilians. He thought too of the folk at Mill Hall farm but all that now seemed a lifetime away. He dismissed all this from his mind as he neared the *Ellie May*.

Don was on deck tidying up some loose bits and pieces, he welcomed Barty on board and showed him where to stow his gear in the tiny after cabin before telling him that they would be leaving in ten minutes' time. He went below and started the auxiliary engine. Barty was surprised to know there was an engine after what Don had said about them but he explained they were an essential for navigation in the confines of the rivers. Soon the boat was making way down the River Orwell towards open water at Harwich and the North Sea. Barty soon recognised the importance of an engine in restricted waters. The engine was cut when they reached Harwich and the sail hoisted

Barty felt quite useless, as the only chore he had been given was to make tea as they finished with the engine. Don was at the tiller expertly avoiding the mud banks and the silted areas. He knew the area so well but he had a chart in front of him to show Barty their position and the various hazards printed on the chart. A man like Don didn't really need a chart, years of experience in these waters had taught him to read the rivers and shores without a chart. Barty was extremely impressed by his knowledge and kept asking questions about the buildings they had passed coming down river, the charts and the boat itself. Don was eager to answer his questions but he felt himself getting a little agitated by Barty's constant talking he was used to the peace and quiet of being away from the noise and sounds of the land" Don't keep calling me Mr McLean" he said in a rather sharp tone, "folks around here call me Skipper"

He noted the irritability in Don's voice and decided to talk less and concentrate more on the charts and the passing coastline. Occasionally Skipper would call on him to take the tiller while he attended to other tasks.

Barty felt quite important standing in the stern of the *Ellie May*, a wherry built in Norfolk in the 1860's, not a big boat but best suited for the shallow waters, rivers and the coasts of East England. She was approximately 70 feet in length and 8 tonnes in displacement and capable of carrying about 25 tons of cargo. She carried a single square sail amidships and an auxiliary engine for use mainly when negotiating the wandering rivers of East Anglia, Barty enjoyed the experience of steering the boat and the peace and tranquillity and the gentle swish as the bow cut through the placid water making about 4 knots, as the estuary widened they saw Harwich ahead; they were a little later than anticipated. Skipper completed has work and came to sit beside Barty, he didn't take over the tiller and he seemed less irritable now and talked freely. He told Barty that they should around the Landguard Peninsula off Harwich at roughly 4pm to 5pm and spend the night at Felixstowe. The stretch from Ipswich to Felixstowe by river is only about 20 miles but they had made a stop at an isolated jetty on the river although Barty couldn't make out exactly where when he looked at the chart. At the jetty Skipper, was met by a man and between them they loaded 12 medium sized crates into the hold while Barty was sent to make three mugs of tea. The three of them sat on deck to drink their tea the only conversation related to the fine weather and the fact that Barty was being given a lift to Southwold before going to Lowestoft to seek employment. Ten minutes later the man drove away in a dilapidated old pick-up truck, Skipper made no comment about the stop and within 30 minutes they cast off to continue their journey. True to Skipper's estimated time of arrival they entered the harbour at Felixstowe after dropping the sail and starting the diesel engine. The change of propulsion was very marked instead of the silence the engine chugged along giving off a sickly, foul smelling vapour. Barty was still at the tiller but Skipper was keeping a very close eye on him now they were in the confines of a busy harbour. He realised that Skipper could have managed the boat on his own and wondered why he had no other crew. Was that why he had offered Barty the lift to Southwold? Why was he putting into Felixstowe for the night, a man like Don McLean would easily manage a night journey up the coast from Felixstowe to Southwold, a distance of about 50 miles without any problem whatsoever? These and other questions entered his mind. He couldn't really ask him what his intentions were, it would appear ungracious to

question him. They slowly entered into the harbour and Skipper took over the steering. He had contacted the Harbourmaster by radio prior to their arrival and *Ellie May* had been allocated a berth at the quayside near the town centre. If Skipper had contacted the harbour office earlier it showed that he intended to spend the night there for some reason, he hadn't mentioned it to Barty. Why was he hiding it? The mystery deepened.
No sooner than they had tied up and snugged down at the quayside for the night, Skipper suggested that Barty should go ashore and buy some food for supper and breakfast next morning. He gave him some money and directed him as to where he should go to buy the 'victuals', as he called them. The shop that Skipper had indicated to him was quite a long walk from the moorings, it was about 30 minutes' walk but it seemed shorter as he was interested in the different crafts in the harbour. He made a mental note of one or two of the larger vessels thinking perhaps there may be work for him. He had promised Skipper that he would crew for him up to Southwold so he abandoned that idea. He found the shop easily from Skipper's directions, paid for the victuals and started back towards the *Ellie May*
During his short absence from the *Ellie May*, Skipper had had a visitor who he welcomed on board. They spoke for a few minutes then the visitor and Skipper manhandled the six crates from the hold onto the quayside. A third man who had arrived with a horse and cart joined them, the crates were quickly loaded and the cart left straight away.
Skipper returned on board to the small cabin the whole operation having taken place in less than a quarter of an hour. Barty witnessed nothing. He boarded the *Ellie May* just as dusk was settling and the quayside was almost deserted. He hailed Skipper for his own safety before proceeding to the cabin, he had been away about 40 minutes, hurrying in back in an effort to keep some warmth in two meat pies he had just purchased.

Skipper made a drink and they ate their supper chatting idly about many subjects especially Felixstowe about which Skipper appeared to have endless information. The stories and the history of the port fascinated Barty and prompted him to ask about Lowestoft and his prospects there but Skipper wasn't so knowledgeable about that town, Barty's final destination. Never once during the long evening did Skipper mention the earlier happenings or the visitor while he was ashore.' As far as he was aware they were still going to Southwold without a cargo but still was unable to understand why they had put into Felixstowe for the night.

The night passed peacefully with only the slight slapping of the tiny wavelets slapping against the hull. Somewhere a distant whistle sounded, probably from the boatyard but acted as a signal for the harbour to awake and slowly, very slowly various boats in the harbour started their duties but Skipper was not in any hurry. They ate a leisurely breakfast and tidied up the decks until 10am. when a well-dressed man called to Skipper from the quay. Skipper didn't invite him aboard but went onto the quay to engage the gentleman in conversation. Barty stayed on board but couldn't hear anything of the conversation that lasted for quite some time and concluded with the passing of an envelope and a handshake before the gent' walked away down the quay.

"Put the kettle on Barty, let's have a brew before we get off about midday, there's been a little change in plans and I've got to go to Lowestoft now if you want a lift all the way?"
Barty had felt a bit disappointed that he would be leaving the *Ellie May* now that they had reached Southwold and he replied with enthusiasm, he was growing to accept this free and easy way of life. As he went to the cabin to make the tea Skipper followed him and put the envelope in a locked drawer saying, "A contract for when we arrive at Lowestoft, some grain to one of the mills". Barty thought his unsolicited explanation quite

plausible and had no need to ask any questions but he hadn't said why the last two clandestine meetings were not mentioned to him, he thought it rather odd but then Skipper knew his business and it was all new to Barty.

    They received harbour clearance just before midday, let go the moorings and made their way towards the harbour entrance under auxiliary engine. The weather was fair with only a light offshore wind and very little harbour movements. Barty was thrilled to be moving on and on reaching the open sea Skipper killed the engine and hoisted the single sail calling on Barty to take the tiller. As they left the lee of the land he could feel the power of the wind as it strengthened causing Skipper to comment that with this favourable wind he expected to make Lowestoft around 5pm to 6pm. As he steered under the watchful eye of Skipper, Barty kept glancing at the chart that he had spread out before trying to match it with the passing landmarks and symbols shown on the map. Occasionally, when it was safe to do so, Skipper would lash the tiller and join Barty to give him advice and instruction in the art of navigation.

As dusk fell, the flashing light from Lowestoft lighthouse could clearly be seen. Skippers estimated time of arrival wasn't far out. Barty had counted a white flash every 16 seconds and estimated they had about 12 miles to the harbour mouth "Well done" praised Skipper as he confirmed his reckoning, "we'll make a sailor of you yet."

    By 7pm they were snugged down alongside the quay, Barty expected to start to prepare supper as they hadn't eaten for some time now but Skipper was in a hurry to go ashore and left within minutes of their arrival. He didn't say anything except, "I shan't be long" as he left the boat. Barty thought his behaviour rather offhand but soon dismissed it from his mind as he started to prepare a meal for his return. Uppermost in his mind was the fact that this was the end of the line having travelled

with Skipper from Felixstowe to Lowestoft. He sat drinking a mug of tea after finishing preparing the supper thinking of what he would do next. He started to pack his belongings ready to leave the boat when he heard to sound of someone on deck. He looked from the companionway and saw the dark figure of Skipper. Barty hailed him and said there was a fresh brew on the stove if he wanted it. They sat in the crew space drinking their tea, Skipper never said a word about his trip ashore, Barty knew it wasn't any of his business so again, he asked no questions. It was then that Skipper spotted Barty's rucksack in the corner of the cabin.
"What's all this?" he said pointing to the rucksack.
"Oh, I've packed my gear as I thought you might want me to leave now we have reached Lowestoft"
"Where are you going?" asked Skipper
"I don't know; I've never been here before but I'll soon find a lodging house or something nearby."
"Nay lad' responded Skipper, "Surely you can stay here tonight and we'll talk about this in the morning"
Barty readily agreed and thanked him for the hospitality he had shown him on the trip north, he hadn't liked the idea of going around a strange town looking for digs late at night.
They finished cooking the supper and enjoyed a large meal, they hadn't eaten for a few hours and after a busy day they cleared their plates.
With everything shipshape, the pair turned in for a well-deserved good night's sleep.

  Footsteps on the deck awoke them at 8am, they had slept so soundly that even the noises about the quay had failed to wake them earlier. Skipper shot out onto the deck, despite his age he was still quite nimble, Barty stayed in the cabin and put on the kettle, he could hear Skipper and another man discussing something but was not able to hear any of the conversation. Skipper returned to the cabin and said, "That's a job for us in a couple of days, let's talk" and seated himself at the table while Barty cooked eggs and bacon for breakfast.

Skipper asked him about his plans for the future, what did he expect to find in Lowestoft? A short lull in the conversation took place that gave Barty a few minutes to think of an answer to the question.

"Now lad, leave things alone for a few minutes I need to have a serious talk with you" He pushed away his breakfast plate and leaned back, and looked straight at Barty with a look that rather surprised him. Barty sat back and poured another mug of tea for them, more for the want of something to do rather than a need for yet more tea.

Skipper could see the puzzled look on his face and continued speaking. "I want to know your plans because I have a proposition for you. If you have nothing particular in mind, I can tell you that working on a trawler is a very hard and dangerous job especially in the wintertime. But I don't believe you have any concrete plans and you don't know anyone in Lowestoft that can help you"

Barty nodded his agreement, and Skipper continued, "I have been watching you very closely since we left Felixstowe. You have been a very good worker, quick to learn and interested enough to want to learn more. I need a mate so if you agree I would like you stay on board the *Ellie May* as mate. I'm getting older now and I would like to think that I had someone to rely on. If you agree we will work out a pay rate for you and then we can discuss our future. I said our future. What do you say?"

Barty was dumbstruck; he hadn't even considered that something like this could happen. He felt good with Skipper and that he had done a useful job even though he knew little about the life, Skipper obviously felt so as well. Barty gaped open mouthed at the offer he could hardly believe.

"Lost your tongue?" enquired Skipper as Barty just sat there with a vacant expression on his face, "Do you want time to think about it?"

"No" he said, "it's just that", he didn't really know what to say, he knew he was being stupid but he had been totally surprised

"Oh yes, yes please, I promise to do my best for you Skipper"

"I know you will, that's settled then, unpack your gear and get it stowed and we'll talk some more when we have done a few jobs There were several jobs requiring attention and it was getting late when they finished and went to the cabin making small talk most of the time.

Skipper said they must both go into town in the morning and register *Ellie May's* new mate with the Department of Employment and get an up to date wage rate. Skipper mentioned the early morning visitor who had offered a contract for a consignment of grain to be taken from Lowestoft to an up-river mill, they would load at the weekend but Skipper wanted all the relevant paperwork completed before they left the port.

They left the boat fairly early the next morning and found their way to the Employment Office. I didn't take long to do the official business and having time to spare Skipper suggested they visited the Chandlers to buy some suitable clothing for Barty for his new job. He was over the moon; his life had suddenly changed from uncertainty to positive employment since accepting the lift from Felixstowe to Lowestoft. No wonder Kaleb (Barty) Bartholomew, mate of the wherry *Ellie May* was so happy!

Having been fitted out with foul weather clothing and a warm jumper Barty took his leave from Skipper to visit a bookshop where he purchased a couple of books on inshore navigation and one of East Anglia from the remaining money he had saved to pay for his lodgings. Having now secured a paid job for the foreseeable future he considered that the money was spent on 'tools of the trade' He was to live on board the boat and split the cost of his victuals with Skipper, which would cut down his expenses considerably.

Weekends were relatively quiet, especially late Saturday and all day Sunday when all harbour activities were limited to minimum movement and any loading or unloading of sea born shipping waited until Monday morning. There were no Dockers at work, each enjoying a weekend at home. This gave Barty a quiet opportunity to study the books he had bought. The cabin on the boat was quite small and when Skipper was ashore, which was frequently, Barty could spread his maps, books and charts without interruption. He surprised himself as his learning progressed, he had never been a keen pupil at school, he could read and write to a good level and his interest in the subject spurred him on. He studied for some time and noted several queries that he wanted to ask Skipper about when he returned. He broke off and made a drink, sat back taking his ease when his mind again started to wander. He remembered his old teacher at the workhouse who actually gave him his basics of reading and writing. He learnt nothing when he became a mudlark except how to steal food whenever he was hungry. He wondered how his young companion Jed Slater from Prospect House was doing, did he stay in his job with the Docklands Light Railway?
He remembered the times sitting on the banks of the River Thames with Jed watching the ships passing along the river and on seeing the many different ports of registry on the sterns, they dreamt of distant lands of which they knew nothing but wished themselves on board many of the vessels. And what about his army mate, Thomas Black, whatever happened to Tom Black? His thoughts made him realise how few his friends really were, he had totally lost contact with everyone including his parents He did remember his farming friends at Mill Hall Farm but he wasn't in touch with them anymore. Skipper now was the only friend he

had and knew he could rely upon. He had taken an interest in Barty since they first met and had now given him a home, a job and was teaching him navigation, with the added bonus of practical 'hands on' experience every time they took the *Ellie May* from her moorings.

He never did find out where Skipper disappeared to every Saturday evening he just assumed that he stayed with friends and old mates in the various ports they visited. This suited Barty fine, no limits or work and Skipper never returned until very late Saturday or even Sunday morning so Barty was taken aback one particular Saturday evening when he returned at 8pm. It was a dark evening; Skipper made a drink and said "Pack up lad, we shall be shifting berth early in the morning"
Barty questioned the reason only to be told that there was some business that needed attention. Barty thought it best not to ask any more probing questions and accepted what he had been told and packed up his books. They had a light supper and made small talk mainly Skipper asking how he was doing with his studies. Skipper answered the questions that Barty had saved for him and showed him how to find various answers on the charts.

There was very little preparation required to make the boat ready for next morning so they went to their bunks before midnight Skipper saying "We shift at 7am. Goodnight" At 6.30am next morning it was still dark and there had been drizzly rain throughout the night so Barty was very thankful for the oilskins they had bought for him from the Chandler's Store. They cast off at precisely 7am and headed from the harbour to a berth away from the town at an isolated jetty not far from the coast where two horse-drawn carts were waiting. The carts, manned by four people were loaded with several large sacks and stood slightly back from the water's edge near a gate in the fence behind them. As the *Ellie May* came alongside Skipper jumped onto the jetty calling to Barty, "Secure her lad then come and join us"

Having done his bidding, Barty went onto the jetty and the six of them started to unload the carts and take them on board to be stowed in the hold. Well over half the load had been stowed when Skipper called Barty over to him. Handing him a large envelope he pointed down the overgrown cart track saying "Follow this track down the back of those trees and you will see a house, give this to the man that lives there and don't be long, we sail as soon as we are laden"

He followed the track and eventually found the house that couldn't be seen from the track, it was further than he had been led to believe and took him about 15 minutes. He knocked loudly on the door of the house that appeared to be uninhabited; there was no sign of life, the whole place seemed deserted. The door was opened quickly but only partially by a man whose features Barty couldn't distinguish. He took the envelope and said, "Tell Skipper I'll be in touch" and with that he closed the door.

He glanced back at the house as he went through the trees and saw no sign of any movement in any of the nearby buildings, the whole place looked grim, rundown and very neglected, sheltering among the trees in the tangled overgrown garden. There was still a light mist as the morning broke. The trip to the house had taken him just over half an hour and as he came towards to the jetty he saw that the four men and their carts had left.

With the cargo safely stowed, Skipper lost no time in casting off, he seemed anxious to leave this secluded area and turned south after rounding the headland. He told Barty to take the tiller while he cut the engine and hoisted the sail. Skipper took over the steering and Barty stood close by him awaiting any order he might give, he was exceptionally uncommunicative, he obviously had something on his mind.

The weather wasn't very pleasant and having listened to the forecast on the wireless it would continue to be overcast with squally rain showers and limited visibility. *Ellie May* was making fair headway, but where? Skipper still hadn't said a word. It was so unlike him to stay silent for so long. A good hour passed before he broke the silence,

"Here lad, take the tiller and keep her steady, head to the wind.

" Where are we heading?" he enquired.

"Just stay on this course and it won't be long before we near Southwold, I'll go and make some breakfast" and with that he went below to the small cabin. The sea was quite lively and he could hear Skipper cursing as he tried to control the production of the breakfast. He eventually succeeded and emerged with a couple of thick bacon sandwiches and two mugs of tea, not quite full when they finally reached the cockpit. Glancing across towards the shoreline he said, "Blasted fog, can't see exactly where we are, take a bearing on the first landmark you see and tell me" It wasn't fog but a heavy clinging mist that didn't look as if it would ever lift. It was the first time that Skipper had given him any responsibility for navigation and it gave him a sense of trust. The wind rose a little during the next half hour and cleared the mist just enough to enable Barty to see a lighthouse on the starboard side. He called Skipper who immediately recognised the flashes, the Sole Bay Lighthouse was about two miles north of Southwold, they had made excellent time. The sea was getting rougher as the wind increased whipping the white-topped spray into their faces. Skipper decided to move closer inshore, he dropped the sail half way down the mast to lessen the speed. He gave Barty a course to steer. *Ellie May* was laden with about 15 tons of grain that had to be kept dry and Skippers preventative measures had the desired effect.

The freeboard increased and the spray ceased to beat in their faces. Wherries were built in various dimensions but mainly for use on the rivers and Norfolk Broads, they were flat bottomed with a shallow freeboard to serve the conditions for which they were built. Skipper told Barty to keep a sharp eye on the shoreline as the East Anglian coast had been subject to cliff erosion and collapse in the past and much damage had been caused to some small coastal villages and to new rocks being exposed and dangerous. With the boat now adjusted to the prevailing condition Skipper relieved Barty at the tiller and sent him to make a few sandwiches.

While busy making the food Barty settled his mind that they were heading for Southwold. He took the food on deck and noticed that Southwold Lighthouse was now clearly visible but they still held a southerly course. The boat was nearer the shore and the roll of the boat was more comfortable as the two men sat at the tiller and ate their refreshments.

Still puzzled as to their destination Barty plucked up the courage to ask. Skipper told him that they were going to a small village named Dunwich. Barty had read about in his book about East Anglia about a village that had been destroyed by the encroachment of the sea.

It was late afternoon as *Ellie May* was passing Corporation Marshes; Skipper came to take over the tiller and a short time later he made a sharp turn to starboard and headed towards the shore. He steered the boat to a short jetty some 80 feet in length, approximately the same length as the boat. This looked to be a long forgotten overgrown spot that hadn't seen much use in years. Skipper called it Sandymount Covert, just to the rear of the Covert was Dunwich Forest to which an equally overgrown cart track lead. The jetty was about two miles from the remains of Dunwich Village. They made fast at the jetty and Barty noticed that the tide was on the ebb and Skipper told him to leave the boat on long lines. In no time the tide had ebbed completely and *Ellie May* was left sitting on her flat bottom on the shingle. There were no signs of life anywhere, no buildings, no pathways other than the track through the Covert to the edge of Dunwich Forest where it disappeared into the trees. A quarter moon had risen and the drizzling rain had stopped, the whole scene was very eerie and visibility was limited, it was till only about 8pm and it seemed as if they had been tied up there for hours. With nothing particular to do Barty started to study his navigation books only to have his attention disturbed by the sound of horses' hooves. And Skipper who had been in the hold, was beside Barty in a flash. He must have the hearing of an owl as he was there in seconds.

Within a matter of minutes several carts drawn by horses came to a halt on the shingle just above the narrow tide line. A group of men, maybe around a dozen, stayed on the carts, silent and unmoving, Skipper too remained silent beside Barty, nobody made a move or spoke, all was completely silent except for the occasional stamp of a horse's foot.

It remained so for at least 5 minutes although it was like a lifetime. Skipper eventually broke the silence and approached the men on the shore after telling Barty to stay on the boat as they would be unloading shortly., As he stood on the boat watching his mind was racing, his thoughts jumbled and mixed, what was happening? Skipper had a word with one of the men who then began to give instruction to the others and they started to position themselves in a short line between the carts and the boat. They began to unload the cargo of large sacks of grain from the hold onto the carts. There was a minimal amount of noise and no talking. Barty tried to count the number of men present but it was impossible as he spotted three other men on the fringe of Sandymount Covert, they were watching the track way approaching the Covert and the stretches along the Marshes. As each cart was load it moved off along the track and into the Forest, each cart not being fully loaded. The whole operation took about three quarters of an hour before everyone had cleared the area. Barty suddenly realised that the cart wheels had made hardly any sounds and the horses hooves made only a soft plodding sound as if they had been muffled., there was no jingling of harness and no one spoke. Skipper came back on board, "That's it lad, let's secure the hold, get below and get something to eat"

His mind was now flooded with questions, "Who were they Skipper?" "Group of businessmen from town. I'll tell you more later"

Barty was unsatisfied with such a brief reply, why were they all so quiet, why were the horses' hooves muffled, where were they going, why had they got watchmen post near the Forest and most of all what did those sacks really contain. He had not taken any part in the unloading, just told to stay on board, so he couldn't guess what the sacks contained but he knew it wasn't grain.

What game was Skipper playing? He had no idea!

With the hold secured they went below to the cabin and Skipper prepared some food, it was nearly 10pm and he was tired and didn't talk very much, he never mentioned the cargo they had just off-loaded but just said, "We will be leaving at full tide tomorrow morning, back to Felixstowe for a load of timber, I'll talk to you in the morning, I'm feeling very tired so finish your meal and get some rest, up at 7am, okay?"

They turned in but sleep didn't come easily to Barty his mind was still in turmoil; he had tried to dismiss all thoughts of what he had seen from his mind without success but he eventually drifted into a deep sleep. It seemed only a few minutes before Skipper was shaking him, "Come on lad, shake a leg there's work to be done" and placed a mug of tea beside him, "Got to catch the tide. Barty recalled that *Ellie May* was flat bottomed and had been lying on the shingle; as soon as she was afloat Skipper took her out from the Dunwich coast onto a southerly course bound for Felixstowe.

Once in open sea Skipper handed the tiller to Barty and went to make some tea and bacon sandwiches. He settled down in the cockpit near Barty and while they ate he started to explain of the actions of the previous night. He thought it prudent to ask no questions of Skipper until he had finished speaking so not to interrupt his story.

He started by telling Barty that, at the age of 48 he had left the Merchant Service and taken a job with a Norfolk commercial inshore carrying business and after a time he had saved enough money to buy a modest house in Ipswich, where his daughter was still living. As mate on a wherry he was quite happy to live on the boat as it saved him the expense of living in a house. Being a careful responsible and prudent Scotsman he took the opportunity to buy a part share in the wherry he operated and after a profitable period of time he was able to buy full ownership of the wherry, the *Ellie May*. Everything went well at first then due to increased running costs, a decrease in trade and the need to pay for a mate he sought other ways of earning money and that was how he became mixed up in the 'freetrade'

Back in Felixstowe when he had offered a lift to Southwold to Barty, Skipper had also been offered two contracts for carrying goods to and from various ports around the East Coast. At that time, he had no mate on board and hoped that Barty might take to the life and sign on. Barty had so enjoyed the change from his previous life in the army that in accepting the offer he found himself drawn to the sea. The change of circumstance that took the boat to Lowestoft was beneficial to them both them, Skipper got himself a reliable mate and Barty, a permanent job, but Skipper had decided not to disclose his illegal activities until he got to know and to trust Barty more.

That time had now come.

The men that had collected the goods last night were 'freebooters, - smugglers, just as he had begun to expect. Skipper had always sent him on a message, deliver an envelope or fetch food whenever unloading was taking place, he now realised that Skipper was only protecting him from 'getting too know too much too soon' – the less he knew the better for him should the Customs men become involved.

The contraband that they had taken from Lowestoft and landed at Dunwich was certainly not grain but tea originally from France. Barty's suspicion was aroused when they unloaded the cargo, as there was no mill at Dunwich and tea was generally shipped in chests, also that he was left on board, as the cargo was off-loaded. It was obvious that such activities couldn't be hidden forever so Skipper thought it better to come clean now before Barty started to ask more questions and maybe not be so discreet in the future. He listened carefully as Skipper explained the clandestine activities that had puzzled Barty but things were almost the same as he had suspected. Skipper needed to earn some extra cash as carrying work had decreased and the *Ellie May* was his sole source of income. He was now in his seventies and this was the only way of life he knew apart from deep sea sailing a trade he was now too old to pursue. Barty felt that he was caught between the prongs of a cleft stick, while he didn't really approve of the illegal trade he had to agree that the past few months had been profitable for him, not just financially but by the way Skipper had treated him, trusted him, taught him, given him food and shelter and latterly a wage. He certainly had no complaints and wouldn't' dream of talking to the authorities. After all, he was an accomplice even though he didn't fully recognise it from the beginning.

The present contract was to pick up a load of imported timber and transport it to a mill, upriver on the east coast, a genuine job! The visibility was murky as they started south towards Felixstowe but the murky weather soon gave way to watery November sunshine and a calm sea. He sat at the tiller in a half daze mesmerised by the behaviour of the boat but his mind was still centred on the future. The gentle slapping of the small waves against the bow somehow gave him a sense of security, a sense of belonging where nobody could touch him; he loved the sea and the way of life that the sea had brought to him. The unlawful side of that life nagged at him as his thoughts wandered. Skipper was busy about various jobs and did nothing to disturb Barty's thoughts. Knowing this charter was perfectly lawful he had ample time to make up his mind whether he would stay with Skipper or look for other employment that had no risks involved.

"We're just off the harbour now lad so I'll take over", Skipper's voice disturbed his thoughts, he had been day dreaming and not paying full attention to his duty so it was with surprise that when he looked towards the shoreline it was nearer than he had expected. Skipper had started the auxiliary engine and came to sit in the cockpit to take the tiller before telling Barty to drop the mainsail. He had radioed ahead requesting a berth by the quay in order to access the pile of timber for loading.

Ellie May was only a small vessel compared with the size of some of the other ones scattered along the quayside. The load was ten tons of short weather boards to be taken to a mill on the River Deben, the load was stacked near a hand crane and the job of loading was done in double quick time with Barty cranking vigorously and Skipper guiding the load into the hold in some order. Occasionally they changed roles, on completion they covered the hold with a large tarpaulin and fastened it down. The work had tired Skipper quite noticeably; he was still sprightly but for a man of his age his strength ebbed fairly quickly. It being Saturday the Dockers finished at Midday, so not on hand to give them any assistance.

They went to a local pub near the dock for a drink and a meal before returning to the boat and sat just beside the cabin discussing Barty's future at length. Skipper emphasised how much he had come to rely on Barty using his age as a lever to try and convince him to stay knowing that he didn't approve of the freetrade. He was in it now so, why not make the most of it while their luck held. He said he would understand if Barty opted to leave him.

Leave him? He couldn't imagine leaving him now, he had been so good to him; a very good friend and he really did need someone to help with the boat. By the time they went to their bunks it was almost midnight and Barty had made up his mind, but he said nothing to Skipper. Good crewmembers were hard to find, to be trusted like Barty was rare, most were just itinerant labourers looking for any kind of work they could find.

They obtained clearance from the Harbourmaster and sailed to the estuary on auxiliary engine turning north to make for the River Deben. The day was overcast and the sea was calm with very little wind to assist them when they hoisted the sail. There was no hurry, the Deben being only a few miles up the coast and the lack of vital work was practically nil, Barty still hadn't given Skipper an answer and Skipper knew that he was weighing up the situation.

It was November and he had been discharged from the army in 1919 aged 21, he suddenly thought he had missed his 21st birthday last September. What with the army discharge and the meeting and travelling with Skipper he had totally forgotten about it, not that he had much cause to remember any of his past birthdays he had had no celebrations as he could think of for many years, such had been the pattern of his life. He had been with Skipper over 12 months now, it didn't seem that long but they had been busy and time had flown.

Skipper had mentioned that he might go to his daughter's house in Ipswich for Christmas but nothing more had been said on the subject. The mouth of the River Deben was soon in view so Barty called Skipper to the tiller position as, according to the chart it was protected by a shifting shingle bar and fast running tides. Skipper told him to stay at the tiller, as the experience of negotiating the shingle bar would be something to be remembered, Skipper would stay close to his side in case of emergency. The waters became a little choppy but *Ellie May* rode the tide well. They crossed the bar safely and very soon were into the relaxing water of the river.

Barty had studied the charts and noted two large towers just south of the entrance, he pointed towards them and looked quizzically to Skipper who told him that they were Martello Towers that had been built for defence in Napoleonic times as they dominated the approach from the sea. Looking ahead he could see a few fishermen's cottages, an inn and a boatyard, this was the small village of Felixstowe Ferry that had only one road that led to Felixstowe Town. They continued up river passing acres and acres of farmland, several boatyards, a gentle relaxing journey from the Ferry to the market town of Woodbridge eventually mooring at the Tide Mill. It was only as they approached the mill that Skipper took over the steering and safely put the boat alongside. Barty stopped the engine and secured the boat to the quayside bollards and Skipper went straight ashore, up to the mill seeking someone in charge. He returned within 15 minutes and told Barty that they would unload the timber next morning.

Having time to spare they decided to have a leisurely meal during course of which there was a hail from the quay. Skipper went onto the quayside and returned accompanied by a well-dressed man whom he introduced as

Mr Arthur Spalding, the owner of the mill. He had called to see his old friend Skipper and invited them both to go ashore to join him for a drink at the local inn. The invite was readily accepted and soon they were seated in the comfortable lounge of the Crown Hotel on Quayside Street, an old coaching inn that retained much of its past character. Mr Spalding and Skipper had known each other for many years having done business together on many occasions. Barty couldn't resist asking what the current delivery of weatherboarding was to be used for.

"Repairs" replied Mr Spalding, "The old mill is starting to show its age badly and I want to replace some of the old corrugated sheets with wood"

The first Woodbridge Tide Mill dates back to 1170 and was reconstructed in 1792 so it was getting on in age. With the popularity of Woodbridge was increasing with the yachting and boating fraternity and visitors, it was in the interests of local businessmen to take advantage of the history and attractions of this lovely part of the County. People wanted to see how flour was produced from grain. They wanted to experience the sights and sounds as the big mill wheels turned to grind the grain as it had done for hundreds of years, the tides drove the big English oak water wheels that turns the machinery to produce the flour, the energy being provided solely by the changing tides.

The whole process of milling interested him so much that questions came one after the other the flow being halted when he was invited to visit the mill after they had unloaded tomorrow. The rest of the evening passed quickly mainly discussing the changes that were taking place in the commercial inshore carrying business and the newly developing leisure trade. The number of working watermills and windmills were declining but people would always need their 'daily bread' so the demand for flour and animal feeds should remain static for years to come, as long as the flat-bottomed shallow draughted wherries were able to navigate the rivers to the mills the two men thought their businesses were safe. A most convivial evening was terminated with 'one for the road' and the company parted.

It was nearly mid-morning when six men arrived to unload the boat. Ten tons of weatherboarding but with a total of eight men unloading and using the quayside crane; the load was quickly brought onto the quayside and taken by handcart to a nearby warehouse. The work was complete when Mr Spalding came to the quay and he and Skipper went to the 'Quayside Café' leaving Barty to sweep out the hold and generally tidy up before settling himself on a bollard on the dock to watch the busy harbour craft going about their duties. The weather was fine but cold but he was quite content to sit and wait for Skipper to return. He was rather a long time so Barty went below to study his books.

It was late afternoon when he did eventually return and Barty was in the process of making a meal, he hadn't eaten all day.

"Do you want to eat now?" he asked Skipper

"Nay lad, I've had a bite with Arthur at the café, I thought I'd be back before now" he replied, "But you know how it is when you get yarning"

"Did Mr Spalding forget my trip with him to the mill? Skipper looked at Barty, "Yes, well no, not really, he only remembered at the last minute and I said you would go tomorrow if that's okay, we're not going anywhere for a day or two."

Barty was relieved to hear this as he had been looking forward to seeing the mill and learning more of how it worked. They spent the next hour or so reading, Skipper - the newspaper and Barty his navigation books, Skipper folded his paper and said, "Let's go for a drink, come on lad, get your coat."

Barty needed no second bidding; he had been hanging about waiting most of the day. They walked off along the quay to Quay Street and 'Ye Olde

Bell and Steelyard', an old building that stood out because of the 'yard' over-hanging the street. Barty's curiosity was instantly aroused.

"What's that?" he said pointing to the yard.

Skipper looked up and said, "Whoa lad, let's get inside afore you start with your endless questions"

Skipper bought a couple of pints of ale at the bar counter and took them to a quiet corner of the taproom where Barty was sitting. The taproom was decorated like a ship's cabin with various articles of nautical paraphernalia dotted about on the surfaces and the walls many of which Barty didn't recognise. Anticipating his next question Skipper decided to get in first.

"That thing outside that you asked about, well it's called 'a yard' When you go back out have a good look at it, it's got a crane above it and chain slings that could lift a wagon before and after it was loaded. The villages all around here still have reminders that agriculture and the river trades worked hand in hand".

He went on to explain what many of the collectibles spread about the taproom were used for in earlier times His explanations were really extended and Barty couldn't remember Skipper speaking non-stop for such a lengthy period ever before and he marvelled at Skipper's depth of knowledge

He had listened intently to Skipper, never interrupting his flow but his imagination was running amok, sheep-stealing, smuggling, he had encountered both but only on a small scale. Skipper related several stories and Barty began to ask questions as his understanding deepened. They engaged in this deep conversation for the rest of the evening, old mates yarning about old times, "Swinging the Lamp" they called it.

 Another bright November day dawned as Barty put the kettle on, Skipper was speaking from his bunk propping himself up on one elbow

"Are you going up to the mill today?"

"If that's okay with you" Barty replied.

"That's fine; it will give me the chance to see a couple of people in town"

At the mill the miller greeted Barty and sent someone to tell Mr Spalding of his arrival. They returned together and walked towards the mill entry, the miller waiting to show Barty around the complex. Mr Spalding introduced the miller but then dismissed him saying that he would show Barty around himself as it would be chance to get to know each other better. He started by apologising for his absence yesterday "I just forgot until it was too late" he said

"That's okay said Barty, "just one of those things. I'm so pleased to be here."

Mr Spalding took him a tour of the whole complex as promised, the barns and stores, the garages and stables where Barty took particular interest in the heavy horses that were kept there, it was an instant reminder of the days spent at Mill Hall Farm before he joined the Veterinary Corps. Finally returning to the mill, Mr Spalding called the miller and instructed him to take Barty and explain all the workings of the mill to him. It certainly was an extended tour as the mill was grinding and, as usual, Barty had so many questions to ask. There appeared to be so many aspects in keeping the mill running and maintained and he was amazed by how few people were employed there. On the second floor of the mill he saw a young man busy attending the huge grinding wheels, some 8 or 9 feet in diameter and bringing sacks loaded with grain, up the hoist from the floor below and loading the bunkers above the grinding wheels. He was working alone with no one to assist in the lifting and shifting of the heavy sacks. Barty took it all in constantly asking questions of the miller. After the tour, they went to the farmhouse kitchen for refreshments. Where Mrs Spalding had provided a plentiful table of tea and cakes and still Barty was asking questions. Mr Spalding realised how much the visit had impressed him and invited him to return to the mill whenever he wanted.

As they were talking a young lady, whose appearance seemed familiar to him joined them and he tended to stare at her unapologetically, he quickly averted his eyes so as not to appear rude but he was instantly struck by her natural beauty. She was about 5 feet six inches tall with long brown hair, about 18 years of age with features that mesmerized Barty from the start. As she entered the kitchen Mr Spalding spoke,

"Ah my dear, let me introduce you to Barty who had brought my new weatherboards upriver, Barty, meet my daughter Sarah."

Barty was almost speechless but managed embarrassingly blurt out "Miss Sarah, so lovely to meet you",

She took a seat at the table acknowledging the presence of her mother at the same time. Mr Spalding sat beside her and told her of Barty's position with Skipper on the *Ellie May*, Sarah had known Skipper for many years he had watched her grow up as her father and Skipper had worked together for a long time.

Barty having led a sheltered life had not encountered many young girls of his own age. He remembered the dairymaids at the farm but they seemed so different from the young lady who now sat near him.

Introductions over the conversation returned back to the mill and then diverted to Barty, Mr Spalding mainly asking him about his earlier life and background. Barty gave a rather diluted account of his earlier life on the farm, his experiences in London and his army service but he didn't go into detail as he was aware that Mrs Spalding and Sarah were both quietly listening. He found himself continually glancing at Sarah and directing his answers towards her, there was little doubt that he was enamoured with her appearance.

The evening drew to a close and after bidding everyone a goodnight, Barty turned to Mr Spalding and asked if he could visit again tomorrow to give a hand to the young man he had seen working at the grinding wheels and at the same time struggling with the heavy sacks of grain hoisting them between to two floors of the mill. Barty said that Skipper didn't need him for a couple of days and he would be happy to lend a hand. Mr Spalding looked at him with a puzzled look on his face. "Which young man was that?" he asked.

"I didn't speak to him but he was wearing brown baggy overalls and a cap" Suddenly Mr Spalding burst into laughter while Barty just stood there looking embarrassed, it was his turn to look puzzled, what had he said to cause such a response? It took a few moments for Mr Spalding to recover from his bout of laughter and Barty felt a further embarrassment when he heard Mr Spalding's say, "That wasn't one of the mill lads, that was my daughter, Sarah", they both looked across in Sarah's direction to see her put her hand up to her mouth to stifle a laugh. "I'm sorry" said Barty, "I didn't realise that it…" His host cut him short, "it's alright, she never dresses to go to work in the mill" Barty saw the fun in Sarah's smile as her father continued,

"You can come anytime you want to, you'll always be welcome."
"Thanks" said Barty hurrying away to hide his blushes. "Thanks for everything."

No wonder he had seen something familiar about her when she had first entered the room, he had not really taken that much notice of the struggling 'young man' in the grinding room and would never have related the two meetings under such different circumstances but there was just enough recognition for him to realise his mistake.

He returned to the *Ellie May* but found it deserted, Skipper had perhaps called for a pint so he sat down with his books but found his was unable to concentrate, he kept thinking of Sarah. No one, ever before had affected him this way, he just couldn't stop thinking about her and was now eagerly looking forward to going back to the mill the next day. Knowing that he was wasting his time trying to study he took to his bunk early that night.

He awoke next morning to find that Skipper still hadn't returned so he left him a note and made his way up to the Tide Mill and straight to the grinding room where he found Sarah busy working where he had seen the 'young man' on the previous day. She was dressed in the brown overalls with a cap pulled well down to protect her hair. They greeted each other and Barty tried to apologise for his mistaken identity of the previous day but she dismissed his apologies saying," It doesn't matter, it gave us all a laugh, it's nice to see you again, come over here and give me a hand". They both worked very hard during the morning hardly pausing to speak unless a question about the work arose. Come midday they went to the farmhouse kitchen just as Mrs Spalding was taking some freshly baked buns from the oven and immediate justice was done to the delicious creations together with a welcome cup of tea, it was dusty work in the grinding room!

Barty left the mill at 2pm, a little worried that he hadn't seen Skipper and to ensure that they weren't due to leave on another trip. Secretly he hoped that Skipper hadn't found another contract yet as he had enjoyed Sarah's company so much that he wanted to go back to the mill again even though they hadn't found much time to talk, perhaps tomorrow he thought.

His hopes were dashed when he found Skipper in the cabin dealing with an amount of paperwork. Pausing for just a second he said "Morning lad, put the kettle on then come and sit yourself down, I've something I want to talk to you about"

He told Barty that he had taken the train to Ipswich the evening before to visit both his daughter and his solicitor. He had registered his business in Ipswich and took the opportunity to attend to a business matter and stay overnight at his daughter's house. In the past, he had spoken at length about his daughter's house that actually belonged to him He let his daughter and her husband and children live there rent free in return for a small amount of work she performed for him, all to do with his business. This arrangement suited Skipper admirably as he spent so much time away working around the coasts of East Anglia. His time with his daughter quickly passed and the following morning he called to see his solicitor a Mr Salmon at his office in Ipswich.

Skipper had come to terms that he wasn't as sprightly as he had been for some time and wanted to ensure that certain arrangements were in place for his daughter and the business. He was with Mr Salmon for almost three hours leaving him with precise instructions as to what was to be done on the occasion of his death and some immediate instructions affecting the carrying business. Barty listened intently but he wasn't hearing anything that he hadn't already been told until Skipper said, "Now listen carefully", Barty stopped what he was doing and concentrated on what Skipper was saying,

"I have told John (Salmon), my solicitor to draw up the following to take effect from next April. I want half a share in the *Ellie May* to be put into your name, you're a good lad, a good worker and my daughter and her husband have no working interest in the boat, He has a good well-paid job in Ipswich and they don't need the money. You must understand that you will share a 50 percent profit on all contracts and a 50 percent liability in all maintenance debts connected to the business. Think very carefully about it for a couple of days and if you agree there are several papers to be drawn up and signed. Let me know by the end of next week. If there are any questions about it don't be afraid to ask. Okay?"

The revelation hit Barty like a thunderbolt. There would be so many questions that would need answering; he knew nothing about the business side of things, not much about the trade at all really. He enjoyed the trips, the freedom of the sea, the way of living, he didn't need much money and Skipper paid him for his work, only a small wage but that satisfied him and suited the life he had found with Skipper. It was quite obvious that Skipper had become fond of him, he trusted him in so many ways and he didn't want his business being bought by a stranger, he had worked long and hard to buy the *Ellie May* in the first place. His mind was full to overflowing and once again he felt that his luck was turning. In April, next year Skipper had said, he could be part owner in a trading wherry with a foreseeable future in the coastal trade and he would be fully employed until then. The future looked rosy but there were so many questions swimming around in his head so he started to make a list of the many queries. He had a full week before Skipper wanted a reply. Other than his present employment with Skipper he had no planes for the future. Prior to meeting Skipper, he had intended to go to Lowestoft to find work in the fishing industry. Now life had something very alluring about it, a chance to stay in the work he had come to love, an offer it would be hard to dismiss and a recent meeting with a beautiful young lady, Sarah Jane Spalding had certainly made an impact on his life. The more he thought about it, the more he was sure he would be doing the right thing to say with Skipper on the terms he had offered.

 The next morning, he asked Skipper if he could go into town to visit the Public Records Office. Skipper asked no questions and just said he would see him later. Barty's mission to the P.R.O. (Public Records Office) was to enquire if there was any trace of his father's whereabouts after his release from HMP Hollesley Colony. The man at the PRO was helpful but unable to give him any information as all records had been transferred to the office at Ipswich. It was still early so he took a train to Ipswich in the hope that the records would show his father's release address.

> "Walter James Bartholomew, date of birth unknown, believed to be 1872 at Aldeburgh, Suffolk. Sentenced to 10 years' imprisonment in 1904 for the offence of larceny of two legs of lamb. Released in 1912 after 8 years served, to a hostel for the homeless in London, aged 30 years."

The information was welcomed but it didn't give him the address of his release and there were so many institutions for the homeless and unemployed in London. He didn't hold much hope in tracing his father. He was rather disappointed with the information; it was what he had expected. It was one more attempt that had failed but would he knew not to pursue that angle again.

He returned to Woodbridge and boarded the *Ellie May*; Skipper was not on board so he busied himself with his navigation books and his thoughts. Skipper returned and told him that they had a contract and would be sailing late afternoon the next day. Knowing that Barty had been to Ipswich he enquired if he had given any further thought to his offer so Barty consulted his list and asked lots of questions. Would he still be able to stay on the boat and pay his keep? What would change if he took part share in the *Ellie May* next April? Would he have to register as a part owner? What would be his basic pay and would he need to open a bank account? So many things to think about! Skipper answered the questions to the best of his ability and the answers prompted even more queries. The next two to three hours were spent talking over the things that were worrying Barty but Skipper seems to have covered most of the subjects with Mr Salmon previously.

Barty was satisfied with all the arrangements and was happy that his present position on the *Ellie May* would continue as it was until next year when more responsibility would fall on his shoulders. His financial position now was stable; he hadn't got a bank account but was quite happy to open one when the time came. Skipper said that if he wished to open a personal account now, that would be fine but he didn't expect him to put any money into the business until April next year and that he should speak to a solicitor before committing himself to anything more. Barty was completely satisfied with everything that Skipper had told him and agreed that he would be more than pleased to get involved in the business when the time came. With all the excitement of things to come he forgot to ask Skipper about the new contract he had taken, he wasn't really bothered but suddenly thought he would not see Sarah for a while. As Skipper was turning in for the night he mentioned that his daughter had invited them both to Ipswich for the Christmas holiday, Barty had never met Skippers family and still thinking of Sarah he reluctantly agreed to spend the holiday with his family, Skipper had been so good in so many ways and he was looking forward to taking Barty to Ipswich. Life was good. He felt that things were now looking towards a bright future and he cherished the idea of asking Sarah for the privilege of an engagement but time was still young and he would not rush things too quickly and frighten her off. She appeared to return his affections but only time would tell.

Work was carried out with renewed vigour, squaring up the boat and preparing her for sailing that afternoon. He went up to the mill to tell them that he would be leaving that afternoon and would see them at a later date, he wasn't sure when as he still had no idea where they were bound. Sarah wasn't there but he was assured that his good wishes would be passed to her on her return.

"Let go" shouted Skipper as Ellie May left the quay and started to nose her way down the River Deben towards the North Sea. Once clear of the harbour Barty took the tiller as Skipper hoisted the single sail and headed for the cabin. It was only at the last minute that Barty asked Skipper for the course, he had been day dreaming again.

"Head for Dunwich" he shouted over his shoulder as he disappeared into the cabin.

Dunwich thought Barty remembering the last visit there where they unloaded the mysterious bales. They had cargo now, why were they going to Dunwich, which was only a short distance away? He had to contain his thoughts as Skipper was still below.

The weather was fine and the sea calm as they made their way up the east coast. Skipper emerged and handed him a set of co-ordinates. He glanced at the chart "Steer west" he said questioningly.

"Yes" replied Skipper, "I didn't tell you we are picking up our contract at sea, about six miles off the coast" and with that he went below again leaving Barty to follow the co-ordinates that he had been given. He was sure that there was a small cargo in the hold but he hadn't seen it loaded, he was about to ask but Skipper had already disappeared below again. He came back on deck well before the boat reached the rendezvous point and within five minutes they saw a sail approaching. Barty identified it as a ketch, two masts, a fore and aft rig, she quickly came alongside and Barty was able to read her name on the stern, *"La Rochelle"* A few words were exchanged between the two masters but Barty couldn't understand the French language. With six men on the *La Rochelle* it didn't take long to transfer their cargo of twenty-four casks and twelve large bales into *Ellie May's* hold, the whole operation taking only twenty minutes. The two vessels parted company and proceeded back in the direction from which they had approached but Barty noticed that a few papers were exchanged, few words spoken, again in French. He had also noted that only riding lights were being displayed while the transfer took place and it was now late dusk. "Steer for Dunwich lad and switch to full navigation lights" said Skipper as he went below with the papers he had been given. "Keep your eyes on the shore and no more day dreaming" he added, "See anything odd call me at once".

On nearing the shore, he thought he caught a glimpse of a flashing light, the intermediate flash persuaded him to call Skipper to the deck.

"Aye, that's it lad, I was waiting for that, I'll take over now, you just keep watch" The sail was dropped and the engine started. The boat glided faultlessly alongside the isolated jetty they had used on their last visit' Willing hands on shore tied her up and in no time at all the unloading had begun. Barty was more aware of what was happening as he lent a hand in the unloading. In the distance he could see a man watching the road near the derelict looking house behind Sandymount Covet. It all seemed very familiar the waiting carts were swiftly loaded and the horses driven away almost silently, Land transport was much more labour intensive than transport by water but Barty appreciated why this particular jetty had been chosen as it was close to the Broads and some commercial barges were more than happy to take a little extra cargo.

The hazard of moving smuggled goods was dependent on the vigilance of the Customs and Excise Officers, there was little chance of danger on this part of the coast as the rivers and roadways were so restricted. Most of the local population of the villages were involved one way or another and always welcomed the odd 'goodie' on which no import duty had been paid they were always ready to assist in a landing and to watch for the Revenue Officers that may be patrolling the area.

The Revenue men were usually stationed nearer the larger ports and often patrolled the more isolated coasts in pairs on horseback. Smuggling took many forms around Britain so the fraternity involved in the trade knew they were relatively safe from the Riding Officers but they took no chances, there were often informers ready to earn cash for the correct information leading to a landing.

The goods having been disposed of, Barty reflected on the aspects of the 'freetrade' in which he had now become accidentally involved. He decided that the risk was minimal provided that he didn't get mixed up with the big boys but he couldn't see Skipper doing that.

His thoughts were interrupted by Skipper's voice as he came back on board.

"We'll get cleared up and stay put for the night, it's back to Woodbridge tomorrow", Barty's heart leapt, he couldn't have heard better news.

They spent a quiet night at Dunwich during which time Barty continued to give more thought to the freetrade, and decided that there was much more he should know about but was reluctant to ask Skipper in case he thought that Barty was prying into his business too much and may arouse suspicions. He resolved to go to a Public Library next time he was in town to research a few points and read the latest news if there was any reported. He had heard nothing in the public houses that he and Skipper frequented from time to time but he never heard anything spoken that alluded to the practice. He did know however that Skipper met with certain individuals to pick up any contracts that were in the offing Although the freetrade appeared to be dying out, here he was today taking part in the activities if only in a small way the trade still flourished in certain places as had been confirmed that very evening.

He went on deck just before turning in and whilst standing enjoying the quiet of the river he was aware of distant voices and saw movement at the old house at the edge of the Covet. He had passed the house before and thought it to be unoccupied or even derelict. He had called there to deliver a package to a man having been directed by Skipper the first time they had visited Dunwich but he didn't know if the man lived there or it was just a convenient spot to meet. He stood and listened for a while and came to the conclusion that the voices he could hear were those of some of the men who had unloaded the *Ellie May* a little earlier. The house was being used as a cache for the smuggled goods, he presumed. It was just off the beaten track, easily accessible for carts and a useful escape route by land and river should the Riding men come calling. He vowed he would have words with Skipper after all, he felt it was his right to know as it was Skipper's fault that he had become implicated.

Skipper was asleep when he returned to the cabin so his questions would have to wait until the morning. He climbed into his bunk, his mind racing, he recalled reading a book years ago, before he joined the army it was a story about smuggling and he remembered how it intrigued him. It was story set in Kent and he vaguely remembered a vicar called The Scarecrow being the leader of a smuggling outfit. His real name was Doctor Syn, he recalled very little else but it had conjured his imagination about the double life such a character would lead. He had been besotted by the lives of smugglers and pirates and resolved that he would read more, but he never did.

 They left the riverside early, destination Woodbridge. They tied up at the same berth they had vacated beside the Tide Mill but not before Barty had asked a few questions of Skipper. He confirmed Barty's suspicions about the old house at Dunwich and told him quite a lot more of the freetrade that flourished along that coast of Suffolk, Barty finished up asking if the Revenue men had ever taken Skipper. Apparently, he had survived a couple of narrow escapes but with the help of the watchers on shore and his knowledge of the inshore topography he had never been arrested. The conversation was cut short by their arrival at the mill and Arthur Spalding waiting there to greet them.

"Come up to the house as soon as you are squared up" invited Mr Spalding as he received the head rope of the boat and secured it. "There's a couple of things I want to discuss with you and bring the lad with you"

Sitting in the kitchen with steaming hot coffee before them they discussed the possibility of taking a ten-ton cargo of barley grain to the Snape and a further forty sacks of milled flour to a large bakery in Aldeburgh. The offer came as a Godsend as they had no work booked for the rest of December. Skipper gratefully accepted the contract immediately and business was swiftly completed. They were just about to leave when Sarah walked into the kitchen

"Ah!" said her father in a rather loud voice, "Here's the young man from the grinding room" his eyes twinkling mischievously, "We were about to leave, there's work to be done".

"So soon" commented Sarah and addressing Barty "Won't you stay for another coffee?"

Skipper butted in saying that he had things to attend to but Barty could stay if he wanted. He needed no second invitation and sat back down at the table while Sarah prepared another drink for him. They stayed talking for a half hour then Sarah had to return to the mill.

Barty made the short walk back to the boat, walking on air all the way! Sarah had been genuinely pleased to see him and had invited him to visit whenever he pleased. With no further contracts for that month he hoped that Skipper would stay at the mooring at the Tide Mill until New Year.

The hold had been swept clean and tidied and the bright-work was being polished as two mill hands arrived at the *Ellie May* bringing a portable hand crane with them. The sacks of grain and flour were neatly stowed ready for transportation to the Snape, the hold covers and the tarpaulins were fastened down, everything was ship-shape and Bristol fashion as the tide began to ebb. They took advantage of the tide to make a swift journey down the Deben, turning north as they reached the river mouth. There was a lively wind blowing and the day was cold and clear. Skipper kept a good weather eye open as he told Barty to tack every so often to keep the boat from losing headway. It was late afternoon when the welcoming flash of Aldeburgh lighthouse was seen well south of the town, switching from sail to auxiliary Skipper skilfully steered into the mouth of the River Alde passing the town of Orford on the starboard side, through the Short and Long Reaches to a jetty at 'The Maltings' just below Snape. Ten tons of barley grain was quickly unloaded and *Ellie May* rested at her mooring overnight before proceeding back down river. The journey down the Alde was very quick as they took advantage of the tide and the shallow draught of the boat to negotiate the winding waters. They stopped at Aldeburgh just long enough to off-load the milled flour then set course for the River Deben and Woodbridge where, by nightfall they were once again snugged down at the Tide Mill.

    Skipper said that he had some paperwork to attend to as they had now finished their legitimate business for the month. He paid Barty his wages it came to quite a sum, putting that to the money he had saved he realised that he ought to put it safely into the bank. *Ellie May* was frequently left unattended and it was unwise to keep his cash on board just in case they had uninvited visitors. Thinking about it he had hardly spent any money at all since he had been with Skipper, just a nominal amount for food, a little on his navigation books and Skipper had bought his working clothes, a thought suddenly struck him, if he was going to Skipper's daughters house for Christmas he would need some presentable clothing, so he decided to go to the shops in Woodbridge at the first opportunity.

It was most fortunate that they had returned to Tide Mill as it gave him the chance to see more of the estate owned by Mr Spalding and to lend a hand at the mill plus, of course he would be able to spend more time with Sarah. Sarah told him that her father had hired another mill hand so that she would no longer be required to work in the dusty mill but return to her original job of administration of the mill and the businesses surrounding the Tide Mill. Today she had found time to be with him and they certainly made good use of that. She asked Barty about his future plans to which he replied that he had no long-term plans but would be staying with Skipper for the foreseeable future. He told her of the offer of a part share in the *Ellie May* next April and that he was very happy with his present position with Skipper. He thought it prudent not to mention his involvement with the freetrade, no one spoke of that except where men got together to arrange the operations. He did mention that he wanted to go to Woodbridge to buy some new clothes and to open a bank account although he had no idea what to do, he had never had to buy new clothes before and knew little about banking. Sarah who had a good knowledge of banking procedures gained through dealing with the Tide Mill accounts, immediately offered to accompany him to Woodbridge. The prospect of spending even more time with Sarah could not be refused, so they made arrangements to meet the next day if her father and Skipper had no objections to them taking time off work.

Barty went up to the house at 9am to meet Sarah both having obtained consent from their respective employers. Sarah looked ravishing and made Barty aware of the of the poor manner in which he was dressed, he had done his best with the few clothes that he possessed but was pleased that he would now get the chance to buy some better ones with the help of Sarah. They took public transport into town where Barty received some enviable looks from other young men when they saw Sarah on his arm. The advice given by the assistant on entering a good class outfitters was well received but it was Sarah's advice that won the day as eventually they agreed on what suited Barty best at the price he could afford however he felt that Sarah had made the greatest impression on what he purchased.

Clutching his shopping they went next to the National Bank. On entering they were approached by a member of staff, "good morning Miss Spalding, can I help you?"

"Good morning" she replied, "My friend here would like to open an account" It was no surprise to Barty that the bank staff knew her. They were led to a small private room and sat opposite the clerk; a number of leaflets were placed in front of Barty.

"Just a few formalities Sir, these are leaflets telling you of our services, now could I please have your full name and address?"

Kaleb John Bartholomew" he relied giving a sidelong glance at Sarah. This was the first time that he had told anyone his full and proper name since he left Mill Hall farm and joined the army, everyone knew him as Barty, Sarah made no comment and just sat quietly as he answered more questions for the clerk, "And your address Sir" he prompted. Barty told him that he really had no fixed abode and lived on board the *Ellie May* so Sarah suggested that he could use the Tide Mill address and she would act on his behalf if ever the need arose. This arrangement satisfied the clerk who completed the forms and asked Barty to sign them. The clerk left the room saying he would be back in about ten minutes. It was evident that the bank staff knew Sarah, as she was the one who conducted the Tide Mill Estates business with them. The clerk returned to say that everything was in order and handed him a receipt for the money he had deposited to open the account.

They stepped out into the main road and went to a nearby teashop for some well-earned refreshments fully satisfied with what had been achieved that morning. He felt like a man of some substance now he had a bank account, a permanent job, new clothes and an extremely notable address, further more he was accompanied by a delightful, intelligent young lady acquaintance. Things couldn't get much better. It hadn't gone unnoticed that Sarah had introduced him to the bank clerk as "my friend" and hoped that very soon he would become more than just a friend. He had also hoped that he could have changed into his new clothes before they entered the teashop but one step at a time.

With time to spare they decided to take a stroll around the local park and he found himself telling Sarah of his interest in navigation and the freedom he experienced whilst sailing around the coasts with Skipper on the *Ellie May* of how he had sat for hours listening to Skipper's stories of the years he had spent as a deep sea sailor asking him about the ports that he had only read about on the sterns of the ships travelling up the River Thames Reaches to the Port of London. Sarah listened intently seemingly understanding his longings and his ripe imagination, she too had known Skipper for a long time and had probably heard many of the stories that he related to her before from Skipper.

By comparison to Barty, Sarah had had a very ordered upbringing, her parents trying to provide everything a young lady from a good family could want. They ensured that the business provided sufficient funds for a good education and that she would eventually inherit a large house connected to her father's business. Furthermore, Sarah had been brought up by her Nanny and had attended the best local school terminating in a college education and qualifications in business administration, English and finally a Business Diploma. She appeared to have been denied the friendship of the local children, of which there had been few and only attended social events culminating from her father's business associates. Barty formed the impression that she had never really had the opportunity to practice her social skills with people of her own age. True, she had met a few mill hands but could find no parallel with any of them they seemed devoid of conversation and ambition whereas Barty, although not educated to her level had an urge to learn, to be involved and most importantly, a good sense of understanding. She felt different about Barty, this strong good-looking lad had only visited the house a few times, they had met infrequently but she has started to look forward to his visits and the time she spent with him.

As they made their way towards the transport home, Barty felt her soft ungloved hand take hold of his hand. She looked up into his eyes half expecting a look of rejection, but no, just a smile and a tightening of the grip. No words were needed; the acceptance was mutual as they boarded the bus home.

Late evening on board the *Ellie May* saw Skipper still working on deck with the aid of the deck lights squaring up loose ends and stowing various tools and equipment into their proper places, he hailed Barty as he boarded asking if he had accomplished everything he needed in Woodbridge. Barty noted that Skipper was moving much slower than normal and said," Are you alright Skipper, you look tired?"

"Aye lad, I'm fine, just squaring off a few things before we go to Ipswich"

Ipswich, - Barty had almost forgotten that Skipper's daughter had invited them to spend Christmas with her family.

Christmas, he was aware of the month but hadn't realised that Christmas was only a few days away. Although he had celebrated Christmas while he was working at Mill Hall Farm he hadn't place much importance on the season, they were just a group of workers getting together for the

celebrations there was no emphasis on family or much on the religious side of the occasion. Work had gone on as usual on the farm and the only token towards the season was the grand dinner prepared and served by dear old Mrs Hudson. He could hear her calling to him now,
"Come on Barty, your dinner's getting cold".
And what a dinner it was! There was no exchange of gifts but there was such a close friendship and a warm atmosphere such that he would never ever forget.

This Christmas would be much different, more of a family occasion and the opportunity to exchange gifts with friends that had become more than just working colleagues. The more he thought about it, the more he realised that another trip to Woodbridge or even to Ipswich town was essential but he had no idea of what to buy as gifts for the others. There would be Skipper and Sarah of course, then Sarah's parents, Skipper's daughter and her husband and the two children. He took the chance to ask Sarah to go back to Woodbridge with him to help him choose something suitable for each of them, except her own of course.

A few days later they again visited the lovely town of Woodbridge which as very busy and Barty was amazed by the myriad of coloured lights and the decorations displayed in the streets and shops. A large Christmas tree dominated the shopping centre that was teeming with happy people greeting each other and beside the tree was a brass band playing carols and Christmas songs with the good folk of Woodbridge joining in the singing. All this seemed overwhelming to Barty as this was the first time that he had been in a town at this time of the year whereas Sarah just seemed to accept the proceedings as normal but she did exhibit her delight when Santa Claus appeared near the tree.

Barty just wanted to stand and watch and listen, his mind flashing back to the workhouse, the lodgings at Prospect House in London, Mill Hall

Farm and the Army as he tried to equate the difference between them, he couldn't, there was no comparison, the promise of Christmas yet to come was so vastly incomparable.

His thoughts were brought back to reality as a voice said "Come on Barty, we'll never get anything done just standing here" and slipped her hand into his and led him around several shops slowly accumulating gifts for friends and family. While Sarah was busy choosing some items of clothing he made the excuse that he needed to go to the toilet. Slipping into the jeweller's shop next door he bought a lovely bracelet for Sarah and carefully put it into his pocket away from prying eyes.

Completely satisfied with their afternoon purchases they repaired to the local teashop for refreshments before returning to the Tide Mill at about 6.30pm to find Sarah's father and Skipper sitting in the lounge enjoying a glass of beer. They were in deep conversation but quickly changed their subject when the couple entered the room. At the same time Mrs Spalding came into the lounge to enquire of Skipper and Barty would like to stay for supper. Mrs Spalding busied herself in the kitchen while Mr Spalding and Skipper stayed in the lounge talking to Sarah and Barty about their trip into Woodbridge. Sarah had managed to secret their purchases and so avoid undue questions but Skipper and Mr Spalding didn't reveal what they had been speaking about prior to the couple's entry. After they had eaten Sarah made the excuse that she had something to attend to in the office, an excuse that gave them a chance to wrap their presents and hide them away again. Time was getting short now, only three days before Skipper and Barty were to leave for Ipswich. Barty had managed to wrap his present for Sarah and to stow it, together with her parent's gifts under the Christmas tree where she wouldn't spot it.

Three days later Mr Spalding drove them to the railway station. *Ellie May* had been secured and left in the care of the mill complex manager who was not married and would spend most of his time looking after the animals and the whole complex, a dauntless job!

From the look of the railway station it appeared that the whole of Woodbridge was making their way to various destinations, it was so busy it took our intrepid travellers quite a time to find a second-class compartment to accommodate them and their two rather large packages – Skipper had been shopping too! Soon after finding their seats and settling down Skipper immediately fell asleep. Barty had noticed that he had been finding physical work very tiring of late and needed to rest frequently during the day. He never neglected his work and kept the records up to date but it was the physical side that was taking him longer to complete. Barty woke Skipper as the train pulled into Ipswich Station.

It was only a short carriage ride from the station to the impressive large detached house situated in St, Margaret's Green. The driveway led to a double fronted house and in the large porch was a decorated Christmas tree and trimmings leading into the hallway where a young woman with two small children was waiting to greet them. Marie Arnold, and her two children John, aged 10 years and Rachel, aged 12 years, hugged their grandfather; it was so evident that they were overjoyed to see him again. They were introduced to Barty who felt that he already knew these friendly people and he hadn't really entered the house yet! There was no sign of Marie's husband Matthew who, Barty later learned was a prominent accountant in Ipswich.

They left their luggage in the hall as Marie led then through to the lounge where they enjoyed a coffee and homemade cakes before being shown to their respective rooms. Barty thought he was in heaven, it was the first time he had ever been in a tasteful room of his own, he had always shared with others, some of whom he did not even know, like Ben Osbourne's lodging house in London! This really must be what heaven was like, everything so clean and ordered and enough space to create a large bed-sit. Silly thoughts it's true but that was how he felt. When Skipper had told him a long time ago that he had a house in Ipswich, Barty had imagined a terraced property or a simple fisherman's cottage, not a large detached doubled fronted house in the centre of town.

It was Christmas Eve and soon after 5pm, Matthew Arnold came home from his office. He was dressed in a dark pinstriped business suit looking every inch the successful businessman that he was, the type of man that Barty had only encountered in official circles. His first impression of Mr Arnold was that of an officious overbearing father that ruled the household with an iron rod but first impressions are rarely correct. After changing from his business suit into something more relaxing Mr Arnold sat with the family discussing the day but mainly showing an interest in Barty and how he was coping with his life as an inshore trader. Barty felt himself warming towards him as his guarded business attitude softened and he became a typical family man. Barty began to understand Matt, as he wanted to be called, when he told of how he longed for a life away from the daily boring routine of office life and dreamed of a more active lifestyle. He obviously envied Skipper who appeared to have led such an exciting life at sea for so many years, always on the move and meeting new people, a life that even now at his age Skipper continued to enjoy. Matt asked many questions of Barty about his past life and his ambitions, all of which he answered truthfully but emphasising the chance that Skipper had given him for a better way if making a living and nurturing his interest in navigation and an understanding of the ways of a seaman.

They talked until late that Christmas Eve, plenty to eat and drink until Marie suggested that the children should hang up their stockings and go to bed before the man in the red suit paid his annual visit! Skipper and Barty emptied the contents of the two large packages they had brought with them and put the gifts into the respective stockings when the children were sleeping and all was quiet. The remaining presents were placed under the tree. Quiet as it was in the house Barty had trouble getting off to sleep. The adrenalin was till pumping and his mind wouldn't settle. He had never known such comfort and after so many lonely Christmas's past he now felt that he was wanted and belonged. He thought of Sarah and her family, how they had accepted him, of Skipper and all that he had done for him, it was he who had introduced him to the life he was now experiencing and to the Arnold family who he had only met a few hours ago. He didn't forget his childhood times, Jed Slater, his fellow mudlark, the people at Mill Hall Farm, his Army Pals, with the good luck that had befallen him he wondered how they had fared through the years and hoped that they had found happiness and satisfactory lives.

A Very Happy Christmas to Everyone. Christmas Day, it was early and he felt as if he had hardly slept a wink when a small boy and a large dog roughly awakened him. John came into the bedroom full of excitement followed by a lively dog taking Barty by compete surprise. John was so excited and that excitement seemed to overflow into Shufftee, the family dog. Barty hadn't met the dog the previous evening, as he had been restricted to the kitchen during the night. John's excitement gradually abated and Shuftee settled down at the foot of the bed with a contented look on his face. Barty glanced at the clock, 5.45am!' time to linger on in bed for a while longer. By 8am the whole family were up and gathered in the lounge enjoying a cup of coffee as they busied themselves opening the gifts that had been piled under the tree. Barty was happy to see that the gifts that he and Sarah had bought were well received, he had had no idea really what Sarah had chosen and wrapped and he had been totally reliant on her choice, he couldn't have done it without her and wished that she could have been there to share the occasion. Skipper who didn't seem to want anything was the hardest to buy for so Barty had bought him a bottle of 'Nelson's Blood' (Rum) and some tobacco for his pipe but the biggest surprise came when Barty received a parcel from Skipper addressed simply "To a good mate" He quickly unwrapped the long package and found a good expensive brass telescope. He was over the moon.

"Now perhaps you will be able to see where you are going instead of where you have been" said Skipper, causing everyone to laugh at his remark. They all knew that Barty was a good navigator, Skipper had told them often enough in his letters to his daughter.

A most relaxing day followed, the whole family except for Marie took Shuftee down to the local park for a walk. Shuftee was a fluffy Old English sheepdog only about 12 months old, still very much a puppy and his playfulness attracted the local children to stroke him and play with him. There was no shortage of children that Christmas morning. New bikes, scooters, footballs and doll's prams were in abundance and Shuftee was soon panting for a drink of water after receiving so much attention from the children, he was something of a celebrity!

They returned home to St, Margaret's Green in good time for a pre— dinner drink before a sumptuous dinner, cooked by Marie and served to them by both Marie and Rachel, appeared on the table before them as if by magic. It was Skipper who found the traditional silver sixpence in his portion of Christmas pudding. It was the best meal that Barty had ever had in his life. Everyone complimented Marie then sat back to enjoy a glass of brandy. Nobody seemed to want to move away from the table but there was the clearing away to be done. Barty offered to give a hand in the kitchen but Marie wouldn't hear of it, "you're a guest in this house" she said, "and guests do not work here" she aimed her remarks at both Barty and Skipper. Very soon after dinner Skipper retired to his room for a rest, it had been a long day and he was feeling quite weary, in fact they didn't see him again until Boxing Day morning. Marie, Matt and Barty stayed up for a long time after a light supper and a drink, just general chat getting to know each other a little better. Boxing Day was pretty much a repeat of Christmas Day, plenty of food and leisure time and for Matt and Barty another rather shorter walk for Shuftee. It took a great deal of effort and energy to keep him fit and healthy and unfortunately the Arnold family were unable to find the time to give him all the exercise he needed. He had been bought as a present the previous Christmas when Matt thought he would make a great pal and housedog but he underestimated the time taken for his care and just how big he would grow. Although he was dearly loved each family member always seemed reluctant to take him out, rain or shine, each finding excuses why someone else should get the job. Matt told Barty of this dilemma and carefully thinking things over he came up with an idea. He didn't say anything then, he wanted to speak to Skipper first.

They had planned to return to the *Ellie May* on the 27th December to start to look for work for the coming months. Barty found it difficult to express his gratitude for a wonderful holiday as they started to make their way to the railway station, but this time there were three of them! During the previous evening the whole family discussed Barty's idea of adopting Shuftee and taking him back to the boat with them. Much discussion ensued but after all the pro's and con's, even the children agreed it would mean a more active life for Shuftee and they would not be saddled with the chore of 'walkies' twice a day.

After the spacious bedrooms that they had occupied at his daughter's house the confines of the cabin on the *Ellie May* were very cramped especially with the addition of a large dog, but this was their home and they soon came to terms with the conditions after discussing the possibility of building a special shelter for Shuftee just outside the cabin entrance. They had arrived home rather late so quickly settled down to sleep, Shuftee being content on a couple of tarpaulins on the floor of the cabin.

It was his growl and bark that woke Barty the next morning He quickly pulled back the hatch to find Sarah, a very early morning Sarah, standing by the cabin, it was barely 7.30am. She greeted Barty and asked after Skipper's health. Barty woke Skipper and put the kettle on to boil. Once he was decent they sat in the cabin while Sarah gave then the news that no contracts had arrived and to invite them both to if they would care to have dinner with them on New Year's Eve at the Tide Mill. Skipper seemed a little reluctant to commit himself at first then after a while agreed to accept the invitation saying that he and Arthur Spalding had a little unfinished business to attend too. Barty recalled that Skipper and Mr Spalding had been in deep conversation a few days ago, when he interrupted them and the subject, wherever it was, quickly changed. Just what they had been talking about he never did find out but on questioning Skipper said that Mr Spalding wanted him to pick up a load for him in the New Year but were awaiting details to be confirmed. There was no work awaiting them on return from Ipswich so any chance of a job was welcome.

"I meant to tell you about that" said Skipper "but while we were planning you came in with Mrs Spalding and Sarah and the time wasn't right to talk of business

Barty was a little surprised "pick up a load" Skipper had said, not deliver it, the secrecy made him think that this was another freetrade arrangement. He didn't question it any further as the final details appear yet to be confirmed. He realised that such a venture wouldn't be without danger but it could be a good money-maker when they needed work

One thing that surprised him was that Sarah hadn't mentioned that it was Shuftee who had announced her presence on the boat. Barty explained all to her and called the dog into the cabin where an instant acceptance by both parties was quickly made.

New Year's Eve and their arrival at the Tide Mill House coincided with several other guests. Skipper was familiar with several of them nearly all were complete strangers to Barty. There were about twelve guests and Sarah's father had engaged a catering company to supply the needs of the assembly leaving him free to make the formal introductions on their individual arrivals. After the formal welcome drinks, the guests were seated at a heavily laden table Sarah was seated next to Barty as he asked the inevitable question.

"Who are all these people, I only know one or two of them?"

"I don't know, there are people here I've never seen before" replied Sarah looking from face to face around the table.

Conversation flowed easily as many of them evidently knew each other but the subject of the conversations was varied as all appeared to be businessmen mingling freely with tradesman and others of no specific calling. Several speeches were made after dinner mainly centred on the commercial conditions in Woodbridge and trade in general.

The speeches completed the gathering broke into small groups, Barty and Sarah finding themselves in company with Mr Spalding, a Mr Gold – solicitor and Ted Moore a local farmer. Informal conversation slowly turned to 'the job in hand'. Both Barty and Sarah were surprised by the developments in the discussions, especially Sarah who had no idea that the gathered people had any connection or interest in the freetrade. Oh yes, Barty and Skipper knew but Barty hadn't realised that the organisation was so widespread. and sat quietly, agreeing with the suggestions made by Skipper but not contributing any observations of his own. Sarah just sat in astounded surprise.

It was very late when they returned to the *Ellie May,* too late to talk so Skipper promised to fill Barty in with the details next morning. After such a magnificent dinner, a few drinks and a lot of words Barty felt tired and was asleep within minutes with a certain excitement swelling within him. He knew that he had been implicated in smuggling before but he hadn't been aware before being unknowingly implicated and certainly not involved in any planning. Skipper had never told him anything and sent him off on errands before any 'crop' (contraband cargoes) was off loaded. Now that he was part of the organisation he had to confess to a thrill at what might happen in future.

'L'Etoile lay snugly at anchor just off a small French village on the west coast of France, she was low in the water and carrying a crop that had previously been loaded at a remote jetty at high tide. Clearance of the low tide mark left her immediately ready for sea. It was a beautiful crisp January morning when the solitary man on deck spied a small single-handed sail boat approaching from the shore. The two vessels came alongside silently and the men exchanged greetings in French. A briefcase was handed to the man on the *L'Etoile,* a few more words and the visitor departed back towards the French coast

The watchman went below after scanning the area to ensure that the coast was clear. Within minutes five more men appeared on deck, weighed anchor and set sail towards the east coast of England.

Meantime, just across the Channel, *Ellie May* was being prepared to make sail. It was late afternoon, just a fair wind blowing and the sea was relatively calm, it was the second day of the new year and Skipper had already explained to him about the forthcoming run. This confirmed Barty's suspicions and the reasons why this run was being undertaken at that particular time of the year. He could feel that surge of excitement again as they made their final preparations and Skipper briefed him on their course and destination. Barty had now become a competent navigator along the coastline of East Anglia.

It was quite unusual for any vessel to be moving as dusk fell but they left the moorings at the Tide Mill unobserved and headed towards the mouth of the River Deben. The tide was low as they approached the estuary and Skipper instructed Barty to stay close inshore where the water was shallow and beaching lightly on the shingle. They stood off for a few minutes when the dark figure of a man appeared, waded into the shallows and boarded the boat. To Barty's surprise he recognised the newcomer as Ted Moore, the farmer who had been present at the dinner party at the Tide Mill a couple of nights ago. Greetings were exchanged between the three men and Skipper gave Barty an offshore position course to steer. He hugged the shore for approximately 30 minutes then took up the course he had been given into the open sea. By the light of a watery moon Barty was easily able to keep the course until he was approximately five miles offshore. Within minutes of reaching the rendezvous position the darkened navigation lights of *L'Etoile* came into view. The French vessel was a two masted ketch with the mizzen for'ard of the rudder head. She hove to, Skipper and Ted receiving their lines and securing fore and aft. Little was said and the work of transferring the crop of bales and kegs to *Ellie May* took about an hour and a quarter by hand as no hand crane was available. Barty counted six men on the French boat, five were helping to transfer the crop while one man, younger than the others kept a constant watch on the seas around then for any sign of other vessels that may belong to the Excise men. Everything was well, most God-fearing men being at home with their families and it was rare to find Excise vessels this far-off shore. Work completed the crews wished each other Good

Luck and a happy and prosperous year ahead and taking the helm Skipper steered towards the English coast, still under reduced lights while *L'Etoile* now ran under full navigational lights. Ted and Barty went into the cabin to make a celebratory drink for a good night's work – so far! Now facing a developing wind *Ellie May* found difficulty in making headway, progress was slow and Skipper was anxious to get inshore before daylight. On nearing the coast Skipper dropped the sail and ordered the navigational lights to be doused as Ted had spotted something onshore that made him suspicious. They were about two miles offshore near the Easton Cliffs just north of Sole Bay. Barty had discovered that Ted Moore owned Easton Farm situated north of Reydon10
and stretching onto the Easton Cliffs below which lay a narrow sandy beach, their landing place. Ted had seen movement on the cliff tops and thought he saw a flink (a warning light) just below the cliff level. They lay quiet with no lights showing when again Ted thought he saw movement on the cliff top and using Barty's new telescope, could discern a few people, some mounted on horses were in deed silhouetted against the waning moon. He was unable to count the number of people on the cliff top but it was reassuring that they hadn't seen the motionless shadow of *Ellie May* lying about two miles off. Ted continued his watch and suddenly reported that the flash on the shore had been seen again. Those on the cliff top could not see the flink. Two other flashes followed telling Ted that it was unsafe to make a landing, as it was the Excise men who were gathered on the cliff looking for a boat trying to make landfall, quickly followed it. How had they found out? They lay still until the early fingers of daylight heralded the new day and as soon as the skies began to lighten Skipper took *Ellie May* further out to sea away from any dangers that the shore may hold, to the casual observer she would be just like any other vessel making its way across the Channel. Skipper decided

to give it 24 hours before attempting to make landfall again. It was late afternoon when they headed back towards the Easton Cliffs. The coast was now clear!

The lay-offshore had given Barty time to reflect on the past hours, someone must have tipped off the Revenue men as to where the landing was due to be made. The coast off the Easton Cliffs are almost deserted at the best of times, there were no attractions at all, the cliffs were very step which made leisure walking awkward and dangerous, there were no buildings of any description in the area. Ted Moore knew this area like the back of his hand, it bordered onto his farm and the small sandy beach below the cliff face could not be seen from the cliff top so it made a perfect landing place. There was ingress and egress via a small sunken passage leading from the cave hidden under the cliff overhang. Ted was well aware of the small cave entrance with accessibility only from the sea. The cave led to a passageway to the sunken shaft that ran up to the surface of one of Ted's fields. This had been a traditional smuggler's run for many years but now almost forgotten since the trade had slowly died down over the past century or more. Barty knew nothing of this run at the time and his mind was centred on who could have possibly be responsible for tipping off the Revenue men. Celebrations for the New Year were still ongoing and the cover by the Revenue men would be depleted, possibly only a skeleton staff so this wasn't an accidental watch.

His thoughts went back to the dinner party at the Tide Mil and the people he had met there. This being the first meeting with most of them he had gained the impression that the majority of them would have some vested interest in the freetrade. He could raise no suspicion against any one so the question remained. Who was the informer?

Ellie May slowly and warily approached the Easton Cliff again, this time there were no warning signals and the boat came to rest in the very shallow water. Six men who had obviously gained access to the beach via the old shaft welcomed them and the work of unloading began immediately until the whole crop had been safely secreted in the sea cave, the six men took their leave through the back of the cave and Tom Moore went with them.

Skipper and Barty stayed in the lee of the cliffs for a further hour before sailing south back towards the River Deben arriving there about mid-afternoon. Barty cleaned himself up and went up to the Tide Mill House to see Sarah, he was 24 hours later than he had said but she asked no questions regarding his delay and he was thankful, as Sarah had no idea of his whereabouts over the past hours. Although it hadn't been said in so many words, Barty felt that the whole business of the past day or so had been unlawful. He was sure she had her suspicions especially after meeting so many unknown 'business men' at the dinner. Something was afoot but nothing was talked about.

Skipper stayed on board the *Ellie May* to square up his 'paperwork', as he put it and then came up to the house at 6pm, just in time for dinner. The evening was spent reminiscing about the past year and the plans for this New Year. The only reference to the past few days was when Mr Spalding enquired of Skipper if his latest trip was successful. The affirmative reply was curt and the conversation was steered away avoiding any mention of the near brush with the Customs and Excise men. Barty had previously had words with Skipper about whom the possible informer could be but Skipper also maintained that he had no idea, "but if I get my hands on him", he failed to complete the sentence. Skipper looked old and tired and the thought of having an informer in the organisation upset him more than he showed.

Tuesday 3rd January 1922, following the New Year celebrations it was business as usual and Skipper arose early and made his way to Woodbridge. He had listed several visits he intended to make so he wanted plenty of time to complete his visits. He left Barty to clear up the *Ellie May* and get everything ready to take the next charter There was nothing pending at the present but it was one of the calls for Skipper to make while he was in town. Taking his time, he called at the solicitor's office, the bank, his agents office and finally to the grocers to buy food to re-stock the boat. Before collecting the food supplies he visited 'The Boaters Inn' where he met with several acquaintances and stayed with them longer than he had anticipated arriving back on board about 6pm. In his absence Barty had finished the special doghouse for Shuftee just beside the cabin hatch making it comfortable and warm for him. Skipper was pleased to have the job done and Shuftee was more than happy with his new quarters.

Skipper stowed away his purchases and called Barty to the cabin, as he wanted to talk to him. He told him that he had been to the solicitor's office to start the paperwork that would make them partners in the carrying business together with all the terms and conditions that would apply They spoke generally about the arrangement and agreed an active date of 1st April 1922, just three months hence, the start of the new financial year. Skipper also settled his account with Barty by paying him his back wages from which he deducted his food bill. Barty was pleased to see that he had an acceptable amount to put into his own bank account. Finally, Skipper said he had been to see his agent and handed Barty a sealed envelope saying that this was his share of the settlement for the job they had undertaken over the new year period just past

Barty thanked him and asked who was his agent. Skipper declined to answer and just replied "all in good time lad, all in good time"

Barty opened the sealed envelope and was quite shocked to see the very generous amount of cash it contained. He found it hard to believe but on questioning the envelopes contents Skipper said, "It's your share lad, look after it"

The freetrade business was obviously quite lucrative, unlawful, but lucrative and here on the east coast, extremely well organised. He felt that there was very little danger from the Revenue men as the shore communications were so good and any imminent danger was quickly alerted all along the coast line when a run was being made. It was a long coast line with many desolate stretches to be patrolled by a very undermanned service.

His mind wandered off again to the Dr Syn books that he had read in his younger days. Dr. Syn lived in a village on the Romney Marches and was the anonymous leader of a fearsome band of smugglers, he was known only as 'The Scarecrow' nobody knew his real identity. His operations were conducted mainly from the shore side whilst he was on horseback directing the runs. In his own communities, he was really a trusted prominent figure, the local parson! Barty felt the thrill of excitement belonging to a similar set up, not as well known or on such a scale as Dr. Syn and the boyhood memories of the adventures of this notorious smuggler would stay with him forever. His memories had whet his appetite to learn more about the freetrade so he often went to the library in Woodbridge to borrow books and he was surprised just how widespread the trade had been in the 18th and early 19th centuries. Now, having been given his first payoff, he could understand why so many were involved in those days and why the practice was still quite prevalent today. Smuggling was still carried out all around the shores of England and many are the stories about those who were brought to justice and their eventual fate. The Customs and Excise Service was slowly expanding and Revenue cutters from England and France regularly patrolled the English Channel in search of offenders.

Barty had always been intrigued by stories of smugglers and pirates and one poem had stuck in his mind for a long time, so much so that he had made a copy of it which he kept in one of his books

The Smuggler's Song.

If you wake at midnight, and hear a horse's feet,
Don't go drawing back the blind, or looking in the street,
Them that ask no questions isn't told a lie.
Watch the wall my darling while the Gentlemen go by.

Five and twenty ponies,
Trotting through the dark
Brandy for the Parson, 'Baccy for the Clerk.
Laces for a lady, letters for a spy,
Watch the wall my darling while the Gentlemen go by.

Running around the woodlump if you chance to find
Little barrels, roped and tarred, and full of brandy- wine,
Don't you shout to come and look, nor use 'em for your play.
Put the brushwood back again – and they'll be gone next day!

If you see the stable-door setting open wide;
If you see a tired horse lying down inside;
If your mother mends a coat cut about and tore;
It the linings wet and warm – don't you ask no more!

If you meet King George's men, dressed in blue and red,
You be careful what you say, and mindful what is said

*If they call you "pretty maid, and chuck you 'neath the chin,
Don't you tell where no one is, nor yet where no one's been!*

*Knocks and footsteps around the house – whistles after dark –
You've no call for running out till the house-dogs bark.
Trusty's here, and Pincher's here, and see how dumb they lie
They don't fret to follow when the Gentlemen go by.*

*If you do as you've been told, 'likely there's a chance,
You'll be give a dainty doll, all the way from France,
With a cap of Valenciennes, and a velvet hood –
A present from the Gentlemen, along 'o being good!*

*Five and twenty ponies,
Trotting through the dark –
Brandy for the Parson, 'Baccy for the Clerk.
Them that asks no questions isn't told a lie –
Watch the wall my darling while the Gentlemen go by*

Rudyard Kipling.

    Barty felt very happy and contented with his lot as he went to his bunk that night. He called at the Tide Mill the following morning at about 10.30am after attending to one or two small jobs on the boat, to tell Sarah that he wanted to go into Woodbridge and did she want to accompany him. He wanted to visit his Bank as soon as possible and to call at the bookshop for a navigation book and a chart for the Norfolk/Suffolk area. By 11am they were on their way, Sarah was happy to have the chance to get away from the Mill for a few hours and to spend some time with Barty. It was a cold January morning as they walked hand in hand along the High Street, Sarah remarked that she was feeling the cold as she had forgotten her scarf and gloves when they left the house in such a hurry. Barty's first call was his Bank and then to a large store to buy a new scarf and gloves for Sarah, a sort of belated Christmas present. As they sat enjoying a cup of tea Barty began to realise just how much he had missed the pleasure of Sarah's company while he was in Ipswich. They spent a long time sitting in the café planning what they would like to do in the near future. Leaving the café arm in arm they took a slow walk along the High Street stopping at whatever shop took their interest until they came to the bookshop. Barty purchased the book and chart that he wanted and was about to leave the shop when he noticed a poster advertising a Horticultural Show to be held in Stowmarket next April. He carefully made a note of the dates and details whilst remembering the times he had attended such shows in the past with his beloved Clydesdale horses. This prompted him to relate his stories to Sarah as they casually strolled along the street. She listened intently asking the odd question here and there and she saw the look in his eyes realising just how much he had loved those horses so she made a suggestion that they arrange to visit the Show when the time came. He was reluctant to agree at first without speaking to Skipper. But it suddenly dawned upon him that on April 1st he would be part owner of the *Ellie May* and in a position to make up his own mind. He could keep that date clear of contracts and make arrangements well in advance, a decision that pleased Sarah immensely

Sarah suggested that it was about time that he started to keep his own diary instead of relying on Skipper to tell him what was happening. They hurried back to the bookshop to a buy a diary and Barty's eye fell upon one of Rudyard Kipling's books. He asked the bookseller if it contained his favourite poem and receiving an affirmative reply he couldn't resist the book and bought it. Was his secret still safe?

He felt that if Sarah really knew about the organisation she would disapprove even though her father was involved.

Although Sarah had some suspicions about his clandestine activities she didn't ask him anything about it or why the poem meant so much to him

Back at Tide Mill House Mrs Spalding informed them that they were just in time for tea. The family took the majority of their meals in the big farmhouse kitchen as Mr Spalding considered the dining room too formal; the kitchen was always warm and welcoming. a much more workable arrangement for Mrs Spalding.

Barty was surprised to see Skipper already seated at the table, apparently, he and Arthur Spalding had met earlier to discuss certain aspects of business and invited Barty to join them. The discussions went on over tea and Skipper announced that the Carrying Company had received no contracts and the next few weeks promised to be no different so he had decided to put *Ellie May* into dry dock for repairs and painting and that meant no income for that time. Arthur had come up with an idea he put to them, he wanted to hire some help at the mill complex to generally tidy up and look after the moorings and a small warehouse close to the dry dock area. It was a job that he had been unable to do before now due to the busy year just past. He had quite a large concern with the work on the moorings, the leisure business, the farm and the warehouses were put together and there weren't enough employees to do everything. Barty hadn't been aware that the whole complex was quite that big. The offer was accepted and the details worked out. Barty and Skipper would be given the use of the small 'Keeper's Cottage' situated beside the mill, rent free as they would be unable to use the boat for a few weeks. They would have to cater for themselves while the work was being undertaken by Mr Spalding's dock employees. All arrangements made seemed most admirable to all concerned. Mr Spalding would pay a small wage to them, more a subsistence as they were being housed rent-free.

Skipper had spoken with his accountant about having *Ellie May* cleaned and painted before their partnership began as the accountant could apply for a better tax relief rate for Skipper as a single crew owner and taking the advantage of Skipper's age. Everything appeared to be in order and the arrangements were accepted to everyone's satisfaction.

    Within a week, they had moved their gear from the boat into Keeper's Cottage, a small quayside building consisting of two bedrooms and a box room upstairs and a lounge area and kitchen on the ground floor. Although the dimensions of the cottage were small they found it quite spacious after the confined conditions on board the *Ellie May*.

The boat was put into dry dock ready for work to commence the following week. It was estimated that the completion date would be roughly the first week in March. The first job for the pair was to remove certain pieces of deck gear and store them in the quayside warehouse to make way for the fitters to remove an amount of planking that needed replacement. Skipper undertook most of the work while Barty carried out many varied tasks at the mill giving a hand to Skipper whenever there was heavy lifting and shifting to be done.

The days were very busy indeed and time passed so quickly that Barty didn't have the time to spend with Sarah as he had envisaged. They managed to spend the occasional evening at the Cottage after they had finished work. Sometimes they would take Shuftee a walk in the fields having been cooped up in the kitchen most of the day he was always ready for a romp. The weekends were little better, they finished work at midday on Saturday but there was always work to be done at the farm whatever day it was.

Work on the *Ellie May* was progressing well and Skipper, being a perfectionist kept a tight eye at all stages. There was a time when looking at the boat, anyone could have doubted if she would ever float again. Barty could find hardly any time to study his books and frequently wished he were back in the peace and quiet of the sea. He felt he was losing time, good practical time, when he could be receiving the benefit of Skipper's advice and guidance and the satisfying, soothing of a calm, clear day on the water,

One evening when Mr Spalding was at home he received a visitor in the shape of Ted Moore, the farmer from Easton Farm. The meeting was very short and purposeful after which Ted asked if he could speak with Barty. Mr Spalding went the few yards down to the Cottage and brought Barty back with him. Apparently, Ted had been told that Barty had served in the Veterinary Corps, having previously worked on a farm on the Isle of Dogs. Sarah had probably mentioned it when she spoke of her and Barty visiting the Show at Stowmarket next April. Ted asked about his experience with horses and when he was told that Barty had won a couple of awards at shows with the Clydesdales, Ted became even more interested. He told Barty that he intended to visit the Show himself and would be showing a couple of heavy horses. Ted had a great interest in breeding and showing the Suffolk Punch breed. The two of them spoke for a long time and the conversation ended when Ted invited him to visit his farm at Easton with a view to helping out at the Show in April. Without pausing to think of anything further he accepted the invitation immediately.

The next day he told Skipper of the plans to which he readily agreed but warning him that contract work should be coming in soon for around that time but emphasised that he would manage as the Show was only of two days' duration and that he was so pleased to be able to help his old friend Ted. Sarah too, was also totally delighted.

Ted's farm was situated above the Easton Cliffs just above the hidden beach where the last landing was made. Easton Farm was reasonably easy to reach via several back routes from Reydon, not by sea though as Barty well knew.

Using the main transport system through the towns and then a local bus, they eventually reached Easton Farm. It had been a long journey and they were both tired After a quick snack they were shown to their rooms with a promise of an early start in the morning.

Breakfast over Ted took them both on a full tour of his farm, the extensive acreage and the many scattered outbuildings. The view from the cliff tops was so panoramic that Barty could easily understand why the hidden beach below was such a valuable landing place and why Ted was such an important part of the freetrade syndicate. Of course, none of this was mentioned to Sarah who stood motionless entranced by the breathtaking views and drinking in the cold February morning air. Returning to the farm house from the cliffs Ted lead them to the stables to show his magnificent stud of Suffolk Punch horses keeping up an endless vocabulary of the virtues of horse breeding and in particular, the Suffolk Punches while Barty fired question after question at him. He was so overwhelmed by the beautiful animals that he found himself asking even more questions just to delay their departure from the stables. It wasn't only Barty that was impressed, Ted also was so totally impressed by his interest and knowledge in the care and well-being for horses and his knowledge of Show procedures that he asked Barty if he would consider being his Show master at Stowmarket next April. Barty looked at Sarah and she could see the excitement in his eyes, a slight nod of her head and Barty had answered Ted's invitation in a flash. Temporary arrangements were quickly mentioned, to be confirmed at a later date. Ted would pick then both up at the Tide Mill on the appointed day and travel together to Stowmarket with the horses in a trailer.

It was getting late when they left Easton Farm and they only just managed to catch their transport by the skin of their teeth. Barty was so contented he felt that he had achieved something special, what was more, Sarah had supported him throughout and was genuinely interested in the future visit to Stowmarket.

Back at the Tide Mill work on the *Ellie May* was developing rapidly, in fact much quicker than had been anticipated and the possibility of completion date being brought forward was good. In the meantime, Skipper and Barty continued to work about the mill and the wharves. Skipper frequently attended meetings in Woodbridge, business meetings to do with the transfer of goods and contracts for the future of which Barty had no working knowledge. While the boat was being refurbished Barty found some extra time to see Sarah and together visit certain attractions around the town but his studies was not forgotten. His sights were set on gaining a full Deep Sea Navigators Certificate in the future but he had still a lot to learn. His association with Sarah had caused him to think of the more distant future. His affections for her grew daily and he included her in all his plans although he hardly ever mentioned much to her for the fear of being rejected. His feelings for her seemed to be reflected as she made every excuse to see him each day if only for a few minutes to enjoy a cup of coffee together. She never brought up her plans for the future either, they were content to be together whenever they were able and neither of them wanted to 'burst the bubble' by being to presumptive. Everything at the mill was fine and Barty's relationship with Sarah's parents became closer. They had on several occasions asked

Barty to use their Christian names but being quite respectful he still insisted in calling them Mr and Mrs Spalding.

Whenever the opportunity arose Skipper would visit the boat to tend to some of the smaller details of the refit and to cast his experienced eye over the general work being carried out and what he saw, he liked.

The mail started to increase as a result of Skipper's visits to town and the diary started to slowly fill with carrying contracts. *Ellie May* should be completed for trials in a week or so and if successful, work would start in earnest. As much as Barty revelled in Sarah's company he was looking forward to getting back on the water.

Early March and the *Ellie May* was handed back to her owners looking immaculate in her new coat of paint all her deck gear looking fresh and purposeful as she left the moorings one morning for her trials. Mr Spalding, Sarah, Skipper and Barty accompanied the chief fitter down river for the tests, everything was fine and the boat responded sharply to the helm and to the auxiliary engine.

That same evening Skipper and Barty vacated their temporary accommodation at Keeper's Cottage and returned to their cabin that seemed to be smaller than ever after living in a room each. Shuftee's comfortable quarters was again sited near the cabin hatch.

A consignment of milled grain was loaded the next morning and Barty felt a great surge of freedom as he took the vessel down river and out into the sea bound for Felixstowe.

Back at sea Barty felt so exhilarated by the conditions and being under sail again gave him time to think of the costs involved as *Ellie May* were in the hands of the fitters. He mentioned the subject to Skipper only to be told that everything was taken care of and he was not to worry. This was the first contract of the season for Mr Spalding and included a return trip to Aldeburgh with a load of timber for a building company. Skipper assured him that all costs for paying for the refit was settled. It seemed obvious that Skipper and Mr Spalding had an agreed arrangement.

The trip to Felixstowe / Aldeburgh and back to the Tide Mill proved to be free of any problems, *Ellie May* behaved perfectly and handled like a new craft over the week they were away. The weather had been very kind and Barty managed to get back into his books with a renewed vigour. Once the boat was secured at its moorings Barty went up to the house to see Sarah who was busy in the mill grinding room. He arranged to see her later after he had attended a meeting at the house with Mr Spalding and others he recognised before the near encounter with the Revenue men. It was only a short meeting and plans were laid for another run very similar to the previous venture and the landing was set to be at Ted Moore's farm, under the Easton Cliffs. This run was scheduled for the first week in April. Barty presumed that he had been included in the plans as he was due to become a partner in the boat in April so he would then share half the responsibility. The responsibilities of part owner ship were many and varied but having thought them through carefully he was ready to play his part, he had no reservations as he knew and trusted Skipper unquestionably.

Barty and Sarah spent the rest of the evening together discussing the forthcoming trip to Stowmarket and what duties he would be expected to carry out for Ted.

As he was leaving the house, Mr Spalding handed him a letter that had arrived during the week he had been away, it was from Mr Smalley, solicitor, of Woodbridge, asking him to attend his office in Woodbridge on the 20th April for the purpose of transferring his part share of the *Ellie May* into his ownership, there were several papers that needed his signature. It was obvious that Skipper had been attending to his part of the bargain but couldn't understand where Mr Smalley had become involved, he understood that a Mr Gold was Skipper's solicitor. He had met Mr Gold at one of the meetings at the Tide Mill and it was only earlier that same evening he had been in his presence at the Mill. He intended to have a word with Skipper next morning as it was getting rather late and he had to get back to the boat.

On rising the next morning, he found that Skipper had beat him to it, he had left a note on the table, "Gone to town, business calls, Skip"

It was late afternoon when he returned and didn't give any clue as to the type of business he had been attending he just informed Barty that they would be leaving tomorrow evening at 5pm. This was the result from the meeting at the Tide Mill the day before so with things to be attended to he decided not to say anything to Skipper until the trip had been completed.

    A thrill of anticipation surged through him as he took the tiller on the evening tide down river, he knew he was soon to be involved in an illegal act. The risk seemed so minimal and he didn't approve of what he was about to do but he had inadvertently become involved and he now was aware that the proceeds were quite considerable. He had a healthy bank balance, a stable way of making a living and the chance to learn a new skill with his navigational studies provided he was able to sit the appropriate examinations.

    Down the Deben and out into the open sea, the plan was exactly as before, the rendezvous point was also the same but the visibility was considerably better this trip so an extremely sharp watch had to be kept for patrolling Revenue cutters from France and England. Ted Moore was on board as usual and alert as ever, the moon was brighter than expected and it was quite warm for an April night. *L'Etoile* was easily spotted and the transfer was swiftly completed and *Ellie May* was soon headed back towards the Easton Cliffs. Ted kept a concentrated watch on the cliffs as they neared the coast, he saw a single flash telling him that the coast was clear. The crop was landed without interruption and *Ellie May* was safely back at the Tide Mill by 8am. A perfect run had been completed.

After brief sleep the pair took lunch together and the opportunity for Barty to ask a few questions of Skipper.

"Who is the solicitor Smalley and why is he writing to me about our pending partnership"

Barty was under the impression that Skipper's personal affairs were dealt with by Mr John Salmon, a partner in the firm of Salmon & Gold, also solicitors in Woodbridge and Mr Edward Gold represented the firm as a member of the group of freetrade members that met at the Tide Mill. Mr Salmon never attended the meetings and Mr Gold always appeared slightly mysterious and hardly ever offered any input at the meetings. Skipper explained that he had been happy with the composition of the freetrade representatives but he had smelt a rat when, after a couple of runs had been planned, the Revenue men had been alerted. There was no evidence pointing to who the informant was but Skipper had noted that Mr Gold appeared to lack interest and he was never present to lend a hand at the landings. Having no trust in Mr Gold Skipper had engaged Joseph Smalley to act for Barty as his personal solicitor in the carrying business adding that if Barty wasn't satisfied he could always change. Barty said he was happy with the arrangements that Skipper had made. Skipper realised that Mr Gold would have access to all his private business papers he was shrewd enough to restrict his dealing with Salmon & Gold to business only insisting that Mr Salmon dealt solely with his affairs. Skipper had no trust in Edward Gold whatsoever. Skipper's explanation had satisfied Barty's question and he would respond to Mr Smalley's letter when the time came.

On the 20th April Barty visited the office of Joseph Smalley as requested. After the due formalities, he produced a sheaf of papers and began to explain the basics of the new partnership, which Skipper had explained to Barty before, carefully acquainting him with all the terms and conditions Barty found it difficult to follow but accepted that these things had to be completed before the partnership was sealed.

Put into a nutshell, Barty would inherit 50% of the *Ellie May* together with a 50% share in the profits and costs of any contracts in the name of Donald McLean (Skipper) and his own name. Furthermore, he would be responsible for 50% of the maintenance costs of the *Ellie May* and any agreed business purchases over £100. He would no longer receive a wage as that would be taken into account through the company trading accounts of a qualified person. Having listened to all the information and asked a few relevant questions he agreed to return to Mr Smalley's office together with Skipper, in two days' time to sign all the necessary papers.

With his head swimming, he slowly made his way back to the Tide Mill. There were so many things he ought to have asked but had neglected to do so mainly because all this was new to him. He had never owned anything of any value before. He realised that he had become part owner at the start of the financial year but that hadn't entailed any paperwork until now. He would speak with Skipper as he trusted him implicitly, he had been like a father to him since they first met, gave him a home and many other things and Barty had never mentioned any of their business, on or off the boat to any other person including the members of the 'fraternity' so Skipper recognised the respect that Barty had for him.

Skipper answered all his questions honestly and those he couldn't explain he would refer to Mr Smalley at the next meeting. Skipper assured him that all the arrangements had been made well in advance for the benefit of both Barty and himself, he didn't want to see his beloved *Ellie May* sold off to just anyone as he had put many years of his life building his business of which he was justly proud.

Much of this hadn't been mentioned to Sarah, especially the latter developments with Mr Smalley that were still ongoing but she was aware that Barty had become part owner since the beginning of the month. She knew of the legitimate business of the boat but nothing of the 'extra work' occasionally undertaken by the 'fraternity'.

That evening he brought her up to date about the meeting with Mr Smalley and she appeared to be extremely happy. He also told her that, should the opportunity arise he would like to sit his Master's Certificate (Inshore) examination in order that he could deputise for Skipper should circumstance ever demand it.

Two days later, Skipper and Barty entered the office of Mr Smalley and signed the relevant papers making Barty officially the co-owner of the wherry *Ellie May* together with the associated company.

A week later Ted Moore came to the Tide Mill to take Barty and Sarah off to the Stowmarket Show. Barty was surprised to see a motor lorry towing a living van and to be told that two further transports had gone direct to the showground, one trailer containing two Suffolk Punch horses. In all the excitement of the previous week they had almost forgotten about the Show but welcomed the chance for a change for a couple of days.

The journey to Stowmarket was uneventful and they soon found the advance party in their allocated position and the grooms looking after the horses in their temporary stables. Sarah and Barty made a hurried tour of the site to familiarise themselves with the layout, the day was still fairly young and many of the attractions were still being assembled and put into their positions.

The preliminary showing of the heavy horses was to be held as the first event the next morning so they spent the remainder of the evening checking over all the equipment and talking with fellow competitors. The grooming began very early, the leathers were waxed and the brasses shone like gold in the morning sun added to which were the colourful ribbons giving the horses a real picture book appearance.

There were three main judges allocated to each of the horse sections. It didn't take long to examine the Suffolks as there were only a dozen competitors entered. The verdict was given within the hour and Mr Ted Moore's entry was forwarded to the finals at 3pm that same afternoon. Barty was so proud as he stood at Ted's side when the announcement was made whilst Sarah and the grooms clapped and cheered enthusiastically from the ringside.

The horses were led away to be unharnessed and fed and rested for a short period. Barty and the crew took a snack meal then began re-polishing all the tack ready for the final showing at 3pm. Several entrants were to compete in the ploughing match to follow but Ted's horses were for the 'Best in Show' category of Suffolk Punch breed.

As the preparations progressed, Barty had his first opportunity to stand back and really "see" the horses. He had seen them before at the farm at the stables but to see them dressed was like seeing them in a different light resplendent in the highly-polished tack and groomed to perfection took his breath away. The Suffolks were smaller than the Clydesdales that he had previously showed but more muscular, some 16 – 17 hands (65 – 70") in height and weighed between 1980 and 2200 lbs, always chestnut coloured, a truly magnificent breed, in fact the oldest English breed of draught horse. With never a moment wasted, the hands of the clock moved swiftly to 2.45pm, time to take up position in the ring. Barty leading his two Suffolks on a loose rein, proudly into the enclosure, Barty stood to the head while Ted nearby just to the rear of his team as the Judges approached. Barty lead the horses one lap of the ring and then presented them before the Judges, different Judges to those of the morning session. They began with so few questions that Barty was surprised but it soon was obvious that their main interest was in the overall appearance and apparent health of the animals. The Judges spent quite a time examining the horses and making copious notes before visiting the next entries leaving them with the solitary remark, "Well done!"

An announcement was made that the complete Show results and awards would be made at 5pm, except for the ploughing match results which wouldn't be completed until the following day. The team felt quite confident as they took their charges back to the temporary stables and turned them loose in the nearby enclosure to graze. Just before 5pm the teams were again brought into the ring still in their dressed state, where the various classes would be given and the winning teams paraded around the ring.

"Ladies and Gentlemen, it is results time at the Stowmarket Agricultural Show" The announcements for the various classes were made and the final, "The final section is the Suffolk Draught Horse Presentation competition. First prize is awarded to Mr George Boswell of Down Valley Farm, Hadleigh, Suffolk. Second place goes to Mr Edward Moore of Eaton Farm, Reydon, Suffolk"

On hearing this announcement our team didn't listen any further, they were delighted. The rosette was appended to the harness and the team took its congratulatory lap of the ring. Ted congratulated Barty saying that second prize was the best he had ever done before and he said that he expected a first at the next Show! High hopes! Needless to say, Sarah was also delighted that the day had turned out so good and that she hoped to be present at the next Show when they win a First!

As they were still celebrating their win Barty felt a tap on his shoulder, turning sharply he recognised the winner of the First Prize team leader who had come over to offer his congratulations. There appeared to be some further recognition as they turned to face each other. The rather tall, fair headed, bearded young man before him held out his hand and said, "Well done Barty, I didn't expect to see you here, how are you doing, do you remember me?" For a few moments Barty was taken aback and the man could see he was struggling to recall where they had previously met. "France" said the young man "Veterinary Corps" that's it! his memory suddenly raced back a few years and he managed to blurt out "Tom, Tom Black" The man grinned and confirmed the recognition.

"Blimey" Barty said, "it's been a few years and I didn't recognise you under that face fungus". They fondly greeted each other, each quickly remembering the time they had spent together in the hell holes of France and Belgium serving with the Auxiliary Voluntary Corps. Their love of horses had led them both into the world of farming where they were able to pursue their common interest Tom was now employed at Down Valley Farm in Hadleigh, not so very far from Woodbridge. He told Tom of his past employment at Mill Hall Farm on the Isle of Dogs, of his present employment with Skipper and the good fortune that had befallen him. Tom had been working at Down Valley Farm since his demob. from the Army. There wasn't much time to talk as the wagons were loaded and ready to move off site. They exchanged addresses and promised to keep in touch with each other,

Skipper was just squaring off a load of flour for transit to Aldeburgh as Barty arrived back on board. He told Skipper of the success at Stowmarket and of his meeting with Tom Black. At 8am next morning

Ellie May had slipped her mooring to take advantage of the ebbing tide to make a swift journey down river. Barty took the tiller and watched as Skipper secured some deck gear prior to making the open sea. He appeared tired and slow in his movements but that may be the result of loading the cargo into the hold the day before. During the whole voyage to Aldeburgh he sat quietly near the tiller but didn't offer any conversation which was most unusual for him. Barty asked several times if he was okay, he insisted he was but he obviously had something on his mind. An overnight stay saw *Ellie May* unloaded and a new cargo od weatherboards taken on board. They left the River Alde next morning, the return journey being a carbon copy of the outgoing one. Skipper was still very quiet but keeping an eye on the weather, the boat's performance and Barty who felt quite confident in his own ability to handle the boat in almost all conditions. It wasn't that Skipper didn't trust in his ability, it was a habit for him to watch everything happening on deck, a habit that was hard to break but something was on his mind and Barty had no idea of what it could be. Throughout the whole trip Barty had performed to perfection and never left the cockpit, the only time Skipper moved was to change to auxiliary engine or make a drink.

They entered the mooring late afternoon and Barty had time to visit Sarah as they would not be unloading until tomorrow.

During his absence, Ted Moore had visited the Tide Mill and left an envelope with Sarah's father to be handed to Barty on his return. The envelope contained £25.00 being his share of the prize money from the Stowmarket Show. He was very surprised as he had expected nothing more than the lift down to the Show and to help with the preparations Accompanying the cash was a card inviting him to take part in other forthcoming Shows, work commitments permitting. Ted had been greatly impressed by the way Barty had handled the horses, how he had dressed them and how he so confidently replied to the Judges enquiries about the care and wellbeing of the animals

When later he was speaking with Mr Spalding he learned that while he and Sarah had been away to Stowmarket for the two days, Skipper had occasion to consult a doctor in Woodbridge. He had asked his old friend Arthur Spalding not to mention the visit to Barty but he thought that Skipper was holding something back and he felt that Barty should be aware of Skipper's condition. Skipper hadn't divulged what the trouble was and when quizzed he just replied "I'm. alright, just getting older!" Mr Spalding asked Barty to keep a good eye on Skipper and to let him know of anything untoward that may appear to affect Skippers capabilities.

The next two weeks were pretty routine, carrying jobs around the coast and only one run to land a crop at Easton Cliffs which went without a hitch. The run took place after a meeting at the Tide Mill when the 'gentlemen' finalised the details of the usual landing place. It was after that meeting, when everyone had gone that Mr Spalding, Skipper, Ted Moore and Barty held a mini-meeting. The four had previously discussed the facts about the informer in their midst. They reached a conclusion that it was probably one of the members and each had their own suspicions about who that informer could be. A lengthy discussion then took place culminating with three of the four participants pointing a finger towards the same person. A further decision was made to change the landing place from Easton Cliffs to the lonely deserted jetty at Dunwich, a site they had previously safely used. The suspect was not to be informed of the change. *Ellie May*, as usual would be manned by Skipper, Ted Moore and Barty and only one other man would be used as a Watchman and would be present on the Easton Cliffs, not at Dunwich. The transport group would be trusted men known only to Ted, none of the team of transport men or the Watchmen were members of the 'inner' committee so they could all be ruled out as the informer. The plans were complicated and several members of the Committee were not required to attend this particular run in any way.

On the night, the transfer of goods went ahead as planned and in the early hours of a clear morning, *Ellie May* was steering toward the landing place at Dunwich. Ted quickly spotted a flash of light from the shore, 'the coast was clear' for the landing which was affected without problem. Meantime, on the Easton Cliffs, the Revenue men supported by mounted soldiers from the local militia waited patiently for signs of a vessel moving along the coastline. Their patience was disappointing and they dispersed soon after dawn.

This incident served to prove that information had been passed to the authorities, but by whom? No one that had taken an active part in the real landing was no longer a suspect, so a further enquiry by the Committee was planned. That wouldn't be for a week or so as *Ellie May* had her legal carrying business to attend.

Late April, Skipper and Barty were recalled to the office of Skipper's solicitor, Mr Salmon in Woodbridge. They duly attended and signed the final agreements creating the new partnership, witnessed by Arthur Spalding and with his agreement and named "Tide Mill Carriers" Celebrations were made at a local pub. It was a momentous day for Barty, now a businessman in his own right and a rosy future ahead of him.

A fortnight after the Stowmarket Show a letter was received from Tom Black that was mainly reminiscent of the time they had spent together in the Army and Tom's life since leaving. He had kicked around for quite a time trying various jobs but finding nothing suitable until he was offered a labouring job at Down Valley Farm in Hadleigh, close to where he had been born. Tom asked if it would be possible for them to meet up again sometime in the near future. Barty's reply would have to wait as he would be leaving the Tide Mill moorings that very morning with a cargo of milled flour for Felixstowe.

It was a drizzly wet morning when they left to start the journey down river. The fine rain was soaking everything and the freshening breeze was causing rippled waves as they cautiously neared the mouth of the Deben.

The weather was uncomfortable and they stayed as close inshore as possible to try to avoid the roughening seas. A little late in their arrival they made fast alongside to await unloading next morning and to embark a load of building materials for Aldeburgh. This contract was the first which Barty felt he had a real interest due to his partnership was really appreciated. Skipper had always accepted any bookings and informed him of the commitments, this time he was consulted about the contract and agreement reached before accepting,

The hiring of *Ellie May* and her crew was becoming less frequent so any working contract was welcome. The development of the railways appears to have drawn away much of the inland waterways carrying trade as access spread from town to town. Luckily many of the mills and watermills were situated well up river from the nearest ports not yet linked by rail and the flat-bottomed boats of Norfolk and Suffolk were capable of reaching these customers just as easily as they had always done. It was generally felt that the river trade would survive for a number of years yet. Barty wondered if this was worrying Skipper who may possible foresee his livelihood dwindling but it wasn't so with his optimistic young partner who would adapt to any changes that the future might hold, He thought about this as they were on route to Aldeburgh and then home to the Tide Mill. Barty always considered the Tide Mill as home, it was a place of security and friends, a place he felt that he could always return to should he ever be in need of help and advice. Secure in his own mind he had even considered asking Sarah if she would consider becoming engaged to him when the time was right. He had even secretly broached the subject to Skipper who couldn't have been happier but advised him to "give it time lad, give it a few months for things to settle down, don't go rushing into things, it's early days yet" Barty understood the wisdom in Skipper's advice and accepted it without question.

A meeting of the "Gentlemen" was to be held the Tide Mill. Skipper. Barty, Mr Spading and Ted Moore all resolved to pay sharp attention to the suggestions of the other members and to note their individual reactions. Apart from the so called' inner circle'. (Skipper, Mr Spalding, Barty and Ted); the Committee consisted of the Reverend Nathan Young – who occasionally provided space at the church for the temporary stowage of goods, the local publican, Mr Bill Oscroft, who performed a similar task, Mr James Gold, solicitor and general organiser, Mr David Pickford, a local haulier and Mr Raymond Butterworth, a local grocer. All these men stood to benefit from the activities and showed an interest in all aspects of the organisation. With the exception of the 'inner circle' any of the other six members could be their suspect informant. Odd occasions arose when one or two of the gentlemen were unable to assist at a run but all consented to give whatever help might be required. The meeting was acquainted with the details of the next run but due to the near miss on the last run with the Revenue men it was decided that a new landing location would be chosen and the Committee informed in due course.

The 'inner circle' made all the arrangements and alerted all the members who would be involved apart from two, the main suspects of being the informant. The two suspects were told that the location was to be a secluded beach to the south of Walberswick known as the Corporation Marshes. In fact, the real landing was to take place at the Easton Cliffs as usual and all the usual precautions would be observed. Of the two men who were given the wrong information, one was not usually involved in the landing but would normally give financial advice after the landing, the other due to medical advice on a strained back, took no part at all.

The meeting with *L'Etoile* was straight forward but with a larger than normal crop of gin, brandy, tobacco and lace. The transaction went extremely well and after the formalities were completed *Ellie May* sailed swiftly on a favourable course towards the landing place at Easton Cliffs. The coast clear signal was spotted by Ted and the *Ellie May* grounded just off the narrow beach under the cliffs to be met by a team of helpers who cleared away all the evidence in record time.

Meanwhile on the beach at Corporation Marshes and the surrounding area, a group of Revenue Men and Militia waited once again for activity that never happened. *Ellie May* was safely back at her mooring by midday.

It was always a good month after a run and the financial settlements had been made and Barty was amazed to receive a handsome cash payment. As a crew member, he had previously been paid varying sums between £30 to £50. Dependent upon the disposal rate. Today he received £150 that included a sum for boat hire, crewing fee and a share of the disposal of the crop. All the expenses had always been borne by Skipper but now a partner 50% of the cost fell to Barty. He was still pleased with the nights' work and the ultimate reward.

Having good reason to visit the Bank, he and Sarah made the now familiar trip to Woodbridge and having deposited his gains they went into the café. It wasn't very busy so, after much thought Barty decided to 'bite the bullet' by asking Sarah if she would consent to be his wife. Somewhat taken aback she hesitated at his proposal, Barty's heart began to sink as she stared into his eyes but said nothing. It wasn't that she had misunderstood his question, more the shock of the unexpected that made her hesitate, the proposal had come out of the blue without any reference and it took her a few moments to comprehend the seriousness of it. Finally, after the initial surprise, she smiled and accepted the proposal. They talked for a while and Sarah asked that they should hold the official announcement for a while as she wished to speak with her father on the matter. She asked Barty to do the proper thing and seek her father's permission, to which he agreed. Before leaving Woodbridge that afternoon Barty took her to the jeweller's shop to choose and engagement ring. He didn't give the ring to her then but they agreed to wait until Sarah's parents had been consulted and the necessary blessings given

Bursting with excitement they talked endlessly on the way home and found her parents relaxing in the lounge. Although they had agreed not to say anything until and appropriate time, their excitement couldn't be hidden and with words tumbling from her mouth Sarah managed to convey her news to them in a fairly coherent manner. Barty stood awkwardly by the door not saying a word. Suddenly, realising his silence he interrupted her flow of explanations by addressing her father and asked for his approval on their pending engagement. As one, her parents rose from their chairs to congratulate the couple, Arthur giving his approval and a warm handshake to Barty while her mother gave him a hug and said that she was not at all surprised after noticing their fondness for each other over the past weeks. They had both grown fond of Barty and to welcome him as a son-in-law would make them very happy They talked long and late that evening and even started to plan an Engagement Party for a couple of weeks hence. The fact that Barty had already bought the ring wasn't mentioned as they didn't want to appear to presumptuous, that could wait until the official date,

During the next two weeks *Ellie May* made some short river trips and Barty had the chance to answer Tom's letter. His days seemed to have filled up more than usual what with working the boat with Skipper, seeing Sarah whenever possible and trying to find time to study but he felt that his life was being fully fulfilled and welcomed each day whatever it held in store for him. He had so much to tell Tom that he thought an early meeting might be preferable and suggested that next week they could perhaps meet in Hadleigh. By return of post Tom agreed and gave a time and place with an offer for Barty to stay overnight at the farmhouse at Down Valley Farm.

Barty took the railway to Ipswich then a bus to the village of Bramford, just off the main trunk road where he was met by Tom who walked him the short distance to Down Valley Farm. Tom had planned an evening out in Hadleigh so after some refreshment at the farm they went into the old medieval town. They didn't get to see much of the town as time passed so quickly. After a dinner at 'The Rose' public house they settled down to enjoy a couple of pints and a long-time reminiscing, it seemed only minutes before the landlord was ringing the bell for last orders, but they did manage to tell each other of their plans. Tom, it seems hadn't really planned anything, he was happy working on the farm.

He had kicked around doing various jobs but had found it hard to settle after leaving the Army. He had been in his present employment for about 18 months where he enjoyed working with the animals and the freedom to work by himself without a foreman or such continually telling him what to do. He knew about animals, particularly horses, he had learned a lot in the Veterinary Corps and took advantage of that, His boss was satisfied with his labours so Tom felt life was being pretty fair with him. Barty told him of his life, how good things had gone for him and particularly of his recent engagement. He even took the liberty of inviting him to attend his Engagement Party the following week. If push came to shove, Tom could even sleep on the *Ellie May* if necessary, after all they had slept in far worse places in the Army and Barty wouldn't be there on the night. Hearing what Barty had told him of his life, Barty sensed an air envy in Tom. Truthfully, he had suffered a hard life growing up as a young boy and whilst in the Army but since meeting Skipper and being offered a lift to Lowestoft by boat his life had changed so much for the better. He could understand why he thought Tom was envious although he hadn't said so, they had enjoyed each other's company in the short time they had spent together and returned to Down Valley Farm where Tom had reserved a spare room in the bunkhouse for him.

A good hearty farmhouse breakfast inside him Barty felt that he could tackle anything, he said his goodbyes and started on his journey back to Woodbridge promising to see Tom again at the Engagement Party. At the mooring, he hailed the *Ellie May* but on receiving no reply, except from Shuftee, he went straight to the cabin to find Skipper in his bunk, fast asleep. He quietly changed his clothes and stowed his gear before Skipper stirred. He was croaky in his speech as he explained that he felt very tired and thought he had a touch of flu. Barty made him some hot soup of which he only drank a little before lapsing back into a disturbed sleep. He slept through the night and got up just after Barty, had a light breakfast of tea and toast before attempting to get dressed. He appeared to be a little better although he said he still felt tired. He dressed then sat back asking of Barty's visit with Tom. It was almost midday when Barty went out on deck to feed Shuftee when he noticed that the boot topping and the hatch coaming had been freshly painted. He immediately understood why Skipper was feeling so tired, he had obviously overdone it, working when he had been warned to slow down. Returning to the cabin to clean up he noticed that Skipper hadn't eaten either. On being confronted with the facts Skipper replied, "I'm alright, stop fussing lad, it's just one of those things" Barty threatened that he would send for a doctor if he wasn't feeling any better by tomorrow. He stayed on board all that day to look after Skipper and to try and tempt him to eat something. He was longing to go up to the house to see Sarah, he had quite a lot to tell her and they had a lot to plan for their future together.

Skipper slept while Barty was studying his books when Shuftee barked and there was a knock on the cabin door and Sarah came in, Barty was so pleased to see her and Skipper dozed on undisturbed, not responding to Sarah's greeting. Barty apologised for not coming to the house and explained how he had found Skipper last evening on his return from visiting Tom. He made a pot of tea while telling her of his visit to Hadleigh, of Toms life and the invite to attend the Party. Sarah readily agreed saying that that he should have some of his old friend's present making him realise that he had no old friends except his recently found old Army mate and Skipper. It was dark when Sarah made her way back to the house, even too dark for Barty to do any small jobs on deck so he turned his attentions to two unopened letters that lay on the table both addressed to 'Tide Mill Carriers' and had been delivered to the house both letters were requests for the hire of the *Ellie May* for contract work on the East coast. Barty checked with his diary to find that both dates were convenient but wouldn't reply until Skipper was able to agree the contracts. He tidied the cabin, made some supper then turned in, Skipper was still sleeping but his breathing was a little more even and he seemed to be better settled than he had over the past few hours.

Skipper was up early the next morning and was reading the two letters when Barty awoke and joined him for a light breakfast, he said he felt much better but was going to take things slowly and asked Barty to respond to the letters confirming their availability on the proposed dates. He carefully replied to the letters in a business-like manner and gave the paperwork to Skipper for approval, and just for fun, remarking that they could do with a good secretary. Barty took the letters up to the house to await collection by the postman and took the opportunity to stay with Sarah for a while as Skipper would be resting. He returned to the boat to find that Skipper appeared to be okay but still complained of feeling tired. He'd had a bowl of soup and was reading a newspaper, he was more like his old self and continued to improve each day but Barty noted that he still tired quickly and often took an afternoon nap when he had the chance. Barty found that he was shouldering more responsibility where business matters were concerned but that served to give him a better understanding of how the business was run. Skipper remarked upon it several times and said how much he appreciated Barty's efforts to keep everything on an even keel. Barty held no regrets about all his time being monopolised in this manner and was grateful for all that Skipper had done for him and for all the advice he gave whenever needed.

Sarah and her parents had been burning a lot of midnight oil planning and making arrangements for their only daughters Engagement Party, they wanted to make it a day that neither of them would ever forget. They hired the best caterers in Woodbridge, the flowers from a local florist while Sarah and her mother tended to the choice of the guests and the sending of the invitations that included many of the immediate family relatives, local business associates, the members of the Committee, with the exception of the grocer, Raymond Butterworth and Joseph Gold, the solicitor, both of whom had prior engagements! Barty's one and only guest was his old Army pal, Tom, who, not living locally would have a room at Keeper's Cottage. With all the arrangements taking longer than anticipated the date was finally set for the first Saturday in June, a week later than originally planned and the invitations were all sent out.

A large marquee was erected in the grounds of the mill and as the guests arrived they were formally greeted and introduced to their host and the rest of the family. Barty felt like a fish out of water, he wasn't used to formal affairs so he stuck closely to Sarah who seemed to be able to cope with everything. The party developed into a large affair, far larger than Barty and Sarah had known but they hadn't been involved in the number of invitations sent out. Any onlooker could see how proud Mr & Mrs Spalding were of their daughter and that was reflected in the party to which they had been invited. Sarah's mother, Rebecca, concerned herself with all the formalities giving Arthur the chance to move among the guests with Sarah and Barty introducing them to the family members and the many business associates that were unknown to the couple. A small band had been hired and played non-stop throughout the evening and into the small hours of the morning when Mr Spalding made the announcement that they had all come to celebrate asking them all to raise their glasses to the engaged couple, his daughter Sarah Elizabeth Spalding to Mr Kaleb Michael Bartholomew. The toast taken and the couple exchanged engagement rings before mingling freely with the guests receiving their congratulations and good wishes for the future, just before Mr Spalding had made the announcement he was handed a note from his wife with Barty's name on it. Nothing more. He had realised that he didn't know Bartys' full name, this was a reminder for Arthur. Barty had noticed that as he made the announcement a few eyebrows were raised as his name was given, nobody had ever known that his real name was Kaleb, they all knew him as Barty, even Sarah showed an element of surprise, she had always called him Barty since Skipper brought him to the mill and he was introduced to the "boy in the grinding room"!

Slowly the guests took their leave and as their numbers dwindled Tom came to speak with the happy couple and to wish them luck. He had spent much time talking with the mill complex workers and had thoroughly enjoyed their company, as a total stranger they had treated him as one of their own. During the celebrations Skipper had sat quietly in a large armchair many people coming to speak with him, but he seemed to want to left to his own thoughts. He was the last to leave and Barty walked him back to the *Ellie May* to make sure he was safely settled before he walked slowly back to Keeper's Cottage to stay there overnight. Tom had already turned in when he got back and Barty got up early in order to talk to Tom before he had to return the Hadleigh, they talked about last night's party and some of the guests but neglected to arrange a future meeting when they could relax more and speak of their own futures without the constant interruptions they had experienced the night before.

After Tom had gone, Barty went to the boat to see that Skipper was alright and found him pottering about doing a few small jobs on deck, he appeared quite lively as he moved about quite freely with Shuftee following his every movement. They had a coffee and talked about the party after which Skipper asked him if he would attend to some paperwork for the post. Barty tried to scan through some of the comments that Skipper had made but found difficulty in deciphering some of his handwriting that had deteriorated badly, instead of the usual neat entries, the comments looked as if a drunken spider had crawled across the pages. It was saddening to see, all his work had always been so neat and tidy, the entries in the boat's logbook was immaculate and so easy to decipher but it hadn't gone without notice that his writing was worsening. He spent a fair time making corrections and re-writing some comments before he was happy that Skipper's work was presentable and understandable. He had to ask a few questions of Skipper to clarify certain points and Skipper readily agreed that his bookkeeping now left much to be desired, he apologised and suggested that they engage a qualified secretary to take over the administrative work. Realising what taking on extra staff would mean Barty was reluctant to commit to the idea and would take over much of the work himself. He did however agree to discuss the idea later after seeking advice from another source so things were left as they were for the present and Barty would cope under Skipper's guidance.

Ellie May had a contract to fulfil the coming week so they both took their time completing the cleaning and preparing to make ready for the trip. Skipper had always emphasised the importance of keeping the boat in tip top condition, not only from the safety angle but also the renovations on the wherry which was all but finished and *Ellie May* was one of the oldest boats still serving. Many had been converted to the leisure industry on the broad waters and rivers of East Anglia. They were also used on the River Thames for pleasure and some had been converted for use as lighters and dumb barges. Traditionally a commercial wherry like *Ellie May* carried a single black sail, the mast being hinged at deck level, known as the tabernacle, to allow the mast and sail to be lowered when the vessel encountered the low bridges of the rivers and waterways. Skipper and Barty kept *Ellie May* looking sharp and Bristol fashion. It transpired that one of the Skipper's main worries was that Barty had no formal qualifications for navigation. To gain such a qualification the applicant must have completed 500 hours under sail with at least eight hours being during the night. True, Barty had more that satisfied these conditions but he hadn't a piece of paper stating the fact.

It came as a surprise when Barty received a small package from the County authority containing a training manual and a date to attend an examination in Ipswich in three weeks' time. He immediately showed the letter and manual to Skipper asking what all this was about. It was about the time when Skipper had been feeling unwell and mentioned it to no one, blaming old age. He realised that if anything should happen to him Barty would have to hire a qualified certificate holder to navigate the boat to keep the business hiring's on course. Skipper didn't want any Tom, Dick or Harry taking over from him and Barty certainly wouldn't welcome such an arrangement so Skipper had decided to apply for the examination on Barty's behalf. The only problem was that he had forgotten to mention it to Barty!

Barty understood his thinking and after a long and deep discussion they managed to clear up many of the problems that could arise.

Skipper could easily verify that Barty had more than completed the required hours from the boat's logbook and he was satisfied that Barty could answer any questions about boat handling, inshore navigation, safety and chart reading to eliminate the need to attend the two-day preparation course. But things didn't work that way. If Barty wanted to gain a certificate he would have to attend the course like any other applicant. He had thought of taking the course several times but he never got around to applying and he was in full agreement with the arrangements.

The discussion of hiring a qualified secretary was again brought up and Barty suggested that Sarah may be interested in taking on the task, she was a qualified administrator and bookkeeper and would find no problem in fitting in to the small trading partnership like the Tide Mill Carriers.

Quietly slipping one evening *Ellie May* made her way to a planned rendezvous with *L' Etoile.* The usual planning had taken place and Ted joined Skipper and Barty on board just prior to sailing. The transfer took place without a hitch but returning towards the Easton Cliffs saw the warning signal, "Coast NOT clear" With all lights extinguished the boat headed north and stood off just out of sight of the cliffs. It would appear that once again someone had given information to the Customs men. This was the third attempt to expose a landing to the Customs and Excise men. Another narrow escape, the situation was becoming dangerous and their luck would not last forever. Who was the mysterious informer?

Rigid observations were kept in case a Revenue Cutter had been deployed and the lull gave them time to discuss their suspicions. Apart from the three of them Arthur Spalding was the only other member who they totally trusted, so who had the most to gain from the membership?

Bill Oscroft had an interest in the liquor that was landed and also provided stowage when needed.

, Raymond Butterworth was pleased to receive any tea and other consumables, David Pickford had religiously supplied transport and had always been prompt and trustworthy. James Gold gave help and advice as needed but never attended a landing. The Reverend Nathan Young's involvement was minimal, giving temporary safe storage at the church for short periods. The trio talked quietly for a long period as they waited for the coast to clear and manged to cut the suspects down to three, James

Gold, Raymond Butterworth and the Reverend. Unable to agree to just one person, they would speak with Arthur Spalding for the purpose of setting a trap to ensnare the guilty party.

Ellie May returned to her mooring twelve hours later than planned having discharged their crop at Easton Cliffs during the early morning daylight hours – a most unusual happening!

It was the day after the trip that Barty was due to attend his examination in Ipswich at 9am. Skipper had taken this into account and had contacted his daughter to make arrangements for him to stay at her house. It was only a ten-minute walk from the house to the Town Hall and after a welcome breakfast he walked down the High Street towards the Town Hall. He was in good time and enjoyed the morning air looking in a few shop windows on his way, He had spent time the previous evening revising some of the finer points of navigation and felt reasonably confident as he entered, the double doors from the High Street. He was shown into a lounge area to join another six or seven men, presumably also candidates for the Basic Seamanship (Inshore) Certificate.

At 9am precisely they were led into a large hall where a dozen or so desks had been set up. The examination papers were distributed and they were given two hours to complete their efforts. Barty couldn't help but notice that most candidates appeared very young and there were three older men who had the air of the sea about them.

Following the examination, they were given one hour for refreshments and told to meet the Wherry Quay for the practical side of the test. They were taken out into a wide expanse of water inside the breakwater in a training wherry that wasn't unlike the *Ellie May*, perhaps a foot or two longer and Barty felt easy about the practical test. With six other candidates to be tested, the examiners could only allow approximately twenty minutes per man performing many manoeuvres and answering innumerable questions.

After everyone had been tested Barty was chosen to take the training wherry back to the quay and make it secure. The candidates were taken back to the hall to collect their gear and then dismissed with no comment other than "Thanks everybody, we'll write to you shortly"

The least he had expected was that each of the candidates would receive some form of criticism or otherwise on their performances. They didn't even get the chance to speak to each other as they were ushered through the door and into the High Street.

It was late when he got back to the boat and Skipper was asking him how he got on as soon as he set foot on the *Ellie May*. It was obvious that Skipper wanted him to do well. Barty told him that he had managed to answer all the questions on the written paper and was more than satisfied with the practical test although he had received no comments whatsoever. Skipper told him that he had every confidence in his abilities or he wouldn't have entered him in the first place. He felt that now Barty was a partner he should have at least the Basic Certificate of Competency and should look forward to taking his full "Skipper's Certificate" in the near future. They had talked of asking Sarah to become their administrator and he said he would mention it to her tomorrow. Before they took to their bunks Skipper brought him up to date with the work schedule as he had been away for almost four days, two on the last 'venture' and two on the course in Ipswich. There was so much to talk about that he felt he owed it to Sarah to spend much of the next day looking at their future and the possibility of her involvement with the Tide Mill Carriers.

It was a lovely sunny morning when he went up to the house to see Sarah. She was busy with her father as he dictated a letter for her to type up and put into the post. He soon made himself comfortable in an armchair at the front of the house where he could see the activities taking place on the quayside while waiting for Sarah to finish her work for her father.

His mind became occupied trying to think of a plan that could possibly reveal the identity of the 'member', who had, to his knowledge, informed upon them on at least three occasions in the past six months. His thoughts proved useless and he was relieved when Sarah emerged from the house and put a tray of coffee on the small table beside him.

"Penny for your thoughts" said Sarah, breaking his train of thought. "Oh, nothing" he replied," Just thinking about that course I've just been on". Sarah sat in the chair opposite him and was quickly immersed in conversation, so much to talk about after their four-day separation but finally he got around to asking her if she would be interested in helping him and Skipper on the administrative side of their business for a small consideration. Without faltering for a moment she consented to help and she wouldn't' want any consideration, she would be most happy to assist as it would make her feel nearer to Barty and his way of living.

Barty was extremely pleased as he knew Skipper would be but he still hadn't mentioned his extra, mainly nocturnal activities although he felt that she had an inkling that he was involved in something with Skipper.

After a very pleasant day with Sarah and dinner with the family he returned to the boat to find Skipper relaxing in the small cabin. On entering the cabin, he realised for the first time just how small it really was, the two of them were living in a space which was only meant for one person. On this type of vessel, the captain usually lived on shore while the mate lived on board and acted as security for the boat. Shuftee was their security and when he was in the cabin movement became almost impossible. He normally occupied his special quarters on deck near the hatchway being allowed in the cabin on special occasions or when the weather was most inclement.

Barty had the idea that he should hire a room in the big house to give Skipper more space and comfort. Having lived in the cabin for several months now, Barty was conscious of his growing possessions, his books, charts and clothing not that Skipper ever complained, he didn't. He didn't mention his idea to Skipper but rather waited until he had made enquiries to Mr Spalding.

He told Skipper of Sarah's acceptance to help and that she would operate from her father's office in the big house. Skipper was delighted, he could see his plans slowly coming to fruition, his plans for the partnership, the boat, the new company, everything was coming together. The house in Ipswich would belong to his daughter and her family and a wave of contentment swept across him knowing that all he had worked for would now be looked after. Everything was almost all in place so he decided to go the see John Salmon, his solicitor in the next few days.

During the next few days, Mr Spalding called a meeting of the 'inner circle' of the Gentlemen's Committee. Ted Moore, Mr Spalding, Skipper and Barty met and formulated a plan which would involve most of the members of the full Committee and the operation would be announced at a meeting of that full Committee at a time yet to be called.

In the meantime, *Ellie May* completed two routine carrying engagements returning to the Tide Mill each evening. The plans for the next 'venture' had been finalised and would involve every member of the Committee plus one or two other trusted men who were in fact, receivers.

The venture would prove to be expensive but if it revealed the identity of the informant it would be money well spent. Any new 'ventures' were to be postponed until their plans had been executed and hopefully the informer found.

The Committee of ten Gentlemen met at the Tide Mill one evening and the Chairman, Mr Spalding warned them of a long session. He told them that the next consignment would be much larger than normal and would consist of about 25 tons of goods. This would be an almost full capacity load for the *Ellie May* and the discharge would require all members to be available for the dispersal of the goods. Each member of the Committee would be required to lend a hand in the operation They were informed that the rendezvous would be about 4 miles off the coast and the landing would be near Bawdsey at the mouth of the River Deben. Due to the size and nature of the crop, *Ellie May* would be lower in the water and not able to beach so extra hands had been hired to transport the goods to shore and then moved by road to a safe stowage. Mr Spalding asked if anyone present would be unable to attend for their part. The only dissenter was Ben Oscroft the publican who had a function booked at his premises that evening. Every man was then detailed for their particular task. Skipper, Barty, Ted Moore and the Reverend would man the *Ellie May*. David Pickford, the haulier would arrange the extra wagons needed. James Gold was to hire two trustworthy motorised cutters from a hire boat business on the River Deben, one in his charge and the other manned by Raymond Butterworth, the grocer. The safe stowage's would be at the grocers' premises, at the local public house even though Ben Oscroft would not be taking part in the venture and at the church.

All aspects of the venture were now detailed and the Chairman asked if they had any questions. The only query was from Mr Gold and Mr Butterworth who enquired who would be manning the two cutters with them and the answer given as two tried and trusted men.

Most people living in the coastal areas had benefitted from the local freetrade in the past, today there was still a good market for the disposal of duty-free goods so the Committees were able to call together quite an army of trusted men at very short notice. A successful run was heavily dependent on the moon and the tides. The meeting was concluded every man knowing the part he would have to play in the operation. The subject of an informant wasn't raised and most thought they had experienced a run of bad luck when the Revenue men showed up at a landing but luck had been with them so far. The two main suspects were both concerned and would be at the centre of the transference from the boat to the shore with the hired cutters.

The mail was delivered to the Tide Mill as usual with one envelope clearly marked 'Personal' for the attention of Mr K M Bartholomew. Barty had a rough idea what the letter was about and with a slight tremble of his hands opened it to discover his Basic Certificate of Competency with a covering letter congratulating him on his success and informing him of an Advancement Course to be held in the County of Suffolk. He was interested in attending if he could afford to but there was no mention of the course fee at this stage. He made careful notes of the suggested materials and books that would be required and resolved that he would try and purchase them on his next visit to the bookshop if the price was acceptable. He was so happy to have passed the course in Ipswich and that made him more determined to try and attend the Advancement Course and could hardly wait to tell Skipper.

Ellie May left her moorings at Tide Mill and proceeded down river with only Skipper and Barty on board. Mr Spalding saw them leave and watched them until they disappeared from sight knowing that they would moor at the isolated jetty hidden from view just before the mouth of the river.

At the same time two men picked up the two hired motorised cutters from the leisure boat yard and met with two others about a half mile down the river, they were Joseph Gold and Raymond Butterworth. The operation they were about to carry out would involve the biggest import the Committee had ever made, not so much in quantity but in value so each man was highly conscious of the consequences of being apprehended. They each knew of the of the estimated time of the rendezvous with a French brig, not the *L'Etoile* and the landfall time was estimated accordingly.

A distance back from the landing place, a large number of men had gathered. They consisted of four Revenue Officers and a contingent of the local militia, some on horseback a force of twenty men in number. It was very clear that the informant had done his work again. All other members of the Committee were home that night except for the crew of the *Ellie May* who were hidden near the mouth of the river. The four men in the motorised cutters waited for others to join them at the pre-determined landing place.

As the estimated time of landing approached the four men secured their boats in the shallow waters and went on to the beach just as the Revenue men moved onto the beach but remained hidden, they had seen the four men come ashore. Time passed painfully slow but there was no sign of an incoming vessel. Well over an hour went past before the Officers decided that they had either been given false information or the landing had been aborted for some reason. They had waited long enough. This had been reported as a big event and was costing the Preventive Service quite a sum of money so they moved in quickly and apprehended the four men on the beach. The cutters were searched and found that they contained absolutely nothing.

Next morning, the *Ellie May* left the hidden jetty and proceeded to Felixstowe to pick up a delivery of provisions for Woodbridge. They wouldn't know the result of the trap until they get back to the Tide Mill. The same evening Mr Spalding called a meeting of the Committee, only three men were absent. Missing were Ted Moore who found the travel distance from Easton Farm to far plus two others of whom there was no news. at such a short notice. Of the two missing men, Mr Spalding had ascertained that both had been arrested at Bawdsey and were now detained at Felixstowe Police Station awaiting interrogation on suspicion of being involved in the illegal transportation of imported goods even though nothing had been found. They could offer no plausible excuse for their presence with the boats during the hours of darkness. No other members of the Committee had been involved in any way as they were either at home or about their own legal businesses. They all had been secretly alerted to the plan with the exception of the suspects. All agreed that the elaborate trap had gone according to plan but of the two detained members they still had no idea which one was guilty. After the Police interrogation, all four men were released on bail, two of them being respectable business men in Woodbridge.

The two men hadn't had any time to formulate an excuse and Joseph Gold said they were on their way to pick up a fishing party that afternoon but one the cutters had developed engine trouble so they had to put into the beach hoping to find assistance but the beach was so isolated that they were unable to summon any help at all.

Raymond Butterworth went along with the same story but not having any time for collusion, the details of their story had many conflicting points. The biggest problem for the Excise men was that they had found no evidence that could have remotely connected them with the actions of landing illicit goods. The real informant would feel safe in the knowledge that something was afoot and it wasn't the first time he had given information and got away with it. But which of the two men was the guilty party. A man of the law or a respectable married local grocer?

As for the two hired men, they were a couple of out of work fishermen, known to the Committee and willing to receive a sizeable consideration for their services knowing the risks they would be taking. They pleaded total ignorance saying they were not told of the purpose. They had been hired, reason unknown but denied involvement with illegal matters. They were discharged after their homes had been searched but no evidence had been gained.

Whilst in Woodbridge, Skipper visited his solicitor John Salmon requesting that he draw up a Will for his signature and acquainting him with the inclusions to be made. He then went to meet Barty for lunch and to buy provisions for the boat. Barty called at the bookshop in search of the books that were suggested by the letter he had received regarding the Advancement Course. He managed to buy two of the books but had to order three others from Lowestoft College that would take approximately a week to arrive.

The qualification he now held was sufficient for him to carry on with his present employment and not rely on Skipper. He had his eye on the future and would like to try and gain the Coastal Skipper's Certificate that would allow him to work on commercial craft of a greater length and an endorsement for operating up to 20 miles from a safe haven – sail or motor. That could take him across the Channel. He already possessed the required experience of 15 days, 2 days as skipper, at least 300 miles and eight night hours. Barty thought that the requirements were perfectly acceptable as he had already completed the majority of them but there would also be a few further subjects to tackle, none of which held any problem for him.

The Course would also include passage planning, day and night pilotage in restricted waters and safety and emergency situations. The minimum duration of the Course would be five days. On reading all this, he decided to write to the Course provider informing them of his qualification and current employment under the guidance of a fully qualified deep sea captain, enquiring if the Course could be undertaken as a distant learning course and attending the practical examinations if necessary. He didn't want to miss time working on the boat and he was loathed to leave Skipper on his own as his physical abilities did not seem to be improving.

The day in Woodbridge had made Skipper very tired, they had done a lot of walking trying to visit many of the businesses connections with the Company.

Back on board Barty made a light snack before going up to the big house to see Sarah, leaving Skipper in the care of Shuftee and to relax with his newspaper.

They hadn't seen much of each other over the past week so Sarah and Barty had much to talk about. The subject of Sarah taking on the administrative duties of the Tide Mill Carriers was being discussed when Mr Spalding entered the room and joined the conversation. He wasn't at all surprised by the development and soon offered good advice to the couple. Barty thought that this could be the golden moment to ask Sarah's father if he would consider renting a room in the big house to him so in order to give more space on the *Ellie May* to Skipper. Mr Spalding said there was plenty of room at the house but he had been thinking about another arrangement It was as if he had been a mind reader and had given their working situation some thought as he told them of his idea.

Sarah already attended to much of the administration of the day to day running of the mill complex and could do with an office of her own.

Currently she was using a small room at the house so her father's suggestion would kill two birds with one stone.

He outlined his plan to them; Sarah should use a ground floor room at Keeper's Cottage and Barty could occupy an upstairs bedroom for himself together with the use of the rest of the Cottage. The only restriction would be that, if a visitor such as Ted Moore required overnight accommodation, as he occasionally did, one bedroom at the Cottage would remain vacant for such use. This was great news for Barty but he knew that Skipper may not approve as he would be loathed to leave his beloved boat. The question of rent was settled, Barty would be charged only a 'peppercorn rent' as Keeper's Cottage was included as part of the Tide Mill business complex and with Sarah to occupy part of the Cottage for business purposes all the terms of letting and occupancy were legally observed. Barty would still take most his meals with Skipper while they were alongside as he felt he could keep a better eye on him without appearing to be over-protective. Apart from that aspect Barty would feel happier if he could still take advantage of Skipper's advice at the drop of a hat, he realised he still had so much to learn both in business and socially. They really had become true partners in every way, a friendship of great trust and dependence and Barty couldn't wait to tell Skipper of the developments in the administrative field and more so in the living arrangements. It was very late when Barty went back to the *Ellie May*, he called softly to Shuftee to prevent him barking as he thought that Skipper would be asleep. He was. All the good news would have to wait until morning. Trying to undress and stow his gear in the dark, in a very limited space, made him wonder why he hadn't thought of renting extra space before now. Over the months, Skipper must have been frustrated several times with the lack of space in the cabin.

The following morning Barty acquainted Skipper with the conversation of the previous evening and when Skipper learnt that he was able to sleep at Keeper's Cottage each night he readily agreed to vacate and give more space in the overcrowded cabin.

After the arrest of Joseph Gold and Raymond Butterworth, the newspapers widely reported the story, as was the way with newspapers they tended to exaggerate the facts and inferred that a quantity of illicit goods had been confiscated from the beach where the two men were apprehended. This was of course, untrue and the men were given bail as no evidence had been found and the story giving their reason for being on the beach were quite plausible but again untrue and not wholly believed by the investigating officers.

On the same day as they were given bail Custom Officers searched their business and residential premises. At Raymond Butterworth's grocer' shop and the living quarters above they found just three chests of imported tea on which no duty had been paid.

At the home of Joseph Gold, they found nothing incriminating but in the cellar of his office in town they recovered a quantity of brandy and tobacco. Neither man being able to give an explanation of how the goods came into their possession or produce receipts for the goods they were confiscated and later charged with receiving and possession of illicit goods.

They were both supposedly respectable business men; their bail was extended to appear in Court the following month.
Many of the townsfolk of Woodbridge and the neighbouring towns had in some way or another, either directly or indirectly benefitted from the activities of the fraternity, in fact a large number were actually involved in the trade in some small way. The trade was not as prevalent as it had been at the turn of the last century when it was quite rife but in these days

of hardly any work and low wages, any small gain by the poorer people from the trade was a Godsend.
Many of the recipients of the small benefits began to shun their dealings with the grocer and the solicitor experienced a drop-in business as both were now considered to have 'shopped' the local Gentlemen and they themselves were feared of getting involved if they were perceived as knowingly purchasing the smuggled items.

   After their appearance in Court, Joseph Gold closed his office in town and Raymond Butterworth suffered great decreased custom so and that lack of custom eventually forced him to get away from the coastal towns moving inland where less people recognised him. Both men had received a substantial fine with a threat of long term imprisonment in default of payment.

   Life at the Tide Mill carried on as usual, with *Ellie May* continuing to attract new carrying contracts that Sarah dealt with in her new office at Keeper's Cottage. Skipper had moved his gear from the cabin and into his new bedroom at the Cottage while Barty remained on the *Ellie May* with Shuftee, his dependable guard dog.

The ties between Sarah and Barty continued to grow stronger and stronger as they now saw each other almost daily and spent more of their leisure time together.

It ws soon after the Court hearing of the two suspect informants that a meeting of the Committee was called to clarify the present position with the organisation. As expected, the eight members present discussed the current items and only when that was completed did the conversation turn to the matter of the two missing members. There had been much speculation in the newspapers but the journalists were not wholly privy to the real facts that were related by Mr Spalding to the Committee that evening. All the details of "the venture that never was" were painstakingly explained and the risk to any member being implicated was non-existent except for the two main suspects. It must be said that Raymond Butterworth was not considered as an informer but had become implicated when interrogated by the Customs Officers confessing of being a good friend of Joseph Gold. He was already known to Customs as having received remuneration for information given to them on previous occasions. Of the two hired men, they each received four months' imprisonment for aiding and abetting, the Customs men really thought they had foiled a landing even though one hadn't taken place. The two hired men each received a sum of money as compensation and their families were looked after by the Committee for the duration of their internment.

The Committee regarded the whole operation as a success having revealed the true identity of the informant and agreed to pay Raymond Butterworth a substantial amount of compensation to help him set up a new business. Joseph Gold received a message warning him of the consequences of exposing the identity of any member of the organisation .in the future. A warning not to be ignored in any way!

A long time passed when all freetrading activities were suspended in the interest of safety. but with the main danger past a further venture was planned to take place within the next month.

Mr Spalding contacted his opposite number in France and they carefully arranged another meeting at sea, the normal format being acceptable. The landing on the English side was to be Easton Cliffs as usual, a tried and tested safe place with the two regular Watchmen being secreted on the cliff top and on the beach below.

Barty received a letter from the College at Lowestoft regarding his application for further training. They agreed that, due to his present circumstances and employment they would send him a modified distance learning course but he would definitely be required to undergo a practical examination their college in Southwold. Should the distant learning course be satisfactory he would be required to spend a week, Monday to Friday, living at the Southwold College for a fee of £100 all inclusive. He studied the paper and signed agreeing to conform with all requirements and returned the letter to Lowestoft College. He was rather reluctant to spend £100 as he had planned to set a wedding day with Sarah and that amount of money would make a big hole in his personal account. On the other hand, if he was successful it would ensure a secure future for them when they were married.

That evening he told Sarah and her father what he had done. Again, Lady Luck was on his side. On hearing his plans, Mr Spalding said he would pay the fees for Barty's Course as he too considered it a safeguard to the couple's future life together and since their official engagement he thought of Barty as his son-in-law.

Skipper was sat on deck with Shuftee reading the paper when Barty went aboard. He told him of his good fortune and Mr Spalding's kind offer to finance the Course. "That's fine" said Skipper "because we have a contract and will be leaving in the morning and I have already decided that you will be skippering the journey to Felixstowe and back to Aldeburgh to gain experience. I'll act as First Mate and I won't interfere unless there is an emergency, you will be making all the decisions for the trip. Okay?" Barty was so pleased with this decision now he can show just how much he had learnt and how much he could be trusted.
The booking had been received by Skipper direct so Barty had to go back to the big house to tell Sarah that *Ellie May* would be sailing next morning. Having passed all the details to her he went back to Keeper's Cottage and so to bed.

An early rise took him back to the boat and they were soon headed down river on the tide, bound for Felixstowe, a journey they had made many times. Barty remained under auxiliary engine until they reached the river mouth then switched to sail. Skipper carried out Barty's directions without question then busied himself doing small job on deck, making sandwiches and tea and generally enjoying the perks of First Mate.

They loaded at Felixstowe, the passage to Aldeburgh was uneventful and Barty gave Skipper no doubts about his boat handling abilities not having once asked for advice. Secretly Skipper was very impressed although he didn't say a word.

It was late afternoon when they returned to the mooring and Skipper reminded him they would be leaving again tomorrow evening for the planned venture. They spoke over supper on the boat of the next venture. Although Sarah didn't know of their nocturnal activities she suspected they were up to something and now that she dealt with the administration of the Company she would soon be asking awkward questions. The last trip, the one they had just done was easily explainable as the contract went straight to Skipper and the details passed on afterwards, but a late departure, when it was dark, how could they justify that? Neither of them wanted to involve her or to lie to her as she was a very honest and trustworthy young lady who knew the benefits from the freetrade but didn't approve of it. They believed they could keep the secret a little longer as Barty, Skipper and her father all had their own personal bank accounts. Sarah kept only the business accounts and due to mutual consent, no records or accounts were kept of the freetrade. All money matters were dealt with by Mr Spalding and the members of the Committee by vote at the regular Committee meetings, reimbursements. compensations, hiring's, disposal and returns from the sale of goods, stowage fees, in fact anything to do with the freetrade if recorded, could lead to suspicion. So, there was little danger from that angle. Mr Spalding always told the members of the financial position and all transactions concerning the organisation. Such were the lucrative returns that no one asked any questions, all being satisfied with their lot and relatively safe in the security of their individual interests. The Joseph Gold affair had been the only time when that security was threatened and fortunately that had terminated without any great loss to their overall assets. Mr Spalding had always maintained that whatever happened he would always be able to supply cash if urgently needed and no man should worry about hardship to themselves or their families should they fall foul of the authorities.

Down at the moorings. *Ellie May* was made ready for sea and Barty made the excuse that the trip was training for his qualification in night navigation. Once again, the meeting with the French boat, *L'Etoile* was perfectly timed on an almost moonless night. The crews worked quickly in a minimum of deck lights to transfer a load of approximately 22 tons of goods, mostly crated.

Business done and farewells exchanged the two vessels headed back towards their respective landing places. *Ellie May* struggled to make good time against a head sea and consequently was a little late before sighting the Easton Cliffs. A little later than estimated. the 'Coast Clear' signal was seen and although the morning light was just beginning to show they managed to unload in the lee of the cliffs. They couldn't be observed from the cliffs but a strong watch was kept in case a Revenue Cutter approached from seaward.

Ted Moore left them as usual returning to his farm via the sea cave and shaft leading up to his land. *Ellie May* was safely moored back at the Tide Mill before midday.

Sarah wasn't in the office at Keeper's Cottage so Barty managed to get some rest upstairs after the busy night's activity. He awoke later, went downstairs to find Sarah in the office tending to the day's mail. She greeted Barty and handed him his personal mail.

He was pleased to receive a letter from the Lowestoft College accepting his application for the distant learning course and enclosing the first part of the syllabus. A quick glance at the subject headings on the syllabus made him feel confident that he wouldn't encounter any immediate difficulties. The practical test date was given as one month hence and a place had been reserved for him at Southwold College as promised. It was clear from the letter that much work was expected from him during the month he commenced the Course. The date he had been given was just prior to his 23rd birthday.

The following two weeks brought a period of no work for the boat so Barty spent his time helping at the mill, doing odd jobs on the boat and studying for his pending examinations. Skipper spent much of his time resting as he was still feeling very tired especially after doing manual work he did however, find the time and energy to spend with Barty explaining the various points relating to his studies and keeping a log book on his studies to remind him of the more important items he should revise regularly.

Ted Moore called to see if he could help out at another agricultural show in the north of the County and having plenty of spare time at the present, he agreed. As before, Ted would collect him at the Tide Mill the evening before the Show, stay overnight at Ted's farm and return the next evening after the one-day Show. Unfortunately, Sarah would be unable to accompany him this time because apart from the horse show there would be a ploughing match and space was very limited in the transport to the Show. Sarah and Skipper would remain to manage the business, of which there was very little at the moment. Skipper would stay on board the *Ellie May* with Shuftee for most of the time and visit the office each morning to collect the mail and instruct Sarah on anything that may require his attention.

The Agricultural Show was a success, the horse presentation gaining second place again but taking a First Place in the ploughing match. Ted was highly satisfied with the results and gave Barty some cash to cover his expenses although he hadn't incurred any! When Barty objected Ted insisted that he take the money saying that he valued his skills and 'know how' with the horses and would like to continue to be able to enlist his help at future shows.

He had been away only two days but in that time the mail had brought three routine carrying contracts which although they were only small jobs and would take them no further than Felixstowe in the south of the County and Aldeburgh in the north, they were work and would relieve the monotony especially for Skipper. It would also mean that Barty would find more time to study and add extra practical experience to his sea log, skippering the boat as he had done on the last 'venture' but of course, that couldn't be recorded. The three contracts were completed without any problems and they were back at the mooring a few days before Barty was due to go to Southwold for his tests.

Taking the railway train from Woodbridge to Halesowen then a bus to Southwold he arrived at the College at 6pm, as arranged, and shown to his room. The written test was due to start at 10am the following morning giving him time for a final chance to revise.

The test was taken in a large hall where fifteen other men were assembled in a bid to gain the Certificate. One or two of the candidates looked very young and apprehensive having only completed the pre-requisite qualification recently and had only the minimum experience at sea. Barty having had almost two years in the inshore trade felt quite confident, he had spent hours and hours poring over his charts and books and with Skippers instructions and backing he had no fears about the paper test. The two-hour test completed, the candidates were given lunch and told to report to Reception at 1pm sharp. From there they were bussed to the town of Southwold and taken to two boats that were tied up below the pier. This was the part of the examination that Barty had been worried about, would he be able to handle a different craft after spending all his time on *Ellie May*? His worries were completely unfounded when he saw the vessels. They were split into two groups, the majority boarding the Thames barge that was tied up ahead of a smaller boat that appeared to be a Norfolk wherry. To his relief Barty was assigned to the wherry. He only then realised that the examinations were for two different Certificates of Competency. Six of the candidates boarded the wherry and after 30 minutes' familiarisation the boat moved off steered by one of the candidates, under the instruction of the examiner.

The weather was fair with a slight breeze and the sea was calm as the boat turned north out of the harbour. Barty had expected the test to take place within the confines of the harbour so he was quite surprised as he knew every nook and inlet of this part of the coast as they passed by the Easton Cliffs. He had learnt of the rock formations and the behaviour of the tides so his confidence was high as his turn came to take the wheel – this vessel was fitted with a steering wheel not a tiller but he soon got use to the wheel as he followed the instructions of the examiner who told him to steer south back towards Southwold, constantly asking him questions all the time. His was the task to take the boat into the harbour, back to the pier and secure it.

The candidates re-assembled in the hall at the College to be addressed by the Principal and told that their examination assessments would be

written up as a report and the results sent to them in a fortnights time. The men taking their tests on the Thames barge would now be seen individually by the Principal and the Examiner, before leaving the College. The six remaining would also be seen by their Examiners but only in respect of their sea test so Barty was led to a small room just off the hall to be greeted warmly by his Examiner where he was asked a few more questions. During this meeting and the whole length of the sea test the two were never introduced, Barty knew the man as Mr Marriott, nothing more. The practical Examiners were not given the name of their candidates either, they were known only by a number. Later Barty discovered that this method of anonymity was employed to ensure that each applicant received a fair and unbiased test,
. There had been times in the past when local notables and wealthy relatives of applicants held some form of sway with the examiners and bribes had been known to have been taken in order to obtain a coveted Certificate. This method ensured that fairness prevailed.

As Barty faced Mr Marriott, he thought that there was something familiar in his demeanour, he felt that they may have met somewhere before but couldn't put a finger on it. He didn't pursue the subject but there was something that rang a bell, the way he spoke, the way he looked, something! Before being dismissed, Mr Marriott told him that his sea examination had been a total success and that he had handled the boat "like a veteran". He now had to wait to receive the results of the written test.

Things were still running normally back at the mill and Sarah was extremely pleased to have Barty back after his course, they were both very conscious of just how much they had missed each other in only a few days. Now that they were seeing each other every day the bond between them was growing stronger and Barty wondered if he should suggest a date for their wedding, they had spoken of it before but Barty felt that the time wasn't right at present. He wanted to give Sarah the security in her life that she had enjoyed with her parents, True, he had just taken one more step up the ladder but he was also very aware of Skipper's condition If his efforts had been successful and he gained the Certificate of Competency, both coastal and seagoing within limits, he would find work quite easily but if anything should happen to Skipper what would happen about the business? He hadn't yet enough money saved to buy Skipper's share or a permanent home for himself and Sarah should they marry too soon. He had talked all this over with her and she said she could understand his hesitations. Since those early days sitting on the banks of the River Thames watching the ships of the world passing up and down, to and from the Port of London Barty had secretly harboured an ambition to take his Seagoing Captain/s Certificate. Just the sight of the ports of registration painted on the stern of the vessels had conjured up visions of exotic foreign lands and the urge to travel. All these dreams were light years away to a young lad working as a farm hand working in the Docklands area. Now, having been employed in the coastal carrying trade for quite some time and achieving his qualifications, his boyhood dreams didn't seem so far away. Perhaps things may still work out for him and Sarah's life together depending on her acceptance or rejection of his ambitions. It was early days and many things could happen before they made their final decisions. At present, he didn't want to be tied to a permanent life at sea, he loved her too much for that and he was happy with his present way of life, just as Sarah appeared to be.

As he entered the office at Keeper's Cottage one morning Sarah embraced him fondly and after a few minutes of small talk she handed him the mail. Most of it had already been opened as Sarah had dealt with the business side of things but there was one envelope addressed to him personally. It was from Tom Black his old Army pal. It was really just a letter to keep in touch as promised but as he read on Barty was saddened to know that, due to the death of his employer things were becoming difficult at Down Valley Farm and the chances were that it may have to be sold as the farmer's wife would be unable to cope with running it. Tom assumed that the job would be safe with the new owners should this be the case. He wrote to say he was fit and well and still maintaining his interests in horse showing although he had been unable to attend the Show at Halesworth recently. He ended his letter saying how much he had enjoyed their time together at their last meeting and hoped they could repeat it in the near future.

The rest of the mail contained three more requests for carrying contracts, two of which were for the same date so Sarah had written to inform them that the date was pre-booked. She had attended to the other letters some of which were demands for payments for goods and supplies ordered for the boat.

When all the business had been completed, Barty, who had been bursting to tell him about the course was able to do so over a cup of coffee. It took rather a long time for him to relate the whole episode to her. She was delighted with the news and suggested they pick up Skipper from the boat and go into Woodbridge for lunch to celebrate his success so far. He was still to hear of the results for the written test. Barty agreed wholeheartedly so they changed from their working clothes and went down the quayside to be greeted by Shuftee sitting on the end of the gang plank enjoying the sunshine. Skipper was also sitting on deck with his breakfast pots still around him, reading a paper as the couple went aboard. He looked well but Barty noticed the difficulty he encountered getting up from the chair. Barty told him the reason for their visit and his success in Southwold and said he would tell him more over lunch. At first, he seemed reluctant to accompany them until Barty suggested a couple of pints prior to lunch. That clinched it! but they would have to wait while he dressed as he was still wearing his pyjamas and dressing gown.

Putting Shuftee on guard they left the *Ellie May,* Skipper was having difficulty in walking so they engaged a cab to take them the short distance into town. Skipper was using a walking stick, something that Barty had never witnessed before, was there something he wasn't telling them? Sitting quietly with a pint of local ale Barty told Skipper about the Course at Southwold College but more especially about the sea test and how it had taken place just off the Easton Cliffs, the area known so well to both of them. Skipper asked many questions, what type of craft was used, how was the test conducted, the interpretation of the charts. He asked about the Examiner, who was he, did Barty think him to be a knowledgeable man? The questions just tumbled from him and it was obvious that Skipper wanted to think he had been given a fair test. As for the question about the Examiner Barty told him it was a man named Marriott but didn't know his Christian name. He gave a brief description of Mr Marriott but Skipper said he hadn't heard of him even though Barty told him that he had appeared so familiar to him and they had met somewhere before. Still Barty was puzzled, his features seemed so familiar it was playing on his mind. He had met so many people in the Army, the farming and coastal communities, it could have been anywhere so he dismissed the puzzle from his mind for the present.

After lunch, he went to the bank to deposit the Course fee that Sarah's father had given him. They then visited the bank where the business account was lodged to find it quite healthy with no foreseeable problems. Barty and Skipper had their personal accounts at different banks for personal reasons but the business account was managed by Sarah at the same branch as the main account for the Tide Mill

By this time, Skipper was beginning to flag he was walking a lot slower although he never complained. Sarah wanted to do a bit more shopping, nothing essential, just a look around the shops really but they decided to get Skipper back to the boat to get some rest as they had a trip the next day. With Skipper safely back on board, Sarah and Barty went to the Cottage to spend some time together.

With Barty at the helm, *Ellie May* gently eased away from her mooring and out into the river. He was having to keep a sharp eye as Skipper wasn't on board, his mate was Sarah!

Skipper had left his bunk that morning not feeling in the best of health but with every good intention that it would be' business as usual' but his tired old legs wouldn't support him and he kept staggering and losing his balance, he would be a liability if the waters should cut up rough. He had wanted to cancel the contract but Barty wouldn't hear of it. Before casting off he had taken Skipper up to the Cottage to be looked after by Sarah's mother. He was quite adamant that he would be able to fend for himself and jokingly suggested that Sarah should accompany Barty on the short trip. To their great surprise, she immediately agreed to go with him. Apparently, she had often wished that she could take a short trip on the boat but never really got the opportunity, now at last a chance had arisen. Preparations for departure were delayed by about an hour and now they were headed down river on an ebb tide which allowed them to catch a little time on their timetable. Other than a days' river trip this was the first time that Sarah had ventured out onto the open sea. Realising that he had a 'greenhorn' as a mate Barty didn't ask much of Sarah but she did surprise him as she responded quickly and capably with the few things he asked of her. After leaving the lee of the land she began to feel a bit queasy due to the motion of the boat but he re-assured her that they would soon feel better when they turned south to take advantage of a stern wind. She started to feel the relief as they made good time towards Felixstowe Harbour and they had caught up on their timetable.

While sacks of grain were loaded into the hold using a hand crane they called at the quayside café for a late breakfast, Sarah could only manage a mug of coffee but said she felt less sick but just wasn't hungry. Back on board they secured the load, squared the deck and left the quay to return to the Tide Mill. Sarah performed her duties very well and said that she was beginning to enjoy the trip but wouldn't want to do it regularly!

Skipper seemed to be a good bit better but he hadn't been far from his bed but it was very obvious that he had been spoilt by Sarah's mother who had been constantly attending him, popping in to see if he was okay and feeding him like never before. Skipper enjoyed the company as it gave him the chance to' swing the lamp' as he regaled her with stories of his early life adventures at sea long before he took to the coastal trade.

Born in 1850 to a seafaring family in Aldeburgh it was understood that Skipper, real name, Donald Mclean, was destined to follow the sea. His parents were living in a small Scottish fishing community and had moved south prior to Skipper's birth, seeking a better life. He was schooled in Aldeburgh and spent his early working life with the local fishing fleet but longed for more. He entered the coastal and cross channel service and eventually obtained his Captain's Certificate. He married his wife Helen in 1895 and were blessed with the birth of their daughter Marie the following year.

Skipper was a product of the age of sail who found it difficult to make the transition from sail to steam but as technology increased he found himself working on steam vessels more and more –steam kettles he called them.

He managed to pass for First Mate on the steamers although his heart was still with the magnificent sailing ships that were slowly disappearing from the oceans. He was spending more time away from his wife and daughter and resolved that when the time was right he would' swallow the anchor'. He saved hard for many years and bought the house in Ipswich for his family, the house where Marie and her family still live. Prior to his daughter's marriage he had tried to settle for a shore job but after trying out several employments he found nothing suitable and those he did try he found mundane and totally uninteresting and boring so he turned back to the sea for a short time.

Realising that his duties lie with his family he again tried shore life and found an opening for a deck hand on a boat belonging to a Norfolk Shipping Company, that specialised in short hauls only The Company quickly noted his qualifications and after offering him more lucrative employment actually listened to his plans to leave the sea and asked if he would be interested in the coastal trade. Accepting the offer, he worked for many years being able to return to Ipswich mainly at weekends. During the week, he lived on board not requiring shore accommodation and he managed to save much of his wages again. Then the opportunity arose for him to put a substantial deposit on a Norfolk wherry he had seen advertised at one of the ship chandler's shops in Felixstowe. He visited the boat and immediately fell in love with the *Ellie May* and began to consider running his own carrying business. He would be his own boss, set his own timetables and be able to visit his wife and daughter whenever he wished. It was only a few months after the purchase of the boat that his wife Helen took ill and passed away.

Skipper was devastated, his whole life seemed to be breaking up with his daughter, still a teenager, he arranged for a distant relative to come and live in at Ipswich to look after her but this arrangement lasted for only two years but it served to settle the problem of Marie's care and took away one of Skipper's main worries for the present. Marie married young and took over the house with her new husband, the distant relative moved out.

Skipper went on to complete his story by telling Mrs Spalding that he had met Barty the day he had been discharged from the Army and they had been together ever since. He regarded Barty more as a son than an employee and that was the reason for offering him the partnership. He knew full well that his son-in-law, Matthew had no interest at all in joining the boating business, he was a successful business man himself. Barty's interest in the carrying company ensured that the future of the business was in good hands and now that he was engaged to Arthur Spalding's daughter, well, everything seemed rosy and he was highly satisfied with all the arrangements and developments that had been made over the past months.

All these revelations were made in the short time that Sarah and Barty were away the details of which were divulged to Barty after he had asked after Skipper's health. Mrs Spalding told him of their time they had spent talking to each other, things that Barty had not known about especially his early life but now he could understand Skipper's love for the sea and how he missed his family and home life so much while he was at sea. Sarah had paid a quick visit to the office to collect the mail and handed one envelope to Barty, it was from Lowestoft College informing him that he had successfully passed both the practical and written tests he had undertaken at Southwold through the distance learning course. Enclosed with the letter was an invitation to attend Lowestoft College for the presentation of the various certificates that he and others had achieved.

While they were discussing the possibilities of attending the Presentation Ceremony Mr Spalding joined them. Barty told him of his good news and he immediately offered to take them to the College on the appointed day. Once again Barty had been successful in his endeavours and agreed that Mr Spalding, Sarah and Skipper would attend the Ceremony. Barty was particularly pleased that Mr Spalding wanted to be there, after all he had paid for the course. Unfortunately, it was doubtful if Skipper would be fit enough to attend as it is a long journey to Lowestoft entailing quite a bit of walking. They talked things over for a while when Mr Spalding told them that he had a surprise for them and asked them to go to one of the warehouses with him.

He opened one of the big warehouse doors to reveal a big black shiny motor car, a bull-nosed Morris Oxford and it gleamed like a brand-new model. It was first manufactured in 1919 and that he had bought it from a fellow associate. Mr Spalding proudly announced that they would travel in style to the Presentation Ceremony. He had been taking a few secret driving lessons when he had first considered buying a car and was happy to drive to Lowestoft. The others had all assumed that they would travel by rail and now it may be possible that Skipper could also be with them. He had acquired the car a few days ago, while the others were away so it really did come as a big surprise to everyone.

The next short contract only took Barty down the River Deben with a grain delivery, he did the trip alone as Skipper was unfit and Sarah couldn't get away from mill business. He found it very hard going on his own, not the boat handling but the strain of loading without help and no hand crane available. It took him a lot longer that he had estimated and on his return Sarah told him not to do any more trips on his own and suggested that the Company hire or buy a small deck crane.

Skipper's legs were still causing him pain and he was spending more and more time at the Cottage. Barty still called at the office every day to keep up with the business and Sarah appeared to have more than enough with her office duties and seeing that Skipper was cared for and fed.

During the next few weeks there were several contracts to be fulfilled but Skipper still wasn't up to taking a trip so Barty had to hire one of the mill workers to help him on the boat. Although the hired hands did their best they weren't familiar with the routines and seemed unable to grasp the rudiments when the boat was sailing under a freshening wind, it was alien to expect a landsman to adapt so quickly to the conditions. Fortunately, the were no heavy winds while he had a mill hand on board so there were no emergencies.

In one of his regular letters to Tom Black, Barty mentioned the manning problem saying that one of the hands couldn't even stand up while the boat was rolling. An exaggeration may be, but it served to show the problem he was addressing. Barty was surprised to hear that Tom had been made part-time as the farmer had died and some of his business sold off, it was now purely agricultural, the cows and the Suffolk Punches were now gone. Furthermore, Tom was looking for accommodation as his cottage was tied and had been part of the sale lot and his part-time wage would hardly support him if he couldn't find full-time employment. Barty mentioned this to Skipper as they were chatting. Skipper said that he felt that he would be a liability if he tried to return to the *Ellie May* and the foreseeable future wasn't looking good. His legs were giving him more trouble and he had taken to a wheelchair for other than very short walking journeys. They talked for a time then Skipper came up with a suggestion that he should ask Tom to go out with him as Mate on the next charter just to see how he fared. Tom was a fit young man, strong and able to pace himself. He had worked on the farm at Hadleigh since leaving the Army but now that the animals had gone he didn't fancy the prospect of being tied to growing and tending field crops only. He was also a man looking for permanent employment and somewhere to live! Barty replied to his letter putting the suggestion to him to which Tom promptly replied that he would be happy to take a trip with Barty "to test the waters" so to speak. Time was no problem and he could travel to the Tide Mill whenever needed.

Tom boarded the *Ellie May* on the evening prior to her sailing. He was bunked in the cabin with Barty ready for an early departure next morning. And, what a morning it was, wet, windy and raining as they slipped the mooring on auxiliary engine. Barty thought what an initiation for Tom, filthy weather and no proper clothing other than an old oilskin and sou'wester left behind by Skipper. Tom was making the best of things though even commenting that it ws good to feel the wind and rain and fresh sea air in his face and not a muddy field in sight. The course was set for Felixstowe so they turned south from the Deben estuary. Progress was slow but steady and they reached the port an hour later than the estimated time of arrival. *Ellie May*, being shallow bottomed had rolled more than normal but Tom seemed unaffected. Barty smiled to himself as he remembered what Skipper used to say about the *Ellie May* "She's that flat bottomed that she will roll on a wet flannel"

The sacks of flour were unloaded and a new cargo of timber embarked before the two of them went to the quayside café for a well-deserved breakfast/lunch. Paperwork completed they left Felixstowe as the tide started to ebb before stopping the engine and switching to sail. Clearing the harbour mouth they headed north carefully avoiding the treacherous rocks just outside Felixstowe when Tom spotted a small leisure cruiser apparently trying to attract their attention. It would appear that the cruiser was heading towards the harbour trying to find the most direct route and had run aground on the edge of the sandbank.

A quick glance at his chart convinced Barty that he could safely approach the cruiser. *Ellie May's* shallow draught ensured their safety but he was very aware of the flow of the ebbing tide. Skipper had always taught him to give the sands a wide berth when sailing in those waters but he still proceeded with great caution as the sands were prone to shift with the alternating tidal undercurrents and he remembered he had a loaded boat. The occupants of the cruiser were a family of four, Dad, Mum and two boys, they were in a hurry to reach Felixstowe as one of the boys was experiencing stomach pains. Barty explained that due to his cargo he would be unable to tow the cruiser off the bank and with consultation of the tidal timetable, it would be about three to four hours before the tide would be high enough for the cruiser to float off. One of the boys was in obvious distress and needed medical attention as soon as possible. Barty explained that he was bound for Orford with his cargo and offered to take the boy and his mother with him and be in Orford before full tide. Taking advantage of the offer they came aboard and made as comfortable as possible in the cabin. The father and the other boy would remain on the cruiser until released by the tide, they were in no immediate danger. When free they would make for Orford and find the *Ellie May* and the latest news on their ailing son.

Ellie May made good time into Orford and Tom immediately found a telephone to call a doctor to the boat, he arrived in double quick time and concluded that the boy had a ruptured appendix and was removed to a local hospital for treatment

The motor cruiser entered Orford about three hours later and fortunately had suffered no damage. Within a short time, the family was re-united.

Barty and Tom finished offloading and because of the delay with the incident they decided to stay overnight in the town and make the trip home the next morning.

At 8pm that same evening they heard Shuftee barking and going on deck, hailing them from the quayside was three members of the cruiser family come to give them the latest news on their other son and to thank them for their kind assistance. They said their son had had an operation and was now in a stable condition. The surgeon had told them that if had they been an hour or so later his appendix would have burst and that would be serious trouble. Mum, Dad and the other son couldn't thank Barty and Tom enough adding that they had saved his life bringing him to Orford so quickly. Tom was really excited that he had been able to help and said that, apart from his experiences in the Army he had never known anything like that before. He was so impressed by Barty's knowledge of the sea, interpreting the charts and his sense of safety it prompted him to offer his services on the boat anytime an extra hand was needed. He had helped to save a life, he couldn't have been happier especially when Barty gave him some money for working as his Mate, a sort of wage to cover the two days they had been away. He had really enjoyed the work and the friendship as well.

Barty told Skipper of the rescue and how good Tom had responded to the circumstances. All three were further surprised to read in the local newspaper an account of the rescue and a formal acknowledgement to their actions from a Mr Alan Jarvis, the father of the two boys. Barty hadn't known or even asked his name and Skipper was pleased to see *Ellie May*, Tom and Barty mentioned in the papers.

The day of the Presentation of Awards had arrived and four people climbed into the Morris Oxford, Mr Spalding and Skipper in the front seats with Sarah and Barty seated in the rear. Mrs Spalding had even made up a picnic basket for them to enjoy on the way and it was a beautiful sunny day. This was to be the longest drive that Mr Spalding had ever made but the road was clear and progress was good except for when passing though small villages where they encountered farm animals, slow tractors and in one village, even a street market. The passengers just sat back and enjoyed the passing scenery, this being a first-time experience for them all, one way or another. Their enjoyment was enhanced by Mr Spalding taking the coastal road wherever possible, a different experience to see the sea pass from the shore rather than from a boat.

Lowestoft appeared to be a large town. As a traditional fishing port, there were many boats in the harbour and the roads seemed to be attracting a large number of people. It was market day. Mr Spalding found many difficulties avoiding farm vehicles, busy shoppers, roads blocked by wagons and stalls. Certain roads were closed to vehicular traffic so he had to ask directions to Lowestoft College which was situated in spacious grounds just outside the main town.

They managed to park outside the College, entered and registered their arrival at the Reception desk, there was only 30 minutes before the ceremony was due to start. Barty was directed to the front of the hall while the others were seated in the main body of the hall, a little behind Barty. There was a quartet on stage playing sea songs for the amusement of the assembled audience whilst nearby the Masters and Instructors were taking their seats facing the audience. Barty was surprised by the number of Certificate recipients present, there must have been well over a hundred there to receive their Awards for various qualifications.

    The Principal arrived and everyone stood as he mounted the stage to take the centre seat. After the Welcome speech, certain introductions were made and the presentations began. Looking at the Instructors on stage, Barty could see his Instructor, Mr Marriott. What was it about this man, why did Barty feel that they had met before he came on the Course? He was still pondering the question when he was conscious of his name being called, interrupting his line of thought

"Kaleb Michael Bartholomew"

He went forward and up onto the stage to receive his Certificate from the Principal who congratulated him on his achievement. Barty looked directly at Mr Marriott and thought he saw just the very slightest sign of recognition on his face. Could he be wrong? Could it be just from the Examination Day; he really couldn't solve the problem

Following the presentation, refreshments were available at the back of the hall. Barty thought he would seek out Mr Marriott in an effort to solve his dilemma. Mr Spalding, Sarah and Skipper, who was in a wheelchair, took their refreshments while Barty searched for Mr Marriott only to be told that he had left the building.

On the way back, Mr Spalding stopped the car at Blythburgh and they sat outside the public house to enjoy the picnic that Mrs Spalding had provided' The refreshments at the College were minimal so they made short work of the picnic before proceeding on their journey home. All together they had had a lovely relaxing day but the exertions proved too much for Skipper who had to take to his bed as soon as they arrived back at the Tide Mill. As for Mr Spalding, he commented on how he felt proud of Barty and on receiving good comments on his driving abilities, he was happy to have been a part of the special day.

The Committee was called to meet on the Saturday afternoon in response to an urgent message received by Mr Spalding's French counterpart which read "Urgent consignment. Monday. Usual route. The message gave no further details that meant that anyone intercepting it wouldn't be able to learn anything, route, time, destination, nothing to help an information probe

Wheels were set in motion immediately but again it was felt that Skipper wouldn't be fit enough to take part so Barty and Ted Moore would again crew the *Ellie May*.

Leaving the moorings by moonlight they made their way down river. Everything was quiet except for the dull chug of the engine and the sound of the bow cutting through the water. There were very few lights on the river banks but even though Barty was now familiar with the twists and turns in the river course he was extremely observant in spotting the isolated landmarks to guide him safely. On reaching the open sea he changed to sail power from engine and his world became even more silent. It was so peaceful and calm, just the lap of the water against the hull and the occasional sound of the light wind in the sail. Ted was very quiet as well, keeping his wary eye on the shore for any sign of a Revenue cutter that may be patrolling the coast. At one-point Ted felt sure that he heard the sound of an engine in the distance. Extinguishing all lights and lowering the sail. Barty let the boat drift idly, barely visible in the watery moonlight. They waited with every nerve fully alert and "Yes", the deep throb of an engine could be heard and seemed to become a little quieter as time slowly passed. A few minutes later the low form of a boat could be seen with several lights illuminating the deck quite clearly. It was a French Revenue Cutter. With her lights illuminating the deck so brilliantly, Ted commented that the crew would have difficulty seeing very far from her own hull. *Ellie May* must be about two miles distant from the Frenchman which was travelling at a fast speed with her searchlight scanning the sea towards the French coast, a good few miles away. Had they had a tip-off?

Ellie May was totally blacked out, silent and almost motionless as they let the tide carry them in an opposite direction. The two occupants didn't move or speak above a whisper, sound carries very fast over water. The Frenchman passed down the coast but *Ellie May* did not move until they were well out of earshot. If they had been intercepted their excuse would have been that they were engaged in a little night fishing, they always carried fishing tackle on board and they were presently carrying no cargo so their excuse could be quite plausible but it was better that they were not stopped as it could lead to many awkward questions and the boat's name should remain as anonymous as possible.

The rendezvous was made albeit a full 30 minutes behind schedule. *L'Etoile* had also been delayed as she had heard the news of the patrolling Revenue Cutter. Apparently, the Cutter had no exact information regarding the position of the rendezvous and were trying to engage with *L'Etoile* as she left her French port but there were miles of coastline to patrol and *L'Etoile* had already left port and was obliged to 'lay to' for a while just as *Ellie May* had done.

During the transfer of cargo, Barty overheard Ted speaking with the French captain which rather surprised him as they conversed in the French language. Barty hadn't known that Ted could speak French, he had never heard him before and indeed never mentioned the fact.

Very few words were exchanged on the *Ellie May* as they headed for the Easton Cliffs, both fully aware that the French authorities might warn the English that something was afoot and they were unable to detect any craft on the French side of the Channel. It was a relief to them both as Ted reported a signal from the cliff top "Coast clear". Safely under the cliffs, the landing party soon unloaded the crop of 20 tons and stowed it in the hidden tunnel at the back of the sea cave. By mid-morning, *Ellie May* was safely moored back at the Tide Mill. No one seemed any wiser that she had even left her mooring the night before. There had been another narrow escape due to the informant on the French side not having the precise information to enable the Customs men to do their job properly. The 'urgent' word had been used in the message that led Mr Spalding to understand that *L'Etoile* was to be subject to a search the morning before the rendezvous date while the ship was at its berth with no cargo or crew on board. It was a blessing that the French side of the organisation had worked so efficiently.

When Sarah arrived at the office she was surprised that Barty wasn't already there. She went to the boat to find him and noted that his bunk had not been slept in. He told her that he had been up all night doing an engine repair and hadn't left the boat. He hated lying to Sarah but there had been no opportunity lately to tell her of his involvement with the freetrade. He still didn't approve of the freetrade but getting involved unknowing in the first place, then enjoying the lucrative returns he couldn't see a way of freeing himself from it. His job would be at risk and now he was a qualified Captain he would find it difficult to secure another berth as such if he was ever caught by the Authorities. He would have to leave Sarah and Skipper, in fact his whole way of living. No, it wasn't the time to tell Sarah yet. His bank balance had become quite healthy and it had been at the back of his mind that he might purchase another wherry to operate along with of the *Ellie May*. He hadn't discussed this idea with anyone, especially with Skipper due to his ill health. No, he must try to keep the secret a little longer.

There had been a mail delivery among which were three contracts for carrying work, these were discussed with Sarah and Skipper who both agreed that they should be accepted and an extra hand would have to be hired as Skipper would be unable to man the boat. Try as they might they couldn't think of a single local man to whom they could offer the post.

Most of the local men who were qualified as Mates already had employment while others didn't fancy a life on the water that took them away from their families. Suddenly Skipper came up with the answer, Tom should be approached to see if he would be interested as his own job on the farm at Hadleigh had become limited. He didn't have a great deal of experience, only the one trip but he knew what the job entailed, he was single, fit and healthy and Skipper had taken a liking to him when they met prior to the last trip.

Barty said he would write to him, offer him the job and if he accepted, could he come to the Tide Mill as soon as possible?

The letter was posted on a Monday morning. On the following Thursday morning Barty was working on deck and Shuftee started to bark as a voice from the quayside cut through the quiet air

"Ahoy *Ellie May*"

Barty recognised the voice of Tom and looked up from his work to see his old pal, suitcase in hand, standing on the quay. He was welcomed aboard and taken to the cabin, they spoke for a while then went to the office at Keeper's Cottage leaving Shuftee in charge. Sarah and Skipper were both in the office so the four of them sat talking about Tom's offered position for two hours.

Tom had packed up his job at the farm on receipt of Barty's letter convinced that he would work with them both without problem. The farmer had told him that he may have to cut his working time at the farm even more or perhaps to lay him off altogether. There were certainly no prospects to be had there so Tom decided just to leave and chance his luck elsewhere so when he received the letter he was overjoyed at the possibility of joining Barty and Skipper.

He was told that the pay wouldn't be much but if he lived on the *Ellie May* as Barty had, there would be no rent to be paid. All terms were fully explained to him and Tom agreed to join the team of the Tide Mill Carrying Company.

A small removal soon took place, moving Skipper permanently into a room at the Cottage and Barty into another room of his own, thus leaving the one spare room for visitors like Ted Moore when he came to stay and Tom would occupy the cabin on the boat together with Shuftee.

Skipper said he would speak to Mr Spalding about paying more than the agreed peppercorn rent as they now occupied two bedrooms and the office of the three-bedroomed building,

Tom moved his meagre belongings into the cabin and after spending a restless night, due to the movement of the boat and the constant slapping of the water against the hull he busied himself next morning familiarising himself with the security of the boat and the various nooks and crannies where certain gear was stowed. He was very curious about several things; after all he was very much a landsman having been to sea only the once with Barty.

Tom was joined by Barty who informed him that they had a routine cargo to pick up from Felixstowe and take to Southwold. The cargo was coal for the few steam fishing boats that were still working there, most of the fishing fleet were now based at Lowestoft, but a job is a source of earning and Barty hated carrying coal, there was a long hard dirty job ahead of them. After delivering the coal, often by hand shovelling, it into skips to be lifted by hand crane from the boat to the quayside, the hold had to be thoroughly cleaned ready for the next load which could be foodstuffs, milled flour or sacks of grain, clean cargo! Barty wondered if this, Tom's first paid work would put him off the job. The trip to Felixstowe was uneventful and a dockside steam crane lifted wagons of coal and tipped them directly into the hold that filled very quickly saving the pair many hours of hard dirty work. Within the hour of loading they were under way again. It was late afternoon when they docked at Southwold which meant that they would be unable to discharge the coal until next morning as there were no carts left on the quay into which they could discharge the cargo.

They spent an uncomfortable night trying to sleep in the cabin, everything had a film of coal dust on it that made even getting some breakfast a double chore having to wash the mugs and plates before and after use. They had managed to shake out their bedding before taking to their bunks. Tom seemed un-phased with all the extra work, he didn't complain once. The wagons arrived on the quayside at 8am and the long process of unloading by hand began. With the aid of two dockside workers it still took five hours to complete the job. The hold and the deck was swept but they would have to wash down once they were at sea. After a good meal in the dockside café they returned to the boat in order to getaway as soon as possible, Barty took the tiller until they were well clear of the harbour and with the sail set. Being well clear of any dangers, Barty handed the tiller to Tom whilst he hosed down the hold and pumped out the dirty water using the hand operated bilge pump. Tom then took over and washed down the deck and cleaned up much the deck gear and polished up the brasses. It was a long, dirty, tedious and boring job but by the time they reached the Tide Mill, *Ellie May* looked more like a traditional wherry than a dirty old collier. She still needed more attention to the paintwork and the cabin but she appeared quite respectable, at least it was a well-paid trip as many carrying services wouldn't move such cargos.

Leaving Tom to tend to work on board, Barty went up to the Cottage to report to Skipper and take the contract paperwork to Sarah. Skipper wasn't there. While the boat was away, Skipper and Mr Spalding had found time for a friendly evening together and yarning about all manner of things. the success of the Tide Mill Carrying Company, the Skipper's health, the Mill complex in general Barty and Sarah and their hopes for the future. Finally, they got around to the subject of the Committee and the need for two replacements for Mr Gold and Mr Butterworth. Mr Spalding said he would call a meeting soon to discuss recent incidents, administration, assets together with the Committee replacements.

When the subject of Skipper's health was brought up, he had to admit that his legs were getting no better and he thought that he wouldn't be able to crew again. This upset him immensely, he loved his boat and hated being stuck on land. He still took a great interest in the working of the boat but he longed to get back the only way of life he had ever wanted but now had to expect to have to slow down considerably.

They had previously agreed a peppercorn rent for Keeper's Cottage so after much discussion Mr Spalding had suggested that he be given light duties about the mill complex doing only jobs he could manage without strain. He would occupy a room at the Cottage permanently so he had access to the office in the same building. This way he could still be involved in the day to day running as a partner in the carrying business, he would see his friends regularly and still feel he was playing a useful part in just about everything including his own upkeep, he just hated the thought of retirement and living alone. True, he could have a good home with his daughter and her family in Ipswich but he knew he would feel like a burden to them, he was too independent to have other people fussing after him. These were his' twilight years' and he was happy, besides he would feel like a prisoner living in a place like Ipswich. He could still earn his keep and give advice about most things nautical and better still he knew how to organise the business with the Committee!

All this was decided over that friendly drink one afternoon in the quiet of the lounge in the big house. It was repeated to Barty when he met the two of them a little later that day. There was just Tom who needed to know his immediate future but they thought there would be no doubt in his agreement.

Returning to the boat, Barty found Tom still cleaning her up and the cabin was in excellent order, everything had been washed and re-stowed in their proper places. Tom made some coffee while Barty asked questions about the trip they had just completed. Tom asked how often they were called upon to carry coal and received the reply that it was only once or twice a year when the usual bulk carriers were unavailable. Tom commented that it didn't really matter but had wondered how Skipper would re-act to all the extra work that involved a similar type of cargo. This comment gave Barty an opening to explain some of the things that had been discussed earlier, the fact that Skipper would no longer crew the *Ellie May* but would live at Keeper's Cottage and would like Tom to live on board as boat keeper/crew for the foreseeable future and, of course he would have Shuftee to keep him company. Barty also told him that Skipper and himself were so pleased with his work on the boat and his performance at sea under many different conditions that they felt he was right for the job if he agreed to stay with them and accept a permanent berth on *Ellie May*. Tom almost fell over himself in trying to find the right words to say how happy he was to accept the offer, he didn't mind the extra work, dirty or not. He said he had enjoyed the freedom he had already experienced which was far better than the rigid timetable he had at the farm. He had thought the position was temporary until Skipper was fit and well again but now he knew that wasn't to be. Skipper had been almost forced to 'swallow the anchor' by his ill health. Tom was very grateful; he just couldn't express it in so many words. As a final seal on the conversation Barty said they must go into Woodbridge and buy some more suitable clothing for him, he didn't want a member of his crew running about looking like a shore side dandy.

Over the next two weeks they took on four more carrying contracts, all of which were successful and requiring no more than two days away from the Tide Mill. Barty took the trouble to show Tom as much as he could concerning the steering and day to day running of the boat, much the same as Skipper had taught him when they first crewed the *Ellie May* together. Tom was hard-working and trustworthy, he relished the days they spent at sea and took to the life whole-heartedly, always asking questions, he had certainly been bitten by the 'sea-bug'.

Mr Spalding summoned the Committee to assemble at the Tide Mill. It was scheduled as a general meeting, at which of course, no minutes would be recorded for obvious reasons. Much business was discussed including that of replacement members for Mr Gold and Mr Butterworth. Mr Spalding told them he knew a long-standing friend and business man, a seed and corn merchant of Woodbridge, who owned a large warehouse on the River Deben and whom he thought would make a good member of the Committee. No one knew the man personally but most knew of him. They agreed that Mr Spalding to 'sound him out' and they would accept Mr Spalding's decision whether to include him or not. The second replacement was more difficult as they really wanted a man with boat-handling experience to replace Skipper. Several names were suggested but no decision was made, each were either family men, sea drifters – men who would work for anyone but were untrustworthy, - or men who were working in the leisure boating sector. Ted Moore suggested that consideration be given to Tom whom he had met and liked. The was a general agreement when Barty explained who Tom was and that he was already working for the Company but it was agreed that the selection remain open until Barty had the opportunity to speak to him and find out his views on the freetrade without revealing any secrets. He would report back to Mr Spalding with his findings and the ultimate decision would be left with him as head of the Syndicate.

Over the next few days *Ellie May* was constantly employed and Barty found little time to see either Sarah or Skipper. He noted that Tom was becoming an excellent crew member needing no prompting in the chores to be done or the handing of the boat. After spending so much time as a landsman, he surprised Barty in his willingness to have a go at all aspects of the trade.

One evening when they returned to the moorings, Barty was given the date of the next 'venture'. It was always given at short notice, when the moon was low, to prevent rumours circulating. Barty didn't mention anything of the 'venture' to Tom as Mr Spalding suggested that he thought it' as just another business trip as usual' but this time during the night.

Tom didn't think it unusual as he had no knowledge of night trading, it had never yet happened to him. The 'venture' was to follow the usual pattern but with Tom replacing Skipper and Ted as an extra hand although he was a permanent crew member, Tom didn't know that either. *Ellie May* was due to leave her mooring as dusk was falling when she would be joined by Ted and Barty. The moon was low as they sailed under auxiliary engine down the River Deben with Barty at the helm and Ted and Tom carefully watching the passing parade of the river banks and any moored craft, the trees looking quite ghostly silhouetted against the backdrop of moon.

The sea was calm as the sail was hoisted and the engine cut. Ted sighted the sail of *L'Etoile*, dead on time as usual and the transfer of goods was made in quick time. The French boat had a small deck crane and carried six men so the combined crews worked quickly and quietly under only subdued deck lighting. Barty carefully watched Tom as he worked and he appeared to want to talk both to him and to the French crew men. Barty discouraged him, telling him they must work quickly and try to maintain complete silence. By this time, Tom had gained some idea of what was happening and was dying to ask more questions. Barty said that he would tell him more when the two vessels parted company then much more when they returned to the Tide Mill and all had been completed without mishap.

On approaching the Easton Cliffs, Ted reported sighting the signal "Coast Clear" so they grounded on the beach under the cliff where they were greeted by several men who swiftly whisked away the goods and into the safe keeping of Mr Pickford, the haulier and the new member, Mr Albert Sutton, the corn merchant, to be secreted in various caches.

A greatly lightened *Ellie May* slid easily from the beach and were back at her mooring after sunrise. It appeared that she hadn't moved all night!

    A catnap and a leisurely breakfast saw Barty and Tom sitting in the cabin discussing the activities of the night. Tom, who was by no means unintelligent had understood all that had happened but felt that he was owed some explanation as to why he had been involved without his consent. Barty told him that he had become involved under similar circumstances, that deep down he didn't agree with the freetrade but now being aware of the benefits to the people living in the towns and the lucrative returns for their dangerous undertakings he accepted it as a part of everyday life in a coastal town. He gave Tom an idea of the money he would receive as a crewman in return for the limited risks taken due to the organisations of the Committee's network of safety measures. Tom had heard of the freetrade, it happened everywhere around the coastal regions of the country. Tom had to admit that he had felt a thrill working on the transfer at sea and realised what he was doing was illegal, he just needed an explanation. Barty told him that his job at the Carrying Company was perfectly safe if he felt he didn't want to take part in future 'ventures' provided that he kept quiet about what he now knew. Should he wish to continue with the freetrade then he would benefit as did all the members. The identity of the people that made up the Committee was kept in utter secrecy and disclosed to absolutely nobody and no records were kept that would that would incriminate any person involved. Barty gave Tom an estimate of the money he had earned that night and what future 'ventures' could hold for him. Tom carefully listened to all he was told and replied by telling Barty that he wanted to continue in his new-found career with the inshore carrying trade and that he was willing to take the risks as crewman on any future freetrade engagements.

Wasting no time at all, Barty left Tom to do a few jobs about the boat while he went to the Cottage to see Skipper. He couldn't say very much as Sarah was present so after a few pleasantries they went to the big house to find Mr Spalding. Barty acquainted them both with the details of the 'venture' and how Tom had responded to the whole trip including Barty's 'pep talk' and his reaction to being 'used' as part of the illegal venture. He finished by saying that he would endorse Toms inclusion into the team as a crew man and a member of the Committee.

They later learned that Albert Sutton had proved himself a useful and willing member and had immediately sanctioned the use of his warehouse as temporary stowage for onward transmission of contraband goods. Before leaving the big house, Mr Spalding invited Skipper, Barty and Tom to have dinner with him and his family at 7pm that evening, an invite that was gratefully accepted.

Ellie May looked spick and span in the misty evening light and Tom was relaxing in the cabin when Barty hailed him as he boarded. He was greeted by Shuftee who left his guard post near the cabin hatch, he always recognised Barty's voice as he hailed the boat, and never barked. Barty told him of the news that he was now the 'venture' crewman and that he was invited to dinner at the big house at 7pm, that evening. They presented themselves a little before 7pm to take drinks with Mr & Mrs Spalding, Ted Moore and to Barty's surprise, Sarah. It was only early that same morning that they had left Ted on the beach at his farm on Easton Cliffs, he had travelled to the Tide Mill after checking the nights' work was safe and secure, Barty thought he had had no chance to sleep at all. Half an hour of small talk dinner was served at 7.30pm and lasted for almost two hours after which Mr Spalding proposed a toast to Tom for his performance on the boat, without mentioning the work they had undertaken. Tom fully understood what he meant, his position and the need for utmost confidentiality.

A most convivial evening ended as Barty and Skipper went back to Keeper's Cottage and Tom went a few yards further to board the *Ellie May*, much to the delight of Shuftee.

Barty visited the boat next morning and had breakfast with Tom, he did so quite often as Tom had no other friends and it gave them both to catch up on the news and the bookings for the boat. Barty intended to go and see his Bank manager in Woodbridge and left Tom around 11am to go to Woodbridge where another pleasant surprise awaited him. The Bank manager told him that his personal account was very healthy indeed and enquired if he had thought about investing some of his savings. For the first time Barty revealed that he had been thinking of buying a second boat, a fact that he had not disclosed to anyone else, not even his business partner. He was amazed how quickly his money had grown, this was his personal account quite separate from the cash held in the Carrying Company account. He spoke at length with the manager and decided to let him research the various avenues where investment could be better than leaving the money in the account at present. Barty himself would look into the possible purchase of a second boat. There could be risks but he was happy to go along with the manager's advice. While he was in Woodbridge he took the advantage to buy a good supply of food for himself and Tom and on returning to the boat, Tom told him that he had had a visitor at the boat. On learning that Barty had gone to Woodbridge the man was invited to await his return about mid- afternoon. The man declined saying that he had an appointment elsewhere and didn't have time to wait. Tom described him as being well dressed, about six-feet tall, slim build, dark hair and a short dark beard, he had no discernible accent. The man's visit worried Barty as he had said that he wished to see him concerning a personal matter. Try as he might he couldn't think of anyone that fitted the description given by Tom, he didn't say he would come back and only stayed on the quayside for the time it had taken to make his enquiry. He went to the office and told Skipper and Sarah of the mysterious stranger, they too couldn't fit the description to anyone they knew and hadn't seen the man on the quayside. Although the incident nagged at his mind he tried to dismiss it, it was the 'personal matter' disturbed him. Who was this stranger?

    Sarah told him that during the next month they had four contracts, all accepted and booked. These were to be normal routine trips around the usual coastal towns except for one that was to take some building materials from Felixstowe to Lowestoft. This journey would be a minimum of four days – the time contracted – entailing a longer trip than they normally made but the contract terms were financially beneficial to the Company, at least these were clean cargos that required little attention after unloading.

Payoff' from the last venture was made via various channels, Barty and Tom's share was paid to them in cash so that it couldn't be traced through any accounts. Barty paid Tom his share together with some outstanding wages with which he was extremely pleased saying that he had received more money for that one venture than he had received for three months' wages whilst working on the farm! He was prompted to ask when the next 'venture' was to take place but of course, Barty couldn't answer that question, as the Committee hadn't met and Barty had to remind him of the need for secrecy and not ask too many questions.

The weather had turned quite autumnal as *Ellie May* left her mooring, the River Deben was placid as they travelled to the estuary. The boat was un-laden and very light requiring extra care in handling due to the pull of the tide. They turned south and as they approached Felixstowe Tom was reminded of his first trip when they received the sick boy from the grounded motor cruiser. In the harbour, they tied up at the stern of a Thames barge that had transported a mixed cargo from the Port of London, part of which was the building material including prefabricated panels to be loaded into *Ellie May* for transportation to Lowestoft.

It was becoming dusk when the boat was fully laden and ready to leave so they decided to remain in Felixstowe for the night and depart at first light in the morning. The sea was very calm, hardly a ripple as they left on auxiliary engine. There was very little wind and a brightening dawn made visibility crystal clear and on reaching open water the engine was stopped and the single sail hoisted. Progress was rather slow due to the lack of wind but everything was so peaceful it seemed as if they were in another world. Passing slowly up the coast, Barty had ample time to show Tom the coastal charts relating to the coast, the landmarks, the lighthouses and safe havens until they eventually sighted Lowestoft Harbour. The trip had taken much longer than estimated but it had been so relaxing they didn't worry about the time. They found their allotted berth but had to remain loaded as the Harbour Master's Office had closed for the day, so they made a hot meal and decided to go for a drink at the public house at the end of the pier leaving Shuftee in charge of the boat.

They were awakened early in the morning by a loud banging on the cabin roof by a Docker who was eager to start the unloading with the aid of a small crane to lift out the large Swedish prefabricated panels.

Cargo off-loaded, Barty went to the Harbour Master's Office for clearance. The Harbour Master told him that a man had called to see him the day before but being late in docking had left him a note which he handed to Barty.

'Unable to contact you, will try again at a later date' It was signed *WJM* nothing more. Barty assumed that it was the same man that had called at the Tide Mill, there was no further clue, just *WJM* and that meant nothing to him. How did this mystery man know he would be in Lowestoft? The Harbour Master just described him as well spoken, tall with a beard. Not much help but it did appear to be the same man.

The journey back to the Tide Mill was pleasant and uneventful, once berthed Barty went to the office while Tom busied himself sweeping out the hold and generally squaring everything off. Skipper was in good spirits but seemed to be having even more trouble with his mobility, he was now using a walking stick all the time. Mr Spalding had taken him into Woodbridge in the bullnose car to see his solicitor, John Salmon. Whatever his business there is unknown but he was happy and content when he emerged. Skipper still longed to get back on the water but knew he could never be agile enough to be anything more than a passenger. He often spoke with his lifelong friend Arthur Spalding about it, they had been friends for many years and were both content in each other's company. Arthur had also started at sea then, being the recipient of an inheritance started his own business and progressed to become very successful. Occasionally he used to take Skipper with him to meetings as he placed much credence on Skipper's sound advice and experience. They had worked together well in the past and were still able to find satisfaction in their connections at the Tide Mill and the more lucrative 'trades' they enjoyed. Altogether, the arrangements with which they were living today had worked for them, one way or another, throughout their lives and was beneficial to them all, even Tom who was now included and was well content with his new employment.

The Committee was called to meet and everyone attended. The plans for the next 'venture' was planned and finalised for the landing of a large shipment of brandy. As the bulk weight of the crop would be fairly heavy, a flat easily accessible landing was necessary, the usual landing under Easton Cliffs being unsuitable. Dunwich beach just below the Heath was chosen as there were roads through Dunwich Forest to easily accessible safe houses. As was normal practice the timings and final details were not given to avoid possible leakage of information.

The moonless night finally came and the well-planned organisation swung faultlessly into action. *Ellie May* was crewed by Barty, Tom and Ted, while on the shore, cart wheels creaked and the sound of horses' hooves, although muffled, made a scuffing sound along the roads converging close to the landing place waiting for the signal to move onto the beach.

The transfer of the goods at sea took place without any problems and as *Ellie May* neared the shore Ted spotted the 'Coast Clear' signal. The boat came into shore as close as was possible, she was low in the water, and men moved quickly and silently, waist deep in the water to gather the casks and carry them to the waiting carts.

Everything appeared to be going according to plan when suddenly, one of the watchers ran onto the beach to warn the gang that Excise men and some local militia men had been sighted coming quietly through Dunwich Forest. They had received a tip-off, but had purposefully left their intervention as late as they were able in order to catch the goods being trans-shipped red handed. The word was passed at speed and although there were still a few casks still on the *Ellie May*, being now higher in the water, she was able to get under way quickly with the use of the engine. Realising that the smugglers were escaping they swiftly swooped on the carts and arrested the drivers while a few men were able to disappear into the Forest.

The unlit boat managed to leave the shallows and into the moonless night without any recognition, to hide her name she had a tarpaulin draped over the stern. How many men had been arrested, no one knew? To return to the beach to try and pick up any men left there would have been foolish. *Ellie May* returned to her moorings, squared off the decks after removing the remaining casks under the grain in the barn and turned in as soon as they were able in case they received a visit from the authorities. Shuftee was on deck and would give early warning should anyone approach. The rest of the night passed without any callers but nobody had much sleep that night.

    Mr Spalding, Skipper, Barty, Ted and Tom, away from the ears of Mrs Spalding and Sarah, met on the quayside that morning to discuss the nights' happenings. Nearly everyone that occupied the front of the big house had been disturbed by the commotion of the boat coming to the quay and of Mr Spalding leaving the house to assist in the hiding of the remaining casks. One looming problem would be the number of questions asked about the nocturnal activities. No questions were asked that morning as everyone was busy with their normal duties and didn't meet each other. By midday it became general knowledge to the people of Woodbridge that something had happened during the previous night as the newspaper headlines announced.

CAUGHT IN THE ACT.
EIGHT MEN ARRESTED BY CUSTOM OFFICIALS.

The headline was followed by a shortened report as this was breaking news. The full facts would be reported in a later edition as the news became available. The article simply read –

"Eight men were arrested on Dunwich beach in the early hours of this morning. After receiving certain information, Customs and Excise men assisted by men from the local militia raided the beach at Dunwich and intercepted a consignment of contraband goods as they were being transferred from ship to shore. The goods were confiscated and the carters were arrested. Unfortunately, the vessel bringing in the goods was darkened down and escaped as H M Customs vessels were unavailable to assist in the raid. At present, there are no clues to the identity of the vessel and no further details of the incident are available at present. Enquiries are continuing".

Mr Spalding immediately called an emergency meeting of the 'inner circle' and included Tom as he had been a first-hand witness to the whole saga. They met in the lounge of the big house for a deep and extended discussion about the whole episode. They concluded that a message should be sent to all Committee members informing them that all activities would be suspended until the conclusion of H M Customs enquiries. During their talks, the 'inner circle' believed one of the helpers on the night, a lookout, a carter, someone had passed the information on to the Customs hoping they would gain a reward greater than the hush money and benefits they had already received. Should the authorities have suspicions and ask questions about the hiring's of the *Ellie May*, it would have to be business as usual, and the books were available. She had been alongside most of that day and was certainly still there at daybreak. The only people who knew of her movements were the members of the Committee and some helpers on shore with the landing and some of them didn't know her actual timing, so the leak must have come from one of those helpers, there was no other explanation. Sarah's suspicions had really been aroused, was it time to tell her the truth? What would be her reaction?

 As it happened, that very afternoon Sarah came down to the *Ellie May* soon after the 'inner circle' meeting had ended. During her visit, she asked Barty why the boats name on the stern was covered. This was a small point he had missed, small maybe but it could have had dire consequences. The name was covered on both sides of the bows and the transom to hide her identity from the Customs men but in their haste to conceal the few remaining casks, it had been overlooked. Barty made the excuse that the tarpaulins had been hung over the bows and stern as they had been scrubbed and were drying. Sarah didn't say anything else but he got the impression that she wasn't wholly satisfied with his explanation. She had started to piece together certain facts and, in future there would be further details that would suggest clandestine happenings.

At his first opportunity, he spoke to Mr Spalding about his daughter who agreed to speak with Sarah that evening. Barty had emphasised that he had tried to keep their extra-curricular duties secret to protect her but now that she was a part of the administration of the Carrying Company, things had become very difficult. He didn't want to lie to her so he would leave the explanations to Mr Spalding, whose advice he totally trusted. Being engaged to Sarah he felt that there should be no secrets. Mr Spalding agreed and just said "Leave it with me."

The following morning, Barty went to the office to be greeted by a remarkably cheerful Sarah. Apparently, she had spent a long evening together with her father who had told her everything about the operations of the Committee and much to his surprise she confessed that she had long held suspicions even before Barty came on the scene. Her father had tried to keep his activities well separate to his family life but they lapped over occasionally She had often wondered why so many business men – members of the Committee -had regularly met at the Mill. She often had heard odd remarks or witnessed small occurrences connected to the Committee but never commented on them but they just led to further suspicions that her father was involved in something more than the milling and boating trades.

Barty lingered in the office for a long time talking to Sarah. There seemed to be an air of easiness between them as if a shadow had been eliminated from their relationship. Sarah was completely 'au fair' with the business administration of the carrying Company and that of her father's businesses but was not involved in the nocturnal activities in any way shape or form. Barty had spoken freely of his business and personal life but confessed that he had found great difficulty in keeping secret the work of the Committee. Now that her father had told her everything following her promise of secrecy, it was if a guarded part of their relationship was no longer a barrier that had to be covered up or lied about. Unknowingly at first, Tom had become an integral cog in the wheel just by being present at the last two ventures', the latter reminding him for the need for utmost secrecy and now, Sarah although not directly involved was subject to that same promise.

Eventually they got down to the real business of carrying and Sarah told them she had received several contracts for the boat, carrying goods, regular jobs, nothing exciting but all good money earners and now that their 'Cross Channel' trade had been temporarily suspended, any well-paid work was welcome.

Remembering his mystery caller, Barty asked if there had been any further contact from Mr WJM but that still remained a mystery.

Skipper was present when Mr Spalding came to the office and declared that they should have a business review if all had time to spare. Sarah told them of a very healthy bank balance and a reasonably good diary suggesting plenty of work in the near future, before Barty announced that he would like to add a second boat to the business. The inshore trade appeared to be picking up even though the railways were getting a lot of new transport routes. Many of the inland and river towns had no railway connection so Barty's idea was discussed at length. They agreed that initial enquiries should be made to try and establish the possibilities and the possible costs. Skipper said he didn't want his retainer pay as a reserve crewman as he was now living at Keeper's Cottage and receiving a small wage from Mr Spalding for his light duties around the mill complex, he requested that his part of the wage bill be transferred to Tom who was due to a pay increase. Sarah was happy with her wage from her father and from the administration work she did for Barty's Company. Barty for his part, was pleased with his share of the returns from his partnership with Skipper, all profits going into the Company account.

Ellie May was in excellent condition and required very little in the way of maintenance, nothing that Barty and Tom were unable to fix between them. Tom was getting more and more interested in navigation and he was a great asset to Barty, he never complained or asked for anything unless it was advice. His living conditions left much to be desired and he spent a lot of his time in harbour studying Barty's books and charts. He was an avid reader, devouring novels one after the other. He often remarked how much he valued his job, the freedom it brought to him and the friendship he had found with Barty and his colleagues. If anyone deserved a pay rise it was Tom. A very important member of the crew was not forgotten, Shuftee was happy with his lot!

On the whole, the review served to show how well everything was working and would in the future now that there were no secrets to hide although the identity of the informer was yet to be traced and as the trial of the arrested men progressed, there was still a possibility of a visit from the Customs and Excise Authority

As Mr Spalding had some interest in the leisure boating trade, Skipper asked him if he could offer any advice on what type of vessel they should purchase, stressing that it would be employed in the coastal trade and the probable asking price for a good seaworthy craft. He agreed to look into the matter and report his finding later. He took this opportunity to ask Barty if he would be interested in skippering a day boat for a sight-seeing trip on the River Deben. Not wanting to miss the experience he jumped at the chance provided that he could take Tom as crewman. Mr Spalding said he had hoped that that would be the case and the trip was scheduled for the end of that month – September. That would give Barty the chance to buy a couple of 'tourist type' books on the River attractions to prepare for any questions that may come his way. He asked Sarah to enter it in his diary to avoid any double bookings. He also wanted to familiarise himself with the craft, the *'Deben Dove'*, a 70-foot passenger boat with 40 seats and a small galley and bar.

A short two-mile trip down the Deben with Mr Spalding, Sarah, Skipper and Barty at the helm with his crew mate Tom soon convinced Mr Spading that he had made the right choice. Barty had no trouble adapting to the diesel engine craft and handled the boat with complete ease and confidence. Skipper enjoyed the short trip as it was the first time he had been on the water for several months and he could just sit back, have a beer and take in the passing scenery.

A week before the tour trip was due, Sarah reminded Barty that his birthday was due on September 21st. He had never celebrated his birthday much, mainly because he had spent so many years on his own and because he had just forgotten! She had made arrangements for the two of them to have a quiet dinner at The Crown in Woodbridge. It was a lovely candlelit venue where they sat to enjoy a first-class meal in each other's uninterrupted company, uninterrupted that is until the landlord brought to their table a beautiful iced birthday cake, Sarah was trying to make up a little on all the times he had not recognised his birthday.

This was the first time that they had found themselves alone in such an intimate setting, so it wasn't long before the conversation turned to marriage. Sarah, who had experienced a perfectly stable and secure upbringing wanted to get married as soon as practicable but Barty, whose life had been anything but secure, wanted to wait a little longer until they had a new boat and trade had settled down so that he could offer her a brighter life. He also hinted that he wanted to know the outcome of the Customs enquiry from the last 'venture'.' Although he felt that they had not been identified he wanted to be sure. He didn't want to marry and then find out that they could be separated in a few weeks' time should he be found, convicted and sent to prison. He remembered the fate of his father. In talking it through, Sarah could see the wisdom in his hesitation and decided not to pursue the subject for the present.

At 10.30pm Sarah's father collected them in the car as previously arranged and took them back to the Tide Mill. It had been a most enjoyable evening but it had given Barty much to think about.

The *Deben Dove* looked resplendent in her coat of fresh white paint reflecting in the still waters of the leisure pool as twenty bird watchers bristling with binoculars and cameras boarded her about three berths away from the *Ellie May*. Barty and Tom were at the gangway to welcome them aboard and issue each one with a life jacket. The group leader asked Barty if they could have a fairly slow passage so that his members could take full advantage of the beautiful scenery along the banks of the river and to take photographs from time to time

The journey down river should be quiet and relaxing but may become a little busier with river traffic as they neared the estuary. The plan was to start the return leg before they reached the sandbar at the river's mouth. It was a beautiful autumn day as the half laden *Deben Dove* left the mooring and nosed her way into mid-river in bright sunlight and Barty could announce that,

"The bar is now open should anyone wish a cold drink"

In charge of the bar was Sarah who had agreed to act as barmaid and also supply any refreshments that were ordered.

The passengers had plenty of space to set up their equipment and settle onto the deck seating. Soon they were passing large farming estates where busy farmers were still harvesting the results of their earlier efforts. They had a perfectly peaceful relaxing outward trip with frequent stops along the way to enable the 'twitchers' to use their cameras and on one occasion, Barty went alongside an isolated jetty to allow some passengers onto the fringes of the marshlands in the hope of spotting a rare marsh bird.

As they approached the shifting sandbar at the mouth of the river, Barty turned the boat and headed towards their scheduled lunchtime booking at a public house near Felixstowe Ferry, a fascinating little fishing hamlet. Landing was easy from the ferry jetty and just to the south was a good view of two Martello towers, built as defence towers in Napoleonic times, they were the focus of many long-distance camera shots.

A satisfying fish lunch provided the passengers with renewed vigour as they boarded the boat to enjoy the panoramic views along the wooded banks, sandy beaches, gently sloping corn fields and lush green marshlands. At convenient places, a few of the braver passengers ventured a little further on shore after landing in one of the *Dove's* small rowing boats. Progress became even slower as the setting sun sank lower and the keen photographers took enumerable pictures of the wonderful light shades and the setting sun.

Later than scheduled they approached the Tide Mill. Throughout the day Barty had pointed out places of interest as they appeared in the landscape. He had taken the trouble to learn the main points to watch for from his tourist trip book and drew the passengers attention using the public-address system. Sarah had coped extremely well in the galley and bar, Light refreshments, tea, coffee, wine and beer being available throughout the day, except at lunchtime and business had been good. As the passengers went ashore at the Tide Mill it was evident that they had enjoyed the days outing as they pressed 'tips' into Barty's hand and made comments that showed their appreciation of the work put in by the members of the crew. After the tripper's departure and the boat had been secured, Barty remarked that he had found the day most relaxing, Tom agreed and said he wouldn't mind a cargo like that every day, no loading and unloading, good company and a lucrative pay off. Sarah had worked hard and didn't have much time to admire the scenery but she said that she felt she had done her bit and would gladly do it again. Including the 'tips' they had received and the hire fees, Barty began to wonder if the leisure industry had more to offer than the carrying trade. It had made a lovely day out and his only regret was that he had not taken Skipper along with them, he would have loved it.

Back in the office, Barty had found that more contracts had arrived in the post that Sarah had not yet been able to attend but there was no further correspondence from the mystery caller. Mr Spalding produced a couple of brochures regarding boats for sale but on perusal they didn't satisfy their needs and were more expensive than they had anticipated. They had spoken quite lightly about their prospective purchase but looking through the brochures Barty realised that he must be more specific about his requirements, much more research was needed before he committed money to the purchase. In his mind Barty thought along the lines of another wherry but the decision wasn't his alone.

Several more contracts were completed before Barty, Skipper, Mr Spalding and Sarah were able to get together on a social occasion and to discuss previous business and family affairs. The subject of marriage arose again but Barty wanted to feel wholly satisfied with the business of the Carrying Company. He dearly wanted another boat so no date was fixed and no one disputed his reasons.

One development was the trial of the eight men arrested on Dunwich beach on the night of the last 'venture'. Without exception, they all attended Court and were sentenced to six months' imprisonment. They were all hired helpers and therefore unable to identify their employers for that occasion. They were hired in pubs by word of mouth receiving their pay from an anonymous third party,

. The employers could not be identified as each man had been paid off by different persons at various locations convenient to each individual.

The Committee had always looked after their men although many were unknown and there was a great trust in them, and so it would be with the convicted men, their families would be cared for the duration of their internment. "Honour among thieves!" As for the Committee, they were thankful that the Revenue cutters were not out that particular night and the authorities didn't intercept until much bulk of the consignment had been landed and spirited away before they swooped on the unfortunate men still at the scene. Further 'ventures' would remain suspended even though justice was seen to be carried out as far as the general public were concerned.

   Life at the Tide Mill fell into a pattern, the quayside was busy with non-stop loading and unloading of visiting vessels, only the leisure trade seemed to be doing well but even they were beginning to feel the drop-in trade as the autumn weather slowly turned colder. It was only a few weeks before Christmas again.

The Carrying Company honoured its contracts and managed to keep a fair timetable even though the wind and weather played a large part in occasionally delaying deliveries by a few hours every so often. The slight slackening in trade gave Mr Spalding, Skipper and Barty a chance to get together and look towards the mill development as a whole. It was clear that the mill would carry on in business without problem, everyone needed flour and weekly deliveries would be made as long as the conditions allowed. So, the Carrying Company under its new partnership was only really in its infancy but looking prosperous. Similarly, the leisure hire business was popular and the next season's bookings were looking good but that was Mr Spalding's' own private undertaking. This lead to the topic of the trip that Barty, Tom and Sarah had hosted for the birdwatchers and everyone had to agree that it ws probably the best financial hire that had dealt with all summer, this gave way too much more thought and discussions.

The question of buying another boat still lingered on, but what kind of boat? It was still viewed as being financially impossible at the present time, it was something to be looked at again in the following year.

During the meeting, Tom called into the office, unaware of the meeting taking place and Mr Spalding invited him to sit in, after all he had been involved with the set-up for a while now and his opinion may be of value. Tom had nothing but praise for the birdwatching trip, how light the work, how enjoyable the charter and how it had proved so beneficial to all of them. Mr Spalding had previously given then a complete breakdown of all the incomings ad outgoings concerned and concluded in asking the question, "Would it be better to invest in a leisure boat instead of another wherry?"

The question created a whole new discussion and the meeting was extended well past the planned time, so far past that Mrs Spalding came to ask if they would like a light lunch while they talked?

Although Barty had had toyed with the idea, it was Toms question that had provoked the subject as Barty had never mentioned it before. It was only an idea in the back of his mind. In conclusion, they promised to meet again in two weeks' time to pool their findings and the possibility that here might be a new extension to the Tide Mill Carrying Company.

After the meeting, Tom returned to the boat, Barty and Skipper spent time together to speak of their partnership and how a new development could affect them but the main reason was to pass some time together as old friends. They reminisced well past tea time when Barty left to return to the *Ellie May* to check that both Tom and Shuftee were okay. He found Tom studying the navigation books again saying that his interest had been invigorated by the possible development of the Company and would, in the future, like to become a qualified Mate.

In the following weeks' Barty and Tom found their research enquires limited as they were away on a couple of trips. They did, however manage to obtain some information from the library at Harwich, where they had business, and from the Public Information Offices in

Woodbridge and Felixstowe. Time passed so quickly and their work occupied most of their time. The second meeting of the group convened and each presented their findings. Mr Spalding had been looking at the costs of a suitable vessel, most of which would require modernisation to upgrade them to meet the Board of Trade Safety Regulations, the results could prove rather costly. Barty and Tom had been exploring a suitable base, perhaps on another river, where the river attractions and the town populations may offer extra trading possibilities; Skipper had been looking at displacement figures, lengths of various vessels and their adaptability for use on nearby rivers for whatever purpose, leisure or carrying. Sarah had been office bound collating all the information they had gained so far and applied the possible income against expenditure, a very difficult exercise not knowing the type of craft or business they would settle to employ. It was accepted that the idea was sound and practicable but other attractions would be needed to supplement the decline in the leisure trade in the winter, for example river fishing, something to think about in the future.

Sarah presented the Treasurers' Report for the Tide Mill Carrying Company which was satisfactory but they decided to get Christmas over before pursuing any new purchases or activities.

The mention of Christmas prompted Mr Spalding to invite everyone to spend it with him and Mrs Spalding at the Mill. Skipper was a little reluctant to accept as he had always spent Christmas with his daughter and family in Ipswich whenever he was able but recognising his physical limitations he decided to accept the invitation, after all. The company of his good friends at the Tide Mill were very much like his own family.

Living at the Tide Mill was like living in a different world, they saw nothing of the festivities in Woodbridge as they prepared for the coming holiday and very little was ever said about the various activities which were staged as part of the attractions of living in a town. As Christmas rapidly approached, Sarah said they should both go into town and buy gifts for the people they knew would be at the Mill at Christmas. Imagine Barty's surprise to see the town dressed for the holiday, he had never seen such a sight before, the town appeared to be alive with a myriad of bright twinkling lights and a magnificently tall beautifully dressed Christmas tree just in front of the Town Hall. All the shops were ablaze with coloured lights and scenes of the Nativity in many windows Sarah had of course, seen such a display several times before living so near a town but as for Barty, well it certainly opened his eyes. Only once before had he experienced the real meaning of Christmas, that was when he was in the Army in France when a short religious service was held at the veterinary hospital. The Service made Barty realise the futility of the war and he was thankful that he wasn't engaged on the front line. His work was as a result of the fighting on the front line, the wounded and maimed animals he was treating that had been arriving daily giving hardly any time to celebrate Christmas. It was only that short Service and a gift containing small comforts from the Red Cross that even hinted that it was Christmas, the fighting and misery had continued for a very long time to come. Barty even remembered the Christmases that he had spent when he worked at the farms prior to joining the Army but during those times there was no communication with or from his parents. He had often wondered what had become of his mother? It was similar with his father. Barty had visited Woodbridge Prison a long time after his father's release but never managed to find a forwarding address. This saddened Barty but now he had a relationship with Skipper and Sarah and his life had taken a new path. He also felt that Mr Spalding, Ted Moore and Tom had become quite dear to him and he resolved that he would make the most of the approaching celebrations with his new-found family.

Sarah and Barty were really busy the rest of the day. They were intending that every guest at the Tide Mill for the holiday would receive a small gift from them. Luckily Barty had Sarah by his side to guide him in his purchases as he had no ideas himself! So many were their purchases that they had difficulty carrying them. It wasn't a long walk back to the Mill but laden as they were, they took a cab back home.

There was only one more contract to fulfil, a two-day trip to Aldeburgh and Southwold with part loads, before the Christmas break. While away in Aldeburgh, Barty took the opportunity to buy his special gift for Sarah, a gold neck chain and locket. The trip went without problem and gave extra time for Tom to take the tiller and ask endless questions about the coast and the charts applicable to that sea area.

The Spalding's were a traditional old Suffolk family and as such they always tried to re- enact some of the old traditional customs related to the County. In some parts of the County, one of the first rites on Christmas Day was "the boiling of the Hackin", a giant sausage that was served with beer and cheese. If the Hackin had not been boiled by daybreak, two young men would fetch the cook and chase her around the village market place as a penance for being idle. In the Spalding household, the cook was always Mrs Spalding and being a lady of punctual habits always arose early on Christmas morning to prepare the Hackin, beer and cheese. Following close to this tradition, before dinner, a group of children would arrive from the village, take off their coat and tie ribbons to their shirt sleeves, decorate their hats with Christmas foliage while one boy with a skin pulled over his head jumped about among the onlookers with a collecting box.

On the same day, also just before dinner, one Suffolk village held a Cold Fair. That village was Coldfair Green near Leiston the village where

Barty was born. Originally it was an animal fair but over the years it had developed into a larger event with roundabouts, boxing booths and a fortune teller from Knodishall, a gypsy encampment about a quarter mile from Coldfair Green, apart from fewer animals it was mainly a funfair. The assembly at the Tide Mill didn't visit the Cold Fair due to the many activities taking place on their own doorstep.

Barty and Skipper had spent the previous Christmas at his daughter's house in Ipswich, a lovely close knit family affair, very well organised and restful. The celebrations at the Tide Mill were much more a public affair with visits from the local traditional dancers, the Mummers and terminating with the singing of Christmas songs and refreshments all laid on courtesy of Mr Spalding, all this before dinner! Christmas Day dinner, what a meal that was, so much excellent fare cooked by Mrs Spalding and her hired helpers after which thanks were given by Skipper with a well-prepared toast to all. Skipper's speech and toast would have given great surprise to the King himself, Skipper's eloquence with words was unsurpassed. Gifts were exchanged and everyone were delighted with all the celebrations that appeared virtually non-stop. To add to a most happy day, Mr Spalding had booked a group of singers to entertain his guests for the remainder of the evening. Barty and Tom had never experienced anything like it before, when the singers had finished their contribution the National Anthem was sung and everyone retired to their respective quarters, Barty and Skipper to the Cottage and Tom to the *Ellie May* to be greeted by the patient Shuftee who had been guarding the boat.

After a short lay-in on Boxing Day, Barty went to the boat and he and Tom spent time tidying up the vessel and making ready for the next trip which wasn't until early in the New Year. There wasn't a deal to be done so they went up to the big house to see if they could be of any assistance there, but apart from odd jobs being carried out by the mill staff there was little that needed attention. The rest of the time between Boxing Day and New Year's Eve was spent just pottering about the mill and the boat and a single journey to Woodbridge for some fresh supplies for the boat. Tom applied himself to some extra studying and taking Shuftee for long walks in the surrounding fields.

New Year's Eve was an exceptionally lazy day, the boat was ready to leave on 2nd January, Barty spent the day with Sarah and Tom got out his books again between taking Shuftee short walks up and down the quayside which was practically deserted. Later. Everyone gathered for drinks and to celebrate the coming of the New Year, the celebrations ending soon after midnight

!923 dawned as a murky, drizzly day, the river running fast and Barty was pleased that their sailing day was tomorrow as he still felt a little jaded from the previous night's celebrations.

January 2nd wasn't much better but he now had a clear head and was looking forward to getting some clean clear fresh air and feel the wind against his skin again., it had been nearly two weeks since their last contract and the relief of getting back to the job felt good. They got under way immediately to catch the fast tide, Barty at the tiller while Tom prepared some breakfast. Safely in harbour they picked up sacks of grain from Felixstowe to take back to the Tide Mill then loaded flour sacks for delivery to Aldeburgh and onward to Southwold. Fully loaded they left the quayside within the hour. The weather had eased; the rain of yesterday had dropped but the wind had stiffened and Barty felt he should stay on deck with Tom to keep an eye on things. Shuftee was restless, he roamed about the deck several times watched constantly by the pair, he was often kept on a lead while the weather was rough but today he had a free run. He didn't seem bothered by his surroundings, many times standing still near the low guard rail gazing at the sea as if mesmerised.

He visited his litter box often, maybe the rich food over the holiday period hadn't wholly agreed with him. He responded quickly when he heard his name called but that could be that the call was mainly meant food in his brain! It seemed odd that his responses were different to his normal behaviour and it worried Barty and Tom who kept lavishing their attentions upon him.

Back at the Tide Mill, Barty went straight to the office to give Sarah his log and the paperwork while Tom stayed on board to check that Shuftee was okay. Once again Sarah told him that he had had a visitor while he was absent. Again, no name or reason for the visit was given and Sarah deduced that it was the mysterious Mr *WJM*. He did however say that he would call again on 7th January – tomorrow! Barty returned to the *Ellie May* to find that Shuftee seemed to be more his usual self, was it something he had eaten that had upset him for a few days or had he been feeling a little seasick?

The morning of the 7th saw them cleaning out the cargo space and generally tidying up when they heard a hail from the quayside and Shuftee started to bark. Looking up Barty saw a smartly dressed man standing on the quay waving. Mr *WJM*?

Barty stepped onto the quay and approached the stranger. There was something familiar about him especially when he spoke.

"Hello", he said, "remember me, Bill Marriot from Lowestoft College"? Barty looked at him carefully, "Yes" he replied, but recognition was made difficult as he had never seen him dressed in other than casual clothing or foul weather gear.

"Yes, of course, I heard that someone was looking for me but I didn't know who, what brings you here?"

"I didn't leave my full name as I didn't want to cause any confusion, I'll explain, is there anywhere we can talk privately?"

"In the cabin", said Barty, "come aboard"

He introduced Mr Marriott to Tom as his old instructor from Lowestoft College the asked Tom to leave them so they could talk privately. Saying he had plenty to do, Tom called Shuftee to him and walked off towards the big house.

Sitting in the cabin, Mr Marriott started to explain he reason for his visit. He told Barty that when he had first started at the College he, like Barty, had experienced the feeling that they had met before. Barty had spent only two days at the College and it wasn't until after Mr Marriott had thought about that feeling of recognition he wanted to speak to Barty. The examination that Barty undertook did not reveal the candidates name as they were tested by number recognition only. Following the practical examination, he had resolved to check the candidate number against the written test papers that he came to a certain conclusion. It was that conclusion that had urged him to try and trace Barty.

At this point, Barty made some coffee as he thought that this could be a long session. Mr Marriott continued saying that he had tried on several occasions to contact him without success. The week after Barty's attendance at the College, Mr Marriott had left the College to serve on sea- going vessel in order to take his Mates Certificate (Sea going) and he hadn't had the chance to follow up his findings except for the times when he found himself near East Anglia.

"Do you mind if I ask you one or two personal questions?" asked Mr Marriott, carefully watching Barty's face for his reactions.

"Not at all" answered Barty, who had nothing to hide.

"Can you tell me your full name and date of birth?"

"Kaleb Michael Bartholomew, but everybody calls me Barty and I was born on 21st September 1898, I was 25 last September"

"Where were you born?" enquired Mr Marriott

"Leiston, Suffolk"

"It's been a long time", Mr Marriott seemed to be speaking more to himself than to Barty. He was silent for a while as if he was thinking things through, Barty just watched him not wanting to interrupt his train of thoughts.

"At last" he murmured and looking straight at Barty he said,

"I think I have some news for you, but just a couple more questions if I may? Where were you before you started on the boats?"

"I was in the Army, the Veterinary Corps, worked on a farm before that and that's about it" said Barty.

"Where are your parents?"

Barty hesitated before answering, "When I was young my father was sent to prison and my mother and I had to move from our farm cottage, Dad was a farm labourer see, Mum had to go to London looking for work, I have not seen either of them since".

There was another long pause in the conversation then suddenly the bombshell dropped.

"Barty, I think I am your father"

Barty was dumbstruck, he had wondered why all these questions were being asked. He could see no connection with anyone or anything in his past who could be looking for him.

"You see my real name is not Marriott, it's Bartholomew, Walter James Bartholomew, folks call me Bill now, I changed my name after I left prison in Woodbridge as I couldn't find work after I was released. I did several jobs over the years but nothing permanent, I was a drifter taking work whenever I could find it and I finished up as a lighter man on the Thames. I eventually got my Bargeman's ticket and applied for the Instructors job at Lowestoft College. There's not much more to tell you at present, I looked for your Mum but I have never found any trace of her, it's just like she vanished into thin air".

After receiving the news that Bill Marriott was his father, Barty thought long and deeply about their conversation, he could see no reason to disbelieve anything he had said, it all fitted in with what he could remember even though it happened so long ago. He accepted all the facts with mixed feelings, how would his new-found father fit into his future life, he was a stranger of whom he knew so very little.

They spent a long time talking together and decided that they would meet again soon. His father had just finished his sea time and was going back to Lowestoft to resume his duties as an Instructor at the College.

Before he left, his father said how pleased he was to have discovered his son again after so many years, it had been about eighteen years since they were parted by fate, neither of them could recall the exact date, those times were in the misty past. As they walked down the gang plank onto the quay Barty said, "I have one more question for you now, do I call you Bill or Dad?" He was feeling a bit awkward but needed to be correct. Without hesitation, he received the reply, "I'd much prefer Dad if that's alright with you, I'm so pleased to have my son back again!"

As his father made his way down the quay side he couldn't wait to tell Sarah and Skipper the news, he was so excited that he even forgot to tell Tom or to say where he was going. For the first time since he was a young lad he suddenly developed a sense of not being alone, he was part of a real family, albeit a small family but this man was his father. He was very close to Sarah and Skipper, who he looked upon as a near family but now he had a real relative, a father, who he had often thought about but never found until today. His father had taken a long time to find him but he had never stopped, their lives had gone in different directions until that chance meeting at Lowestoft College had sown the seeds of recognition in his father and the final contact was made, a stroke of good fortune! Sarah and Skipper were both delighted for him, the elation of finding his father cold be seen in his eyes as he told them all he knew of him which wasn't a great deal but there was much to talk about.

Bill Marriott returned to his old post of Instructor at Lowestoft promising to write to Barty and hopefully set a date for another meeting when they could spend more time getting to know each other a little better. Sarah was eager to meet her future Father-in-Law, of whom she said that he sounded like a lovely man.

Barty had to repeat the whole tale again when he returned to Tom on the *Ellie May*. They talked for a while whilst taking Shuftee a long walk in a nearby field where he was able to run free.

Next morning Sarah came into the office to attend to the mail. It was a cold day and persistent snow flurries led to a limited visibility causing Barty to remark that he was glad the weather was poor and there was no reason to take the boat out. The mail was rather late that day, the postman was certainly feeling the cold after fighting his way through the snow and gratefully accepted a hot coffee laced with rum that Sarah had prepared. They sat around the blazing log fire and the postman was most reluctant to leave the comfort he was enjoying but he was now running a lot later that normal. The conversation had got around to the purchase of a cruise boat but they were still waiting for Mr Spalding to bring back more news about any of his latest findings. Skipper, who had left them to go upstairs to his room before the postman left, re-joined them. He appeared to be in good health but Barty noted the problem he had in negotiating the stairs. He sat in the old armchair and asked if there was any mail for him as he was expecting an important letter but there was only one letter of interest and that was a contract enquiry from a mill owner that was a little different from the usual as it would take them, not to sea but from river to river. Skipper commented that he thought that the coastal trade was getting less as the railways grew and there were more motorised coastal vessels serving the larger ports. There were quite a lot of Dutch vessels trading in and out of the London Docks and even Felixstowe was becoming extremely busy.

A knock on the door brought them back to the moment as Mrs Spalding came to ask if she could get them all some lunch. From her kitchen window, she had seen the postman depart and Tom and Skipper join them in the office, noting the inclement weather she had put a large pan of stew on the stove. Like the postman, they were reluctant to leave the fire and accepted the unexpected treat. Sarah suggested to her mother that when the meal was ready she should put a tea towel at the window and Tom and Barty would collect it at the kitchen door, only several steps across the yard from the Cottage

The meal being ready Mr & Mrs Spalding brought it across, - no signal. "Can you find room for two more?" asked Mr Spalding, "we don't get the chance to eat together very often" They shuffled around the office desk and a small table to enjoy a steaming beef stew loaded with vegetables and dumplings, a real winter warmer. Shuftee was more than happy lying in front of the fire giving his full attention to a large bone from the beef stew. When they had finished their meal, Tom helped Mrs Spalding return the dirty pots to the kitchen. Mr Spalding, out of earshot from his wife asked them to remain together as he has something he wanted to say to them.

    The members of the 'inner circle' were all present, Skipper, Barty. Tom and Sarah directed their attention to Mr Spalding who said he was taking this unique opportunity to speak to them. He told them that he had received a communication from his contact in France. He had never revealed how communications from France were sent or received but whatever the method, it was quick, reliable and precise. He told them of a planned 'venture' to take place within the next three weeks. As usual, the exact date was not given to protect the arrangements. This would be the first 'venture' since the eight men were arrested at Dunwich and that was almost three months ago. Full details would be revealed in due course but the landing pace would be below the Easton Cliffs yet again, one of the safest places on that coast as any signal from the cliffs could be spotted easily from the sea and the beach was hidden from anyone watching from the cliff tops. Ted Moore would organise the landing and dispersal of the crop, in fact everything looked as if it was the recognised routine. Barty, Tom and Ted would crew the *Ellie May*. Other members of the Committee, when notified of the precise details would organise the manpower. The only change to the normal was that *L'Etoile* would not be available for the transfer due to suspicions of the French Customs Service. An unknown named vessel was to replace her. This did cause a little concern as recognition was all important especially as the French Authorities had tightened up their patrols and *L'Etoile* had been searched in harbour as the vessel was suspected of being used for freetrade purposes, nothing illegal had been found. The French side of the organisation had thought it prudent to replace the suspected vessel with a different one.

  In the meantime, *Ellie May* had the river to river contract to complete, the details of which arrived the next day. They were to load a consignment of milled grain at the Tide Mill ready for transportation to Ipswich. A new cargo of timber was to be trans-shipped to Oulton Broad, near Lowestoft on the River Waveney. This would entail a lengthy journey up the coast from the River Orwell, up to Oulton Broad. Barty estimated the time allowed as approximately four days taking into account the loading and unloading times. Sarah had negotiated very good terms for the long journey to compliment the usual carrying charges for the first part of the trip from the Tide Mill to Ipswich They were well stocked for food for the journey but needed some extra supplies for the third mate – Shuftee. He had made several trips on the *Ellie May* and always stayed on deck while at sea. If the weather blew up rough, he was put on a lead and tethered in the cockpit where he was safe as he had a tendency to roam around and the boat had very low guard rails. He was a good guard dog though as Barty and Tom had soon found out, he would soon bark to warn them of any stranger approaching the boat and he was wonderful company to the helmsman in the quiet hours.

Just before his departure from the Tide Mill, Barty had received a letter from his father thanking him for the welcome when they last met and looking forward to meeting again very soon. He had signed the letter "Dad" and that thrilled Barty who immediately penned a short reply to say that he would be in Oulton Broad, unloading timber at the boatyard, on a certain date in three or four days' time., so if he could find time to meet him he would be delighted. Barty left his letter for Sarah to post for him.

The ebbing tide ensured a swift passage down the Deben, turning into the River Orwell to arrive at Ipswich by early afternoon. The flour was soon off-loaded but they were unable to start loading the timber until next morning so after a meal they spent a pleasant evening in the local pub where most of the customers in the tap room spent their time petting Shuftee and feeding him morsels from their snacks. They had taken him to the pub with him as a treat as he hadn't had much exercise during the day and the *Ellie May* was safe at her moorings.

"Early to bed, early to rise" It was getting late when they boarded the boat that evening only to be raised from their limited slumbers by a banging on the cabin roof and Shuftee barking his annoyance at being awoken so soon! The dock workers had arrived.

They started loading at 6.30am and it turned out to be a long job due to the one and only antiquated hand crane on the quay. They slipped the moorings late afternoon and decided to get to Felixstowe and spend the night there as they were both feeling tired.

Heading north next morning they found progress slow due to a strong headwind, each landmark passed agonisingly slow, the mouth of the Deben, the lighthouse at Orford, Aldeburgh, Southwold finally sighting the welcome flash from the Lowestoft lighthouse. It was drawing dusk when they finally berthed in their allotted place on Oulton Broad quay that was crowded with leisure craft. It was an early morning start once again and the timber was unloaded onto some waiting wagons destined for a large building site on the outskirts of the town.

During the process, Barty's father arrived, he was casually dressed and genuinely pleased to see his son hard at work with Tom at such an early hour. He immediately took off his jacket and offered to help with the unloading. The three of them plus one dockworker completed the task before stopping for tea. Barty's father had twice waited on the quayside for the arrival of the *Ellie May* which was late due to the changeable weather conditions en route.

It was Saturday and Bill said he had plenty of time to himself as he had the weekend off from the College. He took them to a nearby café for a belated breakfast before returning to the boat. Barty was surprised by the number and the variety of boats tied up around the quay while further into the harbour he could see coastal freighters spreading their cargos or loading ready for their onward shipping. The three of then strolled casually along stopping occasionally to pay attention to the odd craft that caught Barty's eye. Bill seemed to possess a wealth of knowledge about the vessels and was able to answer most of Bartys questions, he also had a good knowledge of the docks and judging by the number of people that spoke to him, he appeared to be quite a popular man.

Settling down on the *Ellie May*, Bill explained that he had a house near the docks and spent many hours on the quay. Barty was well aware that his father worked at Lowestoft College and had presumed that he lived in at the College, so it came as another surprise to learn that he owned a house on Beach Road, very near Waveney Dock, where they were moored. This revelation led to more questions, where had his father been prior to joining the College and how did he come to gain employment there? Tom produced some bottles of beer from the galley area as Bill said he felt that he owed Barty a full explanation about his earlier life.

He began to tell his story from the time he was committed to Hollesley Bay Prison for the theft of two legs of lamb from Sunrise Farm. Ten years was a long sentence, although he only served eight years during which time he worked mainly in the prison gardens. He had lost his tied cottage at Sunrise Farm so with no income, Barty and his mother went to the workhouse where Barty learned much of his basic education. His wife had left the Workhouse to seek domestic employment in London. He had never heard a word about her since that day and he had no idea what had happened her either.

After his release from prison Bill went to London to search for his wife and tried to find work. He was unsuccessful for a few weeks then managed to find employment on the London Docks. Living in the dockside doss houses but eventually finding a place as a Lighter man on a Thames Barge. He had remained in employment working to gain his Bargee's ticket which he did achieve quite a time afterwards giving him a better wage and enabling him to live in a comfortable Bed & Breakfast near the river. Reading in a newspaper he noticed in the Jobs Vacant section an advertisement for the post of Navigation Instructor at Lowestoft. On a whim, he applied thinking that his qualification may add weight to his application and to his utter surprise he was granted an interview. After further training he qualified for the full post, the rest, as he said was now history.

He had never traced Barty's mother and it was just a stroke of luck that he thought he recognised Barty when he attended his short course at the College.

The more they talked the more Barty realised that his father had had a hard time, he wasn't a persistent thief or even a petty thief, he had committed the theft crime to obtain food for his family in hard times and was caught, and paid the price. He had never again been in any trouble. He had strived to redeem his self-respect, to become an honest hard working man, that he had achieved.

Barty and Tom had listened intently to all Bill had said especially of his time spent at the College, Tom asked many questions as his intent was to gain his Inshore Certificate. They told Bill of their plans and the intention to buy another boat, how they were drawn to the leisure trade and that Skipper was exploring suitable craft and costs. Bill responded by saying that if he could be of any help he would be happy to do so adding that he often walked around the docks and harbour and if he spotted anything that might appeal he would contact them as soon as possible.

Living on Beach Road and near the college he was in a perfect place to hear the latest news from the harbour. Mention of his house reminded Bill that he hadn't told them that he was a member of the Lowestoft Lifeboat crew and had been since just after gaining his post at the College. Barty said it was a job that he had considered on occasions but his present occupation prevented it as he didn't live near a lifeboat station and that he was often away working when perhaps he would be needed. Finding yet another subject of mutual interest, Bill told them of one or two rescues around the coast and finished by mentioning the great disaster at Aldeburgh in December of 1899, a year after Barty was born. Bill remembered it well. For the next half an hour or so he kept them entranced with the story of the disaster and being men who earned their living from the sea they listened intently to his every word.

On that ill-fated December day the Coastguard fired the rockets that called out the lifeboat, Bill was 29 years old at the time, working at Sunrise Farm so the memory hadn't faded. Men had run to man the lifeboat, all the volunteer lifeboat men donned their cork life jackets and foul weather gear and made for the boat. Practically all the village folk had turned out to help launch the sail powered 18-man lifeboat into the rising and treacherous seas. Eventually the launch was made and the boat drew away from the shore to try to reach the vessel in distress but was overturned by two gigantic waves throwing 12 men of the crew from the boat to try to reach the shore. Six crew men were trapped inside the hull and found to be dead when the boat was washed up back on the shore, a seventh man died of his injuries. Bill said he hadn't intended to tell the story but his own involvement with the lifeboats meant so much to him that it brought the report to his mind. He said the whole incident had been intensively reported and documented they he would have thought they would have heard of it, if not then he felt that they should read the history of the incident, Barty fully intended to do that.

It was about tea time when *Ellie May* left the harbour bound for home, she was un-ballasted and responded quickly to the light easterly wind giving them a good headway. They took short turns at the helm giving each a chance to take forty winks but neither of them could sleep. Shuftee, and the other hand slept endlessly. The Channel is a very busy highway at the best of times but they were surprised by the amount of shipping using the Channel during the hours of darkness. Barty and Tom kept the boat well inshore keeping a sharp eye upon the chart, for the landmarks and for other inshore craft. Inshore trade was limited and most traffic preferred to move only in the daylight hours so they were surprised the see the navigating lights of a boat astern of them. They were passing the Easton Cliffs on their starboard side, an area well known to Barty and the following boat was catching up on them fast. Looking at the vessel bows on, it was difficult to see her type but they could hear the throb of her powerful engines. When the boat was roughly 500 yards astern, they were still no wiser to her purpose but it was then they heard a load-hailer. "Boat ahoy, this H M Customs Revenue Cutter *Vigilant*, heave too immediately" Barty and Tom swiftly dropped the sail and the powerful motor launch came alongside., they were approximately three miles offshore. Two Officers boarded the *Ellie May* explaining that they were intercepting craft suspected of being involved in illicit trade. They asked permission to search the *Ellie May* even though they had the right in law, Barty having no objections as they carried no load, he explained their business and proved it by showing the contract they had just completed and off-loaded at Lowestoft. The search was carried out in minutes, the Officers apologised for the intervention and wished them a safe onward journey back to the Tide Mill. Barty was pleased to be able to comply with the Officer's request and thanked his lucky stars that he hadn't been engaged in a planned 'venture'. The engagement worried him a little because this was the first time he had been stopped by the authorities, and near his usual route as well, was someone tipping them off? He thought this unlikely as the details of the next 'venture' had not yet been circulated, perhaps it was just coincidence, he had seen the *Vigilant* before but only around the port areas. He wondered if the French Authorities had been in contact with their English counterparts who had maybe given some false information. Whatever was happening he had noticed the increased activities of the Customs men and read articles in the newspapers about suspected increase of smuggling activity especially along the Norfolk and Cornish coasts. There had been one or two successful operations by the Customs Officials but they were mainly confined to the movement of illegal goods on shore, not at sea. However, Barty resolved to check with the 'inner circle' that all was covered by them ready for the next 'venture'.

The details and the stopping of the *Ellie May* were brought up at the final committee meeting prior to the next 'venture' in three days' time. All orders would be sent to team leaders and the whole venture put on standby while all arrangements were double checked.

Special attention was to be paid by the Watchmen on Easton Cliffs, they would be supported by extra 'hired eyes' looking both to sea and to all routes approaching the cliff tops. Information had been received from the French that the vessel replacing *L'Etoile* would be a two masted brig, the '*Monique*' that was able to carry more cargo and attain a faster speed due to the increased sail area. Her orders were to be the usual rendezvous point and transfer twenty tons of goods to the *Ellie May* then proceed to another rendezvous with an unknown vessel much further north. As far as the *Ellie May* was concerned, she was to carry a crew of four instead of the usual three, Barty. Tom. Ted and Sarah who would be the extra pair of eyes although she would not be expected to handle any of the heavy goods being transferred.

A low moon shed an eerie light over the water as *Ellie May* left the River Deben, the evening was calm and the sea almost as placid as a mill pond. While running north, the engine was needed periodically as the wind was so light and had dropped even more as they left the lee of the land. As they turned east towards the rendezvous point they were obliged to keep to sail only to be able to make any headway and minimise any noise from the engine. Sarah was the first to see a distant signal, an intermittent green flash from the *Monique*, the timing and position was perfect, no waiting by either vessel for the other to arrive. All navigation lights were totally extinguished and the crews worked solely by the light of the watery moon. With well-oiled blocks and pulleys, they off-loaded the goods in a reasonably short time while extra eyes scanned the waters and listened for the sound of approaching engines. Papers exchanged, *Monique* quickly got under way again heading north while *Ellie May* turned westward towards the Easton Cliffs. The two vessels were approximately four miles apart when Sarah's sharp eyes spotted what she thought to be a masthead light coming from the direction of the French coast, some 14 miles away. Immediately Barty extinguished all lights and had the boats name on the transom covered, he had the feeling that the approaching boat was a Revenue Cutter and could vaguely hear the hum of a powerful engine over the calm sea. Had they been spotted by the patrol?

To his great relief, the vessel seemed to stay about two and a half to three miles distant. He had seen the stern light of the *Monique* and turned in pursuit. The Revenue crew had evidently spotted both vessels and chose to pursue the *Monique*, being the taller and the nearest to their present position. *Ellie May* continued silently on her course using only the now freshening breeze for sail power.

The timed green light was directed towards the Easton Cliffs by Sarah who triggered the question "Clear?" Ted verified the reply that came from three different points on the cliffs that had been set by him. "Coast clear" Everything was well.

Barty brought the boat inshore until it grounded and was soon surrounded by a team of men to unload and carry the crop into the cave entrance. With the boat now fully unloaded it was afloat again and left the beach as the tide started to turn and by early morning she was tied up at her mooring at the Tide Mill. Ted had left the boat at Easton Cliffs and returned to his farm. Tom had turned in on the boat with Shuftee quietly guarding the gangway. Barty went back to the Cottage but didn't see Skipper who was still sleeping and Sarah went to the big house, tired out but still excited by her recent experience. Her sharp eyes had been a boon to the operation and she could be said to have saved the night.

    Mr Spalding went to the office that afternoon taking with him the papers the French skipper had handed to Barty from the transfer the night before. He noted all the details he needed and then destroyed the papers for security reasons. He had finished when Sarah joined him, she was still quite excited about her trip and told her father of the appearance of the French Revenue Cutter. He said he already knew but he would endeavour to find out about the occurrence. Sarah busied herself with the mail when Barty came in, apart from a couple of business letters there was one from his father informing him that he had found three river cruisers for sale that looked interesting. He didn't give any further details but suggested that if they could find the time they could meet in Lowestoft and view the boats. Barty was quite taken by the idea of returning to Lowestoft, the port really fascinated him but he must first discuss the suggestion with his partner, Skipper. Although Skipper had quit the sea-life, his knowledge and experience of all things maritime was invaluable. Being steeped in deep sea sailoring and the inshore trade both in sail and steam, his advice would be twice as valuable when it came to purchasing another vessel but first they must consult with their business bank manager. Sarah was busy making up the work diary when her father returned to the office, "News from France" he announced, "I have received an important message from my French friends" He unfolded the message and read,

"A French Customs and Excise Cutter had intercepted a brig, the 'Monique' about six miles off the coast of France. Her cargo of liquor, tobacco and bales of silk had been impounded and the crew arrested on suspicion of smuggling illegal goods upon which no tax had been paid" There was silence for a few moments, then Skipper remarked, "It's getting a bit near home!" Everyone agreed. The newspaper report from France hadn't surprised Barty as the Revenue Cutter was seen to be pursuing the *Monique* after the transfer, although the 'venture' from the English side had been successful, they could still perhaps be implicated in the pending investigation in France and the possible Court hearing. The actual arrest of the *Monique* took place only ten miles away from the transfer point. Had the French cutter pursued the *Ellie May* instead it would have been catastrophic as it would turn out to be for their French counterparts. The topic was explored at length and a decision was made that the 'inner circle' needed an emergency meeting very soon and should include some of the more prominent members of the Committee. This was set for two days hence.

    Mr Spalding, Ted Moore, Skipper, Albert Sutton, the corn and seed merchant, the Reverend Nathan Young, and Barty, all met to discuss the future of the organisation and what course to take should they become implicated in the French proceedings. The meeting lasted for hours until they adjourned to take welcome refreshment supplied by Mrs Spalding at the big house.

The result of the meeting was very hazy as there were so many unanswerable questions but it was ultimately agreed that all future 'ventures' would again be suspended with a view to disbanding the organisation totally. There had been too many near misses and leaked information's lately and the business was becoming too risky to carry on, all the members had legitimate businesses of the own and wouldn't want to jeopardise them. It was generally felt that the Authorities were breathing down their necks and they all had too much to lose should any one of the be questioned.

During this meeting, Tom had stayed on board with Shuftee, he had found it hard to keep his mind on his studies and eventually gave up trying. He tried sleeping but that didn't come either, his mind was trying to come to terms with what had happened. Had they been identified? He would fight with many questions until next morning when Barty came to tell him of the decision of the 'inner circle' that all 'ventures' would be suspended for the time being and possibly forever.

Tom didn't say so but he was relieved at the news but still aware that the enquiry could last for months so the threat would still linger on. He had obviously been thinking about his future because, right out of the blue he asked, "Have you thought any more about buying another boat for river trips?"

Barty thought he must be a mind reader as the subject had been lightly addressed as the result of his father's letter the day before. Barty replied by telling him that he and Skipper would be seeing the bank manager shortly. Meanwhile they should settle down and attend to the carrying business, now to be their main source of making a living

The next few days were spent cleaning and tidying up the *Ellie May*, the first chance they had had to square-off after the last 'venture'. A visit to Woodbridge was also necessary to stock up on the victuals kept aboard and the chance to make an appointment to see the bank manager while Shuftee guarded the boat, not that he was needed as the mooring was on private property and relatively safe.

After buying their provisions they went to The Crown for a leisurely pint and lunch before returning to the Tide Mill by teatime. Barty was able to spend a relaxed evening with Sarah talking of their plans for the future. They had been engaged for quite some time now so their talk soon turned to marriage' a guest list and where would they live after the wedding? Barty still didn't want to commit to a date until he had settled the question of another boat especially now as they seem to have lost a valuable source of income, he wanted to expand and give Sarah a secure life after the wedding. Once again, she seemed to fully understand his intentions. So much to be said and talked about, it was past midnight before she went across the yard to the big house.

After the meeting, word was sent out to all concerned in the stowage of contraband in barns, cellars and safe houses, in fact everyplace where they were kept hidden, that they should be cleared as soon as possible and sold off. All financial returns should be submitted to the Committee to ensure full and fair re-imbursement to all members. This was to be carried out in double quick time and all storage places should, after the disposal of the goods, appear as any normal domestic or commercial premises just in case any miss-led information should lead to their inspection by the authorities. No records of transactions were ever kept by any members and any paper work was destroyed after the necessary actions had been taken. All financial transactions that had ever been made were conducted using cash only. The financial side was dealt with solely by Mr Spalding, a respected business man, totally trustworthy and trusted by all, both commercially and with the closed community. When all traces of the organisation had been completely obliterated and all returns had been made, then the cash share-out would go ahead. Members would receive payments according to their involvement, some, such as the hauliers and watchmen would have already received payment on the night of their call-outs. All this would take a few weeks as the result of the French affair and the possible chance of being implicated was still anxiously awaited. Whatever the outcome, all shares would be paid as and when circumstances permitted. It was to be the end of the freetrade along this coast as it had been known for many years.

Sarah contacted the bank manager of the Tide Mill Carrying company to inform him that Skipper would be unable to keep the appointment made by Barty due to ill health. It was only a short distance to the bank but Skipper was just unable to walk that short distance so the Manager, Mr David Lloyd, would meet them at the Tide Mill tomorrow
They met in the small office at Keeper' Cottage, Skipper, Barty and Sarah, where Mr Lloyd gave them a printed statement of the Company account. Agreeing that the account was in very good terms they discussed the bookings that had already been received and the possibility of a loan should they decide to go ahead with the plan to buy a river cruiser. The time passed quickly and when it appeared that an agreeable result had been reached they concluded the meeting to the satisfaction of all four of them. The agreement had to be left with many open queries all dependent on the cost of the purchase and other factors but generally speaking the arrangements were accepted. Sarah carefully put all the papers relating to the business away after making a special note that Mr Lloyd had made a generous loan offer of £15,000 subject to conditions. Although the business account was quite healthy, both Skipper and Barty were hesitant to commit at this early stage. More research was needed and a suitable vessel found, it's cost, registration and moorings. It was most satisfying to know that the bank was offering the loan but they decided that the offer be left on the table for a couple of months at least.

When Mr Spalding was told of the letter that Barty had received from his father, he straight away offered to drive up the Lowestoft to view the boats. A time and day was arranged but sadly on the appointed day

Skipper was too weak to travel. Barty was extremely disappointed as he placed so much trust and reliance on Skipper' advice. Sarah agreed to go with him but he felt it may be a journey in vain without Skipper, but at the last minute he decided to take Tom along with them, not that he knew that much about buying a boat but more to support him and perhaps remember facts that he was liable to overlook or forget.

What he had forgotten was that Mr Spalding owned a small boatyard at the Mill and had a good knowledge of different types of craft, mainly working boats but he could certainly keep an eye open for a bargain should one be offered.

Bill, Barty's father was waiting for them on the quayside so they went to the Quayside Café for coffee and a chance to look through some pamphlets and papers advertising the sale boats. Bill had planned to visit the three boats during the course of the afternoon but had given no particular time. Luckily the boats were all moored in the inner harbour, just a short walk between them. They spent all afternoon looking over the boats that varied in several ways. The sales representatives were very helpful in supplying each boat's history and assets but they, of course wanted to make a sale! Having spent time on each vessel, one seemed to satisfy what Barty had in mind. Bill turned out to be a great help and had a very good knowledge of boats quickly pointing out any items or defects that could be detrimental to its intended use or quite costly to rectify. Bill did spend a lot of time wandering about the harbour as he lived so near them and he knew several of the men that worked there and spoke freely with them, he really was a great help.

Alter seeing all three vessels, still only one stood out, the same one that had attracted his eye in the first place before boarding any of the others. The *"Pride of Waveney"* was a double deck river cruiser seating forty passengers and appeared to be the closest to what Barty perceived to be ideal. There was no sales rep. present on this vessel and the price was not included in the brochure, it just read P.O.A. (price on application) at the Sales Office. The other two boats they had viewed were unsuitable so Barty decided to go to the Sales Office for the full specification and price. They had all agreed that the last vessel was more suited to their plans and told the salesman they would make further enquiries and get back to him. As Mr Spalding drove them back many more questions came to mind after reading the full spec. on the boat. The salesman had given Barty quite a comprehensive description of the *Pride of Waveney* that would require undisturbed study and Skipper was the man for that. The price he had been quoted was "offers in the region of £20,000" – more than he had anticipated but still within the realms of possibility should Skipper agree.

In the comfort of the lounge of the big house, the group met again, except for Bill and with the addition of Skipper, who had read through the brochures and papers concerning the boat.

"The *Pride of Waveney*", said Skipper, "I know that boat, it used to belong to John Proud who ran a boatyard and hire service in Lowestoft, he died about two years ago, leaving the business to his son. He ran the business into the ground, so to speak, too higher charges and some trouble with the Board of Trade. The business went into liquidation and as far as I know the *Pride of Waveney* has been at her present moorings for about 18 months or so. I expect she will want some looking at now, could cost a pretty penny to put her right. *Pride of Waveney*, yes, I remember her well, she was a lovely craft in her time, how much do they want for her?"

£20,000 or offers in that region" said Barty.

"Fair price dependent on her condition, I'd like to see her"

Mr Spalding volunteered to take Skipper to Lowestoft when he felt a little better, he wouldn't have to walk far as the car could be driven onto the quayside. Sarah would contact the Sales Office and make the necessary arrangements.

They kept their appointment and met Bill and the salesman on the quayside a few days later and paid a return visit to the *Pride of Waveney*. Skipper excelled himself climbing up and down, examining every nook and cranny, he did a detailed examination of the hull both inside and down to the waterline on the outside as far as he was able. For a man so limited in his movements he appeared to be inexhaustible, was so thorough and ably assisted by Bill who revealed a deep understanding of the nature of the craft and was in constant conversation with Skipper. Their combined knowledge was remarkable. Before Bill took up his present employment at the College he had been employed for a while in a boatyard and had certainly learned a lot. Mr Spalding and Barty could only get the odd question in here and there. The salesman in attendance was completely lost for words answering only questions put to him, mainly to do with the current workings of the harbour and the local boat sales, he was out of his depth.

When they had seen enough they adjourned to the Quayside Café for a meal, telling the salesman that they would call at his office before leaving Lowestoft. They lingered in the Café to talk about the prospective purchase. Skipper thought the boat to be a fair purchase but would like to see her out of the water. She certainly needed the hull scraped and painted and there was a fair amount of work to be done but nothing too costly as far as they could ascertain. They agreed that if they could negotiate a price reduction of about £2,000, as seen, she could be a bargain, after all she had been laid up for nearly two years, and did require work to be done. They returned to the sales office and put forward their offer.

"£17.500, as seen" said Skipper.

The salesman hesitated and after a minute or so he replied quietly,

"The craft is still in the hands of the Official Receiver and I shall have to contact them"

"Don't forget to remind them that it had not been in use for almost two years and will require a complete overhaul and paint job while it would be in dry dock. Cash as seen." He emphasised, "I'll leave you my contact address and hope to hear from you soon, in the meantime there may be one or two more questions so Mr Marriott here will keep in touch with you, he lives locally".

He nodded his assent as the trio left his office.

As soon as Skipper was safely in the back seat of the car, he was snoring, tired out from his efforts of the day that had seemed to inject a new rush of energy into him, he had been back in his element and enjoying the environment that he loved and knew so well, boats and water, but it had taken its toll.

By the time Skipper awoke next morning, *Ellie May* was on her way to Southwold with a load of flour, a routine trip. He had spent a long time after getting home last night, thinking deeply about the pending purchase. Much of the decision would be based on the Boat Surveyor's report due next week after dry docking. Should the report be favourable and the offer price accepted, the investment could go ahead with the approval of his partner, Barty. As the sale was down to the Official Receiver, he was quite confident that the offer would be accepted as they would settle for that amount to get the boat off their hands after such a long time. He knew the bank account was healthy and that Barty had been offered a loan if required. With all this and more on his mind he finally fell into a long, deep sleep. It was just prior to lunch time that he managed to get to the office where Sarah was busy with her work. He happened to arrive just as Mr Spalding entered the office. After the exchange of greeting the conversation turned to the visit to Lowestoft. Now that their additional income from their nocturnal activities no longer existed they each needed more legal trade to supplement their incomes. The money that had been made from their freetrade ventures. was kept by Mr Spalding, not in any account and when this was shared out they would be able to deposit an amount into their own personal accounts should they wish to do so. Everything really depended on the boat report and the final decision of the bank manager. They needed another meeting to iron out a few of the minor queries like maintenance budgets, wages for additional staff they would have to engage as Barty was the only one with a valid qualification to take the boats out. It was true that Tom was learning fast but how long would it take him to learn enough to qualify to take his exams? Perhaps a word with Bill might help to get a rough idea of the costs and getting Tom into Lowestoft College. Mr Spalding left the office after making two important offers should they be accepted or even needed. He would be quite willing to loan the money to the Tide Mill Carrying Company, enough for Tom to get to sea-school and the chance for him to buy a share in the Company to defray initial costs, details of which could be worked out later.

Skipper and Sarah talked together for a while and Skipper asked if she would make two appointments for him. He would like his own personal bank manager Mr John Salmon to visit him at the Tide Mill and a similar arrangement to see Mr David Lloyd, the Carrying Company solicitor, but not at the same time.

When *Ellie May* came back to her moorings she had no cargo to unload so Barty went straight to the office, it was getting late and Sarah was about to leave. Briefly she told him of the new diary dates for future trips that prompted him to remark on his return trip from Southwold and the loss of income due to having no cargo. He felt that a wider circulation of the business might prove beneficial. That noted, Sarah made mention of the earlier conversation between her father, Skipper and herself saying that all would be revealed at the next meeting but her present requirement was for a wash, a change of clothes and a good meal, she had been working non-stop most of the day. She invited Barty to take the evening meal at the big house, with the family. They hadn't seen much of each other when they were able to speak freely about things other than work. A quick shower and a change of clothes and Barty went to the big house for a satisfying meal and pleasant conversation with the family then return to the Cottage for a much-needed rest having planned to meet at the office the next afternoon when Sarah had dealt with the mail and paperwork.

Tom was hard at work next morning, cleaning out the hold, polishing the brasses and tidying up the cabin. Shuftee to was hard at work lying near the gangway keeping a silent guard on any activity that came near the *Ellie May*, he had become an excellent 'Keeper of the Plank' alerting Tom of the approach of any strangers. So, it was that very morning, a short sharp bark brought Tom on deck to find Ted Moore on the quay. Ted was passing on his way to see Mr Spalding, they were old friends and had quite a lot of sorting out to do with winding up the freetrade business. They were two very prominent and important characters and it had been previously agreed that they should settle all outstanding business with the approval of Skipper and the Reverend. Ted had just called to say' Hello' and to see if Tom and Barty were keeping well. Shuftee recognised him immediately and settled down to his guard duties again, just managing to keep one eye open!
Ted went up to the big house and he and Mr Spalding were not seen again until 2pm.that day. Mr Spalding's next meeting was scheduled for 3pm, just enough time for a quick bite to eat before Ted went on his way and

Skipper, Barty and Sarah met him in the office to discuss all the points previous outlined.

The idea of sending Tom to sea-school was approved but would also have to be agreed by Tom. The possibility of Mr Spalding investing in the Tide Mill Carrying Company was left on the table until Skipper and Barty had met with the Company solicitor and the two respective bank managers They looked broadly at the budget for the Company and agreed that if they could secure the purchase of the *Pride of Waveney* for the offered amount they would be able to afford the repairs that may be needed, everything now depended on a favourable reply from the Sales Office in Lowestoft.

After the meeting, Barty and Sarah decided to go to Woodbridge to see a movie film that was being shown at the Town Hall. They had both heard and read so much about the moving pictures but neither of them had had the opportunity to watch one before and the new technology was something to be marvel about, they watched in wonderment at this American production of 'The Jazz Singer' starring Al Jolson and May McAvoy the first ever film to have a synchronised dialogue and it was causing quite an interest among the townsfolk. They happily made their way home still marvelling at their first step into the modern age and found it hard to describe the experience to Tom.

Unknown to anyone, Bill had been several times to the *Pride of Waveney*. making notes and plaguing the sales staff to give him access on board, as the representative of the prospective buyer. They agreed and Bill was able to inspect the vessel in more detail. He asked if the boat was still covered by a Board of Trade Certificate allowing the carriage of passengers, he was not surprised to learn that it had expired. He asked when she was last dry docked, the engine ran up, the steering gear checked, were the life jackets included in the sale, there were so many things he wanted to know and the sales staff were getting fed up with his constant questions. Bill was doing his best to find anything that could perhaps reduce the buying price but all his questions were met with the same answer that the boat was still in the hands of the Official Receiver and their hands were tied. This fact was to be Bill's "ace in the hole" as the Receiver's Office had said as the vessel had been laid up for so long and they needed to settle as quick as possible, they would be open to price negotiation with the purchaser, dependent on the Surveyor's Report. That evening Bill wrote all his findings in a letter to Barty stressing that they needed to meet and talk about the situation as soon as possible.

Bill was proving to be a great representative and living in the town he could easily for the time to wander the numerous moored craft and paying special attention should a better sales prospect present itself, but the *'Pride'* appeared to be the only one suitable for their planned purpose. Being at the College gave him the chance to speak with other instructors and research the requirements of a Board of Trade Certificate and the costs and procedures in acquiring any other related documents and licences.

On completion of his research, he wrote to the Official Receiver's Office, as the agent for the purchaser, albeit - self-appointed – giving all the results of his extended findings and asking if they were grounds for a price negotiation.

He received a reply within a few days saying that due to the length of time the vessel had remained unsold and its present deterioration plus the need to settle quickly they would consider a reasonable offer but insisted that an early meeting with the purchaser was paramount.

Good news! It was Bill's weekend off from the College so he put the letter in his pocket and immediately made the journey to Woodbridge hoping that Barty would not be away on a contract. Time was of the essence, he had to speak with Barty and Skipper as soon as he was able. He found them both at the office with Sarah as they rarely left the moorings at weekends. Bill's visit was unexpected but they were pleased to see him and welcomed the news that he had brought with him. Bill stressed the need to meet with the Receivers so Sarah called her father to the office as Bill related the developments. Mr Spalding, an astute business man for many years listened carefully and agreed that they should attend the meeting even though Barty and Skipper had not yet met with their solicitor, that particular meeting was scheduled for Monday, the day after tomorrow, when David Lloyd, the bank manager, would come in the morning and bank manager and Noel Baxter, the solicitor, would visit in the afternoon. Mr Spalding asked Sarah to arrange to visit the Receiver's Office in Ipswich the following Friday as *Ellie May* had a two-day contract on the Wednesday and Thursday. Mr Spalding said he would drive them to Ipswich and at Skipper's request would represent him at the meeting. Even though very little walking would be necessary, it was clear that Skipper was now suffering with his condition

They thanked Bill profusely for all that he had done and kept him informed of any developments. As for himself, Bill felt that he had suddenly become a small part in the interests of his son, not part of the family by any means but able to show that he could play a useful part in Barty's life, it gave him a sense of belonging, something that he hadn't experienced in many a year.

During Bill's visit Barty took the opportunity to mention the possibility of Tom attending the College and Bill said he would find out when a suitable entry course was due to be held   On Tuesday morning, Skipper had a meeting with his own personal solicitor, John Salmon. The office was deserted except for the two of them and they were able to speak freely about Skipper's personal affairs.

2pm that same day saw the arrival of David Lloyd just as Barty reached the office and Barty insisted that Sarah also join them as she was the Company Secretary. The proposed extension of the Company was put to Mr Lloyd and terms discussed. Company funds were very good so dependent on the amount needed in the form of a bank loan, could the arrangements to be approved conditionally?

Barty had said that the new vessel would be based on a north Suffolk river from where they could access the Norfolk Broads with ease, now that trips onto the Broads were becoming more popular especially in the summer months. Mr Lloyd listened to the proposals and tentatively agreed to help as much as possible and to make any provisions that may be called requested. As he left Noel Baxter arrived, a similar story was given to him, and like David Lloyd they were promised every assistance in their efforts to develop the business, everything was dependent on the Boat Surveyor's Report.

On Wednesday morning, the *Ellie May* left with a cargo of flour for Southwold, due to return Thursday with a load of grain for milling. Tom was at the tiller most of the time, busy making notes on the conditions and keeping an eye on his charts. Barty and Shuftee sat in the cockpit just enjoying the extremely pleasant weather.

Friday's meeting at the Receiver's Office was fixed for 11am. Mr Spalding brought the car to the front of the office to pick up Sarah and Barty while Skipper waved them off from the window wishing them good luck at the meeting.

In the plush surroundings of a private room at the Receivers they began their negotiations, Mr Spalding, after explaining his presence instead of Skipper, asked most of the questions while Sarah made copious notes of their replies. A long time passed and the three visitors got the impression that the Officer, a kindly man, was becoming quite anxious and appeared to want the conversation quickly over. He took into account all the points that Bill had noted and after single telephone call, presumably to the vendor, he agreed to lower the purchase price by a further £1,500 to £16,000 but still dependent on the Surveyors Report. Mr Spalding had been a wonderful help in the negotiations, he business acumen coming to the fore in gaining the reduction. Barty believed that had he not have been present no concession would have been gained. The news was given to Skipper on their return home and he was utterly delighted and said that the sooner they made the move to complete, the better. Mr Spalding told them of more savings that could be made if they would let him undertake the repairs to the boat in his own boatyard but that would entail getting *The Pride* down from Lowestoft. The offer was left on the table and the discussion continued. The Company funds would allow for £10,000 to be withdrawn for the purchase and the remainder of the money would be made up from Skipper's and Barty's personal accounts. They each had accumulated a considerable amount in savings from their 'freetrade' activities although such amounts were never disclosed to anyone. Time seemed to pass so slowly while they awaited the Surveyor's Report in order that arrangements could be finalised. Whilst waiting they pursued their business commitments and Tom received a letter from Bill informing him of a Course at Lowestoft College on the same terms that had been afforded to Barty. He would be required to attend the College for three days only as he was receiving 'hands on' tuition while working on the *Ellie May*. Needless to say, both Tom and Barty were happy with the offer and immediately sent an affirmative reply.

News from France was received by Mr Spalding through his usual channel, that the five crew members of the *Monique* had been sentenced to four years' imprisonment each, and the Captain was given five years, fortunately no enquiries had been made in England as to the identities of any other accomplices, so it came as a great relief now that the case was closed.

It was almost a month later when two letters were delivered to the Tide Mill addressed to the Secretary, one from the Official Receiver's Office and one from the Boat Surveyor. Sarah opened the envelopes with bated breath, her concern quickly changing to sheer joy as she read the contents. She immediately called her father, Barty and Skipper to the office and with great delight read them out. Congratulations all round, now they could put their well laid planes into action at last.

Bill, who had been in constant contact with the Sales Office was sent a cheque and asked to make a payment of £1,000 deposit on behalf of the Carrying Company. Having already been given free access to the boat, Bill had been doing small repair jobs, cleaning and painting, in his leisure time and keeping Barty fully informed of his actions. With his knowledge of boats, he turned out to be an indispensable asset to the Company.

To Bill, time passed quickly, his job at the College and his interest in *The Pride* kept him busy but Barty felt quite the opposite. When he was not employed on a contract he spent his time pottering on the *Ellie May* and sitting with Sarah in the office. Time seemed to be standing still and he often wished that *The Pride* was moored nearer as he longed to be involved in the restoration work with his father.

Skipper was very interested in the progress but was unable to assist with any physical work, in fact he was growing weaker and was now very reliant on his wheelchair. He couldn't go far but he insisted in going onto the quay and around the harbour every day to see his old mates and to watch the various crafts using the Tide Mill facilities. He had received a couple of visits from his solicitor, the purpose of which were unknown and usually took place when Barty and Tom were away on the boat.

The time came when all the interested parties to the purchase of the *Pride* were to meet, tidy up a few details and sign the relevant papers. Persons present at the meeting were Skipper, Barty Sarah and Mr Spalding who had driven them to his solicitor's office in Woodbridge, to meet the Vendor's solicitor and a representative from the Sales Office. The Boat Surveyor's Report had proved favourable, the deposit had been paid and a few minor details sorted. Arrangements were made for the final payments to be effected and provision made for *The Pride* to remain at her present moorings on the River Waveney for the duration of the refit. In a short time, all formalities were completed and the papers signed so they all repaired to The Crown Inn, in Woodbridge, to seal the deal. Barty and Skipper were now joint partners in the ownership of two boats.

Back home, Skipper talked incessantly about the expansion of the business and of the future opportunities for the Company. He had got so excited that by the time they had finished he felt exhausted, and had to go and lay on his bed for a while, only to re-appear at suppertime looking flushed and having difficulty in catching his breath, making the excuse that the stairs caused him the trouble. It's true that his mobility was now very limited and his old friend, Arthur Spalding and his daughter had become carers when Barty wasn't around, in fact Arthur had taken him to hospital by car after one visit from his doctor but the staff were unable to find anything wrong, they reminded him he was getting older and gave him some pills. Skipper had asked Arthur not to tell Barty and Sarah of his hospital visit as he didn't want to upset them.

After the meeting at the solicitor's office, Barty wrote to his father telling him of the good news and that he and Sarah would be coming to

Lowestoft to look over the boat again and to determine the best time to have her dry-docked, scraped and re-painted.

The next two weeks saw the *Ellie May* away from the Tide Mill on three routine trips so Barty saw very little of Sarah but she was able to speak with her father of the forthcoming trip to Lowestoft. No further mention of him becoming a shareholder in the Company had been broached but he still had a lively interest in the Company where his daughter was Company Secretary and one of the partners was soon to be his son-in-law. He volunteered to drive them up to Lowestoft as he wanted to see *The Pride* again before she was dry-docked.

On his return, Barty was told of the offer to be driven to Lowestoft as Sarah's father had requested an early start as he had some business to attend to in Southwold. They reached the town in good time where Mr Spalding attended to his business, he hadn't said what it was but Barty knew he had so many interests in Suffolk and just surmised that it was one of those that required his attendance. Being in good time he took them to a local inn for lunch, - 'Daddies' Treat' – arriving at Lowestoft Harbour at 2pm. As they approached the boat Barty was amazed to see the amount of work that had been done since he last visited. The boat looked quite serviceable, tidy, much of her deck housing and fittings freshly painted and varnished. Bill had been hard at work even though the boat hadn't been turned over to them until very recently, he had obviously anticipated no problem and had made himself useful. The purpose of their visit was to ascertain what needed to be done but she looked perfectly sea-worthy but the work was purely cosmetic, she was still in urgent need of dry-docking to check the hull and under water fittings.

As they went back along the quayside they met Bill coming the other way. Barty thanked him for all the work he had done and said how pleased he was to see *The Pride* looking the part. It was also obvious that Bill had spent a fair amount of cash buying paint, varnish and many cleaning products and Barty offered to reimburse him accordingly. Bill said he would give the receipts to Sarah but refused to take any payment for his labours. Had the purchase fallen through he would not have claimed anything as he had been more than happy doing the work he loved so much. He said that he felt he was part of something worthwhile and it filled in his spare time of which he had plenty and what meant more to him was that he was helping his new-found son, the son he felt he had let down so many years ago. Barty felt like a king, everything seemed to be going his way, that wasn't the last of his luck. Mr Spalding had another piece of good news he broke to them as they left Lowestoft. His business in Southwold had to do with settling some debts and credits that had been incurred in the wind-up of the now defunct 'freetrade' organisation the settlement was far better than he had anticipated and he would like to make give a present to the Company by paying the dry dock fees for *The Pride*. He would also like to pay for Tom's Course fees at Lowestoft College which would have to have been paid for by the Company. All this news was overwhelming and Tom was most grateful for the gift as he had expected to have to pay his own costs. The journey home was most enjoyable, what a good day they had experienced and a rosy outlook for all connected with the Tide Mill Carrying Company.

On arrival back home, it was sad news that greeted them, Skipper had been taken to hospital again. Enquiries revealed that he had pneumonia and would be laid up for a week or two

Next morning Sarah and Barty went to Woodbridge Hospital and were shocked to find that Skipper's condition had taken a turn for the worse. He had slept a lot but when he was awake he could hardly find the strength to speak. He looked so small and frail, only a shadow of the man that had offered Barty a lift on the *Ellie May* a good few years ago. Barty had realised that Skipper was ill several months ago, but seeing him almost every day it just didn't appear to him how fast he was deteriorating but seeing the man in a hospital bed looking so vulnerable upset Barty beyond words.

The next few days were spent journeying to and from the hospital and trying to fit in Company business. On one visit when Mr Spalding accompanied Barty he was so shocked at Skippers condition that he couldn't remain at his bedside for long and had to leave the ward. On another occasion, during a visit by Barty and Sarah, Skipper experienced a lucid moment and spoke with them in a low whisper, hesitantly but coherently.

"I want to tell you something important, don't try to interrupt me until I've finished. I think I am nearing my end and I have spoken with Mr Baxter (Skipper's solicitor) and made some arrangements I want carried out. As you know, my daughter, Marie lives in my house in Ipswich with her husband and children, Matthew has a well-paid job and supports his family comfortably. I want to leave my house to my daughter when I go. I have put all this in my Will and Noel Baxter will ensure that it is carried through but the main thing I want you to know is that I am leaving my share in the partnership to you. That means that you will own the *Ellie May* and *The Pride* and all associated subsidies outright. Over the years Barty, you have been like a son to me and I know you will run our Company with success. I want to leave other sums of money to a few people named in the Will that you will not know. Look after Tom and Sarah and I know you will have a happy life together and I am so sorry I won't be there to see you two married. I wanted to tell you all this so you can make any necessary changes before it's too late, Oh, just one condition, sell some shares to Arthur. I think that's about it, I made it in one!"

By this time both Sarah and Barty were in tears yet Skipper seemed to be at ease, as if a load had been lifted from him. Barty tried to reply to Skipper's revelations but was somehow unable to speak, he was stuck for words. Skipper sensed this and just said, "Don't lad, I know, leave it"

All the effort had taken it out of Skipper, Barty had never heard him make such a long speech in his life. He was asleep in a few seconds.

They returned to the big house and Sarah told her father of the visit and what had transpired and he said he would visit Skipper in the morning. On his arrival at the hospital he was given the sad news that Skipper had passed away in the early hours of the morning. He was so saddened by the news of his old pal and wished that he had been there the night before, Skipper, the wise old man, must have had a premonition that the end was near and that is why he had cleared his wishes with Barty and Sarah.

The news at the Tide Mill was greeted with utter grief, although it was half expected, it had come sooner than anyone had thought, He would be sadly missed. Arthur Spalding and his wife Helen had known Skipper for many years ever since the first time he came to the Tide Mill to apply for moorings for the *Ellie May* some thirty years ago, and they had become great friends and business associates. It was reassuring that there would still be a connection with Barty having his Company based at the Mill.

The funeral would be planned by Barty and the Spalding family' the costs being borne from Skipper's own account before it was finalised and closed. Sarah made many telephone calls to friends and relations informing them of the passing of Skipper and the time and place of the funeral.

Skipper had not been a religious man but his last wish was to be cremated and his ashes scattered at sea, a burial befitting a man who had spent all his life at sea and Barty had resolved to make his final wish come true. The decision was made that the affair should be small to try to accommodate the number of guests that could be safely embarked on the *Ellie May* for the scattering of his ashes, the day after the Service in the crematorium on Quayside.

Considering how many people had known in his life, Sarah's letters were sent only to a selected few, mainly his close associates and his own personal friends and family but others may wish to attend the funeral service at the crematorium, but not all would want to go to sea for the burial. After the ceremony, a small wake would be held at the big house.

The day of the funeral arrived and the small chapel at the crematorium was so full that an anti-room was opened for the overflow of mourners. It was a simple Service culminating in the singing of the sailor's hymn, *'Eternal Father strong to save'*. Many people attended the wake at the Tide Mill afterwards and the same local group of singers that attended one Christmas gatherings came to sing more boatman's songs and shanties. Skipper would have loved every minute of the entertainment held in his memory.

Next morning around twenty-five people gathered on the quayside near the *Ellie May* ready to board and take Skipper to his final resting place. Earlier, the Reverend Nathan Young, who had conducted the Service, brought Skipper's ashes to the boat which Barty put safely into the cabin. The river, like the sea was very calm as the boat slowly made her way towards the sea with Tom at the helm and Barty's father standing next to him. Barty was aware that he was carrying roughly twenty-five passengers and mindful of the fact that he had no licence to carry passengers. He could have hired a licensed craft but this was Skipper's journey and it had to be on his own boat, the *Ellie May*. They reached a point about five miles from the Easton Cliffs when the Reverend gave a prayer and blessing, the congregation sang *'Abide with Me'* as Barty scattered Skipper's ashes and some flowers along the coast that he had known so well throughout his long years of association with the Suffolk coast and Norfolk coasts. It had been a moving and tearful ceremony and all the people gathered knew that Skipper would have not wanted any other way, he was at peace now in the element he had so loved.

Work on *The Pride of Waveney* carried on apace, she was docked, scraped, painted and put back into the water Very few repairs had been needed to the hull but the upholstery inside the main covered cabin area needed completely replacing. Her decks were stoned and varnished and replacement fittings were made where required.

Inside six weeks the boat was almost ready for charter and during that time Tom had taken his Certificate examination at the College and passed without problem.

Having two boats in service, Barty had to think about crewing them, careful thought led him to two decisions. The first was to re-name *The Pride* in honour of Skipper. He consulted with Tom, Sarah and Mr Spalding and all finally agreed that she would be known as *'Skipper's Delight'*. The registration papers were drawn up and approval was obtained for the re-naming. Bill arranged for a sign writer to paint her new name, *'Skipper' Delight*. Lowestoft. on the stern and the name on the bows. The port of registration was to remain Lowestoft and she would retain her mooring on the River Waveney.

On a crisp October morning, Mr & Mrs Spalding, Ted Moore, Bill and Sarah, with the crew, Barty and Tom, boarded *Skipper's Delight* for her maiden voyage up the River Waveney to Beccles, an ancient town on the river and nearby access to the Broads of Norfolk. Just before casting off, Mr Spalding christened the boat with a bottle of champagne, naming her and wishing all "Happy voyages".

It was whilst on this trip that Barty's second idea was revealed. With two boats to run he would need extra crew and decided to ask Bill if he would be interested in working for him as Captain of *Skipper's Delight*? He would still be able to retain his job at the College if he wished and plan his charter dates accordingly, weekends mainly being the best time for the hire of leisure cruises. Tom on the other hand was now a qualified mate and could take *Ellie May* out as required when Barty was unavailable. They would still require two casual mates, one for each boat but that should not prove to be a problem. In a quieter moment, Sarah and Barty had discussed their wedding, no date was yet fixed but they agreed to become man and wife in the Spring of next year.

   With the reduction on the purchase price of the leisure cruiser, the dispersal of the 'freetrade' funds and the settlement of Skipper's Will Barty found that his personal bank account, like the Company account were far better that he thought. He had been given so much help it was unbelievable, Mr Spalding, Skipper and Bill had all made things possible and provided the opportunity to be able to offer employment to others. The coastal trade from the Tide Mill although now a little depleted was still thriving and the intermittent hire of one of Mr Spalding's boats for bird watching trips meant extra work for Barty, Tom and Sarah so their incomes looked secure for the foreseeable future. The business in Lowestoft was yet to be tested.

   Keeper's Cottage was eerily quiet, Skipper's room was now empty except for a few sticks of furniture, his personal belongings, of which there was little, had been sent to his daughter in Ipswich. Barty continued to occupy the larger of the three bedrooms and Sarah used the office on the ground floor and she usually confined her visits to the mornings to attend to any incoming mail and general administration for both the

Company and some of her father's work. In the afternoons, she would occasionally do jobs around the mill yard, and met with Barty whenever time allowed to discuss business affairs and to try to settle the finer points they wanted to include in their wedding plans.

Ellie May remained committed to two or three jobs a week each of a minimum of two days per trip. Tom kept his eye on the upkeep of the boat giving time for Barty and Sarah to have the occasional relaxed time in Woodbridge to see a film show, have a drink or just spend some valuable time together. Barty was not one for just idling his time away and would often volunteer to take on work in the mill yard to assist Sarah. One day, Mr Spalding suggested to Barty that he should learn to drive. About three months before Skipper died, Mr Spalding had bought a small lorry, being the only person at the Mill that could drive he sometimes found it difficult to fulfil all his commitments but if Barty could learn to drive, he could, at convenient times be of great help to Sarah' father, who would teach him to within the confines of the farm and the quayside. Barty thought that such an arrangement could be an asset and he agreed. His first lesson was to be on the coming weekend, just for an hour or so when the mill yard, quayside and harbour road would be relatively quiet and free from heavy traffic. Most leisure craft would have left the moorings for the weekend and it appeared to be the ideal time for a novice learner to try his hand. Barty had never had any real desire to drive a motor vehicle and was really looking forward to receiving his first driving lesson but "the best laid plans Of Mice and Men oft times go astray" as the old saying goes, Barty's first driving lesson would have to be postponed.

Sarah had received an urgent letter from Bill who, in turn had received a request from a group of people wanting to hire *Skipper's Delight* for a weekend trip on the Norfolk Broads and needed some advice from Barty. There was not time to reply by post so he decided to travel to Lowestoft and see Bill personally. Mr Spalding was informed and said this was the golden opportunity for him to go with Barty and teach him the basics of driving in the quieter places thus killing two birds with one stone.

Sarah made the necessary arrangements and Tom joined them for the journey. They met Bill at the boat and the details of the hiring were discussed, Bill's delight was boundless and it showed, being in charge of the riverboat seemed to have injected even more enthusiasm into him, if that was at all possible. He had already shown great enthusiasm in the way he had dealt with the organisation of the previous two-day booking for the bird-watchers group. The hire group had given him their proposed itinerary which included an overnight stay in a hotel. From the information that Bill gave him, Barty could see that Bill had done his homework and even given an estimate of the cost of supplying refreshments on the two days. Bill had achieved all the terms and conditions for the hire in two short days as the applicants wanted a reply and costings by the weekend hence the hurried meeting.

They listened carefully to Bill's suggestions and wholly accepted them. If it was possible to provide an estimate of the costings today, Bill would pass it to them personally as he was in contact with the organiser. Sarah would type up the full estimate, excluding the hotel charges then contact Bill by return of post. If the estimate was accepted, Bill would take charge of *Skipper's Delight's* first charter. Both Barty and Mr Spalding asked to be present on the first day of the trip but Bill would be in full charge.

On the journey home, the whole conversation was of the work that needed to be done, especially by Sarah, to make the charter a success.

They were so busy talking that Barty's driving lesson was totally forgotten. On reaching home, Sarah was immediately informed of all they had talked about and set about formulating an official estimate to be sent to Bill by the next post, each item to be individually costed to include refreshments and overnight moorings near their chosen hotel.

Bill would need an extra crew member after Mr Spalding and Barty was to leave the boat after the first day. Once again Bill came to the rescue by saying that he would recruit a fellow instructor from the College to assist.

Tom in the meantime, had had a short one-day trip down the river to deliver animal feed to a local farm where he enlisted the help of a farm hand to unload the sacks of feed. Tom, now qualified, welcomed the chance to get away on his own and enjoyed the peace and quiet of the trip and not having his 'boss' on board for a change., but he still had his good friend Shuftee there to keep him company. Now that Barty was resident at Keeper's Cottage, Shuftee hardly ever left Tom's side.

Sarah contacted Bill and gave him a verbal estimate for the charter that was transmitted to the applicant that day with the promise of a written copy in post that same day. With everything being arranged at such a rush it was hoped that nothing had been overlooked but consoled themselves by thinking any small mistakes or omissions could be accredited to lack of experience and they would learn from them. On completion of the costings, it was sent off next morning to the Chairman of the hiring Committee, copy to Bill who had passed on the verbal estimate and it appeared to be acceptable. By Thursday evening, the Chairman had contacted Bill asking him to finalise the arrangements for their departure on Saturday morning. So much depended on this first charter and everyone worked tirelessly to make it the success it needed to be.

A fine sunny morning greeted the thirty guests that boarded the river cruiser. Bill stationed himself on the quayside, looking every bit 'the old salt' in his navy-blue crew neck sweater with *Skipper's Delight* emblazoned across his chest and a Breton cap set at a jaunty angle, to welcome each passenger as they arrived.

The boat looked great, her fresh paintwork shining in the early morning sun and sporting a dress of brightly coloured flags overall.

Bill steered her out from her mooring into the river 9am prompt with all passengers on board. Mr Spalding and Barty stood beside Bill at the wheel. A volunteer from the College attended the deck duties and Sarah, who had decided to look after the refreshments was busy at the stern end covered accommodation. Bill had obtained the services of a second volunteer from the College who looked after the engine and associated machinery. Barty glanced around him, happy people, the boat looking immaculate and the look on his face showed the pride he was feeling, Good fortune and good friends had made this dream come true. Mr Spalding had noted the satisfactory look on Barty's face and secretly thought that his daughter's future was assured with Barty He also gave a thought to Donald (Skipper) McLean, how proud and happy he would be to see the growth of the Tide Mill Carrying Company as he had envisaged it when Arthur Spalding and himself had first become friends so many years ago. Today was a reward indeed.

Throughout the quiet journey up through Beccles, they encountered much to see and to photograph. One of Bill's co-opted crew, Jim, had helped Sarah to prepare the refreshments that all the passenger enjoyed with their drinks after asking Bill to slow the boat so they could also keep a sharp lookout for any unusual bird or animal sightings finally reaching the moorings near the hotel they had chosen in Bungay. Thirty happy and tired passengers booked into their reserved rooms after thanking the crew for a lovely day on the river. They had been overwhelmed by the sights they had seen on the journey, the diversity of the wildlife but the highlight was when a pair of otters had been sighted on the southern boundary of the Broadlands. As they had passed near Beccles heading for their hotel, Bill had told them a little of the early maritime history of the town dating back to the eleventh century when it was a thriving herring port. Their overnight stay was in a traditional building in the town of Bungay that also had a long history dating back from a great storm in 1577 and a devastating fire in 1688, much of its history was to be found in commemorative architecture in the town. Bill had been very busy studying these histories and the passengers never tired of his constant comments as they passed notable points along the river.

The visit to Bungay was the first time that Barty had ever been there and was delighted with the professionalism that Bill had shown in presenting the charter, the beautiful scenery of the Waveney Valley, the birds and wildlife, the 'laid-back' rate of the river travel, the history and architecture, coupled with the tripper's own choice of a first-class hotel, all added up to a perfect day. Bill had every right to feel that his first charter was shaping up to be a success. As for the performance of *Skipper's Delight*, that was also perfect.

Mr Spalding and Barty would have loved to have stayed on board for the whole trip but they had got to get back to Lowestoft, pick up the car as they both had business to attend the next day. As it was they didn't get home to the Tide Mill until the early hours of Monday morning.

It was just before 6am when a very excited Shuftee barked his greeting to the tired and jaded Barty. Tom was nowhere to be seen on deck but very soon located in the cabin, rudely awakened by Shuftee's barking, they were due to leave early and Tom had overslept. He quickly dressed and put the kettle on to boil. The time didn't really matter that much as Tom had loaded up over the weekend and prepared everything ready for their departure the day before. The *Ellie May* left her berth at approximately 7am with a cargo of flour for Southwold destined to return with sacks of grain for milling at the Tide Mill.

Barty cast his eye along the boat, it seemed like he was seeing her from a different perspective. After being on board *Skipper's Delight*, freshly painted, refurbished and dressed in flags and bunting yesterday, *Ellie May,* although clean and tidy, looked just what she is, a working boat. He made up his mind that she should receive a new coat of paint as soon as the opportunity presented itself and he had consulted with Sarah to find a slot in her bookings as a re-paint would take three to four days to complete. His thoughts turned to Sarah, not for the first time as he realised that he hadn't seen her for five days and here he was off on another short trip.

The passage to Southwold was uneventful but on the return journey that were hailed and stopped by a Revenue cutter, a routine check. Papers and cargo being in order they continued their way thanking their lucky stars, had they have been pulled over a couple of months earlier it could have been a different story.

Back at the home moorings they received news that *Skipper's Delight* had returned safely to Lowestoft and that the Chairman of the hiring organisation had nothing but praise for their treatment over the hire period and assured Bill that he would certainly book him again for future hirings. Bill had attended to all the costings including the refreshments, an account that was settled without question plus an extra £20 for all the trouble he had taken to assure their satisfaction.

When Bill received the money, he deposited it in the Company Bank and his agreed wages and expenses etc. would be settled from the Company Office. The whole charter had been a great success and yielded a better financial return that had been expected.

It wasn't long before a further booking was received, mainly for bird and wildlife watchers up the River Waveney. It was late autumn and the birds were gathering together before embarking on their great migratory flights to the warmer climes. It was a truly beautiful time of the year visually as the heavily wooded valley was looking at its best in the golden dress of the season. Soon all the leaves would be gone, the bookings would cease during the winter and Bill would be busy laying up *Skipper's Delight* until next year. That would mean a lot of work especially as he still held his post at the College so his work on the boat would be limited by the weather conditions. Booking for the *Ellie May* were also slowing down to an average of two a week, enough to keep the Company ticking over but not enough to consider any further developments at present.

This lapse in time did however provide Barty with the opportunity to take his first driving lesson. He quickly grasped the basic control of the car as Mr Spalding slowly explained the workings to him. His first slow and careful movement was quite positive with Mr Spalding sitting by his side he only drove up and down the quayside once or twice. The first attempt on reversing left a little to be desired but that was mainly due to the narrowness of the quay and the limited space for making a turn. After about an hour time was called on this first outing with a promise that on the next occasion to take him around the small harbour road and out onto the public road but only at the weekend when there would be very little traffic about. Barty had only had an hour's tuition, both verbal and practical, but he felt he had achieved something and was looking forward to the next lesson.

The age of motor transport was really taking off judging by the number of cars and lorries to be seen on the roads around the harbour. Barty had been fired up by his early success and told Sarah that he would buy a car when they were married. In pacification, she tended to agree

with him at the same time wondering where they would be living. They sat for a while talking of the wedding in the Spring and the possibilities of a favourable place to live where they could reach the business easily
It would soon be Christmas again, another year gone but looking back over the past year made them realise how well they were doing both in business and their relationship. Reminiscing inevitably brought the conversation back to Christmas. The Spalding's had always celebrated a traditional Christmas as they did the last year before Skipper had passed away and they had expected to spend Christmas at his daughter's house in Ipswich. He hadn't seen Skipper's family since the funeral and he felt uneasy and spending the holiday with them didn't appeal to him very much. He thought how awkward he and Sarah would feel being with so many people they didn't know very well. He was thankful for the arrangement but felt that his 'nearest and dearest' were all here at the Tide Mill so gratefully declined the kind invitation from the Arnold family at Ipswich. Whatever the celebrations planned by the Spaldings, he knew he would be part of it. Sarah mentioned Tom saying that he too should be included as he had nowhere else to go and no known family. It was quite similar with Bill, now that Barty had found his father he didn't' want to lose him again. Sarah said that she would speak to her father about it all knowing full well that he would agree with the suggestions without question. Sarah, like many well-loved daughters could wrap her father around her little finger.

That same evening Sarah and Barty sat in the lounge of the big house so Sarah took the opportunity to tell him of their plans over Christmas and the friends they would like to invite, of course her father agreed and Sarah said she would write the invites tomorrow morning as the *Ellie May* was due out and she would have the time. She wrote to Bill asking him to come to the Tide Mill just before Christmas so that they could exchange views and discuss the Companies prospects in the coming new year, Barty would speak to Tom during the trip to Aldeburgh in the morning.

It was a dull miserable morning as the boat left her moorings but Tom was in a good frame of mind especially when he was told of the invite over Christmas saying that he wasn't looking forward to spending time on his own as he had no known living relatives. He asked if Shuftee was invited as well, he couldn't leave his faithful friend on the boat on his own over Christmas, but that went without saying, Shuftee was part of the family too.

After a slow wet journey, they arrived in Aldeburgh and having unloaded they had time to spare as the return cargo hadn't arrived on the quayside from the outlying farm supplying it. With time to spare they decided to take a walk round the delightful town that was once a thriving port. In 1899, a year after Barty's birth, Aldeburgh had been the scene of that devastating disaster. Distress signals were heard from a ship in trouble during a very heavy storm and during an attempt to launch the lifeboat, one extremely heavy wave struck her broadside and turned her upside down on the beach. The crew were trapped under the lifeboat and for three hours many men tried to free them eventually recovering them but seven of the crew had died.

Barty had remembered reading of the disaster as a boy but it never had a great impact on him being so young but today, as he read more of the history of the incident and seeing the names and pictures of the men that perished brought to him a deep sadness. Being a man who understands the sea in her many moods and knowing that his father was a lifeboat man at Lowestoft brought home to him the impact of the disaster and the suffering endured by friends and families of the crew and the might of the uncontrollable sea. True, there had been many tragedies around the coasts but this one had been on his own doorstep, so to speak and it had a most depressive effect on him. The crews ages had ranged from 21 to 52 years, many being younger than himself.

Returning to the *Ellie May* they learned that their cargo would not arrive until after sunset so they decided to get some sleep and load up tomorrow morning. During the night, they were both woken up by Shuftee's incessant barking, most unusual unless something was bothering him. They quietly and carefully left the cabin to find the cause of the disturbance which had now stopped. With Shuftee still in close attendance they soon found the reason why the dog had been so excited. Curled up in the stern was a man, fast asleep, try as they might they couldn't rouse him, he was obviously under the influence of drink and was trying to find somewhere sheltered to sleep it off. They thought to leave him there for the rest of the night, he was doing no harm and he would be under the ever-watchful eye of Shuftee. They returned to their bunks only to be awakened again, seemingly in minutes, by a dock worker who had come to assist with the loading of the cargo that had arrived unheard late the night before. As for the sleeping man, he had disappeared.

An early finish to loading the boat led to an early departure from Aldeburgh, a town that had impressed both of them with its history and architecture not to mention the sad story of its courageous townsfolk and lifeboat men.

With only one more booking before Christmas, Sarah and Barty had planned to take a full day in Woodbridge to do some much-needed shopping. A slow walk back after the shops had closed, they were nearing the Tide Mill when they heard music, it appeared to come from the direction of the quay. Approaching in the darkening evening they saw a glow around a moored vessel from which the unmistakable sound of a sea shanty was cheerfully filling the air. Barty recognised the lines a large coaster, probably the largest vessel that could enter the quay in safety and seated on a bollard near the gangway was Tom. He had helped with the mooring of the Dutch Trader and was now enjoying the music being made by the six-man crew. Barty and Sarah stopped and were talking with Tom when one of the crew spotted them and came over to speak. On learning that they were from the wherry tied up astern of them they were immediately invited aboard the coaster. It was the birthday of one of the crew and they were gathered on deck to celebrate. The deck was festooned with flags and bunting with coloured lights twinkling above their heads. One of the crew was busy cooking food when a musician struck up a well-known shanty *"Rolling the Woodpile Down"* while they were found a seat and given a celebratory drink.

What a lovely friendly evening, good food, good beer and excellent company of which Skipper would have approved, he would have been in his element.

During the early days when Barty first met Skipper, he used to sit on the deck of the *Ellie May* on a warm sunny evening playing his concertina and singing in his rough gravelly voice. Barty had learned several shanties from him but he never learned to play the concertina.

Sea shanties are almost international especially the tunes, although the words often differ according to the language and the Dutchmen played some well-known shanties in English in honour of their guests. Barty had no voice for singing but gave them his rendition of *"The Leaving of Liverpool",* one of his favourites but one that they all seemed to know. It was a lovely evening, one that brought back many fond memories of Skipper.

Barty experienced his second driving lesson and Mr Spalding took him off the quayside and onto the public road as he had promised. The roads were nearly empty, just the occasional lorry or a horse drawn vehicle and he was able to practice reversing where space wasn't as limited as it had been on the quayside. He did quite well and received praise from Sarah's father for his swift learning skills. On their return to the Tide Mill, the Dutch trader had left, that saddened Barty a little as he was hoping to be able to talk with the crew and learn something of the life they led, both at home and at sea. He had really enjoyed their generosity and friendship and seemingly free and easy way of life.

The final trip for the year had to be cancelled due to heavy weather and repetitive storms in the Channel. This was the week when Bill should have come to the Mill, he was making his own way down from Lowestoft on the Thursday afternoon, three days before Christmas Day that fell on a Sunday in the year of 1927. Lowestoft College had closed down until the New Year and Bill had arranged for a pal of his to occasionally visit the *Delight* to keep an eye on things. Bill was to be accommodated in Skipper's old room at Keeper's Cottage. This would be fine as it would allow Barty and his father to talk freely, there were several questions about the past that he wanted to ask his father when the time was opportune.

Mr Spalding had called for a meeting on the Friday morning at 10am hoping that all could be present, the weather allowing their successful arrivals. As it happened, the winds and storms abated and at 10am sharp all were gathered in the lounge of the big house, Sarah, Barty, Tom, Bill and Ted Moore, sat around the large table enjoying a coffee while Mr Spalding acquainted them with the purpose of the meeting.

"I have been looking at the books and hearing the plans of the Tide Mill Carrying Company" He began, glancing at each person individually around the table to see that he had their full attention. "I personally have no financial interest in the Company so I speak to you today as my daughter's representative as Company Secretary and her pending marriage to Barty. As you know, the Company is so named due to its location here at the Tide Mill, my own business interest. Barty's boat, the *Ellie May* has been based here for many years, long before he became a partner with Skipper, in the Company and has operated for a long time. On the other hand, *Skipper's Delight* has had only one hiring which was very successful and had great promise for the future as a hire boat operating on the River Waveney. I think there will be a marked increase in this type of leisure service holiday in the years to come".

Mr Spalding had been a respected business man over many years, he had inherited the business from his father which included the Mill, the small harbour and moorings, some vacant land and a small but productive road carrying firm consisting now of only two motor lorries. To those that sort it, his advice had always been readily given and trustworthy.

He carried on speaking, "I have only Sarah, we were never blessed with a son to take over the business from me and I'm getting older now and have been doing a lot of thinking lately. I feel that I ought to be letting younger people take over some of my interests and I have one or two suggestions I would like you to consider"

At this point, there was a pause as Mrs Spalding entered the lounge with more refreshments and small talk and speculation broke out between the guests as they helped themselves to the snack provided.

"Right then", Mr Spalding was on his feet again as if to add emphasis to what he had to say, carefully thinking out his words before he continued. "Sarah and Barty are planning to marry in the Spring, about May time I hear, but nobody's told me yet and I would like to be given some indication so that any response to my proposals can be considered by myself as soon as possible. I am now 78 years old".

This revelation came as a surprise to Barty and Tom who had never considered him to be over 56 years, he certainly didn't look his age. "and I realise that I am loading more and more work on Sarah dealing with certain aspects of my business on top of her duties for the Carrying Company, she could do without that extra work. I have also noticed that Barty can often be found about the Mill and stables doing odd jobs, just to help out, more work. As for Bill, he has only been with us for a short time but it has not escaped me that the time and effort he has put in looking after *Skipper' Delight,* repairing, re-painting and everything that has made the boat what it is today, quite unbelievable really and now taking care of it for the Company. What I would like to propose is this – He took a folded paper from his pocket and carefully laid it flat on the table in front of him.

"I have numbered these points so that each may be discussed as a separate item, please listen before making any response at all as some of the items may affect you individually.

Number one, I would like to see the amalgamation of the Tide Mill Carrying Company and the Tide Mill complex into a single business. I would like to see this happen to ensure that my daughter will have security in her future life with Barty and to ensure the continued success of what is now two very successful and viable businesses, if agreeable this to be arranged by the Company solicitor Mr Noel Baxter and that he should retain interest in the new undertaking.

Number two, that I should become a sleeping partner with an interest in the Management Board until the time of my passing or until I become unable to continue to give advice on Company affairs due to ill health.

Number three, I wish Sarah to remain as Company Secretary for the amalgamated companies and the house to become her sole property to be occupied by myself and my wife. For our remaining life.

Number four, the *Ellie May* to be skippered by Tom who, after Bartys marriage to Sarah could move into Keeper's Cottage and the ground floor to remain as the Company Office.

Number five, finally that the Management Committee be increased to represent the various interests of the new business with Barty as Managing Director, Sarah – Company Secretary, Tom – Cargo carrying (water), *Ellie May*, Bill – Passenger, leisure services and myself as a sleeping partner to the new company. I have discussed these proposals at length with Ted who is in full agreement and invited him to take shares in the new company should he wish and to retain his interest should he wish to attend any future meetings of the Management Committee. Those are my proposals and I know that each of you will have many questions which we will deal with after the Christmas holiday. Please write out your questions and bring them to the next meeting for discussion. We have a little under six months before the wedding and I would like to think that we can have everything resolved and up and running before then".

There were a few instant questions requiring one word answers but Mr Spalding fielded the more complex queries by asking again that they think carefully and to write them down for discussion at the next meeting. Mr Spalding closed the meeting by thanking them all for their attendance and wishing them a Happy Christmas. Ted, Sarah and her father stayed at the house, while Barty, Tom and Bill went back the *Ellie May* to talk about Mr Spalding's proposals. Three in the small cabin was very cramped so they made their way to the local pub in Woodbridge for lunch and a pint or two.

Although Barty had met his father on a few occasions he had never had the chance to sit and talk freely of the past. What happened to him after the time he was released from prison until they met again recently.

He knew a few things about him but not enough to satisfy all the missing years. His father spoke quite freely about his life in prison for seven years, he was allowed an earlier release for good behaviour. Eight years for stealing two legs of lamb to feed his hungry family during the bad times when employment was so hard to find and workers were being laid off with no wages and no prospects of new work. He saw his father infrequently during the time spent in the workhouse. When he was finally released, his wife had gone to London seeking work and he had no idea what had become of his son. He looked for employment but to no avail. When prospective employers asked about his work record, he told the truth and they immediately discounted him as unemployable. Combing the London area in his search for work he also went to great efforts to trace his wife after learning that she had been in London seeking domestic employment, in fact he actually called at Mill Hall Farm on the Isle of Dogs only to find that she had made application for work there but had been turned down due to the accommodation problem.

Bill persisted in his search for work and eventually secured a job as an unqualified Mate to a Thames Barge waterman. His main work was in the Port of London with an occasional visit through the Limehouse, Greenwich and Blackwall Reaches, the East India Docks and other associated dock areas. Barty thought of the times that he had sat on the banks of the Reaches watching the ships and boats travelling to and from the docks and wondered if his father could have possibly been on one of the barges, of which there were many. Working on the river gave Bill a chance to improve his lot, so he studied and passed for his Waterman's Certificate. He found part-time work in a boatyard where he gained a good knowledge of boat construction. Reading a London Docks news magazine one day he spotted an advertisement for a vacancy for an Instructor at Lowestoft College, he applied and was called for interview and examination at Greenwich Maritime Museum, exams were being held at various venues around the country and this was luckily near to him. So successful were his results that he was immediately accepted for an extended interview. Being a working licensed Waterman with several years' experience he more than satisfied the Interview Board that he was the right man for the post. He was offered and accepted the opportunity to attend a six-week familiarisation course at Lowestoft College. He completed the six-week course satisfactorily and filled the post of Instructor the following week. He found a small house in Beach Road, Lowestoft to rent and was still living there. The house was near the harbour and his work wasn't too demanding so he found time to wander about the harbour and doing small repairs and odd jobs for the boat owners that were moored there. He got to know many of them and the harbour staff quite well seeing them nearly daily. Barty had known all this before but he now realised just how patient his father had ben until he secured his present position.

During all this time, he never gave up searching for his wife but all without success. He found no contacts or anyone in the London area answering to her name. In the early days, he had assumed that his son was with her but now he had reached the conclusion that he would never see either of them again. He apologised to Barty for all the missing years and stressed how happy he was to be re-united with his son and to feel a small part of the family which he had been searching for so long. Not a very exciting life he admitted but now life was looking rosier with the proposals made by Mr Spalding and suggested that they got together regarding the expected questions that would arise at the next meeting.

They left the pub to take a walk around Woodbridge. The town was dressed for the Christmas festivities, all the shops displaying coloured lights and decorations and the usual Christmas tree in front of the Town

Hall with a group of singers surrounding it. There was a wonderful feeling of peace and well-being everywhere and the three of them enjoyed the spectacle of Christmas laid out in front of them.

What a day it had been, Mr Spalding's proposals, a good lunch in convivial surroundings, good ale and excellent company, they had plenty to think about during the next few days,

Christmas with the Spalding's was, as usual, a very traditional affair. Invites had gone out to many local people to attend a party on Christmas Eve. Barty had never seen so many people at the Tide Mill before. The arrival of the Mummers giving their version of St. George and the Dragon was a great success and carol singers from the local church joined the guests to celebrate the festive season. Mr Spalding had hired a catering supplier for the plentiful food and even a group of cleaners to clear up after the party that ended about midnight.

Several guests stayed overnight including Ted Moore and his wife, who had not been seen since the freetrade Committee had dispersed. A magnificent Christmas lunch was enjoyed by the guests that had stayed overnight after which the rest of the afternoon was engaged in casual conversation, drinking and reminiscing about the year past. The only diversion from the festivities was the attention required by the horses and other animals housed on the small farm on the complex. Barty volunteered to give a helping hand with the job as he fancied a breath of fresh air. Two more volunteers stepped forward to accompany him and what was a small job feeding the stock turned out to be a complete tour of the complex as Ted and Tom both walked the surrounding fields that bordered on the upper reaches of the inner harbour. The following week was spent in much the same manner, there was no business for the crew of the *Ellie May* until next week so the leisure time was used tending the animals and doing odd jobs about the mill. Except for Ted, who had to return to his own farm, they all got together again on New Year's Eve to drink a toast to 1928.

The 2nd of January was a very cold crisp morning of heavy frost and iced up fittings as they brought the boat from her moorings into the river, the harbour not been subject to the tide, Barty felt that it might have been iced over as well. Even Shuftee, who had spent most of the past week in the kitchen of the big house or stretched in front of the blazing fire at Keeper's Cottage, seemed reluctant to leave the comforts for the frozen deck of the boat! It was a routine two-day trip to Felixstowe carrying flour and a mixed cargo for the return journey. They saw hardly any river traffic on the Deben and only a couple of coasters as they neared to port. It was an ideal time to travel and after a week of near idleness it felt good to be back on board and to feel the gentle breeze and the crisp wintery air on their faces, it was certainly blowing away the rich indulgencies of Christmas and New Year.

They arrived back at the Tide Mill at lunchtime on Wednesday only to find that Mr Spalding had called his follow-up meeting for the Friday morning.   In addition to the members of the proposed Management Committee there was one other person present, Mr Noel Baxter. the Company solicitor. Mr Spalding took a seat at the table and welcomed everyone. Prior to the meeting, Mr Spalding had met with the solicitor for some preliminary talks about the papers that Mr Baxter had drawn up outlining the finer points of the proposed amalgamation, its terms and conditions. A copy of the papers was passed to each person present and Mr Baxter elaborated on the more important points. Very few questions were asked during the time it took to go through the fairly lengthy presentation. After a time, Mr Spalding suggested that they adjourn for refreshments at midday and take time to read through the proposals again and to formulate any questions to be brought up during the afternoon session commencing at 2pm.

They resumed shortly after 2pm when there were a multitude of questions, mainly of a minor nature that were most satisfactorily answered by Mr Spalding and Barty, the only intervention was from Mr Baxter when there was a question requiring a legal point. The meeting went on for a further four hours, Mr Baxter making copious notes throughout.

At the closure of the meeting he promised to produce a full resume of all the items appertaining to the successful outcome of a most informative and agreeable meeting. If his new report met with the approval of everyone concerned, he would have the document witnessed and signed and hoped he could have all complete within a month and to be able to announce the new company and partnership.

As the members started to disperse, Mr Spalding called for their attention saying that he had an announcement to make himself.

"Just before we go I would like to say that my daughter has, at long last, given me a date for her marriage to young Barty here", he said pointing at him. "I would like you all to mark your diaries for the 18th May this year and you will receive an invitation in due course" Then, looking directly at Barty he continued, "You have been a good and trusted man since I met you a few years ago, and whatever the final findings of today's meeting I look forward to the agreements in partnership with you in any future dealings. Good Luck to you and to everyone."

Barty felt about ten feet tall, to have such a tribute paid to him in front of friends was very re-assuring and to know that his future father-in-law had, unreservedly accepted him as family, well, unbelievable!

Barty thanked him for his kind words and everyone left the house except Bill, he would have a long journey in front of him and unlike Ted, he had no personal transport and would stay at Keeper's Cottage for another night. Bill welcomed the chance as he had something rather special to tell Barty but that could wait until morning.

Sarah came to the office at the Cottage early in the morning bringing with her a cooked breakfast for Bill who was already up and dressed He was petting Shuftee who had wheedled his way to spend the cold night by the kitchen fire. It was a full hour later when Barty came into the office, Sarah had been listening to Bill who was saying how proud he was of his son and how much he had missed him during the lost years. He was proud of the way he had worked to make something of himself and remarked that his future prospects in business were looking fine especially with the offers that had been discussed recently. Bill was a happy man and he hoped that Barty would accept the news he was about to tell him.

The three of them sat talking with a fresh cup of coffee made by Sarah then Bill started to speak.

"I didn't want to raise this subject until yesterday's meeting had been concluded. It appears that most of the proposals have been successful and I have been entrusted with the job of Manager for the Leisure Services up in Lowestoft but there is something that I have kept secret since we met. I am the owner of an ex. Admiralty MFV (Motor Fishing Vessel) that I have been renovating for quite some time. I bought the MFV as almost scrap from a dealer in Lowestoft about two years ago, and have been working on her ever since. I have almost finished the job now and she is starting to look sharp, she just needs a final coat of paint, the decks caulking and scrubbing before I register her for sea trials. I'm telling you this now because it looks as if I may have responsibilities to a new Company and I shall have less time to tend to the boat. I have thought about this a lot lately and I had intended to hire it out to fishing trips but now, if you agree, I would like to give the boat to the new Company, there is just one problem. I have nearly finished all the refurbishments and the work on her engines, the final clearance rests with the Marine Engineer's department for approval. If the Company could see its way clear to finance the last of the work and the inspection, then the boat could be added to *Skipper' Delight* for hiring. And I could still maintain her in Lowestoft. The cost wouldn't be high as I have financed the bulk of the work over the past two years. At present, she is on a cradle in a field near the river. I will leave you to think about it and if she is not wanted I will put her up for sale,"

This revelation came as a big surprise as Bill had never once mentioned the MFV and the surprise showed in Barty's face. He was dumbstruck! His mind raced with kneejerk ideas but he refrained from making an on the spot decision, he must speak with his partners.

At length, Barty found his tongue and responded, "What an offer but before any decision can be made we must await Mr Baxter's final testament and put your offer before the Committee. Thank you so much for the offer, I think you will understand my hesitation but I think its best that everyone agrees when we have all read the final papers"

Barty said he could see a bright future if the offer was accepted and went on to say that he had been, for a long time considering the possibility of adding another carrying boat to the *Ellie May* but hadn't mentioned it before as he wanted to see all other changes through and to make sure that the Company was fully solvent before he said anything to anyone else.

Bill, a very forward thinking man made no further comments but asked that they didn't say anything to the Committee members for the time being, to which they agreed. It was going to be hard secret to keep.

Friday 18th May 1928, the date seemed to be approaching fast now that it had been announced as the wedding day and it as obvious that Sarah and her parents had had their heads together, nothing that really stood out to say they were planning but small things like the number of times that John Salmon, Mr Spalding's solicitor visited the house for instance. Barty was quite unperturbed by little comments and changes that were being made, after all Sarah kept his diary and she was perfectly capable of handling the everyday business affairs without his questioning or objections although there were one or two things he wanted answering when they next had time to talk together. The diary showed that there were several trips to be undertaken in the next eight weeks so his concentration was on the upkeep of the boat.

Ellie May was looking very ship-shape and Bristol fashion when Barty eventually managed to find a spare afternoon to visit. He found Tom tidying up the decks and preparing the hold to embark a cargo of flour for Felixstowe. Shuftee was, as usual laying near the gangplank with one eye closed, busy guarding the boat from unwelcome callers. On seeing Barty approaching he leapt up and was over the gangplank in a flash, jumping about him as they came back on board where Shuftee resumed his post seemingly exhausted by the sudden burst of energy.

Tom greeted him and went to make a cup of coffee. They sat on deck in the late afternoon sun, it wasn't particularly warm but the tidiness of the boat coupled with the sound of the water lapping idly against the hull made it seem more like a Spring morning, the lack of activity on the quayside added to the feeling of tranquillity making Barty realise how much he missed his life under sail. Problems from the land seemed so small and petty when he was at sea and that he could never take a fully land-bound occupation ever again. He knew how Skipper had loved the sea and how he must have felt when he became physically incapable of pursuing his employment and probably lived his dreams through Barty and the life he was now living.

In the evening, he met with Sarah to talk of their future together and to settle a few queries about the business. Suddenly, he had the presence of mind to ask her where they were to be married and had arrangements for the publication of the Marriage banns been made? At this, Sarah somewhat shocked by the question.

"The banns" she exclaimed, I had completely forgotten about them, but Dad and I have spoken with the Reverend Nathan Young in Woodbridge, setting the date for the wedding but the banns were never mentioned, is that done automatically, I don't know, we'll have to get in touch with the Vicar as soon as possible" There were so many things to think about, mainly concerning the wedding but Barty was happy to leave those arrangements to the family as his prime concern ws the amalgamation of the Companies and the day to day running of the *Ellie May*. Sarah did raise one important point though, a small matter that hadn't been addressed at any meeting. What was to be the name of the new amalgamated business? Sarah was insistent that the name of her father's business be retained in some form together with Barty's Tide Mill Carrying Co. and she suggested to simple name of 'Tide Mill Incorporated' as that represented their many interests. They decided to bring up the name at the next meeting.

As the tide turned the next morning, *Ellie May* left her moorings in the mist of a drizzly day, Tom taking the helm. They had a small cargo of flour for Felixstowe and were scheduled to pick up a full load of timber imported from Sweden to take up the coast and deliver to Oulton Broad adjoining Lowestoft where some new boathouses were being built. That meant an overnight stay in Lowestoft where he would be able to take the opportunity to call on his father and perhaps visit the MFV he has spoken about.

The journey up the coast saw the boat making slow headway due to the fierce alternating winds and choppy seas that breached the low bulwarks on several occasions but luckily not enough to enter the hold. The slow progress led to a late entry into the calmer waters of Oulton Broad. Tom supervised the off-loading of the timber while Barty called on Bill at Beach Road. During the time they had taken to get from Felixstowe, Bill had received a message from Mr Spalding asking if he could attend a meeting at the Tide Mill at the weekend. Barty said that it would be better if Bill could travel back on the *Ellie May* to the Tide Mill instead of having to rely on public transport. He also replied to Sarah to say that Bill would be with him but they may be a little later that estimated due to the weather conditions and a swift call into Southwold to pick up some grain for milling.

It was only a short walk from Bill's house to the field where the MFV was cradled and Tom managed to join them after the unloading had been completed quickly using a small hand crane on the jetty. Shuftee remained on guard on the boat. Within ten minutes of leaving the house they were gazing upon the sight of a well maintained MFV that looked in every way ready for sea except that she was still cradled and about thirty yards from the water. After hearing Bill's description of the boat, it was hard to believe that this was the same boat. The wheelhouse was set above the crew cabin that would sleep about six people and there was a spacious deck area with a few seats and lockers situated towards the stern. It looked in every way highly suitable to serve as Bill had suggested, a sturdy vessel, visually attractive, the fresh paint covering the original Admiralty grey and black.

A small mixed cargo had been loaded into the hold as *Ellie May* left Oulton Broad, through the harbour and took up the course for Southwold. It was a very early start and they encountered very little waterborne traffic, just a few fishing boats that were leaving for the North Sea fishing grounds. *Ellie May* turned south with Bill at the helm, he had insisted on working his way and not be a non-fare paying passenger. It was the first time he had been to sea in the *Ellie May* and Barty sensed his feelings and saw the enjoyment as the strong following wind urged their progress.

In no time at all they rounded the Southwold lighthouse and came to the quayside. They unloaded the small cargo within an hour and would liked to have stayed a little longer as they liked the town so much. Southwold and Aldeburgh, two ancient towns they held so much interest. Barty had once considered buying a house in one of the ports but developments at the Mill had given him second thoughts, how often would he need a house, he was nearly always at sea?

They left Southwold immediately having sailed from Lowestoft at 4am that morning and with a strong following wind had reached the port in a little over two hours so Barty estimated that with favourable weather they should be at the Tide Mill at roughly 2pm. His prediction was correct, almost to the minute but he was obliged to use the auxiliary engine for the upriver journey. The meeting was scheduled for 2.30pm but as they were slightly behind time it didn't start until 3pm. with all five members of the prospective Management Committee being present, Mr John Salmon, representing the Tide Mill Carrying Company, Mr Joseph Smalley, Barty's personal solicitor and Mr Noel Baxter representing Mr Spalding's interests, who had sent the relevant papers to all concerned to enable them to familiarise themselves with the pending proposal beforehand. The meeting lasted for two hours and very few of the proposals needed clarification. The necessary signatures were obtained after minor alterations to the original. Only one question remained, the title of the newly established Company and Barty suggested 'The Tide Mill Incorporated' but Mr Baxter insisted that the new title should be 'The Tide Mill Associates', the name was readily accepted by all.

The members of the Management Committee would remain as previously suggested, Mr Spalding would be a sleeping partner and Barty the Managing Director, Tom was to be Manager of the carrying side of the business and skipper of the *Ellie May*, while Bill oversaw *Skipper's Delight*, as the Leisure Services Manager and would recruit additional staff for the boat as required. Sarah would be the Company Secretary. There would be a few further changes that would affect individuals but not the new Company. Mr & Mrs Spalding would remain in the big house to be joined there by Barty and Sarah when they were married. Tom would take up Barty's old room at Keeper's Cottage while Shuftee was left to guard the *Ellie May* each night as she was moored very close and could easily be seen from the Cottage. John Salmon would now relinquish his interest in the now defunct company and Joseph Smalley would be Barty's personal solicitor, and Noel Baxter would be the sole representative of the Tide Mill Associates. The only person missing was Mr David Lloyd the Bank Manager of the Tide Mill Carrying Company and Tide Mill Trading that was Mr Spalding's business. Mr Spalding said he would speak to the Manager and enquire if he would be willing to oversee the accounts for the newly amalgamated companies. He apologised for neglecting to invite Mr Lloyd to the meeting but he knew that both the accounts were in a healthy state and he felt sure that Mr Lloyd would be happy to accommodate them.

The moment seemed right to mention Bill's fantastic offer so, as the members began to rise they were interrupted by Barty, now standing.

"Gentlemen and Sarah, I have received an offer that is of great interest to me and I also think, that of the new Company". He went on to describe the offer of the donation of the MFV made by his father, he tried his best to tell them of the details but he was that excited that he was unable to speak coherently and called upon Bill to tell them more about the vessel and his intentions.

On conclusion, Mr Spalding, who had chaired the meeting said, "I think this generous offer needs more time to discuss fully, this is really not the meeting for this item as it requires our Bank Manager to be present. This could be an exciting development and I would like to see a little more time given to it. Such a wonderful offer needs to be given proper attention to details and if Bill has no objections perhaps Barty and I could come to Lowestoft to see the boat. He went on to thank bill profusely for his offer and the interest in enhancing the Companies possibilities but he felt that some remuneration should be considered in return. Bill replied, "Thank you, I would have suggested that a couple of members should see *Alacrity* before any decision was made, that is the reason why this topic wasn't raised until the new Company was formed. As for remuneration, I don't want anything other than the cost of the licence and a few refurbishments". The meeting finally closed and they repaired to the conservatory for refreshments before dispersing.

It was business as usual the following week during which Sarah and Barty found time to visit the Reverend Nathen Young at All Saints Church in Woodbridge who informed them that the banns would be read on three consecutive Sundays prior to the date of the marriage. Someone had remembered!

Ellie May was snugged down early on Friday morning before Mr Spalding. Tom and Barty climbed into the car, Barty taking the wheel. They had one other passenger, Shuftee, Barty had decided to give him a treat as he seldom went very far from the boat or the mill complex, he sat in the back seat next to Tom, the first time he had ever ridden in a car. Barty had received a few lessons from Mr Spalding now and he deemed Barty quite capable of taking them to Lowestoft safely even though it would be the furthest he had driven. He was very quiet during the journey as he concentrated on the job in hand, the only time he spoke was to ask Mr Spalding anything was on the approach to a barrier controlled railway level crossing, something he had not encountered before during his tuition.

They arrived safely in Lowestoft and booked into an hotel on the main road. Over breakfast the next morning, Mr Spalding commented on Barty's driving ability making him feel quite proud of himself.
An early breakfast meant that they could meet Bill at the Harbourmaster's Office by 9am. The day was a little overcast and there had been light rain overnight making the ground where *Alacrity* was cradled quite muddy with large puddles, the area around the vessel being hardened by the constant foot-fall about the boat over the past two years. Bill asked them to hold fast for a moment as he climbed the ladder into the boat and re-appeared carrying three pairs of wellington boots and wearing a pair himself. Explaining that he had started to get some kit together for any fishing trips that he hoped would book the *Alacrity* in the future. After donning their boots, they crossed the muddy patch and climbed into the boat where Barty was amazed by the cleanliness and tidiness that was taken place since his last visit. He thought it a crime to tramp with muddy boots over the pristine decks! Mr Spalding and Tom could offer nothing but praise as they were given a full intensive tour of the boat. It was so obvious that a considerable amount of time, trouble and money had been spent on the refurbishment and restoration of the craft, a real labour of love by Bill.

Returning to the hotel they discussed the merits of the *Alacrity* and without hesitation accepted Bill's magnificent offer. Bill wanted no payment for the boat except the financing of the licence etc. that they had already talked about, he wanted to donate the vessel as a token of his happiness in finding his son again and becoming a part of the new Company. In the eyes of the Company that was a small price to pay for such a wonderful addition to them. Furthermore, it was agreed to keep the name *Alacrity* if the Admiralty approved and would ask Sarah to write to them as a matter of courtesy. Their visit to Lowestoft had been a total success and everything seemed to be going well without any hitches or problems.

Sarah was having a very busy time in the office when Barty arrived there the following morning. Having been briefed by her father she had contacted Noel Baxter asking him to draw up the necessary documentation to include *Alacrity* as a Company asset. She had written a letter to the Admiralty regarding the retention of the MFV, s name and her final letter was to the Registration Office at Lowestoft giving all the dimensions and details of *Alacrity* for inclusion on their records whilst applying for her permanent mooring in the port. That letter was not posted and remained undated pending the reply from the Admiralty. Should the retention of the name be refused then a new name would have to be given on the registration documents.

With all the business being up to date, Sarah and her mother went to Woodbridge to choose a wedding dress and accessories for the big day. This venture took a long time and they didn't get home until after 6pm. Meantime, while the exciting shopping trip was taking place, Barty kept Tom company on the *Ellie May* doing odd jobs whilst in the small lounge of the house on Beach Road. Lowestoft, a very contented man was engrossed in setting up dates and arrangements for *Alacrity* to be put into the water and all the attendant tasks to take place. As Bill worked he felt a warm glow that he was now part of a big family business and found a great satisfaction posting the Boat Surveyors final report to Barty.

It seemed an eternity waiting for replies to letters that Sarah had sent but life carried on quite normally. An average of two trips a week kept *Ellie May* and her crew of Barty, Tom and Shuftee fully employed. Mr Spalding was keen to get all the loose ends tided up before the wedding and was constantly calling different businesses and his solicitor in an endeavour to speed things along. The replies may seem a long time coming but the date of the wedding was rushing headlong. Suddenly, everything seemed to be one big rush and the only time Barty felt that things were normal was while he was away at sea on Company business.

Wednesday 16th May, two days before the wedding, messages and replies had started to arrive at long last, each one bringing the news they expected. The Admiralty said they would be delighted that the name of *Alacrity* should be retained so Sarah immediately posted the letter to the Registration Office duly signed and dated. Bill was kept informed of all the developments. He had received a date for the sea trials but unfortunately, they wouldn't take place until after the wedding. Most everything seemed to be falling in place as planned but Barty hadn't planned a' stag do', he had been so taken up with the business interests that he hadn't thought about it. But Tom had!

Barty started to become suspicious when first Ted Moore arrived followed closely by Bill, they greeted Barty, spoke with Tom before going up to the big house to see Mr Spalding for a meeting – or so they said, but Barty had not received a call to any meeting and he slowly started to put two and two together. Not a word was mentioned until Tom said, "Get your working rig off, we're going for a pint we can't let your last bachelor day pass without marking it" Barty changed his clothes and they set off to the local for a pint or two so imagine his reaction to be greeted by a roomful of people, some of whom were complete strangers to him. They were joined by the local folk singers and the evening flowed as freely as did the ale. Barty, ever conscious of his responsibilities managed to remain relatively sober as toast after toast was made to his future married life and the success of the new Company, the Tide Mill Associates.

The marriage ceremony was scheduled for 2pm, Barty felt very nervous. Tom ensured that they enjoyed a relaxed forenoon just sitting and talking of this and that. Come midday, Barty went to his room at Keeper's Cottage to dress into his wedding suit. In no time at all he heard Tom calling him from the mill yard and on going outside he expected to see the car waiting for him but standing in the yard was two decorated carriages drawn by white horses dressed with colourful ribbons, predominantly white. The first carriage was for Barty with three principal guests sitting inside waiting for him, his father, Tom and Ted Moore. He had previously asked Tom to be his best man. The second carriage was for the bride, her parents and two bridesmaids to follow a little later. All this rather overwhelmed Barty as he had expected a small gathering with close friends and relatives of the bride to be among a few invited guests. The Reverend Nathan Young conducted the ceremony before a crowded church, who, apart from family were mostly local traders, business representatives and staff from the mill complex.

The Marriage Register and the Certificate were signed and the photographers took quite a time to settle the guests to form an acceptable line-up before committing the affair to film. The many invited guests then returned to the Tide Mill for a reception in a large marquee that had been erected in the paddock just to the rear of the house.

Barty, who was relieved to get the formalities completed still felt overwhelmed with everything that had been arranged and only found a minute to tell Sarah how beautiful she looked and how proud he was to have married her before the guests started milling around them with their own congratulations. Later, Barty was heard to remark that he had never liked formal affairs but he appreciated all the preparations that had been made for him and Sarah, a day that he would remember forever. As the guests mingled freely, Mr Spalding called for their attention and offered a toast to Mr & Mrs Bartholomew, the happy couple, he summed up the proceedings and presented Barty and Sarah with an all-expenses paid honeymoon in Paris leaving Felixstowe tomorrow the 19th May. Barty did his utmost to reply to his father-in-law's generosity but somehow the words wouldn't come he only managed to utter a stuttered thank you and even that was almost incoherent but it was plain that he was greatly appreciative of everything that had been done to make this day unforgettable. There were things still to be done here and as he started to object Mr Spalding cut him short saying that everything was covered and there was absolutely nothing to worry about, just to look after his daughter and enjoy their holiday.

Mr Spalding drove them to Felixstowe the next morning and dropped them near the gangway of the Cross-Channel ferry that was to take them to France and the start of their future life together. For once in many weeks Barty had nothing on his mind knowing that his friends and new family would look after his interests and a long reassuring smile from Mrs Sarah Bartholomew told him all was well, they were off on their new life together.

But that's another story………..